Merry Band of Misfits

Sebastian Grey

Copyright © 2026 by Sebastian Grey

Published by Bastian House

Cover design by David Ter-Avanesyan/Ter33Design LLC

Proofread by Tenyia Lee

ISBN: 979-8-9946653-8-1
Ebook ISBN: 979-8-9946653-9-8

For all the other Misfits out there...

Prologue

Timing is everything.

Mom used to say that when she taught me to cook. Well, she would probably still say it, but she's dead now, so I can't hear her anymore. Nicholas says I shouldn't start conversations like that because it makes people uncomfortable, but it's true.

Like with eggs benedict. I make really good eggs benedict. The secret Mom taught me is you have to put the hollandaise sauce on at exactly the right time. Too early and the sauce breaks. Too late and the eggs get rubbery.

Timing.

Right now, I am sitting in a van parked across the street from First National Bank. The steering wheel is a little too close to my chest, because Nicholas adjusted the seat for me back when he taught me to drive. I wish he'd taught me how to adjust it. Through the windshield, I can see everything happening exactly like we planned.

"Mozart's ready to play," a voice buzzes loudly in my earpiece.

That's Floyd in my ear. Floyd is part of my Family. You will meet the rest of the Family soon. We are not really related, but we are Family. Except for my brother, Nicholas. I *am* related to him.

I see Floyd in front of the bank. He is sitting in his motorized wheelchair with his remote control for Mozart, which is what he named his little flying drone. Floyd always gives his inventions composer names because he says music and math are the same thing. That doesn't make sense to me, but Floyd is really smart about numbers and notes, so I believe him. And Floyd agrees with me about timing being important.

But today, timing is even more important.

Today, my Family and I are robbing a bank.

I know that sounds bad.

Nicholas always tells me to explain things properly and in order so people understand me better. We're not bad people. We're different, but not bad. We just need money to save our house so we don't get sent away and never see each other ever again. And I believe that sometimes, just sometimes, when you really, really need something, it's okay to do things you wouldn't normally do. Like when I'm cooking and we don't have butter. I use margarine instead. It tastes worse, but it works.

"Set," Garth says in my earpiece. Garth's voice sounds funny through the Bluetooth, but I would never tell him that because Garth is deaf and it would hurt his feelings. He's wearing an orange construction vest and placing orange cones to block the street from police. Garth is the strongest person I know. He almost won a gold medal at the Special Olympics for weightlifting.

In exactly one minute and seven seconds, William will walk into the bank acting like someone else. William's real name is William, but when things get scary, he pretends to be

Mr. Darcy from *Pride and Prejudice* because Mr. Darcy is brave and always knows what to do.

"I have eyes on Mr. Darcy," I say into my Bluetooth to them all. "We're at the point of no return."

That's what Nicholas taught me to say when we trained for this heist. Nicholas is my twin brother, but he's typical and I'm not. Oh, I forgot to tell you...

My name is Vinnie, and I have Down syndrome.

People act weird when they find out we're twins. I always tell them we're not identical. I have Down syndrome; Nicholas does not.

They know.

I see the looks of pity on their faces when they stare at me.

I hate those looks. They make me feel small. I don't like feeling small.

But pity is better than when they laugh and make fun of me.

I see Mr. Darcy walking into the bank now. Time to make the donuts, which is something Mom used to say when it was time to start working.

When I cook, if I mess up the timing, dinner gets burned. When you rob a bank, if you mess up the timing, you go to prison.

I don't want to go to prison.

Prison food is terrible.

"Game time, everyone. Stick to the plan," I tell my Family through the earpiece. "We do this right, it'll all be over in five minutes—"

TAP TAP TAP.

I turn to see a police officer tapping at my window.

Oh shit.

We look at each other through the glass. Both of us shocked.

I'm shocked because I'm robbing a bank.

The police officer is shocked because...well, I have Down syndrome and am driving a getaway van.

I don't know what to do now...

Oh... I think I started telling my story too late. I will go back and start at the beginning like Nicholas says. Please forget what I told you until we are here again later, and imagine it is now—

Chapter One

Six months earlier...

I found Vinnie exactly where I knew he'd be, in the middle of the playground, surrounded by a pack of kids who were hanging on his every word. My twin brother had that effect on children. They saw past the Down syndrome features that made adults uncomfortable and just saw Vinnie as funny, kind, and always eager to play.

Kids are great. Then they grow up...

"Five more minutes," Vinnie called out when he spotted me approaching, not even looking up from the elaborate game of hopscotch he was orchestrating.

"No, now. Let's go." I kept my voice firm but not harsh. This wasn't my first rodeo.

"What if I don't want to?"

Classic Vinnie. Testing boundaries he knew perfectly well existed.

"You know the rules. Time to go home, Vinnie."

That's when I saw the gleam in his eye, the one that meant trouble. Vinnie clocked the parents watching our exchange from their benches, probably wondering why a grown man like me was ordering around someone who looked like he belonged in a care facility.

"I'm tired of sleeping in my cage!" he announced loudly enough for everyone to hear.

That sneaky little fucker...

The parents' expressions shifted from mild curiosity to horror. A few actually gasped. I watched their faces harden as they looked at me like I was the kind of monster who kept disabled people locked up in cages.

"I keep his cage very clean," I deadpanned, playing along despite myself.

The parents weren't buying it. They never did.

"I'm kidding. He's my brother; we're twins."

No one ever believed that either. Can't say I blamed them. The odds of fraternal twins where one has Down syndrome and the other doesn't are what Floyd calls "mathematically disharmonious." Vinnie and I were essentially a genetic lottery ticket, Powerball and all.

I shook my head at my brother's Cheshire grin. He was practically bouncing with satisfaction at having pulled off another performance as we began our trek home.

"I see what you did there," I said.

"Playing?" Vinnie's voice was pure innocence, but I knew better.

As we walked away from what was quickly becoming an angry mob, a small child Vinnie had been playing with broke free from her parents and ran after us.

"You're a mean dumbhead!" she yelled directly at me.

Vinnie and I kept walking, each certain who she was talking to.

"Pretty sure she's talking to you, Nicholas," Vinnie said.

"Definitely talking to you," I shot back.

"Nope. You."

"You."

"You."

By now we were both grinning. It was impossible to stay annoyed when Vinnie got like this. Part mischievous little brother, part criminal mastermind.

If I had only known...

Living with my Family was like being part of an improv troupe that never broke character. You never knew what you were going to get when you walked through the front door. Sometimes it was comedy, sometimes drama, but it was never boring.

As I led Vinnie into the house, I quickly realized that tonight was going to be a disaster.

"Dammit," I muttered, staring at the wreckage that used to be our living room. "I just cleaned up this morning."

Chairs were knocked over, athletic equipment was strewn across the floor, and a trail of dirty clothes led deeper into the house like breadcrumbs in a very messy fairy tale. Vinnie followed behind me, his expression shifting from mischievous to meek as he took in my reaction.

Our house wasn't much to look at from the outside, a modest five-bedroom in a neighborhood that had seen better days, but inside, it was pure chaos. In the best possible way. Every room told the story of its inhabitants. Floyd's engineering projects scattered across the living room table, William's color-coded movie collection arranged with OCD precision, Garth's Special Olympics medals hung in the hall next to Vinnie's collection of restaurant menus from places that would never hire him.

It was eclectic as hell, but it was home.

"This isn't my fault," Vinnie protested. "I was at the park."

I followed the trail of destruction deeper into the house, mentally cataloging who was responsible for what. The dumbbells belonged to Garth, our resident giant who towered over everyone at six-foot-four and could bench press the whole family. The scattered electronic components were definitely Floyd's. He had acquired savant syndrome. The lightning strike that put him in a wheelchair had also augmented his mathematical mind, meaning he could now calculate pi to a hundred decimal places while designing drones that NASA would envy.

"No, but because I had to go find you at the playground, I get to clean up the house again," I said, gathering clothes as I went. "This is why it's so important we follow rules, Vinnie."

The truth was, I didn't mind cleaning up after them. These weren't roommates or clients. They were Family. The kind you'd do anything for, even if it meant giving up everything you thought you wanted in life.

I'd learned that lesson the hard way.

"I'm sorry, Nicholas. I won't do it again," Vinnie said, unable to mask his ear-to-ear grin.

When Vinnie grinned like that, he was usually hiding or planning something. But before I could call him on it, the kitchen lights blazed to life behind us.

"Happy birthday, Nicholas and Vinnie!"

The kitchen was suddenly filled with balloons, cake, and the rest of the Family.

William stood at attention like an aristocrat, his obsessive-compulsive disorder making him count the balloons and separate them into sets of three. Floyd sat in his wheelchair, the lightning-strike scars that spider-webbed across his arms were visible beneath his rolled-up sleeves. And Garth, who communicated more with his presence than most people did with words, looked very pleased with himself as he smiled at me.

William approached first, his spine locked in aristocratic

rigidity. He extended his hand with a formality that came with his particular expression of autism. "Did we trick you, Nicholas? You're not mad, are you?" Then, "It was Vinnie's idea."

"Thanks, everyone," I managed, genuinely touched despite my earlier frustration.

The cake read "Vinnie & Nicholas = 30" with fifteen candles on each side.

"I used the recipe from work," Vinnie announced proudly. "The restaurant sells a hundred of these every day."

Vinnie and I shared a deep breath and blew out the candles together.

"This is really good," I said between bites. "It must be—"

"Vegan," Garth spat with disdain, his voice carrying that distinctive quality that came with his hearing loss.

As a caregiver, I'd converted to a vegetarian lifestyle years ago—and while everyone else grimaced at the first bite, they ate it anyway.

Vinnie, honest to a fault, shrugged. "I know, Garth, vegan was not my first choice, but Nicholas likes to eat healthy, even though we hate it."

William looked away to ask, "What'd you wish for, Vinnie?"

"If I tell you, it won't come true," Vinnie replied.

"That's a silly superstition," William said.

"L-like birthday w-wishes," Floyd added through his stutter.

"No one's talking to you, Floyd," William snapped.

"Settle down, all of you, and I'll tell you mine," I said.

"Don't!" Vinnie protested.

"I wished we could all eat this delicious vegan cake the rest of the week. Oh, look at that. My wish came true. Leftovers!"

The Family groaned collectively. Garth pushed his cake away in disgust.

"I see what you did there," Vinnie accused me sardonically.

The gift-giving started with Garth and William. They pushed forward a container of whey protein powder with a bow taped on top.

"That's from me and Garth," William announced. "Good for his training."

"So's that healthy cake. The Special Olympics are right around the corner, Garth..." I noted, though I knew they weren't buying it. They really hated all things vegan.

Our conversation was cut short by a mechanical whirring as Floyd's mini-drone flew into the room carrying two lottery scratchers. The little aircraft was cobbled together from spare parts, but it flew with precision as Floyd guided it to drop its cargo into my hand.

"I d-did the c-calculations," Floyd explained, his words catching on the consonants. "St-statistically sp-speaking, these have the h-highest pr-probability of w-winning. One to th-three point seven f-five."

"Thanks, Floyd," I said, handing one scratcher to Vinnie.

"These are always a rip off," Vinnie complained. "I don't know why you waste your money, Floyd."

"You can't w-win if you don't p-play," Floyd countered, the stutter making even this simple phrase a struggle.

From the corner of my eye, I caught Garth giving Floyd a meaningful look. Floyd hesitated for a moment, then seemed to make a decision and nodded back.

Floyd's mini-drone suddenly wobbled erratically before diving straight into the vegan cake, sending crumbs and frosting flying everywhere as the propellors gummed up with icing.

"Oops," Floyd said with obviously fake concern. "L-looks like Bach had a m-malfunction."

Garth tried to look innocent, but his satisfied expression gave him away. The rest of the Family struggled to hide their relief at the "accident" that had just solved their leftovers problem.

I suppressed a smile. "So much for healthy cake all week. I see what you did there."

"What a shame," Vinnie said, not sounding sorry at all.

Then came Vinnie's gift, an envelope with a ribbon that he handed me with obvious pride. "This is from me. I hope you like it. Happy birthday, big brother."

"A twenty-dollar gift card for floral arrangements... Just what I wanted," I lied. Not exactly what I'd expected, but I'd learned long ago to trust Vinnie's thought process. It might take the scenic route, but there was always a specific destination.

"Now you can send Rita flowers like boyfriends are supposed to," Vinnie said. Then, as if annoyed that I hadn't put it all together he added, "She says it would be nice to get flowers once in a while."

See what I mean? What seemed mere seconds ago to be total nonsense now not only made perfect sense but showed how thoughtful and caring Vinnie could be. Still, I didn't like being reminded I may have been a bit remiss in my romantic notions with my girlfriend, so I did what siblings do when one shows the other up; I threw it back at him.

"Where's Celia?" I asked, noticing Vinnie's girlfriend wasn't there. "You did invite her, didn't you? It's your birthday too, Vinnie."

Vinnie's expression darkened immediately.

"I don't want to talk about her," he said firmly.

William, Floyd, and Garth exchanged knowing looks.

"Did you guys break up?" William asked as he tried unsuccessfully to mask his delight. Covering, he quickly added, "Celia can be very... How shall I say...?"

"D-demanding?" Floyd offered.

"No, more like bitc—" William started to say.

"Bossy," Garth spoke over him, his deep voice flat but certain.

"That'll do," William finished.

"I said I don't want to talk about that!" Vinnie snapped, louder than necessary.

Whatever was happening between him and Celia, it was clearly more serious than a simple lovers' quarrel. They all laughed, letting the subject go as they returned to eating cake they didn't like.

This was my Family. Messy, brilliant, and absolutely irreplaceable. We'd found each other after the world had broken us, and then we built something beautiful from the broken pieces.

I'd protect them with my life.

As we gathered around the sabotaged vegan cake, I felt that familiar tightness in my chest. The one that came with loving people unconditionally. The one that reminded me every day that I was all that stood between my Family and a world that would tear them apart without a second thought.

It was then that the sirens started wailing outside, and our front yard exploded in flashing red and blue lights.

Chapter Two

At first, I got scared when I saw the police lights flashing outside our house. Nicholas taught me to respect authority figures, especially police officers. He said they are there to help people, and I should always be polite and do what they say. Nicholas said this is extra important for people like me because sometimes police officers don't understand people with disabilities.

Nicholas walked out first with me right behind him.

But then I saw who got out of the police car, and I wasn't scared anymore.

"Oh, it's just Rita," I said, relieved.

Rita Reyes was Nicholas's girlfriend since high school. Even after he quit college to take care of me. Rita was pretty, but in a strong way. She had muscles in her shoulders and arms from working out. Rita had to be strong because she was a police officer, and Nicholas said some male police officers didn't respect women cops.

But Rita proved them all wrong.

The other police officers called Rita "Mother." At first, I

thought they called her that because she took care of all of us, like Mom used to before she died.

But one day I heard Nicholas laughing about Rita's nickname with Floyd. Nicholas said "Mother" is short for "motherfucker," which was what the other cops called Rita because when she fought criminals, *she was one bad motherfucker.* Rita said I shouldn't use that kind of language because it was bad. But Nicholas said it meant the other cops respected her, which was good.

Rita walked up to our porch carrying two presents. She looked very official in her police uniform.

"'Just Rita'? Is that any way to greet me? Happy birthday, Vinman."

She handed me my present and gave me a kiss on the cheek, which I rubbed off right away. Rita always did that even though I told her I have a girlfriend.

"You know I have a girlfriend, Rita," I reminded her.

That always made Rita laugh. But it was not the kind of laugh that makes me feel small. The kind I don't like. Rita always laughed with us, not at us.

"And you know I have a boyfriend," she said before kissing Nicholas.

It was then that William appeared behind me. Whenever William saw Rita, he got weird. William had a big crush on Rita even though he knew she and Nicholas were together. William thought if he waited long enough, maybe Rita would notice him instead. Or maybe he believed Nicholas would mess up their relationship. It's hard to tell with him. Nicholas said this was called "unrequited love" and that William would grow out of it. I don't think so.

William straightened up and his voice got deeper. He was turning into Mr. Darcy.

"'Tis an honor to have you call upon us this fine evening,

Officer Reyes. My own birthday is nigh on half a year from now. I do hope to have the pleasure of your company then as well," William proclaimed.

I told you. Weird...

We were used to William talking like this when Rita came over. He always got nervous around her, so it was easier for him to talk to Rita as Mr. Darcy.

"Easy there, tiger," Rita said, which made William look away and go back to his normal voice. "But it's good to see you too, William."

I opened Rita's present and found a real birthday cake with frosting flowers and everything. Not vegan like the one we had earlier.

"A real birthday cake!" I said, excited.

"Red velvet. Your favorite," Rita replied.

Everyone liked Rita because she treated us like typicals, not like we needed special help all the time. Even Garth, who didn't like speaking, would talk to Rita.

Rita handed Nicholas his present. "Thanks. Want a beer?" he asked as he measured the heft of his gift.

"Still on duty. Open it," she said eagerly.

Nicholas unwrapped his gift and found a thick book about psychology. Some dead guy named Jung. I could see Nicholas get that look he got when he remembered his old life before he had to take care of us. Nicholas used to study psychology in college. He wanted to understand how people's brains work. Nicholas was especially interested in philosophers like Schopenhauer and Nietzsche, more dead guys who had big ideas about why people did things and what made life worth living.

But when Nicholas quit college to take care of me, he had to stop reading those books. He said he didn't have time for that kind of thinking anymore. But sometimes I saw him looking at his old school books late at night when he thought we were all sleeping.

"I haven't read Jung since college," Nicholas said, staring at the book.

"It's all you talked about back then. With things going well with your merry band of misfits, I thought you might enjoy some light reading," Rita said with a smile.

"Jung? Light reading?!" Nicholas said, getting excited like he used to. "Carl Jung identified archetypes we all use in everyday behavior. His work on the collective unconscious is..."

I had no idea what he was talking about. I could tell Rita didn't either. Thankfully, Nicholas stopped talking when he realized he was rambling. Rita was watching him with a look that made me think she was remembering something good.

"Thanks, Rita," Nicholas said earnestly before kissing her.

"What'd they get you?" Rita asked.

"A lotto scratcher. Some whey powder. And a gift card for flowers," Nicholas said.

"The usual then," Rita laughed.

"They also executed a devious plan of a surprise party. Almost as if they had help," Nicholas said, looking at Rita suspiciously.

Rita shrugged, then winked at him. They looked at each other for a moment, and I could tell they really loved each other even after all these years.

They're going to get married. I know it.

The Family was making noises behind me about wanting to go inside and eat cake. Probably because it wasn't vegan.

"Vinnie, what do you say when someone gives you a gift?" Nicholas prompted.

"Oh, right. Thank you, Rita," I said.

"Okay, put it in the fridge. We've already had dessert," Nicholas said.

"C'mon!" Garth bellowed.

"Not a good one," William added.

"R-really?" Floyd demanded.

Rita raised her eye brow at Nicholas. "Nicky, let them eat cake."

This made Nicholas sigh, and we knew that meant he would let us eat cake. The Family stampeded into the house with me, leaving Rita and *Nicky* alone together. I think they were about to have a make out session when I remembered the rule about birthday wishes.

"The birthday boys have to eat the first piece or it's bad luck. Come inside now, Nicholas. You too, Rita!" I called out.

Rita's police radio started making loud noises. She listened to it and made a face.

"Rain check. Duty calls," she said.

"Is it dangerous?" Nicholas asked like he always did when she got called into work.

"Nothing I can't handle." She gave Nicholas a kiss on the cheek then blew a kiss at me, which I ducked. I was mad at Celia, but I was no cheater.

"Be careful," Nicholas called after her.

"And do the sirens!" I shouted.

Rita got in her police car and turned on the sirens as she drove away.

I loved it when she did that.

As we watched her drive away, I could see Nicholas looked sad. He always got like that when Rita left for police work. Nicholas worried about Rita because being a police officer was dangerous, but he was also proud of her because she's so good at her job.

William stood next to me, still watching Rita's police car disappear down the street.

"Someday," William said quietly, "... she'll realize what she's missing."

"Come on, William," Nicholas said, putting his arm around his shoulder. "Let's go inside and finish that cake."

As we walked back into the house, I thought about how lucky we were to have Rita. She wasn't just Nicholas's girlfriend. She was part of our Family too. She understood that we weren't broken people who needed fixing. We were people who did things different. She never made me feel small.

I didn't know it then, but in a few months, we would need Rita more than we ever imagined. We would have to make hard choices about right and wrong, and Nicholas would remember all those philosophy books he used to read. But for now, we were a Family eating birthday cake.

Rita was out there keeping people safe, and we were safe at home because of people like her.

I hoped she would catch all the bad guys and come back soon.

Chapter Three

Smeared icing on empty plates was the only evidence left behind of the red velvet massacre. The caregiver in me gathered them up, surveying the damage Rita's cake had inflicted on our usually manageable evening routine.

"Time for bed, everyone!" I called out.

In the living room, Vinnie sat cross-legged on the floor while Garth's massive frame took up most of the couch, with William perched on the edge like he was ready to bolt at any moment. They were all glued to the TV. The local news was on, and I caught the tail end of the story.

"The police are investigating the robbery of the Second State Bank branch. If anyone has any information, the police are asking you to call the tip line—"

"Bedtime!" I said louder, cutting off the reporter.

Begrudgingly, they turned off the TV, and the familiar bedtime choreography began. Vinnie headed to the kitchen to load the dishwasher. William beelined for the bathroom, but Garth grabbed his shirt and yanked him back, claiming first dibs, much to William's chagrin.

I watched William bounce on his toes in front of the bathroom door, counting his bounces with mounting agitation.

With the TV off, I could hear music drifting from down the hall. Bach's Toccata and Fugue in D Minor. I followed the sound to Floyd's bedroom.

Floyd sat hunched over his desk, his thin shoulders curved in concentration as he tried desperately to salvage his mini-drone. I could see icing mucking up the delicate electronics, collateral damage from its birthday cake kamikaze run.

"Is he salvageable?" I asked from the doorway.

Floyd shook his head sadly, like he was mourning a fallen soldier.

"I f-fear poor B-Bach has m-met his end. Worth it."

"Let me help you get ready for bed."

Floyd took one more moment to memorialize his creation before nodding. I knew how much he hated needing help with something as basic as getting undressed.

I lifted him from the chair onto the bed and began carefully removing his clothes. The fern-leaf pattern of scars across his legs, arms, and back never stopped making me wince. Lightning doesn't just strike—it brands you for life.

Once he was settled, I opened his medicine pill box and checked the calendar on the wall. Each day was marked with either a red X for nightmares or a green check for peaceful sleep. Green checks stretched across the past two weeks. A minor miracle.

"Looks like we might've found the right dosage. Here."

Floyd accepted the pills without complaint, but I saw the resignation in his eyes. The medication helped with the nightmares, but it also dulled the brilliant mind that made him who he was. One more trade-off in a life full of them.

"Who're you building next? Wagner? Tchaikovsky perhaps?"

"Tch-Tchaikovsky? Meh."

"'Night, Floyd."

"'N-night."

Out in the hallway, Garth emerged from the bathroom, all six-foot-four of him wrapped in a towel that looked comically small around his frame.

"So long! What do you do in there?" William demanded.

William finally got his turn in the bathroom when—SNAP!—he yelped as Garth's towel struck him with a perfect rat-tail.

"Stop that!" William protested. Then, at the sight of a now buck-naked Garth, he shrieked, "Put clothes on! My eyes, my eyes!"

Garth left, naked and laughing. Some things never changed, and honestly, I wouldn't want them to.

After Vinnie made his rounds—banging on the bathroom door to hurry William along, checking that Floyd was tucked in, and pointedly ignoring Garth, who'd climbed into bed still naked—he appeared in my doorway.

I was at my desk in the corner, the only quiet space in a house full of chaos, making notes in the ledger while sorting through our group home's bills. The numbers weren't getting any friendlier, but we still had our heads above water.

"Everything done?" I asked without looking up.

"I checked to make sure." Vinnie entered and sat on my bed. I knew his routine. When something was bothering him, he needed time to process before he could talk about it. But I had something that might help smooth the way.

"I made you a gift. Wanted to give it to you in private, so here. Happy birthday, Vinnie."

I pulled out a binder I'd been working on for weeks.

"A book? I don't like books, Nicholas. You know that."

"Open it."

Annoyed, Vinnie reluctantly obeyed. But as he read, his expression transformed.

"These are recipes," he said excitedly.

"Not just any recipes. They're Mom's. I had them laminated, now they can't get destroyed."

As Vinnie flipped through the pages, his eyes misted up. He recognized Mom's handwriting, her little notes in the margins.

"I know she'd want you to be the keeper of her secrets. And I miss her eggs benedict."

Vinnie nodded his head emphatically. "I miss Mom so much. I wish she was here for our birthday."

"I miss her too. But you know, she's watching you from up there," I said.

"I bet she laughed at how we tricked you today. I'm a trickster, just like her." Vinnie laughed as he flipped through the recipe book, and I saw my opening.

"You want to talk about Celia?"

The binder snapped shut. Vinnie set it aside, his mood shifting instantly. "Do you want to talk about Rita?" he shot back with attitude.

"Vinnie, Rita and I are fine. You're ignoring Celia on your birthday. What's happening?"

I watched Vinnie's mind work, trying to articulate whatever was tearing him up inside. But he wasn't ready. Not yet. Unable to process his emotions, he lashed out instead.

"I don't want to talk about that!"

He stormed out of the room like a man on fire.

I waited patiently.

Everything in his own time.

Sure enough, he came back, grabbing the recipe book from my bed.

"I forgot my book. And I shouldn't yell at you, I'm sorry. I love you."

"Love you too, Vinman."

As Vinnie left with his book of recipes, I returned to my ledger. He would ask for help when he needed it, of that I was certain. How long that would take was anyone's guess. I just hoped that whatever was weighing on him was something simple.

It was not...

Chapter Four

Garth's alarm could wake the dead, but somehow Vinnie slept through it in the room next door. My twin could sleep through anything. I wasn't allowed.

The vibrations thundered through the walls at 5:30 AM. All by design to wake our sleeping giant for his Special Olympics training.

By the time I had thrown on clothes and stumbled to the kitchen, Garth was already there in full gym-rat mode, methodically cracking a carton of eggs into a pitcher.

All twelve of them.

<Morning, Garth,> I signed, but he was deep in his pre-workout ritual, focused like a warrior preparing for battle.

That's when Vinnie appeared, already dressed for work, surveying the egg situation with growing alarm.

"I need those eggs, Garth. I'm making eggs benedict!" Vinnie protested, managing to rescue four eggs from Garth's protein rampage.

Garth drained the rest of the pitcher like it was a protein

shake. I looked away, grimacing. A hundred times I witnessed this and it still turned my stomach.

William wandered in, took one look at Garth's Rocky Balboa impression, and his face went pale.

"The chances of getting salmonella are..." William's eyes darted around, frantically looking for Floyd to provide the exact statistical probability. "Well, they're not zero, Garth."

"I can take it," Garth announced in his careful, measured speech. "Gym time."

William counted the remaining eggs. His anxiety mounting. Four eggs left. At a table with three people, this was a crisis of the highest order for him.

"That's not enough eggs, Vinnie," William said, and I could see the meltdown brewing behind his eyes. "I need my eggs."

"You can have toast," Vinnie said casually, knowing full well he'd ruined William's morning routine and not caring one bit.

While Vinnie made breakfast with what was left, I went to check on Floyd.

I found him awake, marking another green check on his calendar. Two weeks running now. The new medication dosage was working, but I could see the trade-off in Floyd's movements, that slight delay in his responses like he was processing everything through fog. We were swapping his nightmares for his sharpness, and I hated that he had to make that choice.

"Nightmare free? Okay then. Let's get you dressed," I said, lifting him from his bed to wheelchair.

Floyd's gaze drifted to his workbench, where the remains of yesterday's birthday cake carnage was scattered among drone parts.

"M-mozart," he said. "I'm going to b-b-build Mozart next."

"Don't use the Blu-ray player for parts this time," I warned.

"If William can't watch *Pride and Prejudice*, he'll have a meltdown."

"We'll see," Floyd said, which in Floyd-speak meant "I'm absolutely going to cannibalize that Blu-ray player the moment you're not looking."

By the time we made it back to the kitchen, Vinnie had worked some kind of miracle with the remaining eggs. He set a plate of Mom's eggs benedict in front of me and scarfed down his own portion in a couple bites.

William sat staring at my eggs like a man watching his last hope die.

"Your job coach will be here soon," I said, checking the clock.

Ms. Violet's signature two sharp honks arrival announcement blared from outside.

"That's her. See you later," Vinnie said, grabbing his binder of recipes.

"And no park today!" I called after him as I slid half my eggs benedict onto William's plate. His relief was so visible I thought he might cry.

"Thank you," he whispered, like I had just saved his life.

Through the window, I watched Ms. Violet's car pull away with Vinnie and Celia in the back seat. The body language between them screamed unresolved conflict. Vinnie's shoulders were locked in defensive mode; Celia kept talking to him, but he was pointedly studying the scenery through the opposite window.

I had seen Vinnie work through disappointment before, but this felt different. Deeper. The kind of hurt that reshapes how you see someone, maybe permanently.

I just hoped Ms. Violet was ready for whatever emotional bomb was about to detonate in her car.

Ms. Violet was my job coach. She helped people like me learn how to work at typical jobs. She was very nice and patient, even when I didn't want to do what she said. But when I got in her car, I saw Celia sitting in the back seat. I forgot we shared a ride to each of our jobs. I decided not to look at her and looked out the window instead.

Celia was my girlfriend and she had Down syndrome like me. I didn't know if she was still my girlfriend because I was mad at her. The Family had been right when they said she could be very bossy. Today she looked upset and bossy.

"I called yesterday, but you didn't answer, Vinnie," Celia said as Ms. Violet drove. "Did you get my messages?"

I looked out the window and didn't answer her. I had turned my phone off because I hadn't wanted to talk to her.

"Vinnie?" Ms. Violet said. "Celia asked you a question."

"I didn't want to talk to her," I said.

"That was yesterday," Ms. Violet said. "Don't you want to talk to Celia today?"

"I do not," I answered, trying to make my voice sound like Garth's.

"I missed your birthday party, Vinnie," Celia said. "You're being a crybaby."

This made me mad.

"It was my party, and I'll cry if I want to," I told her.

I could see Ms. Violet trying not to laugh, but she did anyway. I thought maybe she was laughing at me, which made me feel small. But then I remembered that Rita laughed too, and she never made me feel small, so maybe Ms. Violet was laughing with me and not at me?

I knew that was right when Ms. Violet explained that what

I said was from a famous golden oldie song, and that was why it was funny.

When I didn't say anything, I think she thought I didn't understand, but I really just didn't believe her.

Then Ms. Violet sang the song for me.

She was right. It was funny now that I heard it.

Ms. Violet had a really good singing voice. It might have put me in a good mood. But then Celia started singing with her.

Celia did not have a good singing voice.

"Stop singing! I don't want to be happy right now. I'm mad!" I yelled.

Ms. Violet and Celia stopped singing. Then Ms. Violet asked us, "What are you two fighting about?"

I didn't want to tell Ms. Violet what Celia had done because it was embarrassing, so Celia answered for me.

"I hurt Vinnie's feelings," Celia finally said.

"Well, why don't you say you're sorry, Celia?" Ms. Violet asked.

"I...can't," Celia said.

"Can't, or won't?" Ms. Violet pushed back.

Celia thought about this for a long time. When she made up her mind she said, "I shouldn't have to say sorry, Ms. Violet. I didn't do anything wrong."

Ms. Violet stopped the car at the restaurant where I worked. She turned to look at both of us.

"Celia, if you apologize, everything will go back the way it was," she said.

"I don't think so," Celia said. "But I still love you, Vinnie."

This made me even more mad and confused. How could she love me if she wouldn't say sorry?

"I don't want to talk about this," I said. "I have to go to work, and you put me in a bad mood!"

I slammed the car door and walked fast toward the restaurant. I stopped and thought about what Nicholas would want me to do. He always said we should be nice to people, even when we were mad with them.

I turned around and opened the car door again.

"I'm sorry, Celia," I told her. "I'll turn my phone on tonight. I love you too. Bye."

I closed the door and didn't wait for her to answer. As I walked into the restaurant, I saw Celia waving goodbye to me through the car window.

I loved Celia, but I didn't know if love was enough when someone hurt you and wouldn't say sorry.

Chapter Five

"Vinman! Right on time," Dave said when he saw me.

I walked into the restaurant kitchen carrying my recipe binder like it was made of white truffles. I'd been thinking about showing it to Sous Chef Dave all morning, even during the car ride with Celia when I was mad.

Sous Chef Dave was my friend at work. He was the only person here who called me by my nickname, and he never made me feel small. Dave wanted to be a head chef someday, like the ones on TV who had their own restaurants. He was tall and skinny with tattoos on his arms that looked like kitchen tools and food. Nicholas said Dave reminded him of Anthony Bourdain, but Anthony Bourdain was famous and Sous Chef Dave was not.

"I brought some recipes I got for my birthday," I told him, holding up my binder. "Can we cook one today?"

Dave's eyes got big when he saw my recipe book. "Whoa, that's a serious collection. Let me take a look."

I opened the binder and showed him Mom's recipes. Her handwritten notes were in the margins of every page, little reminders about timing and temperature and how to make things taste just right.

"These are my mom's recipes," I said. "Nicholas put them into a book for me."

Dave looked through the pages carefully, like he was reading something important. "Vinnie, some of these are amazing. Look at this hollandaise recipe...and this one for duck. Your mom knew what she was doing."

I felt happy hearing Dave say that. Mom was a really good cook, and I wanted to be good like her.

"Can we try one? Please?" I asked. "I made eggs benedict this morning and it turned out really good."

"Lemme run that by the boss," Dave said.

"Okay. I will talk to you later then," I said.

I put my recipe book in my locker, but I could hear Dave talking to Chef in his office. Chef was the boss of the whole kitchen. He was a skinny man who never smiled and talked very quiet. I didn't like Chef very much because he looked at me the way parents at the playground looked at me. Like I was something wrong that didn't belong there.

"Chef, you should see these recipes," Dave was saying. "The kid's mom was legit. I think we could use some of these."

"No," Chef said in his quiet voice. He never showed emotions, which made him scarier than if he just yelled.

"Come on, just let him try one. The variation on hollandaise alone—"

"Dave, the young man was hired to unload trucks and rotate dry stock," Chef said very calmly. "A person like him should never be allowed in a proper kitchen. He's a retard. He'll hurt himself or someone else, and then we'll have a lawsuit."

Dave was very quiet a moment, like he was uncomfortable. "Chef, that word is considered offensive," Dave said quietly.

"The accepted term is 'special needs' or a 'person with a disability.'"

I heard Chef say, "There's no harm in using the word 'retarded.' It's not an insult, it's what he is. Now can we focus on running a restaurant?"

Dave didn't say anything after that. I could tell he wanted to, but Chef was his boss.

I felt my face get hot when I heard that word.

Retard.

Chef used it like it was my whole name, like that was all I was. Sometimes I thought that since I have heard that word so many times from so many people in my life that it would not hurt anymore. But it did. It made me feel small.

"What I should do is remind him what his real job is," Chef said. "The truck is here; he should be unloading it right now, not wasting my sous chef's precious prep time."

I heard footsteps coming toward the kitchen, so I hurried to where the delivery truck was waiting. My hands were shaking as I opened the truck's back door and started pulling out boxes.

Dave came out a few minutes later with a sad look on his face. "I'm sorry, Vinnie," he said quietly. "Chef's not in a good mood today."

"It's okay," I lied.

But it wasn't okay. I knew I was good at cooking. I had been cooking with Mom since I was little, and I made meals for my Family all the time. Why couldn't Chef see that I was more than just someone who carried boxes?

Typicals...

"Hey," Dave said, "why don't you show me more of those recipes during family meal?"

This made me feel a little better. At least Dave believed in me.

For the next four hours, I moved boxes and carried them to

different parts of the kitchen. Vegetables went to the walk-in fridge. Canned stuff went to dry storage. Meat went to the freezer. I knew where everything went, and I never dropped anything or put things in the wrong place.

But while I worked, I watched the other cooks making food. They chopped vegetables and stirred sauces and tasted everything to make sure it was perfect. I knew I could do those things too, if someone would just let me try.

During family meal, Dave and I sat in the back alley behind the restaurant. Dave lit up one of his clove cigarettes, which smelled sweet but also burned my nose. I didn't like it when Dave smoked, but I didn't say anything because he was my friend. I didn't have many friends that were typical, and I didn't want to make him mad at me.

The smell made me think about Nicholas. He used to smoke a long time ago, before he had to take care of me and the Family. But when he became our caregiver, he stopped smoking and drinking cold turkey, which is a weird saying. Cold turkeys can't do anything. It made no sense to me, but it did to Nicholas. He said he had to be healthy so he could take care of us. I wished Dave would quit smoking too, but I didn't know how to tell him.

I showed Dave more of Mom's recipes while he smoked.

"This chicken marinade," Dave said, pointing to one of Mom's notes. "She adds soy sauce with the lemon. That's really smart."

"Mom always said cooking was balance," I told him. "Sweet and sour, hot and cold, soft and crunchy."

"Your mom was a smart lady," Dave said.

"She was the best cook in the world," I said.

Dave looked at my recipe book for a long time. "You know what, Vinman? Someday I'm going to have my own restaurant.

And when I do, you're going to be my first hire. Not for moving boxes, for cooking real food."

"Really?" I asked.

"Really," Dave said. "I promise."

That made me feel good for the rest of the day, even when Chef walked by and made his usual comments about how I needed to move faster or how I was in the way. Dave's promise felt like a secret we shared, something good that was going to happen someday.

At five o'clock, I waited outside for my ride home. Ms. Violet came to pick me up. I was happy Celia was not with her.

"Hi, Vinnie," Ms. Violet said when I got in the back seat. "How was work today?"

"It was okay," I said. "Are we going home now?"

"First we have to pick up Garth," Ms. Violet said.

We drove to Cost$hare Warehouse, which was a huge store with a parking lot bigger than our whole neighborhood. I could see Garth way across the parking lot, pushing a long line of shopping carts back toward the store. Even from far away, he looked tired.

Ms. Violet drove up beside Garth and waved at him. He waved at us and went inside to clock out. When Garth came back and got in the front seat, he smelled like sweat, and his orange safety vest was dirty.

"How was work today, Garth?" Ms. Violet asked.

<Hot,> Garth signed. *<Lots of carts.>*

Garth's job looked really hard. He spent all day walking around a hot parking lot, bending over to fix shopping carts and pushing heavy loads across the pavement. But Garth was strong and good at it, even if it wasn't the kind of job that made people think you were important.

"You boys work hard," Ms. Violet said as we drove home. "You should be proud."

It was nice that Ms. Violet thought we should be proud, but I wondered if Chef would ever be proud of someone like me, or if the customers at Cost$hare Warehouse ever noticed how hard Garth worked to get their shopping carts.

When we got to our house, Ms. Violet said, "Vinnie, you and Celia had some problems this morning. Are you going to talk to her tonight like you said?"

"I told her I would," I said, but I wasn't sure I wanted to.

"Relationships take work," Ms. Violet said.

"I'm a hard worker, it will be fine," I answered and got out of the car. Garth followed me, and Ms. Violet drove away. As I walked toward the house, I thought about everything that happened today. Chef didn't think I could cook. Celia wouldn't say sorry. And Dave's promise felt far away, like something that might never happen. I hope the rest of my day is better.

Chapter Six

"Coo coo," Floyd managed, his voice straining with the effort.

"Coo coo," I repeated back, keeping my tone encouraging as I ran Floyd through his speech exercise. I'd been playing amateur speech therapist ever since the state funding cuts made his real sessions financially impossible. A perfect example of how budget cuts target the most vulnerable first.

We'd been at this for twenty minutes, working through the vocal exercises his actual therapist had drilled into me before we couldn't afford her anymore.

"Coo coo," Floyd tried again, marginally clearer.

"Coo coo!" I said, letting my enthusiasm bleed through. "That's better."

That's when William materialized in the living room doorway, his face a mask of barely controlled irritation. His coding had been interrupted, and William handled disruptions to his routine about as well as a cat handled a bath.

"I'm trying to work and I can't," he announced, frustration

edging every word "It's like living in a damn cuckoo's nest. What's happening?"

I set down the speech therapy materials and took in William's agitated posture. His shoulders were locked, jaw tight, fingers already starting their unconscious tapping. The finger tapping was his stimming behavior that helped William cope with his emotions. The way his autistic mind worked made him a coding genius, but it also made him as fragile as spun glass when his environment shifted unexpectedly. "The regular speech therapist costs too much now," I explained. "This is Floyd's new routine."

William's expression suggested this explanation was entirely unsatisfactory.

"Can he practice it with his inside voice?"

William never meant to be cruel. His brain just processed social interaction like code. Direct input, expected output, no room for emotional subroutines. The world saw him as callous, but I'd learned it was honesty without a filter. Very few people enjoy the way the truth sounds out loud. But, I'd figured out the key to redirecting William's blunt social behavior.

"Is that what Mr. Darcy would say?" I asked, knowing exactly which button to push. "Floyd has to practice."

I watched William's face change as he processed this. When William got overwhelmed, he had this coping mechanism that was beautiful to witness. He'd literally become Mr. Darcy from *Pride and Prejudice*. His posture straightened, his voice deepened into cultured formality, anxiety melted away as he slipped on the mask of a confident aristocratic English gentleman who always knew exactly what to say and do.

His mother had given him that book when he was twelve, desperate to find some way to connect with her son who seemed trapped behind walls she couldn't breach. She'd worked double shifts to keep them afloat while William's needs demanded attention she couldn't always provide. That book became their bridge, and more crucially, it gave William a social template for situations that would otherwise paralyze him completely.

"Coo coo!" Floyd said with a mischievous grin.

"Mr. McCallister, my good opinion once lost, is lost forever," William declared, fully inhabiting his aristocratic alter ego. "I cannot work under these conditions. I take my leave of you!"

He swept off toward his bedroom like he was exiting a grand estate, and I turned back to Floyd with an apologetic shrug.

"Sorry, Floyd. You know William's been procrastinating, and his project is due tomorrow."

"I kn-know," Floyd managed. "It's ffffine."

The stutter got worse when he was exhausted, I noted. Another variable to track in the endless equation of keeping everyone functional.

"Think you can handle the vocal exercises solo for a while?"

Floyd started to answer, but got caught on the "Y" sound. "Y-y-y-y..."

Unable to force the word out, he nodded instead. His wheelchair hummed to life as he followed William's path down the hall, still making deliberate "coo coo" sounds that were definitely more about psychological warfare than speech therapy at this point.

Floyd McCallister was a puzzle I wasn't entirely sure I wanted to solve. His entire life before his accident was gone, and the fragments that occasionally surfaced came as nightmares that left him screaming and soaked in sweat. Part of me worried about what would happen if Floyd ever recovered his full memory.

Sometimes the weight of it all crashed down and I had to

recalibrate before someone noticed the cracks. Back in the day, I'd have stepped outside for a smoke, but I had to stay healthy now, so I had traded smoking for breathing exercises. I closed my eyes and started the routine: Inhale for four, hold for four, exhale for four. Lather. Rinse. Repeat.

Being nurse, therapist, housekeeper, mediator, friend, and brother was a lot of roles to juggle simultaneously.

Inhale, two, three, four…

But who else was going to do it?

Hold, two, three, four…

I was the dam holding back the frigid waters of an uncaring world.

Exhale, two, three, four…

I would not break. Even if it killed me.

Inhale, two, three—

The front door banged open, cutting short my meditation. Vinnie and Garth were back from work, and I could hear Vinnie's rapid-fire commentary while Garth's heavy footsteps followed him inside.

Time to shift from amateur speech therapist back to family coordinator. In minutes, the dinner chaos would begin, and I needed to coax William out of his fortress, get Floyd to stop antagonizing him, help Vinnie decide on a meal that wouldn't trigger anyone's dietary restrictions or sensory issues.

None of us could have predicted that instead of setting five plates for dinner, we should have set six…

Chapter Seven

Vinnie had outdone himself with dinner. He'd pulled Mom's chicken marsala recipe from his binder, something that looked simple on paper but had been transformed into pure elegance through her handwritten notes about the deglazing technique and her secret splash of cream at the finish. The mushrooms were perfectly caramelized, the sauce had that rich complexity that only comes from patience and love, and even William was eating without his usual dissertation on food textures. Hell, Vinnie had even made me a vegetarian seitan version that was damn near perfect.

"This is incredible, Vinnie," I said, taking another bite. "Mom would be proud."

Vinnie's face lit up like he'd just won the lottery. "I want to restart my cooking YouTube channel," he announced out of nowhere. "People should know about Mom's recipes."

The table went dead silent. I felt my jaw clench automatically.

"Remember what happened last time?" I asked, fighting to keep my voice steady.

Vinnie's expression collapsed like a soufflé. "The people on the internet made so much fun of me it made me feel small," he said quietly.

The rage still burned in my chest every time I thought about that clusterfuck. It had taken months to rebuild Vinnie's confidence after the internet mob had torn him apart. The comment section had been a cesspit. People called him names, mocked his speech, made jokes about his disability. Not a single goddamn word about his actual cooking. But what made it worse was knowing who'd led the charge. Francis Donahey, a piece of shit from our childhood who'd never outgrown his sadistic streak.

Francis had always been my nemesis. He'd manipulate Vinnie into humiliating situations, mocked him mercilessly, then smoothed it over with fake apologies that somehow made Vinnie forget the cruelty. I'd lost count of how many fights I'd gotten into protecting Vinnie from that bastard, only to watch my brother welcome him back with open arms every single time.

The internet gave Francis and his kind unlimited ammunition with zero consequences. The cowards could destroy people from behind screens without ever having to look their victims in the eye.

Never fucking again.

"Besides," William said, his posture shifting into diplomatic Mr. Darcy mode, as Francis was a trigger for him as well, "... why not publish your mom's recipes in a book instead? That's what Rita suggested, remember?"

"A c-c-cookbook!" Floyd added through his stutter, his eyes lighting up with possibilities. "With st-stories about your mom. We could c-calculate the pr-printing costs and—"

"Real book. No trolls," Garth interrupted.

Then the conversation inevitably drifted to Rita, and I

could see that familiar gleam creeping into William's eyes at the mention of my girlfriend. "Rita could help you organize the cookbook," he said with calculated innocence. "She could come over more often." That was pure William. Any excuse to get Rita to spend more time here.

"She used to have dinner with us three nights a week, Nicholas," William continued in a prosecutorial tone. "It's been weeks since you've invited her. Floyd, verify my calculations?"

"Exactly thr-three weeks, two days," Floyd confirmed like a human spreadsheet.

But it was Vinnie who cut straight to what they all really wanted to know. "You wouldn't need to invite her if you just married her already. Why haven't you proposed?" he asked with his signature lack of filter.

Suddenly all eyes locked on me. The Family smelled blood in the water.

"Have you bought a ring yet?" Floyd asked. "What's the st-statistical probability of Rita saying yes?"

<One hundred percent,> Garth signed. <She loves him.>

"Where will you propose?" William was shifting into planning mode. "It should be romantic. Mr. Darcy would choose somewhere meaningful. Perhaps a garden? Or during a thunderstorm for dramatic effect?"

I was overwhelmed by their absolute certainty that my life should follow some script they'd apparently written without consulting me. So, I did what any family member does when cornered.

I deflected.

"Did you talk to Celia today?" I asked Vinnie.

The effect was immediate and brutal. Vinnie shut down completely, and the Family's laser focus swung away from me like Sauron's Eye finding the One Ring.

"What exactly are you two fighting about?" William asked, leaning forward like he was a detective interrogating a suspect. His autism demanded solutions to puzzles, and Vinnie's relationship crisis was the biggest unsolved mystery in our house.

"Is it about s-s-sex?" Floyd asked.

"Always about sex," Garth said.

Vinnie's face turned red as a ripened apple.

"Well, what then?" William pressed relentlessly. "If Mr. Darcy had a disagreement with Elizabeth Bennet, he would address it directly, with honesty and—"

"You need to read other books," Vinnie muttered.

"Everything relates to *Pride and Prejudice*," William replied with absolute seriousness. "Life is simply a series of social interactions that can be navigated using proper etiquette and—"

———

"I see what you did there," I said to Nicholas. He was trying to get everyone to stop asking him about Rita by making them ask me about Celia instead.

When Nicholas winked at me, I knew I was right.

That's when the phone rang. Our landline, which was weird because nobody ever called our house phone anymore...

Nicholas got up to answer it while the Family turned their attention back to me.

"Come on, Vinnie," William said. "What's really going on with Celia?"

"Did she do something mean?" Floyd asked.

"Murphy residence, hello?" Nicholas said into the phone.

I was going to answer Floyd when I noticed Nicholas. His body got very still, and his face turned white like milk.

I had only seen Nicholas look like that one time before...

My stomach started feeling sick.

Nicholas was listening to whoever was talking on the phone, but he wasn't talking. He just kept nodding while he got whiter and whiter.

The Family saw too.

When Nicholas hung up the phone, the whole kitchen was quiet. He stood there for a moment like he didn't know what to say.

"What's wrong, Nicholas?" I asked. "Who was it?"

Nicholas looked at all of us, then his eyes stopped on Garth. His face was so sad that I knew whatever he was going to say was going to be really bad.

<Garth,> Nicholas signed, *<your mother is dead.>*

Chapter Eight

St. Ann's Cathedral was packed with the kind of people who measured their worth in stock options and diversified portfolios. I kept the Family close as we navigated a parade of the wealthy elite, all draped in designer black and speaking in hushed, reverent tones as they discussed Agnes Cartwright's "generous spirit" and "community contributions." Our arrival sent a ripple of whispers travelling through the crowd like a stone tossed into still water.

I'd gotten everyone into their best clothes. William was in his favorite suit that made him look like a British aristocrat, Floyd in the button-down that covered his lightning scars, Vinnie wrestled with the tie he always bitched was too tight, and Garth squeezed into the only black suit he had that fit his massive frame. We looked respectable enough, but we still stuck out like misfits in this crowd of country club royalty and old money dynasties.

Then Garth stopped dead in his tracks.

I followed his line of sight to the front of the cathedral and the open casket where Agnes Cartwright lay in final repose, dressed in silk and jewelry that cost more than most people's annual salaries. She looked peaceful, like she was taking an afternoon nap, but I could see Garth's hands starting to shake as he stared at the woman who'd been his mother, protector, and anchor to the world. I watched him remove his hearing aids, his go-to coping mechanism when reality became too hard to handle.

I approached him carefully and signed, *<Would you like me to come with you?>*

Garth shook his head with that stubborn independence I'd learned to respect over the years. He walked toward the casket alone, shoulders squared, quietly determined, and suddenly I was remembering the first time we'd met.

Five years earlier...

I sat in the marble-and-mahogany foyer of the Cartwright mansion, surrounded by furniture far older than anyone I knew and more expensive than I ever wanted to know. Agnes Cartwright had called about her son, and from the careful way she'd chosen her words over the phone, I knew this was going to be complicated.

Through the half-open door of her study, I could hear voices. Agnes speaking with someone in those measured, diplomatic tones people use when delivering bad news. I wasn't trying to eavesdrop, but sound carried in these marble-floored palaces.

"I spoke with the headmaster, but he was inflexible," Agnes was saying, her voice stern but not unkind. "St. Andrew's maintains a zero-tolerance policy regarding physical altercations."

"Not...my fault," came a younger voice, careful. "They make... fun of me."

Agnes' tone softened immediately. "I know, honey. But you

need to learn better coping mechanisms. You can't change people with fisticuffs."

The frustrated silence that followed spoke volumes. A fourteen-year-old kid, expelled from boarding school for defending himself against bullies.

The story hit close to home.

"Perhaps I've been handling this incorrectly," Agnes continued thoughtfully. "I recently met a young man named Nicholas Murphy, who's establishing a residential facility for people with special needs."

"I'll be good," came the panicked response. "Please, Momma...don't send me away."

"Oh, Garth, come here."

The pain in Agnes's voice was unmistakable as she comforted her son. Here was a woman caught between love and reality, understanding that the world would never be gentle with someone like Garth but desperate to shield him anyway.

"It's for your protection," she said softly. "I want you to be happy. And safe. I won't always be here to look after you. Do you understand?"

"Yes, Momma."

"That's my good little soldier. I love you." Then—

"Mr. Murphy?" Agnes called out. "Would you join us, please?"

I entered the study to find Agnes composed and professional, while teenage Garth watched me with the wariness of someone who'd been disappointed too many times. Even at fourteen, he was built like a linebacker, but his developmental delays and hearing loss made him a magnet for cruelty.

"Mr. Murphy," Agnes said, "I'd like you to meet my son, Garth. Garth, this is Nicholas Murphy, the gentleman I mentioned."

I approached Garth slowly and offered my hand. "Good to meet you, Garth."

He looked at my hand for a long moment before shaking it with surprising gentleness for someone his size. "You too," he said quietly.

I recognized immediately that Garth had learned that the sound of his own voice was often an invitation for mockery.

<We can talk like this if you're more comfortable?> I signed in ASL.

<You know my language!> he signed back eagerly, a smile breaking across his face for the first time since I'd walked in.

In that moment, I saw past the angry teenager who got into fights at prep school and glimpsed the gentle soul underneath. Someone who just wanted to be understood and accepted for who he was.

I had no idea then that he'd become one of the most important people in my life, or that five years later I'd be standing in a cathedral watching him say goodbye to the woman who'd loved him enough to let him go.

The memory dissolved as I watched present-day Garth kneel beside his mother's casket, his shoulders rippling as he mourned silently.

"Love you, Momma," Garth managed, the words echoing loudly in the hushed space.

As he stood to leave, a woman approached him like a spider who'd been waiting in her web.

I recognized her instantly. Charity Cartwright, Garth's sister, though the family resemblance ended at their DNA. Where Garth was gentle and warm, Charity was calculating and ice-cold. Her practiced smile never touched her eyes.

"I'm so sorry, Garth," she said, pulling him into what looked like a sisterly embrace. "I miss Mother terribly already. I'm glad you came. She would have appreciated that."

Garth barely returned the hug, and I noticed he wouldn't meet her eyes.

Garth made eye contact with everyone. It was how he connected, how he read people's intentions—and lips—when their words failed to reach him.

"Hello, Charity," he said, his voice flat as concrete.

I caught her gaze drift to his ears. "No hearing aids today," she observed with faux sympathy. "On days like this, I almost envy your ability to shut out the world. But you can read lips, and I need you to understand..."

She gripped his chin and forced him to look directly at her. Garth's eyes went wide with something I'd never seen from him before.

Fear. Pure, undiluted terror.

I'd never seen Garth afraid of anything. Not the neighborhood thugs who'd learned to give him a wide berth after a few encounters. Not William's worst meltdowns when he'd scream and throw things. Not even the time Floyd's drone had malfunctioned and nearly taken his eye out.

"I'll always take care of Momma's good little soldier," she whispered, her voice pitched just loud enough for me to catch the veiled threat wrapped in synthetic sincerity.

Brother and sister locked eyes for a moment that crackled with unspoken menace. Then Garth broke away and walked toward us, his face drained of color.

I motioned for the Family to follow Garth while I approached Charity, every instinct screaming warnings about this woman.

Nicholas stayed close to Garth in case he needed support, like he always did when one of us was hurting. The rest of the Family waited with me while Garth said goodbye to his mom at the front of St. Ann's Cathedral.

I loved cathedrals. They made me feel small, but not the bad kind of small that people's stares made me feel. The good kind of small, like when you look at the stars and remember how big the universe is. St. Ann's was beautiful. The ceiling went up and up, and the stained-glass windows made colored light on the stone floor like dancing rainbows.

Even though today was sad, the cathedral felt peaceful. The flowers were arranged in big bunches that smelled like Mom's garden used to smell when it was summer. White roses and lilies and some purple flowers I didn't know the names of.

"It is a most appropriate venue for someone of Agnes's stature to celebrate her glorious journey to the next life," William said in his Mr. Darcy voice. William was going to be Mr. Darcy all day. Funerals made him extra nervous because he didn't know the right things to say to people who were crying.

Floyd's wheelchair made its whirring sound next to me. The sound bounced off the stone walls. "I guess they c-c-can't afford to p-put a r-r-ramp up." Floyd said, sounding annoyed. I looked down at the stairs Floyd was looking at that led up to the casket. I could hear people talking about us in whispers.

Typicals always thought they were being quiet, but they weren't.

"Poor things," one woman said behind her hand.

"Are they supposed to be here?" another person asked.

If typicals could talk about us, then we could talk about them. I turned to the people and said loud enough for them to hear, "You have so much money, but nobody can build a ramp? That's not right!"

Then I heard a man whisper to the priest, "Oh, they're disabled. They must be one of Agnes's charity cases."

"Charity cases" was what typicals called us when they wanted to sound nice but really meant we didn't belong there. It made my face feel hot, but I tried not to let it show. I was going to be strong for Garth. Instead of getting mad, I made my back straight and tried to be like one of the saint statues in the cathedral. Quiet and dignified.

I was thinking about how statues didn't care about what strangers whispered when I saw Garth moving away from his mother's casket. I thought he would come straight back to us, but a woman got in his way.

She had blonde hair that looked perfect, like she spent lots of time making it look that way.

The woman hugged Garth, but something was wrong.

Garth looked scared.

That didn't make sense. Garth wasn't scared of anything. He was so strong he could carry me and William at the same time without getting tired.

But watching this woman hug him, Garth looked like a little boy who wanted to hide. The woman grabbed Garth's face with her hand, like she owned him. When she finally let him go, Garth walked back to us fast. His face was white, which scared me.

I hugged Garth, trying to make him feel safe, like Nicholas made me feel safe when I was scared. I could feel him shaking a little bit.

I looked at Garth and asked, "Who was that woman?"

Garth read my lips and just shook his head no.

I wanted to ask more questions, but Garth's face told me to stop. So I did, because that's what Family does. We respected each other's feelings, even when we don't understand them.

I looked back at the woman and saw her talking to Nicholas

now. Nicholas had his polite face on, the one he used when he had to talk to social workers or doctors who thought they knew better than him about taking care of us. But I could tell from the way he stood that he didn't like this woman.

Nicholas was really good at reading people, better than any of us. If Nicholas didn't like someone, there was usually a good reason.

I watched the woman's mouth moving and her hands waving around, and I knew she must have done something really bad to Garth to make him afraid of her. Something that hurt him in ways you couldn't see.

Garth might talk about it later when we were safe at home, where we didn't have to pretend everything was okay. Where he could be scared if he needed to be, and we would all take care of him until the scared feeling went away.

But right now, in this beautiful cathedral with its colored light and peaceful flowers, I put my arm around Garth and let him know that he had us.

And we had him.

"Charity," I said, keeping my voice respectfully neutral. "Please accept my condolences. Agnes was a remarkable woman. She'll be deeply missed."

"Thank you, Mr. Murphy," she replied, her smile becoming more genuine now that Garth was out of range. "Poor Garth doesn't seem to be handling this very well."

"About as well as anyone could," I said carefully. "Losing your mother is devastating, especially when... How are you holding up?"

"Honestly, I don't think the reality has hit me yet. Thank you for asking."

I studied her face, searching for any authentic emotion beneath that perfectly composed mask. Every tear calculated, every gesture choreographed for maximum impact. Standing there talking to her, I felt like a surfer being circled by a shark in crystal-clear water.

"I should catch up with him," I said. "If there's anything you need, don't hesitate to call."

"Again, thank you, Mr. Murphy."

We'd soon learn that Garth was right to be afraid of Charity.

Chapter Nine

The house felt weird after Nicholas drove us home from the funeral. Like Death had come home with us and made everything quiet and sad. Even getting ready for bed felt different, like we were all moving through beef stew.

I could hear everyone getting ready to sleep in the house. Floyd's room was quiet, which was good because it meant he wasn't having bad dreams. William's room got quiet after an hour, which meant he finished counting all his stuff and went to sleep. Garth's room was the most quiet, and that worried me because Garth usually makes loud noises getting ready for bed because he can't hear himself.

Then I heard Rita's car in our driveway really late. I looked out my window and saw her walking fast to our front door with a small bag. I think she came to help Nicholas feel better because Nicholas was sad about Garth's mom dying. It made him remember when our mom died.

A few minutes later, I heard Rita and Nicholas talking quietly in the hallway, then his bedroom door closed. Nicholas needed to know things could get better, and Rita helped with that.

That's why they were good together.

When one person fell down, the other person picked them up. Tonight, Rita would pick up Nicholas, so I didn't have to worry about him.

I thought about Garth and how he must be feeling. When our mom died, it felt like someone took a big piece of me and threw it in the trash. I was mad and confused and thought maybe it was my fault, even though Nicholas told me lots of times that it wasn't. I remembered being so mad I wanted to hit things, and then so sad I couldn't stop crying, and then I felt bad for being sad because Mom would want me to be happy.

Nicholas helped me feel better. He told me it was okay to feel sad and mad and confused all at the same time. He said there were steps for feeling sad about someone dying, and everyone had to go through the steps, but different people took different amounts of time.

I thought maybe I could help Garth like Nicholas helped me. I had an idea about what to say to him, but I would wait until tomorrow when he went to the gym. Garth always felt better after lifting heavy things. Maybe I would go with him. It would be a good time to talk about feelings.

Then my phone made a Super Mario sound. It was a text from Celia.

Celia: *Hey, Vinnie. Are you in bed yet?*

I looked at her words for a long time before I wrote back.

Vinnie: *Yes. I'm about to go to sleep.*

Celia: *What are you wearing?* 😉

The little yellow face was winking at me, which meant Celia was being flirty. But I was still mad at her, so I decided to be mean back.

Vinnie: *Bra and panties.*

My phone filled up with surprised faces—😮😮😮😮 — which meant Celia was shocked.

Vinnie: *That's what you want, right?*

Then nothing. Celia didn't write back, and the three little dots that show when someone is typing never showed up.

I put my phone down and turned off my lights. Tomorrow was going to be important.

Rita set down her small overnight bag on the bed and started unpacking. The sight of her there, still in uniform but with her hair loose, always struck me as a perfect metaphor for who she was. Official and intimate, strong and vulnerable, the woman who could command a crime scene and then slip into a faded *Brooklyn Nine-Nine* T-shirt that read "You're Doug Judy to my Peralta"—Vinnie's Christmas gift that had sparked an ongoing debate between the two of them about who was the smooth criminal and who was the overeager detective.

I knew she was one of the few people who understood the weight of carrying others. Her father's cancer was in remission now, thank God, but I could see how his cancer scare had changed her, made her more protective of our time together. Rita had this instinct for knowing when to be my anchor and when to let me be hers, a dance she'd mastered while I was still figuring out the steps. She carried her own pain quietly, the way cops learn to, convinced I already had enough weight on my shoulders with the Family.

"What's in the bag?" I asked, closing the door behind me.

"Sleeping clothes. Fresh uniform's in my locker; I'll change at the precinct," she said. "I have an early briefing."

"Damn, I was hoping for sex toys," I deadpanned.

We both laughed, but the humor couldn't quite mask what

was simmering underneath. I pulled Rita into a tight embrace, holding on to her like a lifeline as the day's weight crashed down all at once. Agnes's funeral, Garth's pain, and remembering the loss of my own mother.

"Hey," Rita said softly, her voice shifting into that gentle tone she used when someone needed protection rather than direction. "Talk to me."

"It's just...watching Garth today. It brought back everything about losing Mom. How shattered Vinnie was, how I had no clue what I was doing..."

Rita squeezed my hand. "That's exactly why I know he'll be okay. Garth has you. All of you. When your mom died, you and Vinnie were alone."

She was right, but the protector in me couldn't let go that easily. "What if I fuck it up? What if I miss the signs that he's struggling, or say the wrong thing at the wrong time?"

"Then the Family will carry both of you," Rita said simply. "That's how this works, remember? Speaking of carrying things," Rita said, her tone shifting into professional mode, "what's the group home funding situation now that Agnes is gone?"

I blinked, caught off guard by the question. "Fine. Why?"

"The Cartwright Foundation's been your primary funding source since day one. Who controls that now?" Her questions came in that clipped, efficient manner she used when gathering intel.

"Charity, I assume. But Agnes and I had an understanding. She believed in what we're doing." I shrugged. "I'm not worried about it."

Rita's expression suggested maybe I should be, but she filed it away the way cops do before they've fully investigated something.

I'd always known Charity was selfish and manipulative, but

what I'd witnessed at the funeral was different. Colder. The way she'd gripped Garth's chin. Like watching a spider who'd spent years patiently weaving her web, and now her prey was finally trapped. The thought made my skin crawl, but I pushed it aside. Agnes had legal protections in place. Charity couldn't just sweep in and destroy everything her mother had built.

Could she?

"I hate to ask," I said, the words feeling heavy, "but could you run a background check on Charity?"

"Are you asking me to misuse police resources?" she said, her voice carrying that cop authority even as her eyes danced with mischief.

As I scrambled for a response, Rita winked at me. "Relax. I've gotten very comfortable mixing business with pleasure when it comes to the Family."

I was mortified. "What? I've never asked you to compromise your—"

"You haven't," she cut me off. "Remember when the Family got obsessed with *Finding Bigfoot*?" she asked, already knowing the answer. "They called the precinct every day for a month demanding I investigate and...find Bigfoot. I filled out a fake police report to get them to stop." Rita chuckled at the memory.

"So, you'll do it?" I asked.

"Of course I will," she said. "Rich kids like Charity always have skeletons buried in their trust fund closets. Money makes problems disappear, but it doesn't erase them completely. If there is something, there'll be a paper trail somewhere."

"Thank you," I said, meaning it more than she probably realized.

"You never have to thank me," Rita said, pulling me into an embrace before continuing, "But maybe you can explain the texts Vinnie keeps sending me. At first, I thought they were random, but Vinnie always has a reason."

Rita showed me her phone with Vinnie's latest message.

Vinnie: *What kind of diamond rings do women like?*

I took her phone and scrolled through Vinnie's text chain about diamond ring shapes, princess cut versus round, what women preferred, which ones looked best in different settings.

That sneaky little fucker.

I knew exactly what Vinnie was plotting. He's trying to figure out what ring Rita would like so he could *suggest* I buy one just like it for her. The last thing I needed was for Rita to connect those dots.

Time for tactical misdirection.

"Celia and Vinnie are fighting," I said quickly. "Maybe this has something to do with it?"

Rita's cop instincts kicked in immediately. "What are they fighting about?"

"No clue," I said. "He won't talk about it. Just gets pissed and changes the subject."

Rita scrolled through Vinnie's texts, processing the new information. "Maybe Vinnie wants to get her a ring as an apology for whatever happened between them?"

I saw my opening and took it. "You don't think Vinnie's planning to propose to Celia? That would explain why he's been so secretive about their relationship problems."

Rita's brow furrowed in concentration. "You might be on to something. Want me to talk to him?"

Thank God, I thought but kept my mouth shut. "Vinnie does see you as a maternal figure. He might open up."

"I'll handle it," she said before leaning in to kiss me.

Her kiss started gentle and reassuring but quickly shifted as Rita had other intentions. She'd come here tonight knowing exactly what I needed. Not just emotional support, but the kind of release that could only come from losing myself completely in her. This was her way of carrying me through my grief and anxiety, giving me permission to stop being strong for everyone else.

Even if it was only for tonight.

Rita felt it too, because when we broke apart, her eyes held a promise I knew well. She raised her left eyebrow, her not-so-subtle invitation for sex.

"Those early morning briefings," I murmured as I kissed down her neck, "... how early exactly?"

"Early enough," she whispered back, her hands already working on my shirt buttons, "that we should probably start making the most of tonight."

I pulled her closer, finally allowing myself to stop thinking, stop worrying, stop carrying the weight of everyone else's world for just a little while. Rita's hands were warm against my skin, and for the first time all day, I could actually breathe.

We made love, quietly, mindful not to draw any attention from the Family.

In the morning at breakfast, our kitchen felt all wrong. Nicholas drank his coffee with a satisfied look. That meant he and Rita had sex last night. William ate his eggs, but he was counting them more than usual, which meant he was anxious. Floyd picked at his oatmeal, but Garth refused to eat.

I noticed Rita wasn't here, which meant she left early. That was good for her because she could avoid William, but bad for William because he would miss having breakfast with his pretend girlfriend. I decided not to tell anyone I saw Rita last night. I didn't want to deal with William or Mr. Darcy right now.

And Garth wouldn't drink the big cup of raw eggs I put in front of him. He always drank raw eggs in the morning during training season. It was part of getting ready for the Special Olympics. But today, he just stared at nothing instead.

"It's not your normal routine, Garth," I said, trying to sound happy, "but I thought I could work out with you today."

Nicholas looked up from his coffee with a surprised but happy look. He was always glad when I thought of ways to help the Family without him telling me what to do. It made him feel like he was doing a good job taking care of us.

"That sounds like a good idea," Nicholas said, and I could hear he was proud of me.

Garth thought about it for a long time, then nodded his head a little bit.

"Drink your eggs then," I said. "I put protein powder in them too, to make you stronger."

"Not hungry," Garth said. "Let's go."

The gym was full of people who loved lifting weights so much they looked like they were made of just muscles instead of regular people. The air was hot and sweaty and smelled like metal.

There were mirrors everywhere, which I liked because I could watch myself and make sure I was doing things right. The weights were organized from small to big, which made William happy when he came here because everything was in order.

Garth started stretching in his usual spot by the free weights. I pretended to stretch next to him, but really I was just bending over because stretching was boring and I was already perfect.

"My mom died when Nicholas and I were in high school," I said while I fake-stretched. "Senior year."

Garth kept stretching, trying to ignore me, but I saw him watching my lips and listening.

"I won't lie to you, Garth. The hurt never goes away. I still think about Mom every day. But Nicholas taught me something good I want to teach you. If you're sad, cry. If you're mad, break something, but not something that costs lots of money. You can't keep the hurt inside. It's bad for you."

Garth stopped stretching, and I could tell he was thinking about what I said.

"Nicholas tried to explain the steps of being sad when someone dies, but I forgot most of it. What I remember is that first, you don't believe the person is really dead, then you get mad, then you try to make deals with God, then you get sad, but that's good because being sad means you're almost done and will be okay," I finished.

I didn't tell him that sometimes that took a really long time.

That's when Tony came over and bumped fists with Garth like they always did.

"Garth, my man!" Tony said loud. "What you gonna win this year at the Special Olympics?"

"He's going to win gold for weightlifting," I said.

"Hell yeah, he is," Tony said. "You need someone to spot you, big man?"

Garth pointed at me and shook his head, which meant I was going to spot him today.

"Vinman, you lifting today?" Tony asked me.

I made my arm muscles big and said, "You don't mess with perfect. I'm here for Garth."

Tony bumped fists with me, then laughed and walked away.

Garth went to the place where you do clean-and-jerks and started putting weights on the bar. But instead of his usual circles, he put on way more circles than normal. More than I had ever seen him use before.

"That's a lot of weight, Garth," I said, feeling worried. "That's way more than you usually do."

Garth closed his eyes and lifted the weight. He was trying really hard. It wasn't easy like usual. Maybe that's what I was doing too, I thought. Maybe today I was carrying Garth, like Rita carried Nicholas and Nicholas carried all of us when we needed help.

But then Garth put the weight down and started adding even more circles to the bar. Way more circles. That made even the muscle people stop and look.

"You're going to hurt yourself, Garth," I said, feeling scared.

Garth didn't read my lips or pretended not to. He stood over the bar and got ready to lift. His face got red and the veins in his neck stuck out.

Everyone in the gym stopped what they were doing to watch. Tony started cheering, saying things like "Come on, big man!" and "You can do it! Go! Go! Go!"

Garth yelled really loud like the Hulk and lifted the bar over his head. He held it there and kept yelling and sweat dripped down his face.

But I saw it wasn't just sweat.

It was tears too.

When Garth dropped the bar, it sounded like thunder. The whole gym clapped and cheered. Everyone thought what he did was amazing.

But I saw his tears and knew they were for his mom.

We walked home, and I thought about Garth's tears mixed with his sweat. Nicholas always said that when people we love are hurting, we have to speak up, even when it's hard. I had to tell Nicholas what I saw at the gym. He would know what to do to help Garth feel better.

I was wrong.
No one felt better after what Garth told us.

Chapter Ten

While Vinnie and Garth were at the gym, the rest of us tried to maintain some kind of normal routine. Floyd worked on his latest drone project in the living room, the soft whirring of tiny motors filling the silence like white noise. William affectionately organized his movie collection, counting and recounting his Colin Firth films. I attempted to tackle paperwork for the group home, but found myself staring at the same invoice three times without absorbing a single number.

When Vinnie and Garth returned, the atmosphere shifted completely. Vinnie's usual chatter was muted, replaced by worried glances toward Garth, who moved through the house as if he was sleepwalking, not seeing anyone or anything except his grief. We all sensed that whatever had happened at the gym was significant, but Garth's palpable grief made us walk on eggshells. The afternoon dragged endlessly as we orbited around his anguish, each of us wanting to help but having no clue what to say.

Tonight would normally be movie night. We'd all argue and

negotiate about what to watch. Sports drama? Documentary? Sci-fi? Fantasy?

But tonight was different.

By seven o'clock, we'd gathered in the living room for our weekly ritual. Floyd positioned his wheelchair in his usual spot near the window. William had already claimed the remote and was sorting through his movie options with the reverence of a priest selecting hymns. Vinnie sprawled across the couch, while Garth settled into his oversized chair, still wearing his sweat-stained gym clothes.

Not a good sign.

William, in his infinite wisdom, had selected *Pride and Prejudice*—shocker—as our evening's entertainment. This was his method of healing, since Austen's story had been his emotional anchor through his own trauma. He was scanning for scenes that might mirror what Garth was experiencing, offering comfort through the wisdom of his beloved characters.

"This is the part where Elizabeth's sister runs away with Mr. Wickham," William earnestly explained. "See how Mr. Darcy provides support?"

With awkward tenderness, William placed his hand on Garth's shoulder, mimicking what he imagined the perfect gentleman's consoling gesture would look like.

The sincerity of his effort made me smile.

"He doesn't want to watch this," Vinnie interrupted from the couch. "Put on wrestling. That's what he likes."

"Wrestling offers no therapeutic benefit," William countered. "It's barbaric entertainment. Garth requires emotional nourishment."

Since William extracted all his life lessons from literature and cinema, he began examining his extensive Colin Firth collection for more appropriate viewing material. I watched with fond exasperation as he sorted through DVDs and Blu-rays, each bearing his own creative renaming system wherein every Colin Firth performance became a variation of Mr. Darcy's adventures.

"What about, *Mr. Darcy is a Spy?*" he asked, holding up a DVD of *Kingsman: The Secret Service.*

Garth remained silent.

"*Mr. Darcy Corrects His Speech Impediment?*" he tried, showing *The King's Speech* Blu-ray.

Still nothing.

"*Mr. Darcy Has an Illegitimate Daughter?*" he proposed, waving *What a Girl Wants.*

Floyd snatched the remote from William and switched from the Blu-ray player to broadcast television. The evening news invaded our sanctuary, and we all went quiet as the reporter's voice sliced through our domestic bubble.

"Police continue investigating Thursday's robbery of Citizen's State Bank," the anchor announced grimly. "This is the third bank robbery this month by what authorities believe is the same crew. In each incident, the perpetrators have executed one person inside the bank, apparently at random, before fleeing with undisclosed amounts of cash. Police are warning the public that the suspects are to be considered armed and extremely dangerous and to immediately alert—"

Floyd switched to wrestling, hoping to lift Garth's spirits, but our traumatized friend didn't even register the channel change. He remained trapped in his private purgatory.

Then Vinnie asked what we'd all been wondering.

"Why are you so afraid of Charity, Garth?"

Garth immediately folded in on himself. He shook his head at Vinnie.

"You don't have to tell us anything you're not ready to

share," I said gently. "But sometimes talking about difficult things helps."

Garth looked unconvinced; his mouth pressed into a tight line.

"Would you rather talk about your mother?" I ventured. "Vinnie and I went through losing our mom in high school, so we understand some of what you're feeling."

"I already told him everything I know," Vinnie added helpfully.

I nodded. "That's good, Vinnie. But maybe Garth wants to work through it with all of us. We're Family. You know this is a safe space, Garth."

Garth wrestled with this for a long moment, his internal struggle written across his face. Finally, he gave a reluctant nod and looked down.

"Don't like...my voice," he said.

Dammit. Despite all his progress, all the confidence we'd built together over the years, he'd regressed to his childhood trauma of people mocking how he sounded.

This was worse than I thought.

"Sign it then," I offered. "I'll translate for everyone."

When he looked up at me, he held my gaze a beat too long; I couldn't tell if he was relieved or frustrated by my offer. Then he closed his eyes and took a deep breath, like he was gathering the courage to relive something he desperately wanted to forget. When he opened his eyes, I saw grim determination, and he began to sign.

<Charity...hurt me,> Garth began.

"Charity hurt him," I said as I watched Garth's hands.

<I was little. Maybe four.>

"When he was very little," I translated as he continued. I watched Garth's face contort as he remembered the lost innocence of his four-year-old self.

<Ball broke...Momma's vase.>

"He was playing with a ball... Broke his mother's vase by accident." I saw confusion spread across his features, the confusion of a small child who didn't understand he'd done something wrong.

<Charity came. Very angry.>

"Charity found him and was furious." I saw the fear in Garth's eyes as he relived facing his teenage sister's rage.

<Momma blamed Charity. Said I was too small to reach.>

"Agnes blamed Charity for the broken vase, even though Garth broke it," I managed. "She said Garth was too small to have reached it."

<Charity... Very, very angry at me.>

"Charity was... God, she was so angry with him." I had to pause as Garth's signing became more agitated, his whole body remembering the terror.

<She found me alone. Grabbed me like this.>

My hands instinctively clenched into fists as Garth gripped his own shoulders, demonstrating exactly what Charity had done.

"She found him alone and grabbed his shoulders," I whispered, my voice breaking.

<Shook me. Hard. Very hard.>

Garth's entire body began trembling as he showed us the violent motion. I couldn't speak. I shook my head, fighting back my rage and tears as he relived the abuse.

"She shook him," I finally managed. "Violently."

<'Speak, dummy!' Over and over.>

"She was screaming at him to speak, calling him...'dummy,'" I finished, the words sounded even more vicious spoken aloud.

<Everything spinning. Couldn't...couldn't...>

Garth's hands fluttered helplessly, trying to show the disorientation, the terror, and I felt sick watching him relive it.

"Everything was spinning for him," I choked out. "He couldn't..."

<Then...no more sound. Nothing.>

"And then he couldn't hear anymore," I whispered. "She destroyed his hearing."

The room fell into absolute silence. William had his hands over his mouth. Floyd had tears streaming down his face. Vinnie looked like someone had gut-punched him.

Shaken baby syndrome.

The medical reality hit me like a freight train. Violent shaking like that, at that age, could cause catastrophic brain damage, hearing loss, developmental delays...

All from a few seconds of a spoiled teenager's jealous fury.

<Never want to see her again,> Garth signed with fierce determination through his own tears. *<Never want to speak to her. I wish she was dead!>*

"He never wants to see her again," I translated, wiping my eyes. "Never wants to speak to her." I left out the death wish bit. If it disturbed me, I didn't want to see how the Family would react.

"We'll never let that happen," I promised him, meaning it with every cell in my body. "We're Family. Always and forever."

The Family surrounded Garth, all of them crying like that movie night when William made them watch *Titanic* for the first time.

But looking around, I realized grief had spread through our house like a contagion.

We needed to escape reality.

Fast.

"Come on," I said, standing up and grabbing my keys.

"Where are we going?" Vinnie asked.

"Don't know about you guys, but I could use a pint right about now."

And just like that, the Family's despair evaporated immediately and we all piled into the van.

Chapter Eleven

The Pint & Proper had that kind of unpretentious charm that came from not giving a damn about impressing anyone. The local bar and grill drew a mixed crowd. College students nursed cheap beers at high-top tables, middle-class DINKS celebrated another successful week of dual incomes and no kids, and then there was us. The Family had claimed our usual corner booth, the one with enough space for Floyd's wheelchair and Garth's massive frame.

I know what you're thinking.

How the fuck can a responsible caregiver be reckless enough to give people with disabilities alcohol? Surely some, if not all of them, are on medications that would make booze completely off-limits?

And you'd be partially correct in thinking that.

Our server, Jenny, set down six pints of ice cream and a round of Shirley Temples. "Mint chocolate chip for Vinnie," she announced. "Vanilla for William, cookies and cream for Floyd, rocky road for Nicholas, and..." She struggled slightly with Garth's two containers. "Chocolate peanut butter and strawberry for our champion here."

Garth managed a weak smile. He'd been coming here since he began participating in the Special Olympics years ago, and Jenny had watched his transformation from a terrified teenager to the powerhouse he was today. Despite his current emotional shutdown, the fact that he'd ordered two pints tonight—something that would've been unthinkable this morning—felt like a small victory.

I watched genuine excitement light up each Family member's face as they prepared to dive into their frozen therapy. Even William, who'd been counting and recounting his Shirley Temple cherries with increasing anxiety, seemed to relax.

Vinnie was reaching for his spoon when I stopped him and raised my glass.

"To Agnes Cartwright," I said solemnly. "Beloved mother and trusted friend."

The Family raised their glasses with me. Garth remained despondent, staring at his untouched drink.

"Garth," Vinnie said gently, "you have to drink after a toast or it's bad luck."

Garth looked around the table at his Family, all of us waiting for him, and slowly lifted his glass to ours.

"To Momma," he said quietly, his voice rough with emotion.

We clinked glasses, and I felt some of the tension leave my shoulders. Maybe bringing them here had been the right call. Maybe we could pull Garth out of this darkness after all.

But my relief was short-lived. William had retreated back into himself, huddled in the corner of our booth as he sipped his drink through a straw. Being around this many people in an uncontrolled environment was clearly distressing for him. This wasn't his routine, wasn't his carefully ordered world. But he was fighting his urge to slip on his Mr. Darcy mask because he knew Garth needed him to be present as himself.

"This is like that scene in *Miss Congeniality*," William suddenly announced, spooning up a large bite of vanilla, "where Sandra Bullock eats ice cream after her terrible day, except Mr. Darcy isn't in that movie, which is unfortunate because he would have provided excellent emotional support."

Floyd snorted. "Y-you know Mr. D-darcy isn't r-real, right?"

"He's real to me," William replied. Completely serious. To him, Mr. Darcy was part of the historical record. "And he would approve of ice cream as a coping mechanism. Very civilized."

Vinnie's phone suddenly erupted with Super Mario's distinctive "Mamma mía!" His text alert never failed to make me smile, even in the worst circumstances. He'd chosen it because Mario Kart was his favorite game, the closest he'd ever get to actually driving.

"I bet it's Celia," William said, perking up with the prospect of relationship drama.

"Pussy whipped," Garth blurted with a slight chuckle.

Floyd mimed cracking a whip while making exaggerated swooshing sounds, which sent William into a fit of giggles.

But as Vinnie read his text, his expression darkened.

"It's not Celia," Vinnie said quietly as he turned his phone for me to read. "It's—"

I read the text and spat the name like a curse. "*Francis.*"

Francis: *WTF? The inmates escaped the asylum?*

Francis Donahey and his faithful lackey Scott strolled over to our table. Both thirty-one years old, yet neither had grown up since high school. Francis still had that same cocky swagger, the same predatory smile masquerading as friendship that had been making my life hell since we were kids.

"If it isn't Vinnie and the Tards," Francis announced with theatrical grandeur. "That'd make a great name for a band. You should use that, Vinman. You could tour on the short bus—"

"You're not allowed to call me that," Vinnie interrupted, showing more backbone than I'd expected.

"What do you want, *Francis*?" I asked, emphasizing his name like an insult.

Francis hated his name. He'd developed a complex about having what most people considered a girl's name since childhood. Oh, he tried to spin this elaborate story about how his dad named him after some Johnny Cash song to make him tough enough to take on the world. Nobody bought it, so he rebranded himself as "Frank."

But I knew the truth. And never let him forget it.

His mother had wanted a daughter and had been so set on the name Francis that when her baby came out male, she kept the name.

Francis feigned hurt as he turned his gaze to the Family, all smiles and sunshine. "I was enjoying my night out when I saw my old high school buds, Nicholas and the Vinman, and I thought to myself, 'Frank, ol' boy, why not spread some of your Irish cheer this fine evening?'"

Nobody in the Family liked Francis except Vinnie when he got manipulated, which usually happened when Francis caught him alone. Floyd expressed his disdain immediately.

"Why don't you go f-f-f-"

Francis's eyes widened at what Floyd was about to say.

"...find another table," Floyd finished.

"Hahahaha, for a second there, I thought your balls had dropped, wheelie," Francis laughed. "Here, r-r-ride the rainbow with me. Might help that st-st-stutter."

He tossed a colorful baggie of what looked like gummy

bears onto the table. Vinnie's eyes lit up at the candy and he reached for it. I slapped his hand away.

"What've I told you about that?" I snapped.

"Never take candy from strangers," Vinnie recited automatically.

"I'm not talking to you, Vinnie. That's not candy."

"And I'm no stranger," Francis said innocently.

Francis was a notorious dealer in healer's clothing. Whatever drug you wanted, this asshole had it. Those gummies were weed edibles, and they would wreak absolute havoc with Floyd's medications. With any of their medications. I tried to control myself, remember my breathing exercises. But this son of a bitch was practically begging for a fight.

Inhale, two, three, four...

Francis slid his baggie back into his pocket, loving that he was getting a rise out of me. He could manipulate both Vinnie and me, and it really pissed me off to no end.

Hold, two, three, four...

"I know," Francis continued with practiced charm. "Scott, go buy us a round of drinks so we can reminisce about the glory days." As Scott headed to the bar, Francis called after him, "Better make it a *special* round." He turned back to us. A shit-eating grin on his stupid fucking face. "Amirite? Amirite? Hahahaha."

No one else laughed. Francis clocked our grim expressions.

"What's wrong with you? You're acting like someone died, for Christ's sake."

"Garth's Mom died," Vinnie said simply.

Francis froze and shifted gears. This was textbook Francis, using fake kindness to mask his true nature. He looked at Garth, and his expression shifted to genuine sympathy.

Fuck this guy.

"I'm sorry, big man," he said, raising his drink. "To our

moms, who've always overlooked our faults, but never our needs. God rest her soul."

Francis clinked glasses with everyone, and I watched Vinnie warm to him immediately. Exactly what Francis always did. Confused him with a little kindness so he could torture him later.

Exhale, two, three, four...

"That was nice, Francis," Vinnie said.

I wanted to scream.

"I'm a nice guy," Francis replied. "Wanna come be my wingman? Chicks love a guy who takes care of retar—"

Inhale—FUCK THIS.

"Get the hell out of here, Francis," I said, standing up. "Or we will reminisce like we used to."

I was in full threat display now. Shoulders squared and pulled back, chest expanded, my frame suddenly taking up more space as every muscle tensed for violence. My hands clenched into fists at my sides, jaw tight, eyes locked on Francis. Vinnie and the Family got scared and uncomfortable, but I was lost to righteous rage, that familiar tunnel vision taking over.

Francis, never one to start a fight in an establishment where he could get sued for damages, laughed off my threat with forced indifference.

"You and I remember high school very differently," he said with a smirk.

"Let's make some new memories then, dickhead."

I was about to stomp a mudhole in Francis's ass when William exploded.

"Stop it! Stopitstopitstopitstopit!"

William's outburst was so loud, so extreme, that the entire bar went quiet and turned to stare at our table. Francis, realizing there were far too many witnesses watching him prey upon a group with disabilities, decided to retreat. But not without saving face.

"I'll be saving that dance for you," he said to me.

"Anytime."

As Francis walked away to join Scott at the bar, I turned to see Vinnie's look of disappointment. Floyd shook his head sadly. William was coming out of his anxiety attack, but it was Garth's glowering expression that cut me to the core.

Goddammit...

"Let's go home," I said quietly.

I followed Nicholas out of the Pint & Proper. He wanted everyone in the van so we could leave. But it takes a long time to get Floyd's wheelchair into the van on the lift.

While everyone waited by the van, they said Francis was mean and that Nicholas was good for not fighting him. But I was getting scared as I watched my brother.

Nicholas used to fight lots of people because I have Down syndrome. One time I asked him why, and Nicholas told me that if a bully picked on you, you had to fight back, even if you knew you were going to lose. He said winning and losing don't matter to bullies. What matters is that you hit back, because bullies are scared babies and they don't like getting hurt.

I understood what he meant, but I was still scared. Nicholas taught me how to tell if he was really going to fight or just pretending. If he yelled a lot, it was to scare someone. No fighting then. But if Nicholas got quiet and really calm, then I should look away because he was about to hurt someone.

Or get hurt.

While Nicholas waited for the lift to go down, he saw Francis's car. I knew it was Francis's because his license plate said "CANDYMN."

Nicholas stared at that car and got really calm and quiet.

Oh shit.

Nicholas walked toward the Pint & Proper, and I knew he was going to fight Francis.

I tried to get in his way, but Nicholas was faster than me. He went around me.

"Look away, Vinnie," he said in a calm voice.

"No more fighting! You promised!" I yelled, but Nicholas wouldn't listen.

Then Garth yelled really loud like he did at the gym, "IN THE VAN!"

That made Nicholas stop and look. I could see Garth was really mad at Nicholas. They looked at each other for a long time, then we all got in the van and drove home.

As I drove everyone home, Vinnie and I continued the argument we'd begun in the parking lot. Thankfully, the rest of the Family allowed us to argue without interruption.

"Fuck that guy!" I said, gripping the steering wheel. "You should've let me handle it."

"You're being stupid, Nicholas!" Vinnie shot back.

"Me?! You always fall for Francis's shit, and it's me who has to get you out of the trouble and pain he causes."

"You don't have to fight him," Vinnie answered with finality.

"Vinnie, some people don't understand anything else. He was mocking you."

"I get mocked every day by everyone," Vinnie said quietly. "Are you going to fight all of those people?"

"If it'd make them stop? Yes."

"Mamma mía!" Super Mario yelled from Vinnie's phone. Vinnie looked at it and said, "It's Francis. I'm not talking to him right now."

From the back of the van, William suddenly spoke up.

"Vinnie, give me your phone please."

Vinnie looked confused but handed it over. William read Francis's text and got very angry.

"Mr. Darcy does not approve of bullies," he said in full Darcy mode and began to text. An evil grin spread across William's face as he hit send triumphantly.

The bartender at the Pint & Proper is a friend, who happens to adore Vinnie. He told me this story later. If it isn't true, it fucking should be.

Francis and Scott were downing whiskey shots at the bar, with Francis lamenting how I had tried to start a fight in their fine establishment. The bartender and everyone around them knew Francis had been the instigator, but he was spinning his usual victim narrative.

"Can you believe that guy?" Francis said to Scott. "Bad form."

To get even, Francis decided to pull his usual shit on Vinnie. He pulled out his phone and texted.

Francis: *If your brother needs something to help him relax, gimme a call, Vinman.*

To his surprise, Vinnie answered back immediately.

"What'd he say?" Scott asked.

"I don't speak fluent retard, but God bless him, he makes me laugh," Francis replied. Then he read the text aloud. "'I am. Sofa king. We Todd Ed.' That's what it says. You can't make shit like this up."

Scott chuckled, recognizing the old trick immediately. "What was that?" Scott asked coyly. "I couldn't hear you."

"I am. Sofa king. We Todd Ed!" Francis announced, practically yelling.

The entire bar erupted into hysterical laughter, but Francis hadn't yet figured out why. As he recited the line to himself a few more times, he suddenly got it.

The phrase, when said out loud, phonetically sounded like "I am so fucking retarded."

Mr. Darcy had tricked Francis into announcing to everyone at the Pint & Proper that he was "so fucking retarded." And it made his blood boil.

"You certainly are," the bartender said dryly.

Then the customer sitting beside Francis threw her drink right in his face.

"Fuck you, you ableist asshole!" she snarled.

William's guerilla text fought Francis's bullying better than a physical altercation. Maybe fighting wasn't the answer?

Back home, I was getting ready for bed when I saw Garth standing in my doorway.

"What's wrong, Garth?"

He stared at me in silence. Too long.

<No more fighting, Nicholas. Don't want you dead too,> he signed.

It would've hurt less if Garth had actually punched me. After losing his mother, the thought of losing the closest thing he had to a father figure terrified him. I should've seen it, but rage blinds me whenever anyone takes a shot at our Family.

"I promise, Garth. I'm sorry."

Garth stepped forward and hugged me. Too hard.

What a fucking day.

Chapter Twelve

After the trauma and chaos of the last few days, I found refuge in the peace of restocking our home clinic. It was midafternoon, and I was elbow-deep in bandages, antiseptic, and medical supplies. The Family hated hospitals and doctors. Each of them had dealt with being poked and prodded, seeing specialists, enduring procedures. For Vinnie, it brought back memories of the hell he'd suffered in state care. State care was worse than prison. Prisoners had rights, advocates, and legal protections.

People with disabilities in the system?

Nobody gave a shit about them.

Knowing how traumatic medical care was for people with disabilities, especially my merry band of misfits, I'd gotten certified as a nurse practitioner specifically to handle most of their medical needs in the comfort and safety of our own home.

It wasn't glamorous work—stitching up Garth's split knuckles from pushing heavy carts at his job, treating William's stress-induced stomach problems, working with Floyd's doctors to manage his complex medication cocktail, dealing with

Vinnie's occasional kitchen burns—but it meant the Family could avoid the sterile judgment of emergency rooms and doctor's offices where they were often treated more like curiosities than patients.

Floyd, William, and I were the only ones home. Garth was at work; William was deep in an online hackathon snuggled nicely—and silently—in his room. Rita had swung by earlier to pick up Vinnie for a trip to the Chinese market downtown. She wanted him out of the house so she could crack the case of Vinnie versus Celia.

The Chinese market was perfect. Vinnie would be completely absorbed exploring all the hard-to-find ingredients you couldn't get anywhere else. Aged black vinegar, hand-pulled noodles, exotic mushrooms...anything and everything Vinnie could experiment with. I hoped he wouldn't bring home another durian fruit. They tasted like the delicacy they were, but smelled like a rotting carcass. The Family did not relish that malodorous culinary misadventure.

The doorbell rang, interrupting my durian memories.

I glanced at my phone to check the time. Thursday, 2:57 PM.

With everything Garth was going through, I'd completely forgotten about Floyd's weekly visitor.

Shit.

I put down the gauze I was stacking and headed for the front door, already composing my apology for the delay.

The woman standing on our porch was exactly what you'd expect of someone who spent her days hiking mountain trails and weekends at the lake. Grace McCallister had that kind of natural beauty that came from an active outdoor life. Sun-streaked brown hair pulled back in a practical ponytail and the lean build of someone who could probably outrun me without breaking a sweat.

Grace was Floyd's wife, but he couldn't remember her. She was maybe a year or two younger than him. Today she wore hiking boots, well-worn jeans, and a simple blue sweater that matched her eyes.

"Grace," I said, stepping aside to let her in. "Sorry, lost track of time."

"It's fine, Nicholas." Her smile was patient and familiar after all these years. Grace carried herself with the quiet dignity of someone who'd learned to live with disappointment but refused to let it break her. "How's Floyd doing?"

I led her toward the kitchen, trying to gauge her mood. Grace was deeply religious—Catholic to the core—and she believed with absolute certainty that God did everything for a reason, that He never gave us more than we could bear, and that Floyd would remember who he was whenever the Almighty decided it was time. She clung to her faith like a life-line in a storm of doubt, and while I admired her conviction, I couldn't share it.

God, I wished I could...

In my experience, it was hard work, dedication, and uncon-ditional love that helped people, not some mystical sky fairy that granted wishes to the faithful. I'd seen too much suffering, too many good people abandoned by whatever cosmic force was supposed to be watching over us. But everyone had their own way of processing tragedy to survive. I didn't judge Grace for her beliefs.

I just wished faith would show some proof once in a while, for her sake if nothing else.

"Has he been doing better? What about his nightmares?" Grace asked, setting a familiar card box on the kitchen counter. Through the box's clear plastic window, I could see a collection of *Magic: The Gathering* cards organized in neat stacks.

"He has," I reassured her. "We've actually had a breakthrough. Found the right combination of medications that have eliminated his nightmares for now. Fingers crossed."

Grace's face lit up with hope. "Really? That's wonderful."

"I'm hopeful that since Floyd's been getting restful sleep now, it might help his body heal better. But Grace..." I paused, choosing my words carefully. "Don't push too hard today, okay? He's doing better, but he still doesn't remember anything before the accident."

She nodded, trying to contain her excitement. "I'll keep it casual, promise."

I went to get Floyd. I found him in his room listening to Bach's *Goldberg Variations* through his noise cancelling headphones while he drew the colors of the music on a tablet. I loved staring at his drawings. They were a rare glimpse into his world.

To Floyd, music was color.

Sensing me hovering, Floyd slid his headphones down to speak with me.

"Hey Floyd, you have a visitor," I said, mesmerized by the structured kaleidoscope drawing he'd sketched that made me actually feel like I was listening to *Goldberg Variations* just by looking at it.

Confusion flickered across his face. "A v-visitor? Who?"

"Grace. She's here for your weekly game."

"I d-don't remember scheduling any g-game," Floyd said, but he was already steering himself toward the kitchen to investigate.

I followed behind, settling into my usual observation post by the window. These visits had become a painful ritual that I felt obligated to witness. Partly to protect Floyd from being overwhelmed, but mostly because I understood how much Grace needed this connection, even if Floyd wouldn't remember it.

Grace smiled warmly as Floyd entered the kitchen. "Hi, Floyd, I'm Grace."

Floyd studied her face intensely. "H-have we met b-before? You look...f-familiar." He paused in quiet contemplation. "Are w-w-we related? Are y-you my sister?"

"Yes, we're...related," she almost whispered.

Floyd's expression relaxed slightly. "Oh. Well, it's n-nice to see you-u-u, Grace."

The ritual began exactly as it always did. Grace opened her box and pulled out two carefully constructed *Magic* decks, explaining the game as if Floyd had never played before. Floyd's eyes lit up with genuine interest.

"Y-yes, I love *Magic*," he said, as if he remembered.

I'd watched this scene play out dozens of times now. For Grace, these games brought her back to better days before Floyd's accident. For Floyd, it was an entertaining hour with a forgotten family member who shared his interest in *Magic: The Gathering*.

They played through two quick games, Grace deliberately making suboptimal plays to extend the games whenever she could. Floyd's mathematical mind made him naturally gifted at the strategic elements of *Magic*, even if he couldn't remember ever learning the rules. Watching him calculate probabilities and plan multiple turns ahead, you could see glimpses of the brilliant mind that existed beneath the trauma and medication.

"You're really good at this," Grace said after Floyd won the second game with a particularly clever combination of cards.

"Th-thank you. It feels...familiar somehow."

And that's when Grace made the same mistake she always made.

"Do you remember the Chaos Orb game, Floyd?"

Floyd tilted his head. "Ch-chaos Orb?"

"It was during one of our early games," Grace began, her

voice taking on the quality of someone reciting a treasured memory. "I had this white weenie deck. All these little soldier creatures that would swarm the battlefield and chip away at your life points until you died from a thousand tiny cuts."

Floyd listened intently, his expression shifting between interest and confusion.

"You were facing down my entire army," Grace continued, unable to stop herself. "All those little creatures ready to attack and finish you off. You were going to lose on the next turn, you knew it. But you had this one card on the table...a Chaos Orb. It was your favorite because it had this special rule where you could physically throw the card, and whatever it landed on would be instantly destroyed."

"That s-sounds like a good tactic," Floyd said, but I could see the familiar tension building in his shoulders.

Grace pressed on, "At best, you might have destroyed a third of my army if you threw it perfectly. I was so pleased with myself; I was finally going to beat you. But then you got this triumphant smile. The same one you always got when you figured out something no one had ever thought of before."

Floyd was listening with rapt attention, but his breathing was becoming more rapid. I considered interrupting, but Grace was lost in memory, too caught up in the story to notice the warning signs.

"You picked up the Chaos Orb card and just...ripped it into a bunch of little pieces. I thought you were throwing a tantrum; you didn't like to lose. So, I started to declare victory and do my celebration dance, but you held up your hand. 'It's still my turn,' you said. And then you paid the activation cost and used the Chaos Orb's rule against me."

"R-right," Floyd said suddenly, his voice clearer than it had been all day, "I b-b-blew those torn pieces across your ar-ar-army on the table. All those tiny ripped up pieces of Chaos Orb frag-fragments scattered across the battlefield, each one landing on a different creature c-c-c-card." His eyes looked upward as he accessed memory. "The rule states w-what-whatever the Chaos Orb lands on is immediately d-de-estroyed. There was no rule that says you can't tear the Chaos Orb into tiny p-p-pieces before t-thr-throwing it."

Grace's fingers found the small silver crucifix at her throat. "That's right."

Then Floyd's expression shifted, confusion flooding back. "Wait... Did I just... How d-d-d-did I kno-ow-ow that?"

I watched Floyd's face cycle through confusion, frustration, and something that might have been recognition before sliding into full denial.

"The bases are loaded with two outs," Floyd said suddenly. "The count's three-and-two. That wind's crazy; storm's coming..."

Here we go.

Whenever Floyd started talking about baseball, this play specifically, he was seconds away from a complete reset.

"Floyd," I said gently, trying to intervene before Grace's heart shattered again.

But Floyd's expression went blank. He looked around the room as confusion set in. He pushed the cards away from him and stared at Grace as if seeing her for the first time.

"W-who are y-you?" he asked, anxiety sharpening his voice. "W-why are you h-h-here?"

Grace's face went carefully neutral, though I could feel the pain radiating from her. She straightened in her chair, drawing on reserves of strength to remain calm.

"Floyd, we were playing *Magic* together," she said soothingly, her voice steady despite what had to be devastating disappointment. "I'm Grace, remember? We were talking about—"

"No, we w-weren't," Floyd cut her off, his voice rising in panic. "I d-d-don't know you. I think you s-s-should leave."

Grace stood slowly, methodically gathering the scattered cards. Like she did nearly every week—her terrible, terrible *Groundhog Day*. Her movements were controlled, but I could sense the crushing sorrow she was working so hard to contain. She didn't let a single tear fall. Stoic. Dignified. Somehow that made the moment even more excruciating.

Every fucking week.

I moved quickly, kneeling beside Floyd's wheelchair.

"Hey, it's okay," I said calmly. "Grace came to visit and play cards with you."

"I d-don't remem-member h-h-h-her," Floyd said, his voice small and frightened.

"That's okay. Sometimes we forget things. Let's get you back to your room; I'll put on some music for you."

I escorted Floyd's wheelchair down the hall, leaving Grace alone in the kitchen. In his room, I put on Mozart. The mathematical structure of his compositions always seemed to calm Floyd when he became agitated that he couldn't remember things.

When I returned to the kitchen, Grace was closing her card box, every card accounted for and properly stored.

"I'm sorry," she said without looking up, her voice barely audible. "I pushed too hard again. It felt like old times... For a moment, he was Floyd."

"It's not your fault, Grace. His injuries are complex. We'll keep working."

"He recognized me today, if only for a second. I know it," Grace said hopeful. "That's something."

"Yes, it is," I lied.

"One day he'll remember," she said with quiet determination, though something in her voice suggested she was trying to convince herself as much as me. "At least I get to spend time with him."

I wanted to offer her some hope, some reassurance that her faith would be rewarded. But I'd learned the hard way that false comfort was as cruel as honest lies.

"I'll see you next week?" I asked instead.

Grace nodded, her composure never wavering. "Thank you, Nicholas. For taking such good care of him. He looks well, and I know how much work you put into helping him."

I walked her to the door, watching as she made her way to the modest sedan parked in our driveway. She sat in the driver's seat and cried quietly, unaware anyone was watching. A few moments later, she composed herself, dried her tears, and drove away.

These visits broke my heart every single week. It was grueling to witness Grace's unwavering dedication to someone who couldn't even remember she existed, and Floyd's fear and confusion when he was pushed too hard to remember.

Life is unfair. That's all there is to it.

Grace's car disappeared down the street. I heard Mozart's music drifting from Floyd's room as Wolfgang worked his magic on the brilliant man trapped inside fragments of himself.

A prison with no walls.

Tomorrow, Floyd wouldn't remember Grace's visit, wouldn't recall the pain or confusion. For him, it would be as if none of it had ever happened.

I envied him that mercy of forgetting.

Chapter Thirteen

I loved riding in Rita's police car. I loved everything about it. It had thick bulletproof glass, a computer that talked to other police cars, and a radio that crackled with numbers I didn't understand but sounded important. Most of all, I loved the sirens. Rita knew this, which is why every few minutes I reached for the siren button, she'd smacked my hand away.

"Vinman," she said, not taking her eyes off the road. "Keep your hands away from my siren."

"Just once?" I asked, even though I knew what she would say. "Just a little beep?"

"No beeps. No sirens. No lights." She glanced at me and promised, "Unless we get a real emergency call."

I sat back in my seat and watched the buildings go by. The Chinese market was still twenty minutes away, and Rita was driving slower than usual.

"So," she said, "wanna tell me what you're looking for at the market today?"

I loved talking about cooking almost as much as I loved cooking. "Doubanjiang, a broad bean chili paste that's been aged for years. Not the fake stuff they sell at regular stores. The real kind that costs more but tastes like...like if you could eat time."

Rita laughed. "If you could eat time?"

"Nicholas says to describe food better, and that's what it tastes like. And I need tofu. The really soft kind. Oh! And hand-pulled noodles. The lady there makes them fresh every morning. You can watch her stretch the dough until it's thin like string but strong enough not to break."

"That sounds amazing. What're you making?"

"Mapo tofu. The real kind, with Sichuan peppercorns that make your nose tingle."

Rita nodded like she understood, which was one of the reasons I liked her so much. "Will William eat it?"

I made a face. "William doesn't like foods that have weird textures. That's what he calls anything that isn't smooth or crunchy. No in-between textures for William. The tofu will bother him because it's squishy, but I'll make him some plain noodles on the side. He'll be fine."

"That's thoughtful of you. Nicholas mentioned William's been stressed about work."

"William's always stressed about something. But he's really good at what he does. He writes code that finds mistakes in other people's code, and sometimes he gets paid to play video games all day to find their mistakes too."

"And William is very good at it. Like you are with cooking. What's Celia good at doing?"

"Celia is good at twerking, church, and bothering me," I said. It was the truth, just not the whole truth.

"Bothering you? How does she do that?"

"It's a secret. I can't tell you. Besides, everyone will make fun of me if I tell." I looked out the window. My thoughts were all tangled up like wet noodles.

"What if I promised not to?" Rita offered.

This was a trick question. Rita was good at trick questions, which was probably why she was a good police officer. But I needed to know for sure. "Promise not to tell, or promise not to make fun of me? That makes me feel small. I don't like that."

"Both. You know you can trust me, Vinman."

I studied her face while she drove. Rita never lied to me, not once in all the time I knew her... I wanted to talk about Celia, but it was hard.

"Celia told me she likes girls," I suddenly blurted.

"Celia told you she was gay?"

"No. Not gay. She said she likes girls and she likes boys. That makes no sense. You can't like both!"

Rita was quiet for a long moment. I knew her brain was working, like the computer in her police car. "Actually, Vinnie, you can like both. It's called being bisexual. It's quite common."

"You don't understand," I said, louder than I meant to, and my voice did that thing where it got all shaky when I was upset. "She doesn't want me. I'm not good enough for her."

This was the part I hadn't told anyone, not even me. The part that sat in my stomach like a rock and made me not want to eat sometimes, which was how I knew it was really bad because I always wanted to eat.

Rita took a moment, and I could tell she was choosing her words carefully, like when Nicholas explained my medication to me. "You know you and your brother are different, right?"

"I have Down syndrome; Nicholas doesn't."

"That's right. Your brains are wired differently. There's nothing wrong with that. It's just different. Now Celia, her brain is wired differently too. Instead of just liking boys or girls, her brain likes them both. Do you understand?"

I thought about this. Different things sometimes came in

pairs. That made sense. Hot and cold. Sweet and sour. Up and down. Nicholas and me.

But Rita was saying some people didn't fit into the neat pairs I was used to. I would think about that more later because there something else that was bothering me about Celia.

"I didn't make Celia that way?"

"No, Vinnie. Just like nobody made you or your brother different."

I sat back in my seat to think about that. Celia liked boys and she liked girls. But that didn't mean Celia didn't like me. It meant she just liked more people than me. And that was supposed to be okay?

"I don't understand," I said.

Rita took a moment to think, then asked, "What did Celia say exactly?"

I tried to remember all of Celia's words. "She said she loved me, but she wanted me to know she liked girls too. See?"

"Vinnie, I don't think Celia wants to be with other people, or that she's choosing girls over you. Celia is saying she chose you as her partner, but she doesn't want to hide who she is."

I was still confused. It must have shown on my face because Rita asked, "If Celia wore a mask to hide her Down syndrome, would you be okay with that?"

"No," I said. "That's not Celia."

"That's correct. Celia took off her mask for you," Rita reasoned. "She wants you to know and accept all of her, Vinnie."

I got very quiet.

"That's a lot, Rita," I told her. Nicholas and Rita knew that when I said that, it meant I needed time to think and they needed to leave me alone.

But then I realized something else.

I loved riding in Rita's police car. I loved everything about it. I loved going to the Chinese market. And I loved to talk about cooking. Rita knew all this.

I turned to Rita. "I see what you did there."

Rita's mouth got tight like when she tried not to laugh. "What did I do?" she asked me like she didn't know.

"You drove me in your police car to the Chinese market, got me talking about cooking, all to make me confess about Celia. I see what you did there," I said in my version of her cop voice.

Rita winked at me, and I felt proud I figured out her plan.

I remembered our long argument about us and *Brooklyn Nine-Nine.*

"That settles it, Rita. *You* are Peralta; *I* am Doug Judy."

Rita laughed really loud. I could tell she wanted to say something back, but all she did was laugh. She knew I was right.

Peralta was a cop, just like Rita.

Doug Judy was a criminal mastermind...just like me.

I just didn't know that yet.

Chapter Fourteen

The sound of Rita's police cruiser pulling into our driveway was immediately followed by Vinnie's excited chatter as car doors slammed. I looked up from the paperwork I was completing to see them both walking toward the house, Vinnie clutching several plastic bags like they contained precious cargo.

"Nicholas! Nicholas!" Vinnie called out before he'd even reached the front door. "I got everything! Sichuan peppercorns, silken tofu, a whole fish and—"

"Slow down there, chef." Rita laughed, following behind him with her own bag.

Vinnie burst through the front door with the seriousness of a child at play. "We're making mapo tofu and steamed whole fish! Rita is staying for dinner."

As Vinnie began unpacking his treasures onto the kitchen counter, William emerged from his room, drawn by the commotion. His hair was disheveled from hours at his computer, and he had that slightly dazed look he got when switching from code to reality.

"Officer Reyes," William said, his posture immediately straightening as he slipped on his Mr. Darcy mask. "What an unexpected pleasure to have you grace our humble abode."

Rita shot me an amused look before turning to William with a patient smile. "Hello, William. Vinnie invited me to stay for dinner."

"Splendid!" William declared.

"Everyone, come here," Vinnie commanded. Opening his binder of Mom's recipes, Vinnie turned to the one he had decided to cook. "We have to do everything at the same time or it won't work."

Floyd wheeled into the kitchen, curious about the commotion. "What's all the f-fuss about?"

"Cooking time," Vinnie announced. "Floyd, you're in charge of cutting. William, wash vegetables. Rita, help me with the fish. Nicholas, measure out the stuff for the mapo tofu sauce."

"Yes, chef," the Family said in unison like they always did when Vinnie got like this.

I marveled at how naturally Vinnie took command when it came to cooking. His usual hesitancy disappeared, replaced by the confidence of someone who knew exactly what needed to happen and when. He moved around the kitchen with purpose, delegating tasks and coordinating timing like a seasoned chef running a professional kitchen.

"Floyd, cut green onions and tofu." Vinnie ordered.

"Roger that, ch-chef." Floyd mocked saluted, wheeling over to the kitchen table where the cutting board was waiting for him.

"William, see the black stuff there? On the bok choy? Wash that off."

William began washing vegetables, counting each piece as he cleaned it.

"Rita, get a knife. I'll hold the fish tail. You scrape off the scales," Vinnie explained, holding up the fish they'd purchased.

I measured out the ingredients for the mapo tofu sauce, per the instructions in Vinnie's recipe binder. I finished at the same time Rita and Vinnie were done cleaning the fish. I caught Rita's eye and nodded toward the front door.

"Vinnie, everything is set for you to make the mapo tofu. I'm going to check the mail," I announced.

"I'll go with you," Rita said, wiping her hands on a dish towel. "Vinman, we'll be right back."

"Don't take too long," Vinnie warned. "Timing is everything."

Outside, the early evening air was crisp and clear. I led Rita down the driveway toward our mailbox, grateful for the excuse to talk privately.

"So," I said once we were out of earshot, "what'd you find out about this whole Celia situation?"

Rita leaned against the mailbox, her expression becoming more serious. "Celia told Vinnie she's bisexual. That's what they're fighting about."

I stopped walking. "That's it? That's what has him so twisted up?"

"It's not that simple, Nicholas. Vinnie doesn't understand what bisexuality means. He thinks Celia saying she likes girls means she doesn't want him anymore and that he's not enough for her."

I rubbed my temples, feeling the familiar tension that came with navigating the complexities of Vinnie's emotional world.

"I tried to help him understand during the drive," Rita said. "He seemed to get that she was being honest with him, not rejecting him."

"Did it help?"

"Some. But he's still processing. You know how Vinnie is with big emotional concepts."

"Did he tell you, 'That's a lot'?" I asked hopefully.

"Yeah, he just needs some time." Rita patted my shoulder reassuringly.

The relief that washed over me almost made my knees buckle. I had learned over the years that whenever Vinnie received advice about something he wanted to understand but didn't and responded with "that's a lot," it was his way of verbally allowing himself the time to process the new lesson.

Sometimes that was a quick process.

Sometimes it wasn't.

But it did mean that in time, he'd understand.

Rita studied my face in the fading light. "What aren't you telling me about Vinnie and relationships?"

"Before Celia, Vinnie never had a romantic relationship. People with Down syndrome...they often get infantilized. Treated like eternal children who aren't supposed to have adult feelings or desires. When Vinnie and Celia got together, it was like watching him discover a part of himself he'd never been allowed to explore."

"And now he's afraid he's going to lose that?" she asked.

I nodded. "I think so. He's not just afraid of losing Celia. He's also afraid of losing the person he gets to be when he's with her."

Rita was quiet for a moment, processing this. "That's why the bisexuality thing hit him so hard. It's not really about her liking girls. It's about his fear that he's not enough."

"And with Down syndrome, that fear runs deeper than it would for someone else. He's spent his whole life being told, in a thousand different ways, that he's not enough," I said.

"Nicholas!" Vinnie's voice carried from the kitchen. "The tofu is ready for the sauce!"

"Coming!" I called back.

Rita squeezed my hand. "He'll figure it out. Vinnie always does. Oh, I promised I wouldn't tell you, so shut the fuck up about it until the Vinman brings it up," Rita finished as I grabbed the mail.

I flipped through the mail as we walked back toward the house. Power bill, junk mail, grocery flyer—then I saw it.

The Cartwright Foundation letterhead stared back at me from an official-looking envelope. Without a word, I tore open the envelope and scanned the letter. My worst fears manifesting with each line. I stopped walking in the middle of our driveway, my hands suddenly unsteady.

"What's wrong?" Rita asked, immediately noticing the change in my demeanor. "You're pale as a ghost. If I noticed the sudden change in your body language, your merry band of misfits will too."

Shit. She was right. I glanced toward the house, making sure none of the Family was outside or within earshot. I scanned the letter a second time in disbelief before handing it to Rita.

I watched her face as she read, her expression shifting from curiosity to confusion to mounting anger. Her jaw tightened, her knuckles whitened as she gripped the paper, and by the time she looked up at me, her eyes were blazing.

"What the fuck?!" she exploded. "Is she serious with this shit?!"

"That's what I'm going to find out," I said, surprised by how calm my own voice sounded. "It must be a clerical error. I'll go talk to her, sort this out. Can you watch them until I get back?"

"I'll hold down the fort," Rita said grimly. "Go."

Chapter Fifteen

The Cartwright estate had always been intimidating. A sprawling fortress of old money and older privilege perched on twenty acres of manicured perfection. But as I approached the front gates, something was different. The ornate iron barriers that had stood perpetually open for as long as I'd known Agnes Cartwright were now firmly closed, flanked by security cameras that tracked my van's approach.

The guardhouse, which had sat empty for years, now housed a uniformed security officer, who emerged as I pulled up to the intercom.

"Excuse me," I called through my window, genuinely confused. "Is this still the Cartwright estate?"

The guard, a stern-faced man in his fifties with the bearing of ex-military, nodded curtly. "It is, sir. Please state your business."

"I'm here to see Charity Cartwright."

"Do you have an appointment?"

I blinked at the absurdity of the question. "No. When Agnes was alive, I never needed one."

The guard's expression remained impassive as he retreated to his booth and picked up a telephone. I watched him speak in low tones, nodding occasionally as he glanced back at me through the glass. After what felt like an eternity, he pressed a button, and the gates began their slow, ominous swing inward.

"Drive straight to the main house," he instructed, waving me through.

As I navigated the familiar circular drive, I noticed more changes. Additional security cameras dotted the landscape like electronic sentries. The wildflowers and topiaries that once filled the gardens, which were Agnes's pride and joy, had been replaced by a sterile grass lawn. Even the fountain had been modified. The cherubic figures that once danced in the spray had been replaced with a stark geometric design.

A butler I'd never seen before opened the front door before I could knock. He was tall, thin, and possessed the kind of practiced invisibility that comes from years of serving the wealthy. Agnes had employed a small, loyal staff who'd known her for decades. This man was clearly part of Charity's new regime.

"Mr. Murphy," he said in clipped, professional tones. "Miss Cartwright is expecting you. Please follow me."

The interior of the house had undergone a similar transformation. Gone were Agnes's warm family photos and eclectic art collection, replaced by cold modern pieces. The place now felt more like a corporate office building than a family home. Even the air felt different...cold and unwelcoming.

The butler led me to what had once been Agnes's cozy study, now transformed into something resembling a law firm's conference room. Charity sat behind an imposing mahogany desk, surrounded by a murder of crows masquerading as lawyers. They were all sharp suits and sharper smiles, the kind of legal scavengers who made their living picking apart the vulnerable.

"Gentlemen," Charity said without looking up from the documents spread before her, "we'll continue this tomorrow. I have a personal matter to attend to."

The lawyers gathered their papers and filed out past me. As the door closed behind the last of them, I found myself alone with Charity Cartwright for the first time since the funeral. She was perfectly coiffed, expensively dressed, and radiated manufactured kindness that came from years of careful practice.

"Please, sit," Charity said, gesturing to a chair positioned strategically lower than her own. I realized every detail of this meeting had been choreographed to establish dominance.

I remained standing. "I got your letter."

"Ah yes, the stipend suspension. I trust the language was clear enough for someone of your...educational background?"

Her casual condescension was designed to be infuriating. She was successful; I forced myself to stay calm and focused. "You're canceling Garth's monthly stipend. I had an agreement with your mother."

Charity's smile could have frozen blood. "My mother is dead, Mr. Murphy. Along with any informal arrangements she may have made with her various charity cases." She paused to let that sink in. "I'm sure you understand that legally binding contracts require actual contracts, don't you?"

"We can't afford to eat without that support. The house mortgage alone—"

"Is no longer my concern," she interrupted smoothly. "Garth's trust fund and inheritance have been temporarily suspended pending the completion of conservatorship proceedings."

"On what grounds?" I demanded, though I was beginning to understand the scope of her machinations.

Charity leaned back in her chair, clearly savoring this

moment. "Mental incompetency, of course. My dear brother simply isn't capable of managing his own affairs. Mother was far too soft on him; all that nonsense about independence and dignity." Her voice dripped with disgust. "It's time for Garth to face reality."

"And if he can't prove his competency in court?"

"Then I'll be named conservator of his trust." She said this with casual satisfaction. "It's really quite straightforward."

"You don't need the money," I said, fighting to keep my voice level.

"Oh, it's not about money." She came around the desk and leaned against it, directly in front of me. "Come now, Mr. Murphy. You of all people should understand..."

Charity's words trailed off, as if she was suddenly faced with an unknown variable that had thrown her entire prepared speech off the rails.

"You never tire of it?" Charity sounded genuinely curious.

"Of what?" I countered.

"The whispered ridicule. The embarrassment always looming on the horizon. I may share some of my sibling's tainted genes, but you're a mongoloid's twin."

Her voice took on a pseudo-sympathetic tone that made my skin crawl. "Your brother. Vincent Murphy, correct? Seeing his face every day. The constant reminder of what you could have been had the genetic roulette played out differently. That never bothers you?"

Something white-hot exploded behind my eyes. I'd heard cruel words about Vinnie before, but never delivered with such premeditated malice. *Was she trying to provoke me?* "We're family," I said through gritted teeth. "Nothing else matters."

"I envy your naivety." Charity's bark of laughter was mocking and cruel—like a hyena's.

And it pushed me to my breaking point. Win or lose, bullies will continue their behavior until you fight back. "I'll petition to be Garth's conservator."

"Legal challenges are expensive—devastatingly so."

"I'll find a way." I wasn't about to back down because of money. Charity destroyed Garth's past, I wouldn't let her steal his future too.

"Of course, you will." Her tone suggested she was humoring a particularly slow child. "But discovery is an interesting phase of court proceedings, don't you think? Lawyers and judges delving deep into the recesses of your life. All those sealed juvenile records, those unfortunate incidents from your past that demonstrate a certain...propensity for violence."

My blood pounded in my ears. Those records were supposed to be sealed, buried, forgotten.

"I do hope the court won't look too unfavorably on a potential guardian with such a colorful history. Assault charges, even juvenile ones, can be problematic when determining fitness for caregiving responsibilities."

She knew. Somehow, this bitch knew about the fights I'd gotten into defending Vinnie, about a system that had punished me for protecting my brother.

"Of course, if your true character becomes public knowledge," she continued with venomous sweetness, "you might lose guardianship of your mongoloid twin altogether. That would be tragic."

"Leave Vinnie out of this," I warned, my hands balling into fists.

"But that's exactly the point, Mr. Murphy. He's none of my business. And Garth is none of yours. I believe we've reached an understanding." She returned to her desk and pressed a button. Almost immediately, the butler appeared. "I believe our guest was just leaving. And Mr. Murphy? Next time you'd like to discuss my family's business, make an appointment."

As the butler moved to escort me out, Charity called after me. "Do tell Garth I'm excited to have him home. It'll be just like when we were young."

I wanted to turn around, to say something that would wipe that satisfied smirk off her face. But I knew she was counting on that. Every word, every gesture had been calculated to provoke exactly the kind of reaction that would prove her point about my alleged violent tendencies.

So, I walked out of that house with my fists clenched, knowing I'd just met an enemy who would stop at nothing to destroy everything I loved.

The smell of Sichuan peppercorns and steamed fish greeted me as I walked back into our house, a stark contrast to the soulless shell that had become the Cartwright estate. The kitchen was alive with the sounds of conversation and clinking dishes as the Family cleaned up from what had clearly been a culinary triumph.

"Nicholas!" Vinnie called out from the sink, his face beaming with pride. "Everyone loved dinner! Even William ate the fish!"

"It was delicious," William admitted grudgingly as he thoroughly dried plates. "Though I must say, having my meal stare back at me was rather disconcerting."

Vinnie beamed at the praise. "Fish eyes go cloudy when it's old. Clear eyes mean fresh. I taught everyone how to tell."

"Very educational," Rita said, appearing beside me with a dish towel. "Though I think William might have PTSD from that fish head."

"I do not have post-traumatic stress disorder from seafood,"

William protested with wounded dignity. "I simply prefer my protein sources butchered and pre-packaged in plastic."

I watched this domestic scene unfold around me, knowing it might be one of the last times we'd all be together like this. The normalcy felt precious and fragile, like holding soap bubbles in a thunderstorm.

"Everything okay?" Rita asked quietly.

"I'm fine," I lied, but she saw right through it.

Twenty minutes later, after the last dish had been washed and the Family had settled into their evening routines, Rita and I found ourselves on the back porch. She nursed a beer while I held a non-alcoholic one, both of us staring out at the darkening sky.

"So," Rita said, taking a sip. "How bad?"

"DEFCON 1 bad," I said. Rita sat and listened with rapt attention as I caught her up. After I finished, Rita drained her beer, opened another.

I took a long pull of my fake beer, wishing it contained actual alcohol. "I don't know what to do. Think I'm stuck in denial. Could you arrest Charity?"

"For what?"

"For being a bitch."

Rita laughed knowingly. "Nicholas, if you could arrest people for being a bitch, I'd be in a cell right next to Charity."

Despite everything, I smiled. "Maybe discrimination against people with disabilities then? There's got to be something."

"I wish I could," Rita said, her expression turning serious. "But a woman like Charity always dots her i's and crosses her t's. Without evidence, even making that accusation would be career suicide."

She was quiet for a moment, processing what I'd told her about the confrontation. "How long has she been planning this?"

"I'm not sure. Probably since Garth was born." I ran my hands through my hair, feeling the weight of it all. "Rita, we're in serious trouble. I don't know how I'm going to tell Garth about this. Or the Family. I don't..."

The familiar tightness began building in my chest. I closed my eyes and—

Inhale, two, three, four...

The breathing exercise helped, but only marginally.

"There's no way to make the house payments, to say nothing of living expenses," I continued. "We're fucked. But not the good kind, more like..."

"Prison fucked," Rita finished.

Exhale, two, three, four...

We sat in silence for a moment, both contemplating the magnitude of the crisis.

"I'm still waiting on that background check I ran on Charity," she said. "Could take a few more days to get the results. But there might be a way to buy some time," Rita said.

"How?"

"Go to the bank. Take out a loan against the house. They don't know your funding has been cut off yet."

I considered this. "A small loan could buy us time. Maybe I could change Charity's mind somehow." Even as I said it, I knew I was grasping at straws. "I don't want to believe anyone is that fucking evil."

Rita had seen enough of humanity's horrors in her line of work to know that people could be that evil and worse, but she stayed diplomatically silent on the subject.

"It's worth a shot," she said instead. "Take the Vinman with you when you apply for the loan. Let the bank see exactly who they'd be helping...or hurting."

I stared at her, impressed by the elegant ruthlessness of the suggestion. "Officer Reyes, that's downright diabolical."

"To protect and serve." Rita winked and clinked her beer bottle against mine.

Chapter Sixteen

I checked my phone again. Ten-fifteen. The appointment was at eleven, which gave Vinnie and me just enough time to get across town without raising the Family's suspicions. The last thing I needed was William asking twenty questions about why we were leaving the house at an odd hour or Floyd wanting to tag along for the ride.

I found Vinnie in the kitchen, arranging ingredients for dinner prep. Even when he wasn't officially cooking, he treated our kitchen like his personal kingdom.

"Hey, Vinman. We need to leave in five minutes," I said, keeping my voice casual.

"Leave for what?" Vinnie asked without looking up from the onions he was organizing by size.

"Dentist. They had a cancellation and can squeeze us both in."

Vinnie's hands stopped moving. He turned to face me, frowning. Something wasn't adding up. "We went to the dentist two months ago. Dr. Peterson said our teeth were excellent."

"I know, but this is just a quick cleaning. You know how important dental hygiene is."

Vinnie sighed the heavy sigh he reserved for things he didn't want to do but knew he should. "Do I have to get the fluoride treatment? It tastes like fake mint and makes my tongue feel weird."

"We'll see. Go grab your jacket."

I heard William in the living room explaining to Floyd why his latest code wasn't compiling, their voices mixing with the morning news from the television. Garth was already at work, thank God. The fewer people around when I lied, the better I felt about it. Which wasn't saying much.

Vinnie came back wearing his good jacket, the navy blue one Rita had bought him for job interviews. "I don't like surprise dentist visits, Nicholas. They make me nervous."

"I know. But it'll be quick, I promise."

We made it to the van without anyone asking where we were going. I started the engine and pulled out of the driveway, checking the rearview mirror out of habit. Old paranoia from the early days when I was convinced someone would come and take Vinnie away from me.

Three blocks from the house, I decided it was safe to tell him the truth.

"Vinnie, we're not actually going to the dentist."

"I knew it! I brushed my teeth this morning. And yesterday morning. And last night." Vinnie said, but he sounded relieved rather than angry. "Where are we going?"

"The bank. I need to apply for a second mortgage on the house. Just some boring paperwork stuff so we can have a little extra money." I kept my voice light, like I was talking about picking up groceries.

"How much money?" Vinnie asked, eyes lighting up. "Could we get new appliances? The refrigerator makes that weird noise. Oh, and a Vitamix blender so we can make smoothies for breakfast."

"We'll see what—"

"Nicholas." Vinnie grabbed my arm, his eyes wide with possibility. "We could remodel the kitchen. We could get an island."

"An island?"

"A kitchen island! Like on the cooking shows! I could prep on one side and cook on the other, and there'd be storage underneath, and maybe even a sink in the middle—"

"Slow down there, Gordon Ramsay."

"Who's Gordon Ramsay?"

"Never mind. We'll see what we can afford after we talk to the bank."

Vinnie settled back in his seat, but I could see the gears turning as he planned his dream kitchen renovation. It broke my heart knowing that instead of a kitchen island and appliances, we were fighting just to keep a roof over our heads.

I parked the van and looked at the brick building in front of us. Liberty Bank & Trust looked exactly like what it was, a place where people in suits who didn't need money made decisions about the lives of other people who did.

"Nicholas, should I be Crazy Eddie or Slow Joe?"

Vinnie knew the game. We'd only done this for extreme emergencies, when we were desperate and had nowhere else to turn. Most recently when Vinnie needed emergency surgery and our insurance was stalling on approval.

Vinnie's performances had never failed to get us what we needed. It wasn't fair, it wasn't right, but it worked. And right now, with Charity breathing down our necks and Garth's world already falling apart, I needed it to work.

"Slow Joe," I said. "Crazy Eddie needs work."

Vinnie's face fell. "What's wrong with Crazy Eddie?"

"Remember when William made us watch *Tropic Thunder* for movie night?"

Vinnie's brow wrinkled as he combed through his memory. "The movie with Iron Man in blackface who fought in Vietnam with Zoolander?"

"That's the one. Do you remember what he said that made you so angry?" I prodded.

A few brow wrinkles later, and Vinnie admitted, "Blackface Iron Man said, 'Never go full retard.' Oh, I see what you did there. Slow Joe it is." Vinnie closed his eyes and took a deep breath, like an actor preparing for his entrance. When he opened them again, his entire posture had changed. His shoulders slumped slightly, his expression became vacant, and when he turned his head to look at me, the movement was just a beat too slow.

"Is this...good, Nicholas?" he asked, each word carefully spaced.

"Perfect. You ready?"

Vinnie nodded his slow nod, the one that would make people underestimate everything about him even more than they already did. "Let's go to...the bank now."

We got out of the van and walked toward the entrance. I straightened my tie and put on my best responsible-citizen smile. Vinnie shuffled beside me, playing his part flawlessly.

Just before we reached the door, I felt a stab of guilt. We weren't really lying, I told myself. We were just...presenting the situation in a way that would get us the help we needed. "Make the system work for you," I remembered Rita telling me.

But as I held the door open for Vinnie and watched him shuffle through with his carefully practiced gait, I wondered if I was becoming the kind of person I used to despise. The kind who used my brother's disability to manipulate people.

Or was I simply the kind who had no other fucking choice.

Nicholas sat right next to me in the bank manager's office. Mr. Reece moved some papers on his desk and looked at his computer screen one more time. His red tie was wide and his dark blue suit looked expensive. The bank manager's office smelled like coffee and the kind of air freshener that makes you sneeze.

"Everything looks good, Mr. Murphy," Mr. Reece said, looking to Nicholas.

I made my face look blank and tilted my head to the side the way I practiced at home. "That sounds...good...for me," I said really slow, like each word was heavy.

Nicholas looked at me, then back at Mr. Reece. "He's talking to me, Vinnie." Then Nicholas smiled at Mr. Reece. "But you're right, Mr. Reece. That is good."

Mr. Reece wouldn't look at me even though I was sitting right in front of his desk. It was like I was furniture or invisible. I knew this would happen, but it still made me feel small.

"Vinnie's very excited," Nicholas said. "This means a lot to him."

Mr. Reece nodded but still talked to Nicholas like I wasn't there. "Tell Vinnie that I'm glad to help. We like to support families in need."

"Vinnie can understand you. You can speak to him directly, Mr. Reece."

Mr. Reece's face turned a little pink, like when you say something embarrassing you wish you hadn't.

"Of course, of course," Mr. Reece said with a nervous smile. "It's very good that Nicholas takes care of his..." He looked at Nicholas. "Twin, I believe you said?"

"We are...not identical," I answered for Nicholas.

Mr. Reece looked at me and then to Nicholas and then

back to me. I was used to this. I have Down syndrome, and Nicholas does not.

"Yes, yes, very good of your, um, twin to be building you a ramp for your house." Mr. Reece turned back to his computer, clicking his mouse. "There are just a few more details, and we'll have the loan squared away..."

The clicking stopped. Mr. Reece stared at his computer screen, and his face changed. The banker's smile went away, and his mouth made a straight line. He read something on the screen, then read it again. Like he didn't like what was on the computer.

Nicholas leaned forward in his chair. "Is there a problem?"

Mr. Reece kept staring at the screen like it was telling him bad news. "Mr. Murphy, your account has been flagged."

"Flagged?" Nicholas said. "What does that mean? Who could have flagged my account?"

Mr. Reece finally looked away from the computer, but he looked at Nicholas only, not me. "I regret to inform you that we cannot approve your loan, Mr. Murphy."

Nicholas's voice got tight. "I don't understand. Who could have flagged my account? This has to be a mistake."

"I'm afraid it isn't a mistake," Mr. Reece said. He straightened his papers like he was getting ready for us to leave. "And I'm afraid there's nothing I can do to help."

Then Mr. Reece looked at me. His face looked sorry, but not the kind of sorry that wants to fix things. The kind of sorry that wants you to go away.

"I'm very sorry," he said to me.

All my slow-acting felt stupid now. I wanted to tell Mr. Reece that I wasn't really slow, that I could understand we weren't getting any money from him. But I just nodded my slow nod and said, "That is...okay."

Nicholas stood up and said, "Mr. Reece, I've been banking

here for years. My credit is excellent. I need to know who flagged my account and why."

Mr. Reece stood up too, but slower, like an old man. "I'm not at liberty to discuss the details, Mr. Murphy. Bank policy."

I thought Nicholas might yell and argue, but he didn't. He said, "I think I understand," and his voice was very calm now, which scared me more than when he was loud.

We walked out of the bank into the bright sunshine, but everything felt dark. Nicholas didn't say anything until we got in the van. Then he hit the steering wheel with his hand and said a word that would have made Mom wash his mouth out with soap.

"Nicholas?" I said. "Are we in trouble?"

"Are we in trouble?" Vinnie asked from the passenger seat as I started the van.

That simple question shattered something inside me. All the stress, all the fear, all the rage I'd been holding back since Charity's letter arrived came flooding out like water through a broken dam.

"Yes, Vinnie. We're in serious fucking trouble." I didn't mean to snap as I gripped the steering wheel until my knuckles went white. I was in full panic mode. My thoughts racing so fast I couldn't focus. There was only one person I knew who would and could flag our account. "It has to be Charity. She flagged our account. She made sure we couldn't get that loan. No one else has the motive or resources," I thought out loud.

"Charity? Garth's sister? She's rich. Why would she stop us from getting money?"

"Because she's a sadistic bitch who gets off on making people suffer!" The words exploded out of me. "Because this world doesn't give a damn about people like us anymore. Nobody has any empathy left. Not a single fucking person."

I tried my breathing exercises. *Inhale, two, three—*

"Fuck that. I want to be angry!" I screamed into the void.

Vinnie sat perfectly still, watching me with wide eyes as I completely unraveled.

"It wasn't always like this, Vinnie. There used to be people like Agnes who actually gave a shit about helping those less fortunate. But now? Everyone's adopted the same goddamn philosophy: 'Fuck you, got mine.' Oh, and if you're different, if you've got a disability, or if you have the extraordinary bad luck of being poor in this rigged game of capitalism, then you're labeled a failure. You're disposable. The American Dream? Work hard, play by the rules, and you'll be rewarded? Bullshit! I've worked my ass off for years, sacrificed everything, kept the Family together. And what's my reward? Charity steals Garth's inheritance and then blocks us from even borrowing against our own fucking house! I can't get a loan to save the people I love, and now we're going to lose the house and everybody's going to be forced into state care or worse!"

My righteous rant hung in the air like a death sentence. I realized what I'd just revealed.

Fuck.

Vinnie wasn't supposed to hear that part yet.

Vinnie went very quiet. When he finally spoke, his voice was barely audible.

"State care?"

I knew exactly what state care meant to Vinnie. What it had done to him before I'd gotten guardianship. The bruises. The way he'd flinch whenever anyone raised their voice.

"Vinnie—"

"Family meeting. When we get home," Vinnie said with quiet determination.

"No. If they find out we're going to lose the house, they'll panic. William will have a complete meltdown. Floyd will reset. Garth..." I shook my head. "I can't do that to them. Not yet."

"They need to know, Nicholas."

"Just give me a little more time. Let me try to figure something out first. Please."

Vinnie stared out the window for a long moment. I could see him wrestling with the decision, remembering his own terror from his time in state custody.

"How long?" he asked finally.

"Give me tonight to sort this out. Tomorrow, we'll tell them everything."

"Promise?"

"Promise."

That night, I sat at my desk staring at the ledger that contained our financial death sentence. The numbers hadn't magically changed in the past six hours. We were still broke. We were still going to lose everything.

Rita had called earlier with news from her background check on Charity Cartwright. Turns out the Cartwrights owned a lot of land in the state. And even more banks. Rita warned me her plan wouldn't work now, and I simply didn't have it in me to tell her I had learned that the humiliating way. No sense drowning Rita with fear, anxiety, and dread too. We were fucked.

That's when I remembered Floyd's birthday present.

The lottery scratcher sat on my dresser exactly where I'd left it weeks ago, pristine and untouched. Like it had been waiting for this exact moment.

I picked it up with hands that were surprisingly steady.

The rules were simple: match three symbols, win one million dollars. One million dollars would solve everything. One million dollars would save the Family.

I found a quarter in my pocket and positioned it over the first symbol.

Please.

I scratched. A cherry appeared. I checked the winning combinations; cherry was one of them.

My heart started hammering as I moved to the second symbol.

Please, please, please.

Another cherry.

Holy shit.

Two out of three. One more cherry and we were millionaires. One more cherry and Charity Cartwright could go fuck herself. One more cherry and the Family would never have to worry about anything again.

I closed my eyes and whispered a prayer to whatever cosmic force might be listening.

"If you're out there, I don't ask for much. But I am now. Please..."

I opened my eyes and positioned the quarter over the final symbol. This was it. This was our salvation.

I scratched.

The silver coating fell away to reveal...a lemon.

So close. So goddamn close it felt cruel now.

"I tried mine too," Vinnie's voice came from the doorway. "I didn't win either. I told Floyd those are always a ripoff."

Before I could respond, Vinnie walked over and dropped a wad of cash onto my desk. "This is all the money I've been saving up for cooking school. Is it enough?"

I looked at the pile of crumpled one-dollar bills. Maybe seventeen dollars total... My heart broke completely.

"We need more than seventeen dollars, Vinnie. Where is everyone?"

"Eating dinner."

I took a deep breath and stood up. There was no putting this off any longer.

"You were right, Vinnie. Time for a Family meeting."

Chapter Seventeen

The dinner dishes were still warm in the drying rack. As usual, it fell to me to gather everyone around the kitchen table for the conversation none of us wanted to have. The living room television droned in the background, some mindless evening programming that usually served as white noise for our post-meal routine.

"Family meeting," I announced, pulling out my chair.

William immediately stiffened. "This isn't the scheduled time. Family meetings occur on the last Sunday of each month at 7:00 PM, after evening cleanup but before recreational activities."

"Coo coo!" Floyd chimed in with a mischievous grin, knowing exactly how to push William's buttons.

"This is important," I cut him off, settling into my chair. The gravity of what I was about to tell them pressed down on me.

The authority in my voice must have registered because the kitchen went dead quiet. Even Floyd stopped his teasing.

Vinnie took his usual seat beside me, but I could feel the tension radiating from him. He knew what was coming.

I took a breath and jumped into the abyss.

"Charity has taken complete control of the Cartwright Foundation," I began. "She's terminated Garth's monthly stipend, effective immediately."

William's reaction was swift and indignant. "That's impossible. Wills are legally binding documents with established beneficiaries and—"

"None of that matters," I interrupted. "Not for people like us. Charity owns the banks, has unlimited resources, and an army of lawyers backing her, and it gets worse. Her plan is to have Garth declared mentally incompetent."

Floyd's face went ashen. "She c-can't be that evil—" He stopped mid-sentence as his gaze shifted to Garth, remembering exactly how evil Charity could be.

"If the court finds Garth incompetent," I continued, "Charity gains legal guardianship. Garth would have to move back in with her."

Garth's entire body went rigid. I watched the color drain from his face as the full implication hit him. His hands clenched into white-knuckled fists. Then his fists slammed onto the table like thunder, making everyone jump.

"I hate Charity!" he bellowed, his voice raw with fury and despair.

"There's more," I said, waiting for Garth's breathing to steady before continuing. "Without that monthly support, we can't make the mortgage payments. Can't afford utilities, groceries, basic living expenses. We've got maybe three months before we're completely broke."

Floyd's voice was barely a whisper. "What h-happens to us?"

This was the part that was killing me. The part I'd been dreading since I'd walked out of Charity's office.

"Nothing good. Garth ends up with Charity. The rest of you..." I swallowed hard. "State care."

The reaction was immediate and devastating.

William shot up from his chair and began pacing, his counting becoming audible as panic overtook him. "One-two-three-four-five... I could get a second job, maybe find the money... Six-seven-eight-nine..."

Floyd gripped his wheelchair armrests so hard his knuckles went white. "I could s-sell my chair. Buy us t-time. I think I could b-build another one from sc-scratch..."

Garth just sat there now, catatonic again, staring at nothing as the prospect of living with his abuser haunted him.

"None of that will be enough," I said, crushing their desperate hope. "I've run the numbers a dozen times."

<hr>

Nicholas's words made my stomach hurt. I watched William pacing in the kitchen. Floyd was holding on to his wheelchair really tight. Garth was quiet. But something else was in my head.

From the living room, the TV was talking about something that made me listen.

"...the bank robbers have struck a fourth bank. It appears to be the same crew responsible for three previous robberies this month and—"

I tried to listen to Nicholas, but my brain kept going back to the TV.

Something was happening.

Something I needed to understand.

"This isn't fair!" William yelled. "We've done everything right, followed every rule—"

William was right. We always followed rules. So many rules. Rules about medicine. Rules about work. Rules about being nice to typicals who were mean to us.

What if we stopped following rules?

That thought felt scary.

"The r-rules are rigged!" Floyd yelled. "The whole f-fucking system is—"

Floyd was right. The system was rigged. Nicholas always said that. When the world was mean to people like us, which was lots, Nicholas got mad and said the system was rigged.

If the system was rigged...

Maybe we could stop following rules?

"Language," William said, even though he was scared.

"Fuck language!" Floyd yelled back. "Our wor-world is en-ending!"

Floyd was right. We were going to lose everything. Our house. Our Family. Everything good.

Charity didn't follow rules. She did what she wanted. Nothing bad happened to her.

Everyone kept yelling. From the living room, the TV kept talking about bank robbers. I kept listening to both.

"...police believe the perpetrators escaped with an undisclosed amount of cash and remain at large..."

My brain was working hard. William always talked about that old game *Tetris* where blocks fall down and you make them fit. He said the best part was when that long straight piece came down when you needed it.

That happened in my head. The long straight piece fell down.

"As it stands, we have about sixty days before the bank forecloses and we get evicted. I know none of this is easy to hear, but we have to face reality and—"

I knew what we had to do.

I hit the table hard like Garth did.

"No!"

Everyone stopped yelling and looked at me. I was so mad. Like Nicholas when he got mad, but this was my mad.

"It's not right!" I said, looking at Nicholas. "I won't let this happen!"

Nicholas used his soft voice, the one he used when he thought I didn't understand big things.

"Vinnie, we've talked about this. If you have an idea, now's the time, but there's simply no way we can find enough money to stop foreclosure."

I looked at everyone. William stopped walking and looked at me with hope. Floyd was leaning forward, waiting to hear what I would say. Garth was looking at me too.

"We can stop it," I said, "if we rob the bank."

Everyone's mouths opened wide. Nicholas looked at me like I said I could fly.

"We can't rob a bank!" William said, his voice getting all high and squeaky.

"We can," I said. "Not just any bank. One of Garth's sister's banks."

For the first time since his mom died, Garth sat up straight. His eyes got bright, like when he lifted heavy weights.

But Nicholas shook his head. "Vinnie, you know that's wrong."

"No," I said. "Charity took Garth's money. Her bank has that money. If we rob her bank, we're taking back Garth's money. That's not wrong. That's right."

Nicholas looked at me like he didn't know me. I could see him thinking, trying to find what was wrong with my idea.

Then he said, "Okay, what happens if we get caught, Vinnie? If you think state care is bad, prison will kill you. All of you."

"We won't go to prison," I said. "No one will believe we robbed a bank. We're retarded, dumb, no one even likes to look at us, and when they do, they see no evil. If we do the job right, they never will. It's perfect."

Nicholas opened and closed his mouth like a fish drowning on land. I could tell he thought my idea made sense but didn't want it to.

"It's what you did today," I said. "At the bank. You asked me to act slow so Mr. Reece would feel sorry and give us money."

"That's different—" Nicholas started.

"It's the same," I said.

"No, Vinnie," Nicholas said loud. "We're not talking about this anymore!"

"But Nicholas—"

"I said that's enough! The TV said those robbers killed people!" Nicholas yelled. "Is that what you want? You want to become murderers?"

"We won't kill anyone," I said. "We're not bad like those people. We'll just take Garth's money. And then give the money to the bank so we keep our house and save Garth."

"It's not that simple!" Nicholas yelled.

"Yes, it is!" I yelled back.

We looked at each other. Nicholas looked angry and scared. But I wasn't going to change my mind. I was right.

So, I said the thing I knew would make him understand.

"Nicholas... *Always protect your family.*"

Nicholas's face went white. He knew those words. They were his words. The most important words he ever said to me.

I watched him remember. I hoped this would make him say yes.

Nicholas stood up, walked out, went to his room and slammed the door so hard the house shook.

I never saw Nicholas slam a door like that. Ever.

The kitchen was quiet. Everyone looked at me like they didn't know what would happen next.

I didn't know either.

Chapter Eighteen

I sat on the edge of my bed, staring at the door I'd slammed three hours ago like some pissy teenager. The merry band of misfits robbing a fucking bank...it's completely absurd.

Through the walls, I'd heard the Family go through their nightly routines, albeit quieter than usual. No arguing over bathroom time. No William counting his way to sleep. No Floyd's drone humming late into the night. Just silence, and it was my fault.

I couldn't face them. Not yet. How the hell was I supposed to convince Vinnie that his plan was not only wrong but would destroy them all? And what alternative could I offer? Nothing. I had absolutely nothing.

I crept out of my room and made my way to the kitchen, grabbing a non-alcoholic beer from the fridge. The house felt different when I walked through it. Even when we were fighting, I couldn't stop being their caregiver.

I checked William's room first. He was curled up in his bed, breathing steadily, his hardback copy of *Pride and Prejudice* on his nightstand like a protective talisman. Floyd's room next.

Asleep too, his breathing peaceful; Garth must have helped him into bed. The nightmares were staying away and that was something.

Garth's room was next. The big man lay sprawled across his oversized bed, taking up most of the space, but sleeping soundly.

Finally, I paused at Vinnie's door. My twin lay in his bed, deep in slumber, his recipe binder on the nightstand beside him.

Always protect your family.

My own words, thrown back at me by the person I'd said them to. The person who'd inspired them.

I leaned against the doorframe, watching Vinnie's peaceful face, and suddenly I was nineteen years old again, standing in a very different doorway, discovering exactly what those words truly meant...

Eleven years earlier...

Spring break, baby! I was practically dancing as I strolled through the sterile hallways of Meadowbrook State Care Facility, car keys jingling in my pocket, Ray-Bans perched on my head like I was some kind of campus celebrity. Which, honestly, I kind of was. Dean's List three semesters running, starting quarterback for our intramural flag football team, and still dating Rita, who had followed me to college.

Sure, I felt guilty leaving Vinnie here while I lived it up at college, but Mom had been clear about her priorities before she died. Education first. Get the degree, get the good job, then Vinnie and I could be together again. The plan was solid. I'd power through college in three years instead of four, graduate summa cum laude, land some corporate psychology gig, and then Vinnie and I would get a place together. Easy peasy.

Until then, Vinnie was safe here. State care wasn't ideal, but it was temporary. Professional. Regulated. What could go wrong?

I'd barely visited because, honestly, these places depressed the hell out of me. All those institutional smells and sad faces. Spring break was calling, my friends were already en route to Fort Lauderdale, and Rita was waiting for me back on campus. We'd been getting serious, talking about moving in together after graduation. Life was a fucking amusement park, and I was riding every ride.

Such a good brother, right?

I found Vinnie's room and knocked before pushing the door open.

"Nicholas!"

Vinnie's face lit up like it always did when I came to visit. He was lying on his narrow bed, staring at the ceiling, but he scrambled up to greet me with the enthusiasm of a puppy who'd been chained in the yard and rarely received visitors.

"Hey, Vinman."

When we hugged, Vinnie flinched. A subtle movement, but I'd grown up with him. I knew every one of his tells.

"What's wrong?" I asked.

"I hurt my back. It's nothing," he said quietly, not meeting my eyes.

Something felt off. I turned him around and lifted his shirt, revealing a dark bruise that covered most of his lower back.

"How'd you get this?"

"I don't know," Vinnie said, his voice small and defeated.

That wasn't like him. Vinnie always knew how he got hurt. He was clumsy sometimes, but never secretive about it.

"Are you done with college?" Vinnie asked suddenly, his eyes bright with hope. "Is that why you're here? To get me so we can live together now?"

The eagerness in his voice made my words catch in my throat. "Not yet, buddy. It's spring break. I'm on my way to meet some friends at Fort Lauderdale and figured I'd stop by and visit the Vinman."

I watched the light die in his eyes.

"Oh," he said quietly. "I see." Then, after a pause he said, "I wish you would go back and finish college first, Nicholas."

Looking back now, I realize that moment should have told me everything.

Vinnie was protecting me from the truth so I could keep living my carefree college fantasy. He was sacrificing his own safety for my education. But I was too selfish and stupid to see it.

"How're they treating you?" I asked, though I was already thinking about the drive to Florida, about which bars we'd hit first.

"Okay," Vinnie said. "They won't let me work in the cafeteria."

"They don't know what they're missing then. Want to play a game or something? Where's your phone?"

"They took it. I play on it too much."

That was strange. Before I could ask more, a burly orderly entered the room.

"Vincent, time for your bath—" He stopped short when he saw me. The man was in his thirties, built like a bouncer, with the cold eyes of a predator.

More importantly, I saw the look of pure terror that flashed across Vinnie's face.

Something was very, very wrong here.

"Sorry, didn't know he had a visitor," the orderly said with practiced professionalism. "I'll come back later."

Every protective instinct I'd developed over twenty years of being Vinnie's brother was screaming warnings. This guy was a threat. But I needed to know exactly what kind of threat.

"No, it's fine," I said casually. "I was just leaving." I turned to Vinnie. "I'll try and stop back by next month. See you then, Vinnie."

Vinnie's face crumpled with disappointment, but he nodded obediently. As we hugged goodbye, I noticed something that made my blood run cold... Restraints attached to his bed. Leather straps, worn from use.

"Bye, Nicholas," Vinnie whispered.

I walked out of that room like nothing was wrong, playing the part of the carefree college kid who had places to be. But the moment I hit the parking lot, I leaned against my car and lit a cigarette with shaking hands.

Restraints. Bruises. Terror.

I knew what those signs meant. I just hadn't wanted to see them. Hadn't wanted my perfect college life disrupted by ugly realities.

What kind of brother does that make me?

Ten minutes felt like enough time. I crushed my cigarette under my heel and marched back inside.

I opened Vinnie's door quietly and saw the orderly struggling to force a defiant Vinnie into the bed restraints.

"Hold still, dammit!" the orderly snarled. "I don't have time for your shit, Mongo!"

He struck Vinnie across the face.

The sound of his flesh hitting Vinnie's flipped a primal switch in my brain. The orderly noticed the open door and turned to see me standing there.

Everything went very quiet in my head.

Serene.

My entire world tilted on its axis.

Waiting for my next decision...

"Look away, Vinnie," I managed to say before I let violence take over.

I don't remember much about the fight itself, just the satisfying way the bastard crumpled when I broke his arm.

And his begging for me to stop as I beat him like he'd beaten Vinnie.

I didn't stop.

An hour later, I sat in the back of a police cruiser with a fresh shiner blooming around my left eye. In the front seat sat Detective Raul Reyes, Rita's father. The only person I could think to call when the facility decided to press charges.

"You broke that orderly's arm," Detective Reyes said without preamble.

I had known Rita's father for years, but never in this capacity. Detective Reyes was an oak. Steady, deeply rooted, unshakeable. His quiet authority came from decades of dealing with humanity's worst impulses.

"Good. He won't be hitting Vinnie anymore with it," I spat.

"I'm not saying what you did wasn't right, but it sure as hell wasn't smart." His voice carried no judgment, just the patient tone of someone who'd seen too many good people make bad choices for the right reasons. "Now, I convinced them not to press charges—"

"Convinced them?!" I exploded. "After what they did, they should be in jail!"

Detective Reyes absorbed my outburst without flinching. I could see where Rita got her unflappable composure under pressure.

"That's going to take time. And your outburst makes it harder." He turned to study my face. "They're not going to press charges, as long as you don't."

I scoffed and stared out the window. *Fuck this world.*

"The way I see it, you're looking at a fork in the road." His tone was fatherly without being condescending. "Best make the right choice."

"Why are you helping me, Detective Reyes?"

He was quiet for a moment, and I could see him weighing his words as someone who'd learned what you said mattered as much as what you did.

"My daughter sees something in you. I trust her instincts." He paused. "Don't make her wrong."

Two hours later, after the paperwork was filed and Vinnie was discharged into my custody, we stood next to my car in the nearly empty parking lot. Vinnie looked confused and lost, clutching a plastic bag that contained everything he owned.

"Are you taking me to college now?" he asked hopefully.

"No, Vinnie. I'm not going back to college. I'm dropping out."

Vinnie's confusion deepened.

I couldn't look at him as I asked the question that was eating me alive, "Why didn't you tell me they were hurting you?"

Vinnie was quiet for a long moment. "Going to college was important to you. It was important to Mom too." He shrugged with that heartbreaking innocence that defined him. "Besides, I'm okay. The Vinman can!"

Tears stung my eyes. I pulled out my pack of cigarettes, then looked at Vinnie...really looked at him. The bruises. The fear that still lingered in his eyes. The way he'd endured hell so I could have heaven.

In that moment, something from my philosophy classes suddenly racked into 4K focus. There was this paper by Schopenhauer I'd struggled with all semester, "On the Basis of Morality," where he posed a question that had seemed purely academic at the time: *How can a human being so completely participate in another's suffering that they spontaneously sacrifice their own wellbeing, even their life, for that person?*

My professor had told this story about a cop who saw someone about to jump off a bridge. When the cop grabbed the jumper, he got pulled over the edge himself. The cop's partner had to grab them both to save them. When asked later why he didn't let go, why he'd risk his own life to save a stranger, the first cop said, "I couldn't let go. If I had let that man die, I could not have lived another day of my life."

Standing there looking at Vinnie's bruised body, I finally understood what Schopenhauer meant. It wasn't about heroism or moral duty. It was the sudden, overwhelming realization that you and the other person are connected in a way that makes their suffering yours. That the separateness you think exists between us is just an illusion.

Schopenhauer's single point of meditation.

Vinnie's pain *was* my pain. His safety *was* my safety.

We are one.

In that moment, I became an adult.

I crushed the cigarette pack and threw it down. "I'm sorry, Vinnie. I'm so sorry. I should've never left you with the state. I'm taking care of you now."

"How?" he asked simply.

"I don't know. I really have no fucking idea." I turned to face him fully. "But if you learn nothing else from me, Vinnie, learn this: always protect your family."

The next morning, I woke before everyone else and made my way to the kitchen. If this was going to be our last normal day together, I wanted it to count.

By the time I'd finished cooking, the house smelled like everything the Family loved most.

"Breakfast is served!" I called out.

One by one, they appeared, hair disheveled, eyes heavy with sleep, but drawn by the promise of their favorite foods. They took their usual seats around the table, but the atmosphere was different. Cautious. Like they were waiting for the other shoe to drop.

"I owe you all an apology," I said, remaining standing while they settled in. "I yelled at you last night when you were already scared and hurting. That was wrong of me. I'm sorry."

They ate in silence, waiting. They knew me well enough to recognize when an apology was just the opening act.

"There's something human beings experience called fight or flight," I continued, pacing slowly around the table. "It's an evolutionary response that helps us survive when we feel threatened. When we're cornered, our brains tell us to either fight back or run away. Charity has our backs against the wall."

I stopped pacing and looked at each of them in turn.

"I've accepted there's simply nowhere to run. It's time to fucking fight."

Vinnie looked up from his eggs benedict. "Does that mean you'll rob the bank with us?"

I took a deep breath. "I'm still not convinced this isn't complete insanity. The risks are enormous, and if we get caught..." I shook my head. "But yeah. As long as we vote unanimously."

The table went dead silent. This was it. Our moment of truth.

"Garth?" I asked.

His massive hands slammed onto the table with vengeful delight.

"Count me in!" he bellowed.

"That's one," I said, nodding. "Floyd?"

"The odds of s-s-su-successfully robbing a b-b-bank are approx-prox-imately three-thousand-seven-hundred-twenty-to-one," he announced. "But you can't w-w-win if you don't p-p-play."

"That's two," I said, turning to the most unpredictable vote of all. "William?"

William had gone completely pale. His hands were shaking as he gripped his fork, and I could see the familiar signs of an anxiety attack building behind his eyes.

"I can't," he whispered. "I can't! It's too dangerous!"

He started to push back from the table, ready to bolt, when Vinnie reached over and gently touched his arm.

"What would Mr. Darcy do?" Vinnie asked quietly.

William stopped short. I watched his entire posture transform as he straightened in his chair, drawing on the strength of his literary hero. When he spoke again, his voice carried the authority of a man who'd found his courage.

"There is, I believe, in every disposition a tendency to some particular evil—a natural defect, which not even the best education can overcome," he quoted. Then, meeting my eyes directly he declared, "Count me in on this dubious endeavor."

"Three," I said, my throat tight with emotion. "Vinnie?"

"You know I'm in. What about you, Nicholas?" he asked.

All eyes turned to me.

Fuck it.

"I guess we're robbing a bank."

Chapter Nineteen

As we cleaned up our breakfast, the Family buzzed with anticipation about Vinnie's plan to rob a bank. Our decision was less than ideal, but it appeared to be our only option. As the last dish was put away, Floyd announced, "I need to g-g-go to TechWorld. I'll n-n-need some components for the bank robbery."

"We don't even have a plan yet. What could you possibly be building?" I asked.

"For starters? A police scan-scanner," Floyd said. "We c-c-can't devise a plan until we've gathered intel."

"Can I come?" Vinnie asked, perking up.

Before I could answer, William claimed, "I'm coming too, even though this is an unscheduled outing."

Garth wanted in as well.

A half-hour later, we were packed into the van like conspirators heading to a secret meeting. Floyd's wheelchair was locked into position behind me in the driver's seat, Vinnie rode shotgun, William fidgeted with his seatbelt behind him, and Garth was silent but alert in the back. Ever since breakfast, our conversation had revolved around our decision to rob a bank. The prospect had cast a ray of light through the dark storm clouds hanging over us. But now that the initial excitement was fading, reality was creeping back in.

"Do you really think we can pull this off?" William asked as we hit the main road.

"Of course, we can," Vinnie stated matter-of-factly.

"William, wh-wh-what do you mean?" Floyd pressed.

"I mean, look at us. We're not Ocean's Eleven, more like Ocean's Forty-Seven," William proposed.

"I see what you did there," Vinnie said.

"Seriously, how are *we* going to rob a bank?" William asked.

From the rearview mirror, I watched the Family look at each other as they pondered William's question. We were all asking the same thing privately. Everyone except Vinnie, who had convinced himself we could do it for reasons I had yet to understand.

Garth finally spoke first. "No other choice."

"I'm just saying," William continued, "It's very easy to *say* we're going to rob a bank, but it's an entirely different thing when you have to rob the bank *with your own hands.*"

"Typicals d-d-do it, why can't we-e?" Floyd asked.

"Typicals do a lot of things we can't do," William countered.

"We voted. We decided. That's that, William," Vinnie answered stubbornly. I could tell he was getting aggravated with William pissing on our parade.

But William had a point.

How the fuck were the merry band of misfits supposed to rob a bank? Was this how people crossed that line between desperation and felony? A string of small decisions leading to a violent break with societal norms? Was this how criminals were born?

"It's only been a couple hours, we'll have time to plan later," I said, more to convince myself than anyone else.

"I can't go into the bank. I know my limitations; I'd be caught for sure," William confessed shamelessly. "Mr. Darcy would not do well in prison..." he finished.

"I'm n-n-not much better," Floyd added as he looked down at his legs.

"How do typicals do it?" Vinnie asked quietly.

"They train for years," I said. "Professional thieves study their targets for months. They plan, they practice, they make contingency plans for their contingency plans. They have time."

"W-we have sixty days," Floyd said.

"We don't have superpowers, we have disabilities," William said with finality.

William's pessimism had become infectious.

"Maybe William's right," Garth said deflated.

The van fell silent except for the engine's hum.

In the passenger seat beside me, I caught a glimpse of Vinnie staring out the window as he processed our situation. His face cycled through emotions I couldn't quite read. My moral compass was spinning like a coked-up prima ballerina; I couldn't imagine what his was doing. Everything I'd believed about right and wrong, about the system working for those who worked hard and followed the rules, had been shattered in Charity's office.

As I pulled into the TechWorld parking lot, I realized I agreed to this course of action, but as we discussed it further...it seemed impossible for me and the merry band of misfits to actually pull it off.

. . .

TechWorld was Floyd's version of Valhalla. Sprawling aisles of electronic components, computer parts, and gadgets that existed somewhere between cutting-edge technology and expensive toys.

"Cir-r-cuit boards are in aisle three," he proclaimed, navigating toward the components section.

Garth followed Floyd, ready to reach anything on high shelves, while William trailed behind them, walking on his toes and counting the items in displays. I stayed at the back of the group, keeping watch—an old habit from years of shepherding them through public spaces.

Vinnie had wandered off by himself to study a display of graphics cards we didn't need. From his posture, he was either working something out in his head or sulking because William had tried to drink his milkshake in the van. Either way...

Everything in his own time.

As I watched my Family navigate through the store, helping and accommodating each other, I realized William was right. This was never going to work.

Having selected the components he needed, Floyd headed toward the register with Garth and William in tow. "Vinnie," I called out as we headed for the exit. "Time to go."

Vinnie looked up and headed toward us, "Coming, Nicholas."

Back at the van, we patiently waited for Floyd's wheelchair ramp to lower. The Family had gone quiet again, as if returning to the van brought back our last conversation. It was all fun and games to fantasize about what you'd do if your life was a movie. Sure, plan a heist, rob the villain, roll credits.

Real life wasn't a movie. And I wasn't the only one thinking this.

"I don't think we can do this," William offered. "I know we

voted. I stand by my vote. But we simply can't pull off a bank heist. What do you all think?"

The Family slowly pondered William's question. I could see the seed William had planted earlier had germinated and convinced them all that running a heist was beyond their capabilities. Floyd's shoulders slumped in his chair. Garth closed his eyes, his head sinking as he accepted the realization. I figured it was my cue to guide us back to sanity.

"I agree with William," I told them. "I don't think we can—"

"We can and we will," Vinnie interrupted.

"Vinnie, we don't know what we're doing. We aren't criminals," William pointed out.

"We are now," Vinnie said with unmistakable pride.

To our collective shock, he lifted his shirt and showed us the brand-new graphics card he'd just shoplifted from TechWorld.

A five-hundred-dollar graphics card, no less.

My eyes went wide, Garth grunted in surprise, Floyd's jaw dropped, and William gasped.

"You stole that?!" William practically shrieked.

Floyd looked around the parking lot as if the authorities were already on their way to haul us all off to prison. "Five-hun-hun-hundred dollars is larceny!"

Even Garth shook his head at Vinnie's revelation.

I was about to tear into him when Vinnie raised his hand to silence me.

"We do have superpowers. Follow me," Vinnie said before marching back into TechWorld.

The Family followed me back into TechWorld. I could hear Floyd's wheelchair making its quiet robot noise behind me and everyone's footsteps on the hard floor. But I didn't turn around to look at them because my brain was working like when I cooked and had to remember exactly what spice came next.

I needed to show them, not tell them.

The owner was behind the register. He was maybe the same age as me and Nicholas but with gray hair that was trying to leave his head. His glasses made his eyes look bigger than they really were, like a cartoon. His TechWorld shirt was too small around his belly.

I walked up to the counter and did what I always did when typicals were about to get mad at me. I let my shoulders drop down like I was carrying something heavy. I made my face look sorry before anyone was even mad yet. I stared at the floor instead of his eyes because that's what made typicals think they were in charge.

"Excuse me, sir," I said, and my voice cracked a little like it did when I was scared. "I think I made a big mistake."

The owner stopped working on his computer and looked up at me. I watched his face change the way they always did. First, he saw just another customer. Then he saw my face, and his expression got soft and sorry. The way typicals' faces always got when they saw I had Down syndrome.

I knew that look. I had seen it a thousand times before.

Pity.

"What can I help you with, son?" he asked in the voice typicals used when they thought I couldn't understand big words.

I was thirty years old and he called me "son." That's what people like me were to typicals. Forever children who always needed help.

I showed him the graphics card I was holding and put it on

the counter. My hands shook a little, because I was acting and because talking to authority figures always made me nervous, even when I wasn't in trouble.

"I was deciding if I buy this graphics card or not, but then my Family said time to go, and I walked outside with it without thinking. I'm very sorry. I didn't mean to take it."

The owner's eyes got big when he saw the graphics card. Five hundred dollars was expensive. Way more expensive than anything I ever bought before. Then he looked back at me, and I could see him trying to decide if I was lying.

I don't know why, but my brain suddenly thought about Mom dying in her hospital bed and how her hand felt cold when I held it. Then I thought about Garth crying at the gym about his mother dying. Then I figured it out. My brain was making me think about sad things so I would cry in front of this typical.

I looked away and wiped my eyes as I said, "I'm very sorry, sir. Please don't call the cops. I don't want to get in trouble. I didn't mean to steal. I promise."

I watched the owner's face while he decided what to do. He picked up the graphics card and looked at it, then looked at me again. His eyes got softer. His mouth made a small smile.

He was seeing exactly what every typical saw when they looked at me. Someone too simple to lie. Someone too innocent to steal. Someone who needed help, not punishment.

That's all any of them ever saw.

I blinked at him with my sorry eyes and waited. I knew what he would say before he said it. Typicals always said the same things.

"Well, I appreciate your honesty," he said in the voice people used for little kids and dogs. "Not many people would come back to return something like this."

He put his hand on the graphics card but kept looking at me like I was a good dog who brought back a tennis ball.

"Are you going to call the police?" I asked, making my voice small and scared.

"Oh no, no. No need for that." He smiled bigger now. "I can see this was just an accident. These things happen."

The owner put the graphics card behind the counter and looked at me with those eyes full of pity. I had seen those eyes my whole life. From teachers who thought I was cute. From doctors who talked to Nicholas instead of me. From strangers at the grocery store who whispered about me to their friends.

"You know," the owner said, leaning forward like he was telling me a secret, "there aren't many people in the world as honest as you anymore. You're a good kid."

Kid. There it was again.

"Thank you, sir," I said, still looking at the floor like I was ashamed.

"You have a good day, son. And don't you worry about this anymore, okay? Just be more careful next time."

I nodded like a child who had learned a lesson and walked back to my Family.

The Family was standing by the door looking at me with their mouths hanging open. They heard everything. They saw everything.

They knew I stole five hundred dollars and watched me give it back, and then watched a typical thank me for doing it.

Now they knew.

We walked to the van without talking. Nicholas kept looking back at the store like he couldn't believe what just happened.

I could tell they were all thinking about what they saw and wanted to talk about it. But I made them wait. I wouldn't talk until we were in the van where no one could listen. When the van doors closed, I said, "Now we can talk."

"What the hell just happened back there?" Nicholas asked as he started driving home.

"You saw what happened," I said. "I took something expensive. I gave it back. He thanked me."

"But why?" William asked. His voice was confused and a little scared.

"To show you that you're all wrong," I said. "About the bank. About what we can do."

Floyd was shaking his head. "I d-don't understand. You st-stole something and gave it back. How does that help us, Vinnie?"

"Because you all keep saying we can't rob a bank because we're different. You keep saying we don't know how and that we're not smart enough or good enough because of our disabilities."

I looked around at my Family. Nicholas was listening. Floyd had turned in his wheelchair to face me. William had stopped his fidgeting. Garth was looking at me too. "You think being different makes us weak. But you're wrong. Being different makes us invisible. Everyone in the store was watching us and I stole it with no one seeing."

I watched them try to understand what I meant. I could see them thinking.

"That man back there at TechWorld. He looked at me and saw someone too dumb to lie. Too simple to plan anything. Too broken to be a criminal."

I let that sink in for a moment.

"That's what all typicals see when they look at us. They don't see people who can think or plan or do dangerous things. They see children who always need their help."

Nicholas was driving slower now. "Vinnie..."

"I'm not finished," I said. "Listen to me. All my life, typicals have talked to you instead of me. Talked about me like I wasn't there. Treated me like a child even though I'm thirty years old. Remember at the bank? Mr. Reece wouldn't even look at me."

"Fair point," Nicholas said quietly.

"They do it to all of us. They see Floyd's wheelchair and think he's helpless. They hear Garth's voice and think he's stupid. They see your counting, William, and think you're crazy. And when they see my face, they think I'm retarded."

I watched my Family remember all the times people had treated them like that. All the times people had made them feel small.

"That's our superpower," I said. "They made us invisible. You're right, William, we can't rob a bank like typicals. No, we'll rob it like misfits."

I felt something change in the van. The Family was starting to understand.

As Nicholas pulled into our driveway, I looked at my Family's faces one at a time. They weren't scared anymore. They weren't talking about how impossible it was. And they were looking at me differently too.

I didn't understand it yet, but I had taken my first steps into becoming the leader of the Merry Band of Misfits.

Chapter Twenty

Back home, the Family had claimed their usual spots in the living room. Vinnie sprawled across the couch, still riding the high from his TechWorld demonstration. Floyd worked on his electronics project at the card table, tiny components spread across its surface like technological confetti. William sat rigidly upright in his chair, while Garth occupied most of the oversized recliner.

"First things first," I said, settling into my own chair. "We need to pick a specific bank. And it can't be any of the ones those other bank robbers have already hit."

William immediately perked up. "I've been researching those robberies online," he announced with pride. "The perpetrators kill one person during every robbery and wear happy face masks to conceal their identities, which is why the media has dubbed them the Happy Face Killers."

The name sent a chill through the room. Floyd's hands paused over his circuit board.

William continued, his voice taking on the clinical tone he used when discussing uncomfortable facts. "The motive appears to be unknown, but according to surviving witnesses, the killings seem random. They've hit four banks across the state, and police expect more robberies and murders in the future."

I felt my stomach lurch. We were planning to join the ranks of bank robbers during what appeared to be a crime spree by actual murderers.

"That's good for us," Vinnie said suddenly, his matter-of-fact tone cutting through my growing dread.

We all stared at him like he'd lost his mind.

"What do you mean 'that's good for us'?" I asked carefully.

Vinnie leaned forward on the couch, his expression earnest and focused. "Think about it, Nicholas. The police are looking for the Happy Face Killers. They're looking for people who wear masks and kill people and steal money from banks. That's what they expect bank robbers to look like."

He gestured around the room at all of us. "We don't look like the Happy Face Killers. He paused, searching for the right words. "To them, we look like people who need help getting dressed, not people who rob banks."

Floyd's eyes gleamed with understanding. "He's r-right. The Happy Face Killers are l-like an umbrella."

Vinnie thought about what Floyd said for a moment before working it out aloud. "The police will be so busy trying to catch the real bad guys that they won't even think to look at us. We'll be hiding under their umbrella. I see what you did there, Floyd. Yes."

I had to admit, in his twisted logic, Vinnie had a point. The Happy Face Killers were generating massive media attention and police resources. Every law enforcement agency in the state would be focused on catching violent criminals who fit a very specific profile.

A profile that definitely didn't include my merry band of misfits.

"That's all I could find through conventional internet searches," William finished. "Perhaps Rita would know more, given her profession. You should press her for details, Nicholas. Maybe invite her over for dinner?"

Rita.

The mention of my girlfriend's name detonated in my mind like a hydrogen bomb. In all the excitement and terror of the day, I'd completely forgotten the most obvious problem with our plan.

I was dating a cop. And planning to rob a bank.

What the fuck was I going to do about her?

I could feel the Family's eyes on me, waiting for my response, but my mind was racing through scenarios. How was I supposed to hide something this massive from Rita? She could spot deception from three counties away. And even if I could somehow keep it secret, what happened when our bank robbery inevitably made the news? When she connected the dots?

Inhale, two, three, four...

Then again, maybe I was getting ahead of myself. We didn't even have a solid plan yet. Hell, I still had nagging doubts about whether we could pull this off at all. Life was so turbulent right now that I could only handle one crisis at a time.

Exhale, two, three, four...

I pushed the Rita issue to the back burner and focused on the immediate problem.

"Let's worry about selecting our target first," I said. "We need a bank that none of us have any connection to, but that Charity owns."

"What about the one that rejected us?" Vinnie suggested with obvious relish. "Mr. Reece was kind of a dick."

"No," I said firmly. "Mr. Reece knows me. It has to be somewhere we don't normally go."

Floyd turned to Garth. "You gr-grew up with Agnes and the C-Cartwright estate. Do you kn-know anything about their b-banking business?"

Garth's expression grew thoughtful as he considered the question. I could see him searching through memories, trying to find something useful. Finally, he nodded slowly.

"Maybe," he said. "Not sure if it helps."

"Tell us," I encouraged.

"Long story. Easier to sign," Garth said and began signing. I positioned myself to translate for the Family.

"When Garth was little..." I began, watching Garth's story unfold through his gestures.

Fourteen years ago...

Little Garth squirmed in his mother's arms as Agnes tried to keep him still in the cramped room. The space was lined with metal boxes from floor to ceiling, each one secured with dual locks.

"The safety deposit box room," I explained to the Family as Garth continued his story.

Agnes was speaking to teenage Charity with the serious tone she used when discussing important family business. Garth could read lips even then, and he understood that whatever his mother was explaining was very, very important. He knew because Agnes scolded Charity for not paying attention.

"Young lady, you need to listen to me," Agnes said sternly. "This is crucial information."

To keep Garth occupied, Agnes had given him a foam keychain that the banker had handed her when they'd entered. Little Garth did what most children do with squishy toys. He immediately put it in his mouth and began chewing on it as he watched the conversation unfold.

Agnes pulled out a long metal box from their safety deposit box and opened it for Charity to see. Inside was more cash than little Garth had ever seen in his life.

"Two million dollars," Agnes explained to her teenage daughter. "Your father had some less than reputable business associates."

Charity's eyes widened. "Why are you showing me this?"

"Because this money is an insurance policy," Agnes continued. "Your father has enemies, and this is in case anything nefarious were to occur. Sometimes you need fast cash that can't be traced to make problems disappear."

Agnes made Charity memorize the safety deposit box number, repeating it over and over until the teenager could recite it perfectly.

Little Garth chewed his keychain and committed the number to memory, not understanding its significance then, but knowing it mattered to his mother.

Garth said, "Security box October 30, '55."

"Ten, thirty, fifty-five?" I asked for clarity.

Garth nodded, "Dad's birthday."

"Do you remember the bank's name?" I interrupted, hope building in my chest.

Garth shook his head, signing that he'd been too young to pay attention to details like that.

My heart sank. "Damn. If we knew which bank, stealing

from a safety deposit box would be easier than cracking a vault. And two million would solve all our problems."

As the Family continued discussing the missed opportunity, Garth's eyes went wide, and he suddenly bolted from his chair.

"Garth?" I called as he hurried toward his bedroom. "Where are you going?"

We could hear him rummaging through his belongings, boxes being moved and drawers being opened. After several minutes of increasingly frantic searching, Garth emerged triumphantly.

In his massive hand was the most disgusting thing I'd seen in months.

The foam keychain from his childhood memory was barely recognizable. Fourteen years of stress chewing had reduced it to a mangled, discolored mass that looked like it belonged in a biohazard container. The original foam had been compressed and reshaped by countless teeth marks, and the surface was stained with God only knew what.

"Je-Jesus Christ, Garth," Floyd said, recoiling in his wheelchair. "That's d-disgusting."

"Why did you keep that?" William asked, clearly distressed by the sight of something so unhygienic.

Garth looked slightly embarrassed but determined. "Momma gave it to me," he explained. "Helps when stressed. Like how it feels."

Despite my revulsion, I felt a pang of sympathy. Garth had kept this gross memento because his mother had given it to him, and because the texture provided comfort during anxious moments. It was touching and nauseating in equal measure.

"We'll get you a proper stress toy," I promised. "But first, can you read anything on that thing?"

Garth held the chewed-up keychain closer to the lamp,

squinting at what remained of the original printing. The Family gathered around, everyone trying to decipher the mangled text.

"First..." Vinnie read slowly, "National..."

"Bank," William finished. "I can make out most of an address too."

My pulse quickened as the pieces fell into place. "That's it," I said quietly. "That's the bank we have to rob."

Floyd was already calculating possibilities. "Two m-million dollars would solve all our pr-problems and then some."

"That kind of money would be enough to save the house and hire a real lawyer to contest Charity's guardianship of Garth," I added.

"And get a kitchen island," Vinnie added.

"The poetic justice is rather satisfying," William added with unusual emotion.

"Before we get ahead of ourselves, I need to do reconnaissance on the bank," I said. "Study their layout, security measures, staff routines. All of that."

"Another field trip!" Vinnie exclaimed.

"No," I said firmly. "We're too conspicuous traveling together. I need to do this alone."

Floyd immediately offered a technical solution. "I could b-build you a spy camera pen. Record everything in r-real time for remote viewing."

"Or I could just set my phone to record as I walk around," I suggested.

Floyd considered this for a moment, then nodded appreciatively. "That's a m-much more elegant solution."

"I'll research the bank's digital footprint," William announced. "Perhaps I can access some useful information through...alternative channels."

Vinnie looked around the room, clearly feeling left out of

the technical planning. "I'll be the getaway driver," he declared.

"Vinnie," I said gently, "you can't drive."

"I'll learn!"

"That's not a good idea. Driving is complicated, and we don't have time to—"

"I'm an excellent driver," William suddenly announced in a flat, robotic cadence that was nothing like his usual speech pattern.

Oh fuck.

Floyd immediately picked up the reference, grinning wickedly. "D-definitely an excellent driver."

"Course, I'm an excellent driver," Garth added in his own version of the monotone delivery.

"No!" Vinnie exploded, his face flushing red with anger. "We are not doing this!"

But the Family was already committed to their favorite form of teasing. They'd discovered years ago that nothing got under Vinnie's skin quite like *Rain Man* references, and they wielded that knowledge with surgical precision.

"Definitely, definitely an excellent driver," Floyd continued, his stutter magically disappearing as he imitated Dustin Hoffman's performance.

"I'm not saying anything from that stupid movie!" Vinnie shouted. "And I never will!"

"Course, definitely not. Definitely not saying anything," William replied in perfect Rain Man cadence.

Vinnie's reaction was explosive. "That movie is so old!" he raged, his voice cracking with emotion. "But typicals still shout 'Rain Man' at me and laugh."

He was gesticulating wildly now, his frustration pouring out in words.

"Dustin Hoffman has autism in that movie. AUTISM! Not

Down syndrome! They're not the same thing! Every typical thinks autism and Down syndrome are the same. They are not! I can't count toothpicks. I can't do math tricks or memorize phone books. I have Down syndrome, not autism. But that movie made every typical think we're all the same."

The room had gone completely quiet.

I felt a surge of protective anger for my brother, mixed with admiration for how clearly he'd articulated something that had been bothering him for years.

"I hate that movie," Vinnie finished. "I will never, ever say any of those quotes. Ever."

Despite the seriousness of Vinnie's speech, I caught William trying to suppress a grin. Floyd was biting his lip to keep from giggling. Even Garth looked like he was fighting back laughter.

They loved Vinnie, but they also couldn't resist the temptation to tease him when he got worked up. It was normal sibling behavior, the kind of gentle mockery that came from affection rather than cruelty.

Everyone burst into laughter, including Vinnie. Then he realized what he was doing, shook his head and declared, "We need to get serious. If we're really doing this, we should watch a heist movie tonight. For research."

"Excellent idea," I said. "What do you all think?"

"*Ocean's Eleven*," William suggested immediately. "The Clooney version, not the Sinatra one. Much more sophisticated."

"*The D-Dark Knight*," Floyd countered. "Heath L-Ledger's Joker has the best b-bank robbery scene ever filmed."

Garth surprised everyone when he suggested, "*Despicable Me.*"

We all looked at him with confusion.

"They steal the moon. All Minion movies are heist movies," he said defensively.

After an exhaustive debate, the Family decided they really couldn't argue with that.

"*Die Hard,*" Vinnie announced with finality.

"*Die Hard* is an action movie, not a heist movie," I protested.

"Professor Snape is stealing bearer bonds from Nakatomi Plaza," Vinnie argued. "That makes it a heist movie. I wish Rita liked *Die Hard*, but she doesn't. *Die Hard* is Peralta's favorite movie. If she did, she would definitely be Peralta to my Doug Judy."

As the Family continued their passionate debate about which movie would provide the best educational value for our criminal endeavor, I found myself oddly comforted by the normalcy of it all.

At least we had a direction now. Tomorrow, I'd drive out to First National Bank and do reconnaissance. Tonight, we'd watch criminals on screen and pretend we knew what we were doing.

The Family decided on *Despicable Me.*

Chapter Twenty-One

"I'm coming with you," Vinnie announced from the couch, where he'd been organizing his recipe binder.

The next morning, I found myself pacing around our living room, checking my phone and mentally rehearsing my reconnaissance plan for First National Bank. The strategy was straightforward. I'd drive over alone, walk around like any other customer, record what I could with my phone positioned in my shirt pocket, and return home with enough intel to plan our approach to the safety deposit boxes.

Simple plans had the best chance of not going completely to shit.

"No, you're not."

"Yes, I am."

I stopped pacing to face my twin brother. The stubborn set to his jaw said he'd already made up his mind. "Vinnie, we've talked about this. Together, we're too conspicuous. We're Solo and the Wookiee."

I could see Vinnie processing the reference. Back when we were kids, Vinnie and I used to theater hop during those brutal summer afternoons when our house felt like a furnace. We'd buy tickets to one movie, then spent the entire day sneaking into other theaters. Three or four films for the price of one, with free air conditioning and unlimited popcorn refills? Yes, please.

It had been perfect until puberty hit and I shot up like a magic beanstalk. Suddenly, a six-foot-tall typical guy accompanied by his smaller twin brother with Down syndrome became impossible to miss. We were a walking spectacle everywhere we went. Much like Han Solo and Chewbacca were most places they went, we imagined.

"Everyone remembers Solo and the Wookiee," I finished.

Vinnie's expression shifted to faux outrage. "You're the Wookiee."

"I'm not the Wookiee. *You're* the Wookiee."

"I'm definitely not the Wookiee."

"You."

"You."

Before I could continue the familiar rhythm, Vinnie held up his hand. "You're right. We go in separately," he said, his tone becoming serious.

I blinked at him. "What?"

"You get typical customer stuff. I get invisible stuff."

I found myself nodding despite my feeling that Vinnie had a different plan in mind. "The Family can stay in communication with us through earbuds. Give real-time feedback."

"I don't want voices in my head," Vinnie said quickly. "I need to think. You talk to them." A beat later, he slid on a pair of sunglasses and stated, "I work alone."

Did he just "I work alone" me?

"Alright," I said, grabbing my keys and wondering how long he'd been carrying those sunglasses around. "But Vinnie, your invisibility has limits. Don't push it."

· · ·

Later that afternoon, we sat in the van across the street from First National Bank.

"Give me a few minutes, Nicholas," Vinnie said, checking that his phone was positioned correctly in his shirt pocket. "I want them to think I came by myself."

"Remember what I said about limits," I warned.

"I'm not typical, but I'm not stupid either."

I watched Vinnie cross the street and disappear through the bank's entrance. While I had no idea what he was planning, I stuck by my plan to KISS—keep it simple, stupid. I'd wait the agreed time, then enter as a regular customer. Tell the teller I needed quarters for laundry, mundane enough to avoid suspicion, legitimate enough to require service. My phone would livestream from my shirt pocket while I surveyed the layout.

Simple. Clean. Low risk.

When enough time had passed, I activated my earbud and heard the familiar chaos of the Family.

"T-t-testing, testing," Floyd's voice crackled through. "Nicholas, can you h-hear us?"

"Loud and clear."

"Excellent," William chimed in, barely containing his excitement. "Our maiden reconnaissance voyage. Most thrilling."

I approached the bank's entrance, phone streaming as I pushed through heavy glass doors. The interior was exactly what I'd expected, polished marble floors, vaulted ceilings designed to inspire confidence, and that hushed atmosphere that made you automatically lower your voice.

To my right, a row of teller windows behind protective glass. To my left, customer service desks where employees handled loans and accounts. Straight ahead, a waiting area with leather chairs. And in the back corner, partially hidden by a decorative pillar, the entrance to what had to be the vault area.

"Ho-ho-holy shit," Floyd's voice buzzed in my ear. "Look at that s-s-security setup."

I casually turned, letting my phone capture the network of security cameras positioned throughout the space. "Eyes everywhere," I murmured under my breath.

"I count six so far," William observed through the earpiece. "No obvious blind spots."

I was the fourth customer in line, which gave me time to study the layout more carefully. The teller area was protected by thick security glass with speaking slots and document passes. Behind the tellers, I could glimpse part of the cash handling area, though the vault itself remained hidden.

That's when I spotted Vinnie.

My brother was casually wandering the customer area, like someone exploring a museum. A security guard glanced at him, took in his Down syndrome features, and immediately dismissed him as a non-threat. A teller looked up from her paperwork, saw a harmless disabled guy wandering around, and went back to whatever she was doing. Even the customers waiting in line seemed to look right through him.

Exactly as predicted. He'd become functionally invisible.

Then the branch manager caught sight of Vinnie. She was a woman in her fifties whose carefully managed appearance screamed career banking professional. Grey hair in a practical bob, sensible shoes, and a name tag that read "Mrs. Patterson, Branch Manager." She'd probably been working in banks since before most of her employees were born.

And she was approaching Vinnie with the expression of an elementary school teacher when they saw a lost child in the hallway.

I held my breath.

"Can I help you with something today?" I heard her ask.

Vinnie turned to face her, and I watched his entire posture

shift. Shoulders slumping slightly, expression becoming more open and vulnerable. He was slipping into character.

"I want to open...a bank account," he said, spacing his words carefully. "But I don't know if I can trust...this bank to keep my money safe."

Mrs. Patterson's expression immediately softened. "Are you here by yourself today?"

"Yes," Vinnie replied with obvious pride. "I live by myself and have a job. I want a bank account, but I'm scared...to give my money to people I don't know."

Jesus fucking Christ. He's brilliant.

Mrs. Patterson's professional demeanor melted into something approaching maternal warmth. Here was this independent young man with Down syndrome, trying to navigate adult responsibilities on his own... Bless his heart. Every protective instinct she'd ever possessed was activating.

"You know what?" she said, her voice taking on that encouraging tone people used with children. "Would you like me to give you a tour of our bank? So you can see exactly how we keep everyone's money safe?"

Holy fuck.

"That would be...very nice. Thank you," Vinnie replied, his gratitude sounding completely genuine. "My name's...Joe, but most people call me...Slow Joe. I don't like that. What's your name?"

"Good to meet you...Joe," she said. "I'm Mrs. Patterson, but you can call me Margaret."

I watched in amazement as Margaret Patterson, the branch manager for First National Bank, began escorting Vinnie around the building, pointing out security features and explaining procedures with the patience of a kindergarten teacher. She brought him closer to the teller windows than any regular customer would ever get, showed him the vault door, even let him peer into restricted areas.

Mrs. Patterson showed Vinnie how deposits were processed and explained the vault's security systems. All while my brother nodded earnestly and asked innocent questions that prompted even more detailed explanations.

"Look at that," William said quietly. "She's walking him right past the safety deposit box entrance."

I could hear Mrs. Patterson explaining, "These special rooms are where customers store their most valuable possessions. Individual boxes that only they can access with their personal key."

Vinnie was gathering intelligence that would have been impossible for any of us to obtain through conventional means. And Mrs. Patterson was helping him do it, convinced she was performing community service like the upstanding pillar of society she surely believed she was.

"I need to think about this," Vinnie finally said after the tour concluded. "This is a very important decision."

"Of course it is," Mrs. Patterson replied warmly. "You take all the time you need. And when you're ready to open that account, you ask for me personally. I'll make sure you get our very best service."

As Vinnie thanked her and headed for the exit, I watched Mrs. Patterson return to her desk, radiating self-satisfaction. Absolutely certain she'd just made the world better.

Mrs. Patterson had no fucking clue she'd just given detailed security intelligence to a criminal operation being led by a man with Down syndrome.

Vinnie passed me in line, our eyes meeting briefly. He gave the slightest nod before disappearing through the exit.

"Next," the teller called.

I approached with my rehearsed request. "I need rolls of quarters for laundry," I said, sliding a ten through the slot.

The transaction took thirty seconds. Long enough for my phone to capture the cash handling area, not long enough to seem suspicious. I pocketed the quarters and headed out.

This might actually fucking work.

Back home, the living room had been transformed into something resembling mission control. The Family had rearranged furniture to accommodate Floyd's spread of electronic components, William's laptop setup, and what looked like hand-drawn floor plans scattered across every available surface. Garth was training at the gym. The Special Olympics were coming up, and he was throwing everything he had at it this year. He'd earned silver three years in a row. He was determined to get the gold this year, and I wasn't going to let planning a heist stop him from achieving his dream.

"That was incredible," William announced before we'd even sat down. "Absolutely magnificent, Vinnie. You were like a master spy."

"She g-gave you more intel than most criminals g-get in months," Floyd added, his excitement making his stutter almost disappear.

"I recorded everything," Vinnie said proudly, pulling out his phone. "She showed me where all the important stuff is."

I settled into my chair, still processing what I'd witnessed.

William was already pulling up video editing software on his laptop. "Vinnie, if you can transfer that recording to me, I believe I can code the bank's interior layout into a virtual reality environment."

I raised an eyebrow. "Since when do you know VR?"

"Since this morning. I've been researching heist methodologies." William's fingers flew across the keyboard. "If I can create a virtual model of the bank, we could practice the entire operation repeatedly without ever setting foot in there again until the actual heist, which is ideal."

The concept was brilliant, but I could see the obvious problem. "VR headsets cost serious money. Money we don't have."

"I could try to b-build one," Floyd offered, "but that would take w-weeks we don't have."

I felt that familiar tightness building in my chest, then I decided to let that go completely. There was no half-assing this. Time to turn our bow into the wake of madness.

"Actually," I said slowly, "given our timeline, we should probably use whatever credit we have left to buy whatever equipment we need for this job."

William looked concerned. "Isn't that financially risky?"

"Not really." I shrugged. "If we fail, we're either going to prison or losing the house anyway. Might as well burn through our credit to try and save our hides."

William's face brightened suddenly. "The return policy on VR headsets is fourteen days. If we take turns purchasing and returning the same unit, we could train extensively while minimizing costs."

"That's..." I paused, impressed despite myself. "...actually pretty clever."

"D-devious too," Floyd added with obvious approval.

"Now," I continued, "we have the basic bank layout, but we still need eyes on the safety deposit box room. We didn't get any video inside the safety deposit box room to see where box 103055 is located. Someone has to actually rent a box to get access."

The room went quiet as everyone processed the implications.

"Has to be someone who looks typical," Floyd decided. "Nicholas, m-m-me, or William."

"Not me," William said immediately. "Too many triggers in that environment. I'd blow our cover for sure. I'm sorry."

"With my chair, I'm too conspicuous," Floyd added. "Bank employees r-remember motorized customers."

That left only me. "But I'm the only one who can drive. I have to be the getaway driver."

"I told you already, I'm the getaway driver," Vinnie said firmly.

"Vinnie, you can't drive."

"I can learn." He turned to face me directly. "You could teach me."

I opened my mouth to explain why that wasn't practical, then stopped. The words died in my throat as I realized what I was about to do.

Shit.

I was about to dismiss Vinnie's capabilities without giving him a chance to prove himself. Just like every typical who'd ever looked at him and assumed he couldn't handle responsibility. Just like the branch manager who'd treated him like a child while he gathered intelligence that would make professional criminals weep with envy. Of course, Vinnie noticed.

"You don't think I can do it, do you, Nicholas?" Vinnie asked in a defeated tone that made me die a little inside.

"You're right," I said. "There's no reason you can't learn to drive. I'll teach you."

Vinnie's face lit up. "Really?"

"Really, Vinman."

"The Vinman can!" Vinnie cheered in celebration.

"I'll build earpieces for everyone on a secure channel so we can talk freely," Floyd announced, already sketching modifications to our gaming headsets. "Real-time c-communication during the operation."

William grinned. "You're turning into Q from James Bond. Though for the record, Sean Connery was clearly the superior Bond, regardless of what anyone says about Daniel Craig's supposed emotional depth that I just don't see."

"So, we have our roles defined," I said. "Vinnie learns to drive and handles getaway. William builds our VR training environment. Floyd creates communication equipment. Garth provides muscle if things go sideways."

"What about you?" Vinnie asked.

"For our next step, I need to find a disguise, get a fake ID to match it, and rent us a safety deposit box at First National Bank. Just another typical day at the Murphy residence, right?"

Chapter Twenty-Two

With Garth at work and the rest of the Family deep in their respective preparations, I figured it was the perfect time to tackle what might be our biggest logistical challenge thus far.

Teaching Vinnie to drive.

I found him in the living room watching *The Fast and the Furious*. "Ready for your first driving lesson, Vinman?"

Vinnie turned off the TV and said with complete confidence, "I'm ready to show you how good I am at driving, Nicholas."

There was something in his tone—not excitement exactly, but a certainty—that caught my attention. Like he was stating an established fact rather than expressing hope about learning a new skill.

"Show me how good you are?" I repeated slowly. "Vinnie, have you driven before?"

"I know how to drive," he said, casual and certain—the same tone he used when discussing cooking techniques. "You'll see."

I felt my eyebrows climb toward my hairline. In all our years together, Vinnie had never mentioned any driving experience. But there was something about his calm assurance that made me pause. Maybe this wouldn't be the disaster I'd been mentally preparing for.

"Alright then," I said, grabbing my keys. "Let's see what you've got."

Not much later, we sat in our van in an empty parking lot behind the abandoned mall. I'd climbed into the passenger seat while Vinnie settled behind the wheel with the kind of purposeful movements that suggested familiarity.

Vinnie fastened his seatbelt, then reached up to adjust the rearview mirror. He checked both side mirrors, fine-tuning their angles like he'd done this countless times before. His hands found the steering wheel and positioned themselves at ten and two, just like they taught in driver's education.

"Vinnie, who taught you all this?"

"TV and movies," he replied, still adjusting his position. "I've been watching people drive for thirty years. It's easy."

My cautious optimism was quickly being replaced by concern, but I was still mesmerized by his apparent competence. When he turned to me expectantly, I found myself handing over the keys, genuinely curious to see what happened next.

"Here you go."

Vinnie took the keys with the same confidence he'd shown throughout his preparation. He located the ignition, inserted the key, and turned it...

Without actually starting the engine.

Then he began pressing the brake and gas pedals intermittently, like he was testing their responsiveness. His eyes moved between the mirrors and windows as he slowly turned the steering wheel left and right, navigating some invisible obstacle course.

"You know, Nicholas," Vinnie said conversationally as he continued his elaborate pantomime, "I've been thinking about Celia. She told me she's attracted to both girls and boys, and I think I hurt her feelings. I want to make it up to her. I want to say sorry. Maybe I could drive us somewhere nice for a date."

I sat there, completely bewildered, watching my brother "drive" while the van remained motionless and silent in the parking lot. He was having what appeared to be a perfectly normal conversation while simultaneously performing what he clearly believed was the act of driving a vehicle.

The steering wheel continued its gentle left-and-right motion. His foot kept working the pedals in random patterns. His eyes checked the mirrors like he was navigating rush-hour traffic instead of sitting stationary in an empty lot.

"What the fuck are you doing, Vinnie?"

"I'm driving," he replied, as if this should be obvious. "See?"

And then it hit me. A realization that made me want to laugh knowing full well that I could not.

Vinnie had learned to mimic what people *looked like* when they drove in TV and movies. The posture, the hand positions, the mirror checks, the multitasking conversation... He'd absorbed every visual cue about driving behavior. But he had absolutely no concept whatsoever of what driving actually *was*.

"Vinnie," I said slowly, "this isn't driving."

His hands stopped moving on the wheel. "Yes, it is. This is exactly what people in TV and movies do when they drive."

"That's what driving *looks like*, but it's not driving."

The defensive tone crept into his voice immediately. "I'm

doing everything they do, Nicholas. I'm turning the wheel and pressing the pedals and checking the mirrors and—"

"But the engine isn't running." I stopped him. "Vinnie, driving isn't just...performing the motions. You have to understand what those motions *do*. The car has to be on. You have to watch for other drivers who might not be paying attention to where they're going. You have to judge distances and speeds and reaction times. You have to understand that this van is a three-thousand-pound weapon that can kill other people, and yourself, if you don't know what you're doing."

By the time I finished, Vinnie had gone very quiet. His hands had dropped from the steering wheel to his lap, and he was staring straight ahead, overwhelmed.

"That's a lot," he said quietly.

I felt my shoulders sag as the familiar phrase registered. Vinnie's way of telling me, and himself, that his brain needed time to properly process what he'd just learned. That he understood this was important, but it was too much to absorb all at once.

Maybe I couldn't teach Vinnie this skill after all. If only I knew someone who was professionally trained to drive and teach...

Oh shit.

I did know someone.

"You know what, Vinman?" I said, switching to the gentle voice I used when he was having a rough day. "That's enough for today. We'll keep practicing, but how about Rita and I double date with you and Celia tonight? Rita's coming over for dinner anyway. We could all go to the same spot, but do our own thing, so you two can have your privacy."

Vinnie's expression brightened considerably. "Sounds like a plan."

At the prospect of a date night, Vinnie's frustration melted away, we exchanged places, and I drove us home while Vinnie texted Celia.

Chapter Twenty-Three

I stood in front of the bathroom mirror, running a brush through my hair for the third time and wondering why I was putting this much effort into a double date at Celia's favorite spot, the Hole Story Mini Golf & Arcade. Tonight's real mission wasn't romance. It was convincing Rita to teach Vinnie to drive without raising suspicion about why we suddenly needed this skill. My plan was to frame it as Vinnie wanting to focus on learning something new to cope with losing his home, which wasn't entirely untrue but felt manipulative as hell.

"Nicholas!" Vinnie's voice carried down the hallway. "I need help!"

I set down the brush and found Vinnie standing in his bedroom doorway, holding two shirts like he was weighing life-or-death decisions. In his left hand, a perfectly reasonable black polo shirt that would look great for a casual date. In his right hand, a *Brooklyn Nine-Nine* T-shirt featuring Doug Judy with the words "The Pontiac Bandit" printed across the chest.

"I can't decide," Vinnie announced seriously. "I really like this one." He held up the *Brooklyn Nine-Nine* shirt with obvious affection. "I was thinking about wearing it to prove to Rita that she's Peralta and I'm Doug Judy."

"Vinnie, isn't tonight about taking Celia out to make up and say sorry?"

Vinnie's expression shifted as he processed this. "Oh. I forgot." He handed me the *Brooklyn Nine-Nine* shirt. "Fine. Help me with the black one."

As I helped him button the polo shirt, making sure the collar lay flat, I decided this was the perfect opportunity to address the elephant in the room.

"Vinnie, tonight's very important for a lot of reasons. You're making up with Celia, which is great. But there's something we absolutely cannot talk about."

"The heist," Vinnie said matter-of-factly.

"Exactly. Not one word. Not a hint."

Vinnie nodded, but I could see that look in his eyes that meant he thought I was being overly cautious.

"I'm serious, Vinnie. Remember that movie you love, *Fight Club*? What's the first rule of Fight Club?"

"You don't talk about Fight Club," Vinnie recited automatically.

"Right. Except this is Heist Club. And what's the first rule of Heist Club?"

"You don't talk about Heist Club." Vinnie's expression became more serious. "Okay, okay, I get it, Nicholas."

I finished adjusting his collar and stepped back to examine my handiwork. He looked respectable, date-appropriate, and most importantly, like someone who definitely wasn't planning a heist.

Celia said the miniature golf course felt like two scoops of her favorite nostalgia. That didn't make sense to me, because none of us played golf, but the Hole Story was Celia's favorite place. We always had a good time here. Celia and I were three holes ahead of Nicholas and Rita, which was perfect because I needed to talk to Celia without them listening.

Celia lined up her pink golf ball at the windmill hole. She was wearing her fluffy yellow dress that made her look like sunshine, and her hair was in a ponytail that bounced when she walked. I loved watching Celia play miniature golf because she got very serious about it, like it was real golf on TV.

"Celia," I said while she was concentrating on her shot. "I'm sorry I got mad at you when you told me you like girls."

She stopped looking at her ball and looked at me instead. "Really?"

"Really. Rita helped me understand. You're not choosing girls over me. You're just telling me who you really are. That doesn't mean you don't like me anymore."

"Vinnie," Celia said, "when I told you I like girls and boys, I wasn't saying I don't love you. I was saying...I trust you. I trust you enough to show you all of me. The parts I hide from my family. The parts I hide at church."

Celia's eyes were wet like she might cry. "I can't say sorry for being honest with you," she continued. "That would be like apologizing for trusting you. I won't do that. Even if it means you stay mad at me."

"I understand now, and I'm not mad anymore," I said. "I love you."

Celia put down her golf club and kissed me right there by the windmill. Her lips tasted like the strawberry lip gloss she always wore. When we stopped kissing, she picked up her club and made her shot. The ball went through the windmill perfectly and stopped right next to the hole.

"Nice shot," I said.

"Thanks. Your turn."

I lined up my blue ball and hit it too hard. It bounced off the windmill and rolled back to where I started. That's what always happened when I tried to show off for Celia.

"Try again," she said, not making fun of me like some people would.

This time I hit it softer, and the ball went through the windmill and stopped near the hole like hers did. We both got our balls in the hole and walked to the next one, holding hands. Celia's hand was warm and fit perfectly with mine.

"The Halloween Smash Ball is coming up," I said as we walked past the pirate ship hole. "We were the best-dressed couple last year. Super Mario and Princess Peach."

"We were," Celia said with a big smile. "Everyone said our costumes were perfect."

"Will you go with me again this year?" I asked.

Celia stopped walking and kissed me again. "Yes! I already have some costume ideas. We have a few months to figure it out."

"I'll think of some ideas too," I said.

But my brain was thinking about something else. Something I promised Nicholas I wouldn't talk about with Celia.

Heist Club.

I wanted to know if Celia would think what the Family was doing was right or wrong. Maybe I could ask her without really asking her, like Rita does sometimes?

We got to the next hole, which had three bears sitting around a table with bowls in front of them. It was the Goldilocks story. That gave me an idea.

"Celia," I said while she put her ball down. "Do you remember the story about Goldilocks and the Three Bears?"

"Of course. She broke into their house and ate their porridge," Celia said.

"Well, what if the Three Bears were mean to Goldilocks first? What if they stole her porridge and she was just taking it back?"

Celia looked at me funny. "That's not how the story goes, Vinnie."

"I know, but what if it was? Would it be okay for Goldilocks to take the porridge back if the Bears took it from her first?"

Celia thought about this while she made her shot. "Two wrongs don't make a right," she said.

"But what if no one else was going to help Goldilocks and she was going to starve? What if she asked the police and the police said they couldn't do anything?"

"It would still be wrong to steal," Celia said. "Even if someone was mean to you first."

My stomach felt heavy like when I ate too much ice cream. If Celia found out what me and the Family were planning, would she think I was wrong? Would she still love me if she knew I was planning a heist?

I thought about Garth and how scared he looked when Charity grabbed his face at the funeral. I thought about how we were going to lose our house and get split up. I thought about how the police couldn't help us and no one else was going to save our Family.

Maybe Celia was right that two wrongs don't make a right. But sometimes when everything else was wrong, someone had to do something to make it right, didn't they?

That was a lot.

"Okay," I said to Celia. "You're right."

I didn't want to fight about Goldilocks anymore. I wanted to think about fun things.

"How about we go as pirates this year?" I said. "I could be a pirate captain and you could be my first mate."

Celia's face got happy. "That sounds perfect! I love pirates."

We finished playing miniature golf, and I didn't think about Heist Club anymore. I thought about Celia in a pirate costume and how pretty she would look.

Rita and I had fallen behind Vinnie and Celia by design, giving them the privacy they needed while keeping them in sight. We'd just finished the castle hole. Rita sunk her putt in two strokes while I'd needed an embarrassing four when I caught sight of them at the windmill hole.

"Don't look directly," Rita murmured, pretending to study her scorecard. "But they're having some kind of serious conversation over there."

I casually glanced over while lining up my ball at the lighthouse hole. Vinnie was gesturing and talking animatedly about something while Celia listened.

"Think they're working things out?" I asked, keeping my voice low.

"Hard to tell from here. But at least they're talking instead of—" Rita stopped mid-sentence as we watched Vinnie and Celia kiss by the windmill. "Well, that answers that question."

Relief flooded through me like a drink of ice-cold water on a blazing hot day. One crisis averted. Rita must have seen it on my face because she smiled and pulled me close for a kiss of our own.

"There," she said against my lips. "Now you can stop worrying about those two."

"God, I hope so," I said, meaning it. "Between the house

situation, Garth's grief, and watching Vinnie torture himself over this relationship... I was starting to feel like a one-man crisis management team."

Rita squeezed my hand as we moved to the next hole. "You're not alone in this," she said.

I squeezed her hand back. "I know," I said. "Things are just all fucked up. It breaks my heart to look at Garth and know that I can't stop his abuser from becoming his legal guardian."

Rita, still holding my hand, pulled me to a stop. "Wait, run that by me again," she demanded, looking me square in the face.

"Fuck, I didn't tell you. There was a lot going on that day," I covered, not wanting to reveal that the real reason I forgot to tell her about Charity and Garth was Heist Club. "According to him, Charity shook him so hard when he was young that she gave him shaken baby syndrome. She's responsible for Garth's deafness and developmental disability."

"Were they playing or did she do that on purpose?" Rita inquired.

"The latter. And now with Agnes gone, Charity wants to get her claws back into him."

"Do you or Garth have any evidence to prove her abuse?" Rita asked.

"It was over a decade ago," I said. "It'd be Garth's word against Charity's, and since Garth is intellectually disabled, we know how that'll play out..."

"Her background check came back clean too," Rita said. "Almost like it was scrubbed."

"I'm researching if there's another way to legally fight her without losing Vinnie, but so far I've come up empty," I lamented. "Though Garth did mention something weird."

"Weird how?" Rita asked.

I decided to take a chance, tell Rita about the Cartwright

"insurance policy" hidden away without revealing the whole truth.

"Garth said his mom kept two million dollars in untraceable cash somewhere in case of emergencies. He couldn't remember where, but he asked in case we could use that to save him from Charity now," I said sadly. "What kind of people just keep two million dollars in cash lying around in case shit hits the fan?"

"Criminals." Rita's investigative wheels were spinning, "Maybe I need a bigger net. I was only looking at Charity... Maybe I should look into the Cartwright family itself."

"You think there's something to what Garth said?" I asked as I set my golf ball down and lined up my next shot.

"Only a hunch, don't get your hopes up," Rita said.

I swung and watched my golf ball glide into the hole. "Your turn," I said as I retrieved my ball.

She paused, seeming to weigh her words carefully. "Actually, there's something I wanted to talk to you about. Now that Dad's in remission and my brother's moving back to help, me and Dad think it's time I found my own place."

I stopped walking. "Really?"

"Nothing fancy. Just a small apartment where I can have some independence again." Rita's voice carried that careful neutrality she used when she wasn't sure how someone would react to news. "It would mean we could have some real privacy a few nights a week. No more sneaking around your house trying not to wake the Family."

A grin spread across my face. "You mean we could actually be as loud as we want?"

Rita elbowed me in the ribs playfully. "Privacy at last. It's been way too long."

I was about to make another suggestive comment when Rita's expression shifted, becoming more serious. "And if your house is foreclosed on, I thought you and Vinnie could crash with me until you get back on your feet," she offered.

My heart stopped. I didn't know what to say to such a generous offer. I tried to think of something that would genuinely convey my feelings. "I love you" didn't seem like enough, but it would have to be.

"Do you know how much I love you?" I said, my heart aching as the woman I loved made room for both me and Vinnie in her world. I pulled her into a bone crushing hug.

"So much that you're breaking my ribs," she said between gasps.

I loosened my grip and kissed her gently.

"Thank you, for inviting us into your home," I said, "but I hope it doesn't come to that."

"If it does, you have a place. I hope that takes some of the stress off your plate."

"It does." I wrapped my arm around Rita's waist as we walked to the next hole. I looked at her sideways and could see Rita was screwing up the courage to tell me something else.

"I know things have been really stressful lately..." She paused, seeming to weigh her words carefully. "And I don't want to add to your stress, but the department's putting together a task force to hunt down the Happy Face Killers, I'm sure you've seen them on the news? The robbers who've been hitting banks all over the state?"

I forced myself to keep my expression neutral. "They've killed someone at each bank, if I heard right?"

"Yeah. Bunch of animals. They're still at large, and honestly, the department doesn't have much to go on. I can get on the task force..."

"That's a dangerous job," I said, worried for her safety.

"It is, but if I can get on and we manage to catch the Happy Face Killers..." Rita's eyes lit up with ambition. "It could be the case that gets me the promotion I've been chasing. Detective before thirty, just like I've always planned."

My girlfriend wasn't just a cop. If she got on this task force, she'd become a cop gifted with state-provided resources to specifically hunt bank robbers. The same type of crime the Family was planning to commit in roughly six weeks. The reality of what was happening finally struck home.

Fuck. Fuck. Fuck.

Should I tell her? Should I warn her away from the task force somehow?

But even as the thought crossed my mind, I knew it was impossible. Rita was a cop to her core. Asking her to avoid a high-profile case would be like asking her to stop breathing. And telling her what we were planning would destroy not just her career, but everything we'd built together.

I was on my own with this one.

"Then you should do it. Join the task force," I said, the words tasting like ash. "You've earned this shot, Rita. Don't let it pass you by."

Rita blinked, clearly surprised. "Really? I was expecting you to push back. Worry about me getting hurt or something."

"I'll always worry about you," I said. "But I'm not going to stand in the way of your dream."

She pulled me into a tight hug. "You're always surprising me, you know that?"

You have no idea.

"Speaking of surprises," I said, desperately needing to change the subject before my poker face cracked, "I was hoping you might be able to help me with something."

"What's up?"

"Vinnie wants to learn to drive." The words came out smoother than I'd expected, probably because they were actually true. "He's really latched on to the idea since we found out about potentially losing the house. I think it's his way of feeling like he has some control over his life."

Rita's expression softened immediately. "Makes sense. Big life changes make people want to feel more independent."

"I tried teaching him myself, but you have the training, you know all the traffic laws," I looked at her hopefully, "would you be willing to give him some lessons?"

Rita's face lit up. "Of course! I'd be happy to help."

"Thank you," I said, meaning it more than she could possibly understand.

As we finished our hole and moved toward the next one, I caught sight of Vinnie and Celia again. They were holding hands now, walking toward the pirate ship hole with obvious happiness.

At least that's working out.

Rita glanced ahead and noticed how far Vinnie and Celia had gotten. "They're really taking their time with this course," she observed. Then she turned to me and her left eyebrow raised with its familiar invitation I'd come to know and love. "Think we have time for a van quickie?"

Despite everything weighing on my mind, I felt my body respond immediately to the suggestion. Rita's ability to compartmentalize never ceased to amaze me. From bank robbery task forces to spontaneous putt-putt parking lot sex in thirty seconds flat.

"I'm always up for some secret nooky," I said, already leading us toward the exit.

Chapter Twenty-Four

"Nicholas," William announced without looking up, "I present to you the fruits of my labor."

William sat with his laptop at the coffee table, surrounded by empty energy drink cans and crumpled notebook pages covered in his meticulous handwriting that meant he'd been coding for hours. He mirrored his laptop screen with the television. What I saw made my jaw drop.

On the screen was a rough but recognizable three-dimensional model of First National Bank's interior. The basic layout was all there. The teller windows with their protective glass, the customer service area, the waiting room with its leather chairs, and in the back corner, the partially hidden entrance to what had to be the vault area. William had even included the decorative pillar that obscured part of the view.

"Holy shit, William," I said, genuinely impressed. "This is incredible. How did you manage this so fast?"

William's posture straightened, visibly proud, though I caught a flicker of something else in his expression. Conflict? Maybe guilt? "I utilized the bank's architectural plans from the city planning office, cross-referenced with Vinnie's recorded intel, and employed a game engine to render the environment." He paused, his voice becoming quieter. "It appears I have a natural aptitude for... criminal planning."

The way he said it made it clear he wasn't entirely comfortable with this newly discovered talent.

Floyd wheeled closer to get a better look at the screen. "The d-d-details are impressive. You can see the c-camera positions, the t-teller stations..."

"I can add more detail as we gather additional intelligence," William continued, clicking through different views of the virtual bank. "The customer movement patterns, security protocols, timing sequences... But I'm limited by what we currently know."

I studied the model more carefully, noting the blank space where the safety deposit box area should be. That conspicuous gap reminded me of exactly what our next step had to be.

"This is brilliant work, William. But you're right about needing more intelligence. Specifically, we need eyes on the safety deposit box room."

"That task falls to you, I presume?" William asked, though we all knew the answer.

"Yeah," I said, "I've been doing some research on the best way to create a disguise good enough to fool facial recognition software and bank employees and yet simple enough that I can learn how to apply it myself."

Vinnie perked up from his spot on the couch. "You could get a fake mustache and glasses!"

"Or theatrical makeup," Floyd suggested. "Pr-prosthetics to change your facial structure."

"I was thinking along those lines. There's that Halloween 365 store downtown... They usually employ film students who know special effects makeup. Maybe I could get a lesson, pick up some realistic prosthetics."

"You can be that *Top Gun* pilot guy from *Mission: Impossible*," Vinnie added. "He's always wearing rubber faces."

"The Phantom of the Opera!" William declared with theatrical flair. "Half your face could be concealed, very mysterious and—"

"Guys," I interrupted, though I couldn't help but smile at their enthusiasm. "I need to look like a regular businessman, not a Broadway character. The whole point is to blend in, not stand out."

Floyd nodded thoughtfully. "But once you r-r-rent the box, we n-need to understand the locking mech-mechanism."

"How do you mean?"

"Safety d-deposit boxes use a dual-key system," Floyd explained. "The customer has one key, the b-bank has another. Both are required to open the box. But we don't know if First National uses tr-traditional turn keys or electronic locks."

"What's the difference?" I asked.

"If they use electronic locks, we're up sh-sh-shit creek. Full s-s-stop," Floyd said. "Digital systems and their v-v-vulnerabilities are closely guarded by their man-manufacturer. But if it's tr-traditional turn keys..." He shrugged hopefully. "The odds are in our favor of picking the locks manually."

The implications tied my stomach in knots. The technical challenges were stacking up fast.

But that was a problem for Future Nicholas. Present Nicholas had to focus on getting into that room.

"First things first," I said. "I need to scout that Halloween store, figure out what kind of disguise I can pull off. Then I need to..."

The words stuck in my throat as the full reality of what came next hit me.

"I'll need a fake ID to match whatever identity I create," I finished with growing dread.

And there was only one person I knew who could get me a convincing fake ID that could fool a bank. The same person who'd been tormenting me and Vinnie since childhood, who'd humiliated Vinnie online, who represented everything I despised about people who preyed on the vulnerable.

Francis fucking Donahey.

The thought of having to ask that piece of shit for help infuriated me. I could already picture his smug smirk when I showed up needing his services. The way he'd leverage my desperation, probably demand some kind of humiliating favor in return.

But what choice did I have? I couldn't exactly walk into a bank with a fake mustache and my real driver's license. Nor would I allow my real face to be recorded anywhere inside the bank I was going to soon rob myself. And finding another source for quality fake IDs wasn't exactly something I could Google.

Goddammit.

I was going to have to crawl to Francis, hat in hand, and beg for his criminal connections. The irony was thick enough to choke on. The real definition of irony, not whatever the fuck Alanis Morissette believed. The man who'd spent years calling my brother a retard would now be helping us commit the crime of the century.

Future Nicholas was getting upset.

"Nicholas?" Vinnie's voice cut through my rage spiral. "You okay?"

"Yeah," I lied. "Just thinking through the logistics."

That's when I heard the distinctive two-note chime of our doorbell. I glanced at my phone, and my heart sank.

Shit. Thursday, 3:00 PM.

Floyd's weekly visitor.

Grace!

"Everyone," I said quickly, "we need to hide Heist Club now. Grace is here."

"W-who?" Floyd asked.

"You'll meet her in a minute, Floyd, just hide your stuff and go to the kitchen," I said.

Everyone else knew exactly who Grace was, and the living room exploded into organized chaos as the Family rushed to conceal all evidence of our criminal planning. William stopped his laptop from mirroring with the TV, snapped it shut, and shoved it under the couch cushions. Floyd began gathering scattered notebook pages while Garth helped move electronic components back to their usual spot.

Within sixty seconds, our mission control had been transformed back into a normal living room where a family might gather to watch television or play board games.

I opened the front door to find Grace, looking as outdoorsy and windswept as always. The familiar box of *Magic* cards was tucked under her arm.

"Grace," I said, stepping aside to let her in. "How are you doing?"

"I'm good, Nicholas. Beautiful day for a hike, though I spent it indoors grading papers instead." She smiled. "How's Floyd been this week?"

"Better. The nightmares are staying away, which is huge progress."

I led her toward the kitchen, where Floyd was already positioning himself at the table. He looked up as we approached, his expression politely curious.

"Floyd," I said gently, "this is Grace. She's here to play *Magic: The Gathering*."

Floyd studied her face. "Have we...played before?"

"Yes," Grace said simply, setting her box on the table and beginning to unpack the familiar decks. "We play every week. You're quite good at it."

"I do enjoy card games," Floyd said, his interest clearly piqued by the sight of the cards. "The strategic elements appeal to me."

And so began their weekly ritual. Grace explained the game as if Floyd had never played before, walking him through the basic rules and mechanics with infinite patience. Floyd absorbed the information like a sponge.

The rest of the Family had hidden in their rooms, while I settled into my usual observation post by the window, half watching their game and half keeping an ear out for any signs that Floyd was becoming overwhelmed or agitated.

"You know," Grace said after she won the second game with a particularly clever play, "this reminds me of Angel Falls."

Floyd tilted his head with interest. "What's that?"

Grace's eyes brightened as she remembered, "We used to hike. Long trails, sometimes overnight camping trips. There was this one waterfall we discovered, Angel Falls. If you time it just right, get there about an hour before sunset, the way the light hits the water...it looks like the whole waterfall is on fire."

I watched Floyd's expression shift as Grace spoke. Something was changing in his eyes. It wasn't the usual polite interest he showed when people told him stories about his past, but something deeper. Recognition, maybe. Or at least the shadow of recognition?

"The trail to get there is brutal," Grace continued, "steep switchbacks, loose rock, places where you have to scramble over boulders. But you always pushed us to go faster, said we had to make it before the golden hour ended."

Floyd's breathing had changed. His hands, which had been casually shuffling cards, went still.

Grace went on, encouraged by his obvious attention. "Said the difference between a good shot and a great shot was all about timing. Being in exactly the right place at exactly the right moment."

"The magic hour," Floyd said suddenly, his voice clearer than I'd heard it all day. "Twenty minutes before sunset, when the l-l-light is warm and horizontal. That's when the w-water-waterfall looks like liquid f-f-fire."

Grace's breath caught. For a moment, hope blazed in her eyes like a gamma ray burst.

Floyd continued, his words coming faster now, as if he was chasing a memory before it could escape. "You had that old C-C-Canon camera with the telephoto lens. Al-always complaining about carrying the ex-extra weight on long hikes, b-b-but you'd never leave it behind because..." He stopped abruptly, confusion flooding his face. "How do I kn-know that?"

I felt my own breath catch. This was the furthest Floyd had ever gone in remembering Grace, in accessing any memory from before the accident. For a moment, it seemed like he might actually be breaking through.

Then Floyd's expression went blank. His eyes lost focus, and when they refocused, he was looking at Grace like he'd never seen her before in his life.

"I'm sorry," he said quietly, that familiar panic creeping into his voice. "Who are you? Why are you here?"

Grace's face crumpled and a tear streaked down her face before her practiced composure reasserted itself. She wiped the tear away and straightened in her chair, drawing on reserves of strength I couldn't begin to imagine.

"It's alright, Floyd. We were playing cards together. I'm

Grace." Her voice remained steady despite what had to be crushing disappointment. "Would you like to continue our game?"

"No," Floyd said firmly, pushing the cards away. "I think... I think you should leave. I don't feel well."

Grace nodded, gathering the scattered cards and returning them to their proper decks. "Of course," she said. "I hope you feel better soon."

I walked Grace to the door, my heart breaking for both of them. Every week, the same cycle. Hope, breakthrough, then crushing reset. I didn't know how she kept coming back, how she maintained that faith that someday Floyd would remember and stay remembered.

"I'll see you next week?" she asked.

"Of course," I said.

Grace walked to her car. As she sat in the driver's seat, I saw her crying as she drove away.

I found Floyd in his room a few minutes later, sitting in his wheelchair and staring out the window at nothing. Mozart played softly from his speakers.

"Hey," I said softly. "How are you feeling?"

Floyd turned to look at me, and there was something different in his expression. Not the confusion or fear I usually saw after his resets, but something more thoughtful. Questioning.

"Nicholas," he said slowly, "d-do you know who I r-really am?"

The question arrested my attention immediately. In all our years together, Floyd had never asked me directly about his past. He'd accepted his condition, lived in the present, seemed content to let his previous life remain buried beneath the trauma of the lightning strike.

"I know a little," I said carefully. "You were an engineer

before your accident. A very successful one. You worked on complex systems, cutting-edge tech."

"What k-kind of engineer?"

I sat down on the edge of his bed, choosing my words carefully. "I'm not sure."

"And the l-l-lightning? What happened to me?"

This was the part I'd always dreaded discussing. "You were struck during a severe thunderstorm. The electrical damage to your brain caused retrograde amnesia. You lost access to most of your memories from before the accident. But it also gave you enhanced mathematical abilities, how you see music and math now. Acquired savant syndrome."

"A trade," Floyd said quietly. "I los-st who I was, but gained s-s-something else."

"That's one way to look at it."

Floyd was quiet for a long moment, staring out the window at the gathering dusk.

As I left his room and headed to the kitchen to start dinner, I couldn't shake the feeling that something fundamental had shifted in Floyd. The calm acceptance he'd maintained for years was cracking, replaced by a hunger for truth that might be more dangerous than his nightmares.

What I didn't know then—couldn't have known—was that Floyd had already made a decision. That night, while the rest of us slept, he would flush his evening medications down the toilet and begin the dangerous journey back to his buried self.

The man who emerged from that decision would change everything for all of us. But first, he would have to survive the process of remembering who he used to be.

Chapter Twenty-Five

I sat next to Garth listening to Charity's lawyer drone through the final items of Agnes Cartwright's last will and testament. The man had the personality of wet cardboard and a voice that could put an insomniac to sleep, but I forced myself to pay attention. This list of assets was important.

The Cartwright estate library smelled like old money and older secrets. Leather-bound books that had never been read, mahogany furniture polished to a mirror shine, and that particular staleness that came from windows that were never opened because the air conditioning was always perfect.

"To Garth Cartwright," the lawyer continued without inflection, "the family residence located at 2247 Windermere Lane, with all furnishings and contents therein, subject to the terms and conditions previously outlined regarding conservatorship proceedings—"

Of course there are strings attached.

"—various investment portfolios totaling approximately $32 million, currently frozen pending resolution of said conservatorship proceedings—"

Strings? Or strands of Charity's web she'd been spinning her entire life?

"—and personal effects as designated in Schedule C."

The lawyer adjusted his reading glasses and turned to Charity, who sat across from us in an elegant black dress, her expression a careful balance of grief and triumph.

"To Charity Cartwright," the lawyer continued, "liquid assets totaling approximately $478.7 million, controlling interest in the Cartwright Foundation and all associated holdings—"

I watched Charity's perfectly manicured nails tap against her armrest. She was bored. Bored at her own mother's will reading because she'd already known exactly what she was getting.

"—and safety deposit box number 103055, First National Bank, along with customer key and all contents therein."

There it is.

My heart rate spiked, but I kept my expression neutral. Confirmation. The box existed. It was real. And now it was legally Charity's. I'd started to worry that Garth had misremembered or that the story about his childhood memory was just a false hope we'd been clinging to. But it wasn't a snipe hunt, it was real.

The lawyer droned through a few more administrative details before finally closing his leather portfolio with the kind of finality that said "my billable hours are complete."

Charity stood immediately. "Thank you, Gerald. Please send the paperwork to my office. I'll review everything and have it back to you by Friday."

Gerald the lawyer nodded and gathered his things, clearly eager to escape the emotional minefield of a family estate division. Smart man.

As he left, Charity turned to us with a smile that belonged on a velociraptor.

"Oh Garth," she said, her voice dripping with synthetic warmth. "I'm so happy Mother left you the house. Of course, once I'm your legal guardian—and I will be, let's not pretend otherwise—I'll manage it properly for you. We wouldn't want you making any...unfortunate decisions about such a valuable property. I'm sure 'Momma's little soldier' understands."

Garth's hands clenched into fists on his armrests. I could see him fighting the urge to sign something that would definitely be inappropriate for the occasion. Or worse.

Charity shifted her predatory attention to me. "Mr. Murphy, I do hope you understand this is all for Garth's protection. Mother was far too permissive with him. Someone needs to ensure he's...properly cared for. Especially now, with all these assets at stake."

Don't give her the satisfaction.

"I understand completely," I said with a calm I didn't feel. "Agnes loved Garth and wanted him to be taken care of."

"Exactly," Charity said, missing my implication entirely. Or most likely not missing it at all. "I'm so glad we're on the same page. Now if you'll excuse me, I have a conference call with the foundation board. Garth, darling, stay as long as you like. This is your house now."

She swept out of the library like a queen dismissing her subjects, leaving Garth and me alone in the oppressive silence.

<She's going to take everything,> Garth signed, his face contorted with grief and rage. *<Just like she took my hearing. My childhood. Now she takes Momma's house?>*

His hands dropped to his lap, but his eyes drifted toward the staircase leading to the second floor. There was something in that look, not quite longing, but something deeper. A need.

Garth's shoulders tensed. He turned back to me, and for a

moment I thought he might refuse. His jaw worked like he was chewing on words he couldn't quite form. Then slowly he signed: <I want to see Momma's room.>

Garth led me through the Cartwright mansion like a ghost touring his own haunted past. Every hallway held memories, every room a story. I noticed more changes Charity had already begun making—security cameras in corners that hadn't had them before, paintings removed from walls leaving rectangular shadows—the gradual erasure of Agnes Cartwright's warm presence.

We climbed the grand staircase to the second floor, Garth's footsteps becoming slower, more reluctant as we approached a specific door. He stopped outside it, his hand hovering over the doorknob like it might burn him.

Garth took a deep breath, turned the knob, and pushed open the door to his dead mother's bedroom.

The room was exactly as Agnes must have left it. A four-poster bed with cream-colored linens, a vanity cluttered with jewelry boxes and perfume bottles, photographs on every surface showing Garth at various ages—always smiling, always with his mother's arm around him. The air still held the faint scent of her perfume, something floral and expensive that probably had a French name I couldn't pronounce.

Garth walked to the center of the room and just stood there, taking it all in. His shoulders began to shake, and I realized he was silently crying. I moved to his side but didn't touch him, giving him space to grieve.

After a moment, Garth walked to the vanity and picked up a silver-framed photograph. He showed it to me—a young Agnes, maybe thirty, holding a toddler Garth, who was laughing at something off-camera. Joy radiated from both their faces.

<First time she learned sign language,> Garth signed, setting down the photo to tell me the story. <I was seven. Doctors said I would never communicate. Momma didn't believe them. Got me an ASL tutor. I learned fast.>

He moved to stand in front of the vanity mirror, and I watched him remember.

<She practiced here. Every night. In this mirror. Her hands were clumsy at first. Couldn't get the shapes right.> Garth demonstrated awkward, incorrect signs, showing me how his mother struggled. <She was frustrated. Angry at herself for not being perfect right away.>

Then his signing became fluid, graceful.

<But she practiced every night. Sometimes for hours. And then one day...> Garth's expression transformed, showing wonder and love. <She signed, "I love you." Perfect. Beautiful. Like she'd been signing her whole life.>

His hands formed the sign—the universal "I love you" that even people who didn't know ASL recognized.

<First time we really talked. Right in this room. I told her I loved her too. We both cried.> Garth touched the mirror gently, as if he could reach through glass and time to touch his mother's hands again.

I felt my own throat tighten. <My mom did something similar with Vinnie,> I signed without knowing. <Not sign language, but...teaching him to cook.>

Garth turned to face me, giving me his full attention.

<We were maybe six or seven. Vinnie wanted to help in the kitchen, but he was clumsy. Broke dishes. Spilled ingredients. Got frustrated so easily.> I closed my eyes, remembering. <Most people would've given up, told him to go play, that cooking was too complicated for someone like him.>

<But your momma didn't,> Garth signed.

<No. Repetition is very important to Vinnie's learning. She patiently showed him again and again. How to crack an egg without getting shell in the bowl. How to measure flour. Basic stuff that typical kids pick up without thinking. But for Vinnie, every small success was a mountain climbed. And every success built up his confidence.>

I smiled at the memory. <First dish he made perfectly was scrambled eggs. Simple, right? But when he served them to Mom and they were actually good—not undercooked or burnt—she cried. I didn't understand why she was crying over eggs.>

<What did she say?> Garth asked.

<She looked at me and said, 'Your brother can do anything if someone believes in him.' Then she looked at Vinnie and told him he was going to be a great chef someday. And you know what? She was right. Vinnie's the best cook I know.>

Garth nodded slowly. <Mothers see potential. Not limitations.>

<Yeah, they see who we can become, not who the world says we are,> I ruminated. <Agnes saw you, Garth, not your disabilities. My mom saw Vinnie, not Down syndrome. That's what makes them special. That's what we remember when they're gone.>

We stood in comfortable silence for a moment, two men bound by the shared experience of mothers who'd loved unconditionally and were now memories.

Then Garth's expression shifted, becoming more focused. He walked to Agnes's dresser with purpose.

<Not just here for memories,> he signed. <Momma kept her valuable jewelry in secret place. Maybe safety deposit key is there too.>

Hope flared in my chest like a struck match. If Garth found that key, we wouldn't have to run the heist at all. We could just walk into First National Bank, use Garth's inheritance rights or some legal loophole, and access the box. No disguises, no drones, no risk, no prison.

Please let it be here. Please.

Garth approached the vanity mirror and ran his hands along its ornate frame. His fingers found something, pressed, and a section of the frame clicked open to reveal a small compartment.

Inside was a jewelry box—ornate, antique, the kind of thing that probably had its own insurance policy.

Garth lifted it out with reverent care and set it on the vanity.

I held my breath as Garth lifted the lid.

Inside were photographs, old ones, showing a younger Agnes with a man who must have been Garth's father. Letters tied with ribbon. Small treasures of a life lived and lost.

But no key.

Why would anything be easy?

<We should go,> I signed, <before Charity comes back.>

Garth nodded and carefully stashed the letters into the small of his back and returned the jewelry box to its secret compartment. He took one last look around the room, then followed me out.

Chapter Twenty-Six

The bathroom had become my makeup lab, its surface splattered with makeup brushes, sponges, foundation, medical adhesive, makeup remover, and the remnants of six hours' worth of trial and error. Silicone prosthetic pieces painted to match my face lay scattered across the counter like puzzle parts waiting to be applied. My own reflection stared back at me, currently sporting what I hoped was my best attempt yet at becoming someone slightly different.

The YouTube tutorials I delved into had been a revelation. Hours of watching spy experts, special effects artists, and film students break down the science of prosthetics and facial recognition had taught me more than I'd expected to learn. The key insight was elegantly simple. I didn't need to become completely unrecognizable. I just needed to change enough primary facial landmarks to confuse the geometric mapping that facial recognition algorithms relied on. The first landmark I needed to change was the distance between my eyes and nose bridge, which was altered by the silicone extension that I held in place on my nose as the medical adhesive dried. The second landmark was the width of my face at the cheekbone level, which I subtly modified with padded silicone cheek extensions that blended seamlessly to my face. These two changes alone would create what one particularly helpful TikTok creator called "facial geometry confusion." The software would struggle to match the proportional relationships of my altered face against any stored images of my actual face.

The nose bridge extension had taken three tries to get right, but now it sat flush against my natural bridge, adding those crucial three millimeters that would throw off facial recognition algorithms. I wiggled the nose extension, testing whether the medical adhesive had finally dried. It did not move, and I carefully released my hold. I looked into the mirror at my widened nose and fake cheek bones and realized I was starting to look like a convincing stranger.

"How's this one look?" Vinnie called from my bedroom, where he'd been patiently waiting with his phone ready to document my progress.

"Getting somewhere," I called back, carefully applying the color-correcting makeup that would blend the prosthetics seamlessly with my skin tone. "Give me two more minutes."

I stepped back from the mirror to gauge my work. The person staring back at me looked familiar enough to be related to Nicholas Murphy, but different enough that even someone who knew me well might do a double-take. More importantly, the changes were subtle enough that they wouldn't draw unwanted attention from bank employees, security guards, or customers.

"Alright," I said, leaning out the bathroom door. "What do you think?"

Vinnie looked up from where he'd been scrolling through the dozen photos he'd taken of my various attempts, his eyes widening as he took in my latest transformation.

"Whoa," he said. "You look like...not you."

"That's exactly what we're going for." I settled onto the edge of my bed while Vinnie held up his phone to capture the final result. "The prosthetics don't have to fool people who know me well. They just have to confuse facial recognition algorithms in case anyone checks security footage at the bank, or if witnesses are questioned. They won't remember Nicholas Murphy, they'll remember," I struck a pose, "Diego Locksley, small business owner."

"Nice to meet you, Diego Locksley," Vinnie said as he took photos, his expression growing more serious as he worked. "Nicholas, can I ask you something?"

"Shoot."

"Since we decided on Heist Club," Vinnie began, then paused as if he was working out how to phrase something complex. "I've been thinking. If we fail, we might go to prison."

"Prison is definitely a possibility," I said.

"I never thought about going to prison before," Vinnie continued, speaking carefully as he worked through something big. "But now I am, and there are things I want to do."

I paused cleaning prosthetic glue residue from my fingers. "Like what kind of things?"

"Driving is in the top three for sure," Vinnie said, warming to the subject. "And becoming a real cook at a real restaurant, not just someone who carries boxes."

"But you're already learning to drive. And you cook for the Family all the time."

"That's not the same," Vinnie said with surprising firmness. "Learning to drive and driving places by myself—those are different things. And cooking for strangers—also different."

"It sounds like you're talking about a bucket list," I said. "The kind of list people make of all the things they want to do before they die."

"A bucket list," Vinnie thought out loud. "Why a bucket? That makes no sense."

"I think it comes from the expression "kick the bucket," for when someone dies."

Vinnie thought for a moment and said, "Yes. A bucket list."

I found myself genuinely curious about what else might be on Vinnie's list. "What's number one?"

Vinnie was quiet for a moment, his expression becoming more thoughtful. "I'm not sure. What's on yours?"

"Never really thought about it, Vinnie," I said, though the conversation was making me increasingly aware of how much we were all risking. "Right now, I need to focus on creating a believable disguise so I can get a fake ID and rent that safety deposit box."

Which brought me back to the task I'd been dreading all day.

"The prosthetics are working," I said, gesturing to my altered face. "But I still need someone who can create a convincing fake driver's license to match this look. And there's only one person I know who has those kinds of connections."

"Francis," Vinnie said quietly.

"Francis fucking Donahey," I confirmed, feeling my jaw clench automatically at the name. "And now I have to crawl to Francis and beg for his criminal services when all I want to do is beat the ever-loving shit out of him."

Vinnie thought about that a moment before managing to say, "Maybe don't say that last part to him. Francis can be nice sometimes."

I stared at Vinnie a long moment as my mind replayed all the memories I had of Vinnie and Francis. Each and every one of them ended with Francis laughing and Vinnie being humili-ated, and yet my twin still looked for good in a person who simply was not. Francis had nearly destroyed Vinnie back in high school. It was the only time I was actually afraid Vinnie might hurt himself.

The memory of that homecoming talent show was as vivid and painful as if it had happened yesterday.

Twelve years earlier...

I sat in the bleachers of our high school gymnasium, waiting to see Vinnie perform in this year's drama club homecoming talent show. Vinnie had joined the drama club to help with his communication skills. Unfortunately, Francis was in the drama club too, most likely practicing and honing his budding psychopathy like little psychopaths do when they're spawned.

Vinnie had been talking about this specific performance for weeks, practically glowing with pride that Francis Donahey had asked him to be part of his act this year.

"It's a song from that old movie *Young Frankenstein,*" Vinnie had explained to me over dinner. "I'll be perfect as the monster. It's going to be very funny. We're going to bring the house down, Nicholas!"

I should have known something was wrong. Francis never included Vinnie in anything unless there was a cruel punchline waiting. But Vinnie had been so happy, so excited to finally be part of something that made him feel accepted. And he had lines. I hadn't wanted to crush that joy with my suspicions.

The act began with Francis taking center stage in a bow tie and tails, perfectly channeling Gene Wilder's mad scientist character. Scott flanked him as his assistant, both of them playing their roles with theatrical flair. Then Vinnie shambled on stage in monster makeup, and the crowd immediately started chuckling at his appearance.

What the audience didn't understand—what I was only beginning to realize with growing horror—was the context of the scene Francis had chosen. In *Young Frankenstein*, the "Puttin' on the Ritz" number was a tragic comedy bit where the scientist tries to prove his monster is civilized by having him perform in public. The humor comes from the monster's speech impediment and his inability to pronounce words correctly, making him sound developmentally disabled when he sings.

Francis knew exactly what he was doing.

"Ladies and gentlemen," Francis announced with a showman's grin, "I present to you my greatest creation! A being of tremendous power and...limited vocabulary!"

The crowd laughed. Vinnie beamed, thinking they were laughing with him.

Francis launched into the song with professional timing, his voice carrying across the gymnasium: *"Have you seen the well-to-do, up and down Park Avenue..."*

Then came Vinnie's cue. He threw his arms wide and bellowed in his natural voice, but exaggerated just enough to emphasize his speech patterns: *"PUTTIN' ON THE RITZ!"*

More laughter. Bigger this time. Vinnie's smile grew wider.

I felt sick.

Francis continued, building the performance toward its climax, his every gesture designed to set up Vinnie for maximum humiliation. The crowd was eating it up, not understanding they were watching calculated cruelty disguised as entertainment.

"Dressed up like a million-dollar trooper," Francis sang with dramatic flair, *"trying hard to look like Gary Cooper..."*

Vinnie threw himself into his response with complete commitment, his voice cracking with effort and enthusiasm: *"SOOPER DOOPER!"*

The gymnasium exploded. Students were on their feet,

applauding and laughing until tears streamed down their faces. It was the biggest reaction of the entire talent show.

And that's when I saw it happen.

Vinnie's expression began to change as the laughter continued, as he realized it was going on too long, too hard. His smile faltered as understanding crept across his face. These weren't appreciative chuckles at his performance... This was the kind of laughter that came from watching someone make a fool of themselves without realizing it.

I watched my brother's joy die in real time, replaced by a humiliation so profound it was physically painful to witness. His shoulders sagged. His head dropped. The light that had been shining in his eyes for weeks simply...went out.

Vinnie ran off the stage in tears.

Francis took his bow to thunderous applause, basking in the success of his carefully orchestrated cruelty. The crowd cheered for what they thought was brilliant comedy, never understanding they'd just participated in the systematic destruction of a gentle soul.

I broke Francis's nose with one punch that night.

The memory faded, leaving me back in my bathroom, staring at my prosthetic-altered reflection. Even now, years later, the rage felt fresh and immediate. Francis had taken something pure and hopeful in Vinnie and twisted it into a weapon against him. He'd used my brother's disability as a punchline, turning the entire school into unwitting accomplices in his cruelty.

Vinnie quit drama club the next day and spent the rest of high school flinching every time someone yelled "Sooper Dooper" at him in the hallways. The depression that followed had been so severe I'd genuinely feared losing him to it.

Francis had scarred my brother for life for a fucking laugh.

And I'd broken Francis's nose for it. The only reason I hadn't been arrested was that we were all still minors, but it had gone into my sealed juvenile record. The same record that Charity was now threatening to expose.

"I'll go with you," Vinnie said, pulling me back to the present.

"Absolutely not."

"But—"

"Vinnie, if you're there, Francis won't be able to stop himself from making a run at you. It's what he does. It's who he is." I met his eyes directly. "And if Francis makes fun of you, I will beat the shit out of him. And then we'll be fucked because we won't get our fake ID, and I'll probably go to jail for assault. I'll be nice to the asshole, don't worry."

Vinnie's expression fell, but he nodded reluctantly. "You're right. Francis is an asshole."

"Francis is a cancer," I corrected. "But right now, he's a cancer I need something from."

I looked at myself in the mirror one more time, studying the subtle changes the prosthetics had made to my facial geometry.

"Take a few more pictures," I said. "We need to compare all of them and pick the best one to use for the ID photo."

Vinnie raised his phone and motioned for me to stand in front of a blank white wall and started snapping shots. "This one's really good," he said, showing me the screen. "You look like a completely different person, but not in a weird way."

I scrolled through the photos he'd taken over the past several hours, comparing the various iterations of my prosthetic experiments. Some looked too obvious, others hadn't changed enough to fool recognition software. But this latest attempt struck the right balance.

"This is the one," I said, pointing to the clearest shot. "Natural looking, but different enough to matter."

"Perfect," Vinnie said, saving the photo to a separate album. "When are you going to talk to Francis?"

"Tomorrow, probably. Get it over with before I lose my nerve."

What I didn't know was that Vinnie had made a plan of his own.

Chapter Twenty-Seven

I needed to talk to someone about my plan to get a fake ID, but not Nicholas. Nicholas would say no and then worry about me, which would make everything worse.

"I'm coming to the gym with you. I hope it isn't cardio day. I hate cardio day," I told Garth while he was getting ready in his room.

Garth looked surprised. "Everything okay?"

"I need to talk to you about Nicholas and Francis," I said. "But not here. Too many ears."

Garth nodded and finished putting on his gym clothes. "Today's cardio, but switch to weights. We can talk."

We walked to the gym together, and I could see Garth was giving me time to think about what I wanted to say. That's what I liked about Garth. He didn't make me talk before I was ready. And I had a lot to think about while we walked.

At the gym, Garth went to his usual spot and started putting circles on the bar. Not as many circles as the day he cried about his mom, but still more than I could ever lift. I sat on the bench next to him and watched him get ready.

"Nicholas has to ask Francis for a favor and I don't want him to," I said while Garth checked his grip on the bar.

Garth paused and looked at me. "What favor?"

"Something for our plan." I looked around to make sure no one could hear us. "A fake ID. Francis is the only person Nicholas knows who can get us one."

Garth lifted the bar, pushed it over his head, and held it there, then dropped it. He was thinking while he worked out, which was something Garth did when problems were complicated.

Garth added more circles to his bar. "Nicholas hates Francis," Garth said. "Francis is mean to you."

"I know, I know." I watched Garth lift the weights again. "If Nicholas goes to see Francis, they'll fight. Nicholas promised he wouldn't fight anymore, but Francis makes him so mad he can't help it. They're like Batman and the Joker. Always fighting."

Garth put the weights down and wiped sweat from his face with a towel. "Francis is Nicholas's nemesis. Find another way."

"I said that already. Nicholas says Francis is our only option." I felt frustrated just thinking about it. "I don't want Nicholas to break his promise. Fighting makes him different."

"Why not ask Francis?" Garth said. "Without Nicholas?"

I thought about that. Everyone knew where to find Francis. Francis was always at the park with Scott. Nicholas told me Francis was a bad person who sold bad things, but Nicholas never told me what Francis sold. All I knew was never to take candy from Francis.

"Francis will ask why I need a fake ID," I said. "He'll want to know."

"What you tell him?" Garth asked.

An idea had been growing in my head. "I have an idea, but

I need your help. Will you come with me to the park after we're done here? I want a meeting with Francis."

Garth smiled. "Got your back, Vinman."

That made me feel better. Garth was the muscle of the Family, and having him with me would make Francis be nicer.

We finished our workout faster than usual because we both wanted to get to the park. As we walked there, I told Garth about bucket lists.

"Nicholas said I was making a bucket list yesterday," I began. "It's all the things you want to do before you die. Or before you go to prison."

"What's on yours?" Garth asked.

"Definitely learning to drive. And cooking at a real restaurant where strangers eat my food and like it." I thought about what else was important to me. "What about you? What would be on your bucket list?"

Garth was quiet for a while. When he talked, his voice was serious. "Win gold. Special Olympics. This year."

"You'll win gold," I said. "I know it. You're the strongest person I know."

"Strongest in world," Garth said with a small smile.

We could see the park now. The playground had swings and a slide and monkey bars, and there were picnic tables where people played chess. Francis and Scott always sat at the same table with a chess board, but they never really played. They moved pieces around while they talked to people who came to see them.

Francis had lots of treats on the table. Gummy bears and brownies and pixie sticks all spread out like it was Halloween. Scott was eating a brownie and laughing at something Francis said.

"Let me do the talking. If Francis is mean, grunt and cross your arms," I told Garth as we walked toward their table. Garth nodded.

Francis saw us coming. His face got happy and surprised, which was how Francis always looked when he saw me. Like seeing me was the best part of his day.

"Well, well, well," Francis said with a big smile. "If it isn't the Vinman and his amazing friend. What brings you gentlemen to my office today?"

I knew Francis was being fake nice, but part of me always wanted to believe he was really being nice. That's what Nicholas meant when he said Francis was good at confusing me. Francis made mean things sound friendly and friendly things sound mean.

"Hi, Francis," I said. "I need to ask you for a favor."

"A favor?" Francis leaned back like he was interested. "I'm all ears. What can ol' Frank do for you?"

I looked around to make sure no one was close enough to hear us. "Not a regular favor. A criminal favor."

Francis laughed really loud. "I've known you my whole life, Vinman. You don't have a criminal bone in your body."

I gave Garth a look. Garth grunted loud and crossed his arms just like we talked about.

Francis stopped laughing and got serious. "Criminal favor, huh? I see you brought your muscle." He nodded at Garth. "Vinman, are you trying to break bad?"

"I don't know what that means, I need a fake driver's license," I said quietly.

Francis stopped smiling. His face got confused. "What the fuck do you need a fake ID for?" he asked in his high voice.

I had practiced this part in my head during our walk. "Remember when medicines were hard to find when the whole world shut down? We had a friend who couldn't get enough of her medicine and had to get a fake ID to make sure she didn't die. One of my medications is going to be hard to find soon. I need to stock up. I need a fake ID to buy extra while the pharmacy still has it."

Francis looked at Garth, then back at me. His face got serious in a way I didn't expect. "Yeah, I remember that shit. Supply chain fucked everyone over. It took months to find any Adderall. Fuck that shit. What a fucking mess."

"I need my medication," I said and nodded my head.

Francis was quiet for a moment. He looked at me, and I could see something change in his face. Not fake nice anymore, but real. I think.

"That's smart planning, Vinnie," Francis said as he side-stepped Garth and put an arm around my shoulder. "Can't trust the system to take care of people like you and me. The whole thing's rigged against us. Oh, they act like they care, but when push comes to shove, we're the ones left hanging, aren't we? All we have, Vinnie, is each other and our little village."

I listened to Francis talk, and part of me thought he was right. The system had been mean to us lots of times.

Francis picked up a gummy bear and squeezed it between his fingers. "That's why you gotta look out for yourself, Vinman. That's why you gotta be smart and get what you need however you can get it. We gotta take care of ourselves, don't we?"

I nodded, but I felt confused listening to Francis. He sounded like he really understood how hard things were. He sounded like he cared about us being treated badly. But I also remembered all the times Francis had been mean to me, all the times he made fun of me, just like the system he was talking about. For a moment, Francis sounded like he was on our side. Like he was fighting for us instead of against us.

It was a lot.

"I'll get you your fake ID," Francis said. "Five hundred dollars."

I took a deep breath. "I don't have five hundred dollars."

"That means we got ourselves a problem, Vinman," Francis said flatly.

I was expecting this. "We are both businessmen, Francis. Surely there is something we can work out?" I said exactly like I rehearsed it. Criminals said this a lot in movies. And when they said this, the two people usually teamed up together.

Francis looked me up and down. And then he and Scott looked at each other a long time, like they were talking without talking. Whatever they didn't say gave Francis an idea.

"Here's the thing," Francis said. "My usual delivery guy is a fucking no show. Left me hanging with a bunch of time-sensitive deliveries that need to go out today."

Francis leaned back and looked at me like he was deciding something. "Tell you what, Vinman. You help me out with these deliveries, just three stops, real quick, and I'll cover the cost of the fake IDs myself. We're a village right? We help each other out."

I looked at Garth. Garth looked at me, and now we were talking without talking.

"What kind of deliveries?" I asked.

"Some products for some clients. Nothing complicated. All you gotta do is hand them their package, they give you money, you bring it to me. Easy as pie. Then I get you the fake ID."

I thought about Nicholas and how much he hated Francis, and how Francis always made fun of me. But I also thought about how we needed this fake ID and how Nicholas might get hurt if he had to ask Francis himself.

"Two IDs," I said and held out my hand to shake on it.

"You drive a hard bargain. Good man." Francis shook my hand, then Scott handed Francis a backpack from under the table. Francis opened it, showed me the three small boxes, then zipped up the backpack and handed it to me. I put on the backpack and Francis said, "First delivery is to The Permanent Marker, it's a tattoo parlor about six blocks from here. I'll text you the details."

Garth and I started walking toward the tattoo parlor address that Francis texted me. The backpack felt heavy even though it was light. That was because I knew we were doing something bad.

"What we're doing is bad," I said to Garth as we walked.

"Pretty sure, yeah," Garth agreed.

"I don't want to do it, but we have no choice. If we don't, Nicholas will never get the fake ID from Francis. Then you have to live with Charity for the rest of your life, and the rest of us get sent to state care. They beat me in state care, Garth."

Garth patted my shoulder.

"Which would you rather do?" I asked without judgment. "Make deliveries or lose the Family?"

"Make deliveries," Garth said.

"Do you have a problem making the deliveries if they're bad?"

"Not really," Garth said. "That or live with Charity. I hate Charity."

I thought about that. Maybe good and evil didn't really exist if you were in trouble? Maybe when bad things happened to you, you just did what you needed to survive? Did that make you bad, if you're forced to do bad? Maybe, but maybe it also just made you survive.

Before we could talk about it more, we arrived at The Permanent Marker. The tattoo parlor had dark windows and neon signs. I texted Francis I was here and soon my phone made its Super Mario sound. I checked it.

Francis: *Ink. Back room. Knock three times.*

"The man's name is Ink," I said to Garth. "I think that's called 'on the nose' for a tattoo artist."

We went inside and found our way to the back room. I knocked three times like Francis said. The door opened and there was Ink, covered in tattoos and piercings, looking at us like we were ghosts.

"Who the fuck are you?" Ink said, staring at me and Garth. Mostly me.

I opened the backpack and held out the box. "Francis sent us."

Ink looked at his package, then he looked back at me. And my Down syndrome face. "I see that, but..." Ink kept staring as he continued, "Your face... Frank's using people like you as mules?"

"I don't know what that means," I said honestly. "I have a delivery for you."

Ink shook his head for some reason and said, "This is either genius or the dumbest idea Frank's ever had."

"It's my idea, and it's genius," I said. "Because of 'my face,' I'm invisible. No cop would ever search me."

Ink opened his mouth to speak, then closed it. He got very quiet, like me when I'm working out something in my head. Then he nodded to me and said, "Respect."

"Thank you. Now pay up," I answered immediately.

Garth held out his hand. Ink quickly counted out money and gave it to Garth. We left.

On the bus to the mall, I kept thinking about what we were doing. "People seem to only like good things until bad things happen to them," I said to Garth. "When bad things happen, they do whatever they want and don't care if it's good or evil."

"Like we are now?" Garth asked.

"Yeah. I was talking with Celia. She says two wrongs don't make a right and bad is bad no matter what. But Celia doesn't know about your sister. If someone was trying to force Celia into state care, I wonder if she would think differently about robbing a bank if it saved her?"

Garth thought about that. "Probably."

I disagreed, but didn't say so. I didn't think Celia would rob a bank. Celia was very religious. People who are religious believe in good and evil a lot. Or do they believe in good and evil a lot until bad things happen to them, and then it doesn't matter? I didn't know the answer. I couldn't decide if Celia was right or wrong.

We got to the mall, and I felt my stomach get tight. I didn't like the mall. People yelled mean things when they saw me. But today we had to be here.

I texted Francis, and my phone made its Super Mario sound when he texted back.

Francis: *Becky. Pink hair. Table near Panda.*

We found pink-hair Becky sitting at a table. She was on her phone. When we walked up to her, she looked at us and her mouth opened wide in surprise.

"I'm here for Francis," I told her.

"You mean Frank? You're my delivery?" she asked, looking very surprised.

"Yes," I said, handing her the box.

"I just... I wasn't expecting..." She looked at me and Garth. "Sorry, I don't mean to be rude. I'm just surprised a person like you works for Frank."

"It's illegal to discriminate against people with disabilities," I said with a serious face.

Becky's face turned white. "Oh my God, I'm so sorry, I didn't mean—"

Then I smiled at her so she would know I was joking.

Becky relaxed and laughed a little. "You got me. Okay, that was good." Then her face got serious again. "Look, I'm not a bad person. I just want to go out with my friends. They'll only let me hang if I bring party favors. That's all. It's no big deal."

"As long as you have the money it isn't," I said, trying to sound tough.

She gave us the money, and we left.

"Becky was rationalizing," Garth said to me as we walked out of the mall. "She knows it's bad, she does it anyway."

"If everyone does that," I said as I thought out loud, "is there really any reason to care if something is good or bad? Just do what you want and rationalize like pink-hair Becky."

We walked to the frat house. It was close to the mall, and I could hear loud music coming from inside. I wondered if Nicholas partied like this when he was in college and I was in state care. It looked like an old movie where people have crazy college adventures.

"They don't care about good or bad," Garth said. "Just drinking and partying."

"Yeah," I agreed. "They will definitely make fun of us. Be ready."

My phone made its Super Mario sound after I texted Francis we were here.

Francis: *Carl. Pledge. Front yard.*

We waited outside the frat house. A boy came stumbling out. He was drunk and looked very young. When he saw us, he put away his phone and just stared at me like he was dumb.

I held out the box. "Francis sent us. You're Carl?"

"Holy shit," Carl said, staring at Garth and then at me. "I never thought retards could have jobs. That's so cool, man. You wanna come inside and party with us?"

"We just want the money," I said.

Then Carl did something I didn't expect. He tried to rob us. Carl grabbed the box from my hands and said, "Yeah, sure. Whatever, retard." He started to run back toward the house without paying.

But Garth moved really fast. He grabbed Carl by his shoulders and lifted him up so his feet didn't touch the ground. Carl's eyes got really big.

"The 'retard' was speaking," Garth said, holding Carl's face close to his.

I watched Carl swallow slowly as he looked at Garth. I didn't like hearing Garth say that word, but I understood he was using it ironically. Real irony, not Alanis Morissette. Nicholas says she doesn't understand that word.

"Show me the money," I said to Carl.

"Okay, okay!" Carl yelled. "I'll pay!"

"You pay double," I said. "Since you tried to rip us off."

"Double? That's not fair—"

"Stunt on this ho," I said like Dexter.

Garth made a growling sound low in his throat and lifted Carl up higher.

"Fine! Double! I'll pay double! Just put me down!" Carl said.

He gave us double the money. We left him there and walked back to the park.

"We just robbed him," I said.

"He tried to rob us first," Garth said.

"So, that makes it okay then?" I asked, hoping Garth could clear this up for me.

"It does for me," he said, which didn't help as much as I wanted.

But what Garth said made me think of Celia. She did not agree that it was okay to do bad even if someone did bad first.

When we got back to Francis, he looked happy to see us. We gave him the money, but we kept the extra Carl gave us without telling him. We earned that ourselves.

"Look at you two," Francis said, counting the money. "Natural born delivery boys. We might have a lucrative future doing business together, Vinman."

"I just want the fake IDs," I said.

Francis pulled out his phone and started typing. "Alright, alright. Keep your shirt on. Lemme text my guy," Francis said as he texted. "Bingo, you're all set. My man's a modern-day da Vinci. Get him your pics, and he'll have you taken care of by end of week, I guarantee."

My phone made a Super Mario sound. I looked at it. Francis had texted me his contact's information.

"Nice doing business with you, Francis," I said.

"Want some candy for the road?" Francis asked, pushing some baggies filled with candies toward me and Garth. "Got all kinds."

"No, thank you," I said. "We came from the gym earlier."

Francis shrugged and put a gummy bear in his mouth. "How's Nicholas doing these days?" he asked while he chewed. "Tell him Frank sends his best regards."

"I will. Thanks, Francis," I said.

As me and Garth turned to leave, Francis looked up with that mean smile I remembered from high school. "Actually, tell him Frank sends his best *retards* with his best regards."

Just when I thought Francis was being nice, just when I

thought maybe he really cared about helping Garth and me, he did that. He said that mean thing and smiled like hurting my feelings was funny.

Maybe Nicholas was right.

Maybe Francis was an asshole and that was all there was to it.

"We have to go now," I said as I turned to leave.

"Remember, Vinman," Francis called after us as we walked away. "Any time you want a job, all you gotta do is ask."

Garth and I walked home without talking much. I was thinking about what we did today and how good it felt to solve a problem by myself. Francis was mean, but I got what we needed. The fake ID would happen, and Nicholas wouldn't have to fight Francis.

All day I kept asking Garth if what we were doing was good or bad. But now I understood something. People in movies always had to make deals with bad people to get what they needed. That's what I did today. I made a deal with Francis, made some deliveries, and now our heist could move forward to save the Family.

I don't think Celia is right.

Chapter Twenty-Eight

The heavy bag swayed back and forth as I worked through my combinations, each punch landing with the satisfying thud of leather against my gloved fists. Jab, cross, hook, uppercut. The rhythm was meditative, a way to channel the rage that built up daily watching the world treat my Family like second-class citizens.

I'd installed the bag in our backyard years ago, ostensibly for everyone's benefit. "Physical exercise is important for emotional regulation," I'd told them, spouting the kind of therapeutic bullshit I'd learned in my truncated psychology studies. The truth was simpler and more selfish. I needed somewhere to hit something that wouldn't get me arrested.

In the early years of caring for the Family, I'd carried so much fury it felt like swallowing molten metal. Every condescending doctor, every cruel stranger, every bureaucrat who treated my people like inconveniences... It all accumulated in my chest until I thought I might explode. The bag gave me somewhere to put that rage.

My own personal *Hadouken.*

To my surprise, the Family had embraced it. Even William, who'd initially protested that introducing "instruments of violence" into our peaceful home was barbaric, eventually started using it. Turned out Mr. Darcy was quite the pugilist when the mood struck him.

Today I was working Francis Donahey's face into the leather. Every jab was his smirking mouth. Every cross was his dead eyes. Every hook was payback for years of psychological torture he'd inflicted on Vinnie.

Jab, jab, cross.

Francis held the key to our fake ID, and I was going to have to swallow my pride and ask the bastard for a favor.

Hook, uppercut, jab.

That was exactly the kind of sadistic game Francis loved. Dangling hope in front of someone who needed it, then yanking it away at the last second.

Cross, hook, cross.

My combinations grew sharper, faster, as the anger built. The bag shuddered under the assault as I pictured Francis's reaction.

"Nicholas?"

I spun around to find Vinnie standing at the back door, watching me. Careful. Assessing. Reading my emotional state.

"What's wrong?" he asked, stepping into the backyard.

I pulled off my gloves and wiped sweat from my face with a towel. "Why do you ask?"

"Whenever you get mad or someone in the Family gets hurt, you hit that bag like it owes you money."

Despite my foul mood, I laughed.

"I'm pissed about having to ask Francis for help," I admitted, unwrapping the tape from my hands. "Every fiber of my being is screaming at me not to do it, even though I know I have to."

"I already took care of it," Vinnie said matter-of-factly.

I stopped unwrapping and stared at him. "What?"

"The fake ID will be ready by the end of the week. I took Garth and had a little talk with Francis. Made him an offer he couldn't refuse."

My jaw dropped. "Did you just watch *The Godfather*?"

Vinnie's expression grew slightly smug. "I've been watching a lot of movies and TV with William. He says you can learn everything you need to know from film and television."

"I'm not sure that's entirely accurate," I said slowly, though I had to admit I was impressed. "But what did you tell Francis? How did you convince him to help?"

"I know you think Francis is bad," Vinnie said, his voice taking on a thoughtful quality. "But sometimes being bad is what you need, isn't it? That's why we decided to do bad things. To save the Family. I did the same thing. I made a deal so you wouldn't blow it by punching Francis in the face."

I felt a mixture of pride and unease. Pride that Vinnie had taken the initiative to protect me from my own worst impulses. Unease that my brother was becoming increasingly comfortable with manipulation and moral ambiguity.

"What exactly did you tell him?" I pressed.

"I made Francis feel sorry for me," Vinnie said with a shrug. "I know he's mean to me a lot, but he's been nice to me too. I figured I could use that."

The casual way he described manipulating Francis was alarming. When had Vinnie become so calculating?

"What picture did you use for the ID?" I asked, suddenly remembering the crucial detail.

"The good one." Vinnie pulled out his phone and showed me the screen. "This one."

I nearly had a heart attack. The photo showed my first disastrous attempt at applying prosthetics.

"Vinnie, my nose looks like Picasso placed it. It's all crooked and..." But the words trialed off into silence as I clocked my twin grinning ear-to-ear. "You're fucking with me, aren't you?"

"I'm fucking with you," Vinnie said, grinning widely. "Of course I used the good one, Nicholas."

He swiped to another photo. The final result from yesterday's makeup session. Clean, professional, subtly altered but believable.

"Jesus Christ, Vinnie," I said, my heart rate returning to normal. "You got me."

But as my relief faded, I found myself studying my brother's face. The easy confidence, the calculated misdirection, the way he'd played me like a violin. Vinnie was evolving, adapting, becoming someone I wasn't sure I recognized.

But was that bad?

"Rita agreed to teach you to drive tomorrow," I said, needing to change the subject. "I thought you might want to practice without me hovering."

"I want you to come," Vinnie said immediately. "Rita's nice, but you're my brother. I need you there."

The simple sincerity in his voice reminded me that despite his growing sophistication, Vinnie was still my little brother who wanted his twin nearby for moral support.

"Alright," I said. "But whatever happens with Rita, we follow the first rule of Heist Club. And what's the first rule of Heist Club?"

"You don't talk about Heist Club," Vinnie recited immediately.

. . .

Dinner was leftovers heated in the microwave. A far cry from Vinnie's usual culinary productions, but nobody complained. We were all too excited about the fake ID development to care about leftover food.

"So let me get this straight," William said, pausing between bites of lo mein. "Vinnie walked up to Francis Donahey and convinced him to arrange a fake identification document without Francis knowing what it's actually for?"

"Pretty much," Vinnie said proudly. "I tricked him into thinking we needed it to get medications, like people had to when the world shut down."

"That's bloody brilliant," William concluded.

Floyd was impressed. "Criminal m-mastermind, Vinnie. You're like Ttony ffffucking Soprano."

"Doug Judy," Vinnie corrected.

I watched the Family celebrate Vinnie's success and felt that familiar mixture of pride and terror. We were really doing this. We were really planning a heist. And somehow, my brother with Down syndrome had just outmaneuvered the most manipulative bastard I'd ever known. Without my help whatsoever.

"This brings up an important point," I said, setting down my fork. "What we're doing is serious. Life-changing serious. We can never, ever talk about it outside this house. Especially not in front of Rita."

The mood sobered immediately.

"Perhaps we should formalize our commitment," William suggested, slipping on his Mr. Darcy mask. "A gentleman's agreement, as it were."

"Like the mafia?" Vinnie asked, his eyes lighting up. "We could make a pact!"

"Alright," I said. "Let's make this official. From this moment forward, what happens in Heist Club stays in Heist

Club. Nobody talks to anybody about anything we're planning."

"Sn-nitches get st-t-titches," Floyd said, and I could see the phrase taking root in all their minds.

"Snitches get stitches," William agreed solemnly.

"Snitches get stitches," Garth rumbled.

"But what if someone interrogates us?" Vinnie posed the question.

"If that ever happens, knock on wood it won't, but if any of us get caught or questioned by the police, we say exactly one word: 'Lawyer.' Does everyone understand?" I asked them all. After watching each of them solemnly nod, I turned to William and said in the deepest, most threatening voice I could muster, "Where were you on the night of October 11?"

William crossed his arms and simply said one word, "Lawyer."

"Vincent Murphy, do you know the whereabouts of your twin brother on the night in question?" I demanded.

"Lawyer," Vinnie replied with ease.

"Mr. Cartwright, are you aware we have security footage of you robbing a bank?" I shot at the big man.

<Lawyer,> Garth signed with a grin.

Floyd beat me to the punch as he replied, "Law-wyer," before I could ask him anything.

Satisfied, I raised my water glass. "To Family. Always and forever."

"To Family," they echoed.

I was floating in that space between sleep and consciousness when the screaming started. At first, my brain tried to incorporate it into whatever dream I'd been having...distant sirens, maybe, or some television show Vinnie had left on too loud?

But the sound was too raw, too primal to be anything but real human agony.

I bolted upright, instantly alert, and heard it again. A blood-curdling shriek that seemed to shake the walls of the house. The sound was coming from Floyd's room.

I threw on a shirt and ran down the hall, arriving at Floyd's door at the same time as the rest of the Family. Through the thin walls, we could hear thrashing and what sounded like furniture being knocked over.

I pushed open the door to find Floyd in the middle of what looked like a waking nightmare. He was sitting up in bed, eyes wide open but clearly not seeing the room around him. His face was contorted in terror as he screamed and clawed at something invisible.

"Floyd!" I called out, approaching slowly. "You're safe. You're home."

But Floyd couldn't hear me. He was completely lost in whatever hell his mind had constructed, screaming the same words over and over:

"It's never coming back! It's gone! Gone!"

I tried to get close enough to calm him down, but Floyd lashed out blindly, his fists swinging at phantoms only he could see.

"Garth," I said urgently. "I need you to hold him still. He's going to hurt himself."

Without hesitation, Garth moved forward and gently but firmly pinned Floyd's arms to his sides. Even in his massive grip, Floyd continued to struggle and scream.

"William, get my medical bag from the closet," I ordered, my nurse practitioner training kicking in. "Black bag, top shelf."

As William scrambled to follow my instructions, I knelt beside Floyd and tried to assess his condition. His pupils were dilated, his breathing rapid and shallow, sweat pouring down his face.

"It's never coming back!" Floyd screamed again, his voice hoarse and desperate. "Gone! All gone!"

William returned with my medical bag, and I quickly located a sedative and syringe. My hands moved with trained efficiency as I drew the medication, though my mind was racing with questions. Floyd had been stable for weeks. His nightmares had stopped completely. What the fuck could have triggered this?

"Hold him steady," I told Garth as I positioned the syringe. "This will help him sleep."

The injection took effect quickly, and Floyd's struggles gradually subsided. His screaming faded to whispers, then to quiet sobs, and finally to the steady breathing of sedated sleep.

I checked his pulse and breathing one more time before stepping back. The room felt eerily quiet after the chaos of the past few minutes.

"Is he going to be okay?" Vinnie asked quietly.

"He'll sleep through the night," I said, though I wasn't sure about much else. "But I don't understand what happened. He hasn't had an episode like this in weeks."

I looked down at Floyd's peaceful face, so different from the tortured expression he'd worn just minutes before. Whatever demons chased him in his dreams, they'd found him again.

And only he knew why.

Chapter Twenty-Nine

Vinnie and I were back at the abandoned parking lot that stretched out before us like a concrete ocean, marked only by faded yellow lines and the occasional weed pushing through cracks in the asphalt. It was perfect for driving lessons. Plenty of space, no traffic, and if Vinnie crashed into anything, it would probably be an improvement to the scenery.

Vinnie sat in the driver seat of our van, gripping the wheel like he was driving Rainbow Road and a blue shell was locked onto him.

Rita occupied the passenger seat in full instructor mode, while I leaned forward from the back seat so I could participate in the conversation.

"I'm disappointed, Rita. I wanted to learn to drive your police car," Vinnie announced. "Peralta would definitely let Doug Judy drive his car."

Rita laughed. "First of all, Peralta has never let Doug Judy drive a police car in any episode of *Brooklyn Nine-Nine*. Second, you are not Doug Judy, and I am definitely not Jake Peralta."

"You're totally Peralta," Vinnie insisted. "You're both cops who follow the rules but sometimes break them for people you care about. Like Doug Judy."

"And you think you're Doug Judy because you're a criminal mastermind?" Rita asked with obvious amusement.

"The Vinman is a smooth criminal," Vinnie replied with complete seriousness.

I watched this familiar banter with affection. Rita and Vinnie had been playing this game for years now, and somehow it never got old. The fact that my girlfriend could engage with my brother's obsessions about a sitcom without condescension was one of the many reasons I loved her.

"Alright, Vinnie," Rita said, shifting into teaching mode, "let's start with the basics. Remember what we talked about. This vehicle is a weapon that can kill people if you don't respect it."

As someone who'd taught defensive driving to rookie cops, Rita patiently walked Vinnie through the fundamentals. Check your mirrors. Press on the gas pedal. Get a feel for how easy or hard it is to push. Now, do the same with the brake pedal. Okay, now press your foot down on the brake and turn the key all the way until the engine starts.

I watched Vinnie remain laser focused as he absorbed every word, asking clarifying questions and repeating instructions back to her. His learning style was methodical. He needed to understand not just what to do, but why each step mattered. And then he needed repetition. A lot of repetition.

Two hours later, we'd achieved what I considered a minor miracle. Vinnie could start the van, put it in drive, creep forward at roughly the speed of continental drift, then put it back in park and turn off the engine. It wasn't exactly Formula One racing, but it was progress.

"I did it!" Vinnie announced proudly after completing his

fifth successful circuit of moving ten feet forward and stopping. "The Vinman can drive!"

"You can operate a motor vehicle at very low speeds in a controlled environment," Rita corrected gently. "But yes, this is a huge accomplishment. I'm very proud of you, Vinnie."

"This is definitely off my bucket list," Vinnie said, beaming.

The moment he said it, my heart stopped. Rita would zero in on that phrase like a heat-seeking missile. *Bucket list? Vinnie, why are you making a bucket list?*

"Bucket list?" Rita asked, right on cue. "Vinnie, why are you making a bucket list?"

Vinnie froze for a moment, and I held my breath. This was exactly the kind of slip that could unravel everything. I saw Vinnie glance at me from the rearview mirror as I silently mouthed the words "Heist Club" without Rita noticing.

"Well," Vinnie said slowly, "I've been thinking...about Garth and his dead mom. And then I thought about my dead mom and started thinking about what I want to do before I die. Like driving. And cooking for people in a real restaurant where they pay money for my food."

I relaxed slightly. Those were safe answers, believable reasons for someone to think about life goals.

"That's very healthy," Rita said approvingly. "Everyone should think about their goals and dreams. What else is on your list?"

Vinnie was quiet for a moment, his expression becoming more serious. "I want to have sex."

Wait, what?

Rita and I exchanged surprised looks, both of us caught off guard by Vinnie's response.

"I don't want to die a forty-year-old virgin like Steve Carell in that movie. I have ten years before that happens. I need to get a move on," Vinnie continued, earnest as ever. "I feel all these emotions when I'm with Celia. My body gets all hot and tingly, and I want to touch Celia all over. But I'm afraid because I don't know what to do. I don't want to hurt her or me. I think my body is saying I want to have sex with Celia, but I don't really understand what having sex means. That's why I wanted to ask you guys in private, since I know you have sex a lot."

Rita's eyebrows shot up in surprise. "How do you know we have sex a lot?"

"We all know," Vinnie replied. "You're very loud."

I felt my face burning with embarrassment, while Rita covered her mouth to stifle what sounded like a mixture of mortification and laughter.

"We should probably work on that," I muttered.

"It's not a bad thing," Vinnie added helpfully. "It sounds like you're having fun. Or maybe wrestling. Sometimes it is hard to tell."

Rita was now openly laughing, and I found myself chuckling despite my embarrassment.

"Alright," I said, recovering my composure. "So, you want to have sex. Have you asked Celia if she wants to have sex with you?" I asked.

"Not yet. I wanted to talk to you both before I asked her," Vinnie said sincerely.

"What do you think sex means, Vinnie?" I tested.

Vinnie's expression became thoughtful. "I think it's when two people who love each other, like me and Celia, cuddle a lot and spend time alone together and make funny noises. And maybe you have to be naked? I'm not sure about that part."

Rita and I exchanged glances. Vinnie's understanding of sex was about as sophisticated as George Lucas's understanding of romance.

"You've watched porn on the internet before," I said carefully. "What questions do you have about what you've seen?"

Vinnie's face scrunched up in frustration. "The internet is not helpful! It's very confusing. I don't look like those people. They are tall, have crazy abs and huge muscles. My body's not like theirs. I don't know what sex is supposed to look or feel like for someone like me. There's no representation for people with Down syndrome in porn."

Rita burst out laughing! The kind of guffaw from someone who'd just heard an unexpected truth.

"There isn't, Rita. I've looked," Vinnie said in an earnest tone.

That made Rita laugh even harder. She waved at him to stop as she tried to catch her breath.

In all my years of caring for Vinnie, helping him navigate the complexities of adulthood, this particular challenge had never occurred to me. He was absolutely right. There wasn't appropriate representation for people with disabilities in pornography.

"I'm sorry," she gasped between fits of giggles. "I'm not laughing at you, Vinnie. I'm laughing because you're absolutely right, and it's something I've never thought about before. Of course, you'd want to see other people like you. That's totally understandable."

"So, my body parts work the same as typical people?" Vinnie asked hopefully.

"Yes," I said firmly. "Your body works exactly the same as everyone else's. The physical mechanics are identical. You have nothing to worry about, Vinnie. First and foremost, don't be afraid of sex. Talking about it with us and your partner is important and will make the experience better for you because you'll understand what you're doing. Remember that old reality show *Sex Sent Me to the ER?*"

Vinnie laughed, "Yeah, those people broke all sorts of weird things."

Rita and I both laughed, "Yes, well those people did not discuss sex enough and didn't educate themselves about sex, and they ended up in the hospital."

Rita chimed in, "You're already doing way better than those people, Vinnie. You're learning about sex now, and if you have questions in the future, just ask. Now, on the topic of porn, what you've seen in porn is not what sex is like. You know that, right?"

"Then why do people watch it?" Vinnie asked.

Rita and I shared a look, she shrugged her shoulders, so I took over, "It's a fantasy, Vinnie, you know, like wrestling? No one can really take a diving elbow drop to the head from the top rope and continue to wrestle. But wrestling makes us feel good watching it, even though we know it's not real. Porn is the same way. It looks real, but we know it's really a big exaggeration made by actors who have been paid to do some crazy things."

"I understand," Vinnie nodded. "This is helpful. Please keep going."

I took a deep breath and launched into what felt like the most important sex education conversation of my life. I explained the physical mechanics as clearly as I could, using clinical terms but keeping the language accessible. I talked about how sex was an expression of love and intimacy between consenting adults, how it was supposed to feel good for both people involved, how it required communication so both partners knew how the other was feeling, and finally that he needed to have patience. "The first time can be awkward as you and your partner learn about each other—what you like and what you don't like," I said.

Rita jumped in to emphasize consent. That both people

had to enthusiastically agree to every aspect of what happened, that either person could change their mind at any time, and that respect and care for your partner was the most important part of the entire experience.

"If it is a woman's first time, like I think it is for Celia," Rita explained, "she might experience some discomfort, but only at the beginning. It's natural and will go away very quickly."

"I don't want to hurt Celia," Vinnie said, shaking his head.

"It happens to all women the first time, Vinnie. It's unavoidable. But if you communicate properly, Celia will feel your love and support and you'll get through it together, and then it will all feel amazing. Trust me," Rita explained.

"And always use protection," I added. "Condoms prevent both pregnancy and sexually transmitted diseases. I'll teach you how to use one when you're ready to learn."

"Most importantly," Rita said, "you need to make sure Celia wants the same thing. This isn't something you can surprise someone with or convince them to do. It has to be something you both want and talk about together."

Vinnie listened with the same intense focus he'd shown during his driving lesson, asking clarifying questions and making sure he understood each concept.

"That's a lot," he said finally.

"It is a lot," Rita agreed. "But it's important information. If you have any more questions, again, we're always here to answer them. There is no shame in discussing any aspect of this with people you love."

"I'm proud of you for having this conversation with us, Vinnie," I said, hoping to keep the lines of communication open. "Talking about sex with us and your partner is healthy and necessary."

"It was uncomfortable, but I learned a lot. Thank you both," Vinnie said.

As we switched places after the driving lesson and headed home, I found myself reflecting on how much Vinnie had grown. A few months ago, he'd been content to let me handle all the complex aspects of his life. Now he was asking deep questions about relationships, taking initiative with criminal contacts, and pushing himself to learn skills I'd never thought he'd master.

It was thrilling and terrifying in equal measure. But mostly, it filled me with pride. Vinnie was becoming the independent adult I'd always hoped he would be, even if his path toward independence was leading us all toward a heist.

Rita reached over and squeezed my hand after we got home. "Think they'll figure it out?" she asked quietly.

"Vinnie and Celia?" I considered the question. "Yeah, I do. Vinnie deserves to experience everything life has to offer. Even if it does complicate things."

"*Especially* if it complicates things," Rita said with a smile. "Those are the most worthwhile."

I squeezed her hand back, grateful once again for a partner who understood that loving my Family meant supporting all aspects of their growth. Even the awkward, complicated, thoroughly human parts.

Chapter Thirty

I sat cross-legged on my bed, eyes closed, allowing myself to get lost in my breathing exercises.

Inhale, two, three, four...

Floyd was in his room tinkering with his communications system he was constructing for the heist, the soft sounds of his toils drifting down the hall. I'd learned to read those sounds over the years. The intermittent silence of his careful movements when he was focused, the frustrated sighs when something didn't fit right.

Hold, two, three, four...

William was deep in his coding zone, muttering occasionally at his laptop as he perfected our virtual reality training environment. When William was in flow state with his programming, the rest of the world disappeared.

Exhale, two, three, four...

Vinnie and Garth had headed to the gym again. Their second trip this week. Part of me wondered if they were bonding over their shared membership in what I'd started thinking of as the Dead

Mom's Club, processing grief through shared experience. But another part suspected Vinnie was beginning to believe he really was Tony Soprano and wanted his muscle nearby for whatever scheme was percolating in that increasingly devious mind of his.

Inhale, two, three, four...

For once, I wasn't using the breathing exercises to manage stress or anxiety. This was pure indulgence. A moment of actual peace in a life that rarely offered such luxuries. No one needed medical attention, emotional support, or conflict resolution. No one was having a meltdown, a panic attack, or a medication reaction.

Hold, two, three, four...

Caregivers don't get days off. We're like mothers in that respect, always on call, always responsible for someone else's wellbeing. Even when I slept, part of my brain stayed alert for sounds of distress from down the hall. Floyd's nightmares, William's late-night counting spirals, Garth's occasional sleep walking episodes, Vinnie's processing struggles. I'd trained myself to recognize the subtle audio cues that meant someone needed help.

But in these stolen moments of quiet, I could remember what it felt like to exist solely for myself. To breathe without calculating whose needs came next. To think about my own wants and fears without immediately prioritizing everyone else's.

Exhale, two, three, four...

All of Vinnie's talk about bucket lists had gotten me thinking about my own. What would I put on a list of things to accomplish before I died? Marriage to Rita was obviously at the top, but our lives were so complicated right now that adding wedding planning to the mix was asking for trouble. We'd talked about it in abstract terms during late-night conversations, both of us understanding that timing mattered more than desire.

Most people's bucket lists contained harrowing, frightening activities. Skydiving, mountain climbing, swimming with sharks... The kind of adrenaline-fueled experiences that made you feel alive instead of just watching life slip past. Extreme sports that proved you were living rather than merely surviving.

But my existence was fundamentally different from most people's. I was responsible for five human beings, counting myself. Doing anything dangerous was completely out of the question. Who would take care of the Family if I broke my neck bungee jumping or got eaten by a great white shark while pursuing some stupid thrill?

I couldn't even process that thought without feeling physically ill. The Family came first. Always had, always would. That wasn't martyrdom or self-sacrifice. It was reality. When you loved people the way I loved mine, their wellbeing became inseparable from your own survival.

If I was brutally honest about what I really wanted, what would make my bucket list complete...it wasn't an extreme sport or exotic travel. It was something much simpler and infinitely more precious: I wanted to wake up one day and have someone tell me that they'd taken care of all the day's problems and I didn't have to worry about anything.

Just once. Just for a day. Have someone else take care of me.

Wouldn't that be fucking nice?

The front door slammed with enough force to rattle the windows, followed by Vinnie's voice calling out their arrival. I opened my eyes and returned to reality, the meditation session officially over.

"Nicholas!" Vinnie's shout from the living room carried that particular excitement that usually meant either very good news or impending disaster. "We're back!"

I stretched the kinks from my back and made my way out of my bedroom, expecting to see two sweaty guys in gym clothes needing post-workout hydration and complaining about the locker room being too crowded or the equipment being monopolized by typical gym rat bros.

Instead, I found Vinnie and Garth looking remarkably fresh and conspicuously un-exercised. No sweat stains, no gym bag smell, no signs of physical exertion whatsoever.

"You're not wearing gym clothes," I observed. Garth was in his regular street clothes, and Vinnie looked like he'd spent the afternoon shopping rather than lifting weights.

"We didn't go to the gym," Vinnie said, barely containing his excitement. "We went to pick up your fake ID from my contact."

"Francis's contact," I corrected automatically, my guardian instincts bristling at the idea of Vinnie claiming ownership of criminal connections.

"My contact now," Vinnie replied with unmistakable satisfaction, his chest puffing out slightly. "I know a guy, like other criminals always say."

He pulled a driver's license from his pocket and handed it to me, watching my face carefully for approval. I examined the card, noting the quality of the printing, the feel of the plastic, the way the holographic elements caught the light. Whoever Francis's guy was, he did exceptional work.

The photo was perfect. My prosthetically altered face looked completely natural, professional even. The changes were subtle enough to pass casual inspection. I looked like someone you might sit next to on a plane without giving him a second thought.

"Diego Locksley?" I read the license aloud.

"You said you liked that name," Vinnie said with a shrug.

"It was a joke, Vinnie," I explained gently. "It was a mix of Don Diego and Robin of Locksley."

Vinnie looked at me blankly.

"You know, Zorro and Robin Hood? We're kind of stealing from the rich and giving to the poor, get it?" I prodded.

Vinnie considered this for a moment, his brow furrowing in that way it did when he was processing information that didn't quite click. Then he shrugged again with Vinnie pragmatism. "I get you're Diego Locksley now."

I compared the fake license to my real one, marveling at the craftsmanship. The attention to detail was remarkable. Proper microprinting, correct font weights, even the right kind of wear patterns around the edges. I wished I could ask Rita to examine it with her law enforcement eye, get her professional assessment of whether it would pass police scrutiny. But that would require explaining why I needed a fake ID in the first place, which would unravel everything we'd worked toward.

"This is good enough to rent a safety deposit box," I said, sliding the fake license into my wallet next to my real one. "I can go to the bank today and get the intel we need."

"Today?" Vinnie looked surprised, his excitement shifting toward concern. "Don't you want to plan more?"

The question revealed how much he'd grown. Old Vinnie would have been pushing for immediate action, unable to process the complexity of preparation. New Vinnie understood that successful operations required careful planning and patience.

"We can't plan any further until I do recon," I said. "Every day we delay is another day closer to foreclosure."

I headed toward the bathroom to apply my disguise, already running through the mission in my head. Walk into First National Bank as Diego Locksley, rent a safety deposit box, get left alone in the room with access to all the boxes, and film everything Floyd would need to determine if this heist was even technically feasible. If it wasn't...

I can't think about that now.

In the bathroom, I began applying prosthetics, my hands moving with freshly acquired efficiency while my mind worked through contingencies.

As I blended the edges with color-correcting makeup, I found myself creating a psychological profile for Diego Locksley. According to spy experts on socials, cover identities worked better when you could inhabit them completely, become the person rather than just wearing their appearance like a costume. Who was Diego Locksley, the man behind the legend? The legend? Now the guy's a legend? I couldn't play a legend.

Diego was an importer-exporter. No, wait. What did he import? What did he export? Shit, I couldn't decide on specifics, and vague answers would raise red flags with bank employees trained to spot suspicious activity.

Fine, he was an architect. Wait, was I unconsciously channeling *Seinfeld*? Might as well call myself Art Vandelay and be done with it.

No, Diego Locksley was a collector of rare and expensive antiquities. Specifically, vintage toys and prototypes. He dealt with private collectors and museums, handling pieces worth tens of thousands of dollars that needed secure storage while he arranged authentication and sales. It was the kind of eccentric but lucrative hobby that would explain both his need for a safety deposit box and any nervousness he might display when handling valuable items.

That'll do.

I examined my reflection, adjusting the final details of the disguise and testing my cover story. "Good afternoon," I said to the mirror, then thought about William and his Mr. Darcy mask and tried again. "Good afternoon," I said in a slightly different voice, with a hint of nervous anxiety to my tone. "Locksley. Diego Locksley, collector of fine vintage toys."

The disguise was working. The person staring back at me looked like someone I might trust with rare collectibles, someone who understood the value of discretion and proper storage. Time to make the donuts, as Mom used to say.

I emerged from the bathroom to find the Family gathered in the living room like a war council, eager to hear the operational details. Their faces showed a mixture of excitement and anxiety that reminded me how much they were all invested in this working.

"Where's your wig?" Vinnie asked immediately.

"I still need to put it on, but here's the plan," I announced, reaching for a small duffel bag to carry into the bank as part of my cover. From inside it, I pulled burner phones for everyone and handed them around. "These are for Heist Club and only Heist Club. I'll call one of you when I'm in the safety deposit box room. Floyd, you'll need to walk me through exactly what measurements and photos you need for your technical assessment."

Floyd nodded eagerly, "I'll need d-detailed images of the loc-locking mechanisms, box measurements, and d-dimensions."

"Uh, yeah, we'll get whatever my phone can get," I said.

That's when William suddenly jumped up from the couch, his face going pale as he pointed toward the front window in abject terror.

"Rita!" he hissed. "She's pulling into the driveway!"

Fuck.

I touched my altered face, mentally running through the time I needed to safely remove my disguise—which wasn't happening. The medical adhesive required careful removal with a special solution or I'd end up with destroyed prosthetics and chunks of silicone stuck to my skin that would be impossible to explain.

The doorbell rang.

Rita was waiting right outside.

"I can't get my makeup off in time. What the fuck are we going to do?" I whispered, panic eclipsing my usual calm.

Vinnie looked around the room, his gaze settling on my prosthetic nose. Something clicked behind his eyes.

"I know what to do," he said confidently.

"What?" I demanded as Rita's knocking became more insistent.

"We're going to do what blackface Iron Man said to never do," Vinnie said seriously.

"Whatthefuckdoesthatmean?" I whispered harshly.

"Don't worry, just stall," Vinnie said, pushing me toward the front door with gentle but firm pressure.

"Stall?! How am I supposed to stall? Where are you going?" But even as I protested, I was already moving toward the door, unconsciously trusting my brother's instincts despite my terror.

I opened the door and stepped outside, trying to keep it closed behind me as I greeted Rita with what had to be the most awkward smile of my adult life.

"Hey," I said, attempting casualness and failing so spectacularly that I might as well have been wearing a sign that read "I'm definitely hiding something."

Rita took one look at my face and her expression shifted through confusion to concern to professional suspicion. I watched her investigative instincts engage, cataloging details and inconsistencies.

"What the fuck, Nicholas? Why are you wearing all that makeup?"

I'm scoping out a bank so I can rob it later, I didn't say, though the truth burned in my throat like acid.

I could feel my brain scrambling for plausible explanations while my heart hammered against my ribs. "Oh, I guess you won't like me when I'm old like this?" The words came out sounding exactly as lame as they were, a desperate deflection that fooled absolutely no one.

"The makeup doesn't make you look old," Rita said, studying my altered features. "It makes you look like you're somebody else. What's going on, Nicholas?"

I was frozen in Rita's headlights, unable to move forward or back, trapped between confession and catastrophe. I didn't know what the fuck to do or say, and I was seconds away from confessing everything when—

The front door suddenly burst open behind me like an explosion!

"Nicholas!" Vinnie shouted with theatrical urgency. "Hurry up! We need to finish filming!"

Rita and I both turned to witness the most magnificently ridiculous sight I'd ever seen. Vinnie had somehow managed to take the extra prosthetic noses I'd been practicing with and apply them to the entire Family in what couldn't have been more than ninety seconds. The results were absolutely chaotic.

Vinnie had one crooked nose glued to his forehead at a completely wrong angle. William sported noses attached to his cheek and chin, making him look like some kind of surreal art project. Garth looked like Frankenstein's monster with two nose prosthetics glued to his neck. Floyd was filming the entire spectacle with his phone as he directed their impromptu performance like Tarantino.

"We're making a movie!" Vinnie announced with infectious excitement, waving at Rita like a producer greeting a potential investor. "Rita, you can be in it too! Come in. We'll glue noses on you!"

I stood there with my mouth hanging open, simultaneously horrified and impressed by my brother's lightning-fast problem-solving.

"We're filming our version of that *Twilight Zone* episode 'Eye of the Beholder,'" William explained, getting into character with enthusiasm that was only partly feigned. "Where the woman in the hospital is getting surgery to look like the monsters of her world. But in our version, everyone has weird noses instead of pig faces."

The Family began making exaggerated expressions and moving around the living room while Floyd directed them.

As Rita watched their ridiculous performance, I felt the full genius of what Vinnie had just accomplished. In ninety seconds, he'd transformed a catastrophic security breach into a harmless art project. He'd taken our biggest liability—my obvious disguise—and made it invisible by surrounding it with intentional absurdity. My twin brother was fast-tracked to becoming a criminal mastermind right in front of my eyes.

But was it enough to fool a trained police officer with years of experience spotting frauds and cons?

Rita laughed, her confusion melting into amusement as she watched the Family's antics. "You guys are ridiculous. I'd love to stay and be part of your misfit movie, but I'm still on duty." Her expression suddenly brightened with obvious excitement. "Actually, I popped by to tell you the amazing news, Nicky. I got the task force position! I'll be hunting down the Happy Face Killers. Isn't that fantastic?"

My heart dropped straight through the floor, but I forced enthusiasm into my voice despite feeling like I might vomit. The irony was palpable. Rita would be hunting the exact bank robbers we were using to camouflage our own bank heist.

I managed to say, "Congratulations! That's incredible! You're going to catch those bastards."

The Family joined in to share their congratulations with Rita as I tried to stay calm and smother the impending volcanic explosion before it erupted and spewed molten fear, anxiety, and dread onto us all.

Rita kissed me, then her radio crackled with dispatch codes. "I have to run, but maybe later we can celebrate properly? Just the two of us?"

"It's a date," I said, kissing her back and hoping my lips didn't taste like lies.

Rita took one last look at the Family, and their prosthetic noses, and shook her head with an indulgent smile before heading back to her patrol car and her mission to catch criminals like us.

After she left, William turned to me with uncharacteristic seriousness. "Rita is now part of the task force assigned to hunt down the Happy Face Killers," he said in an even and measured tone.

I nodded slowly. "It would appear so."

Rita would be using every skill, every instinct, every tool at her disposal to hunt down criminals exactly like us. If we got caught, Rita wouldn't just be arresting strangers. She'd be arresting me.

"Nicholas, the chances of Rita and her task force hunting us down are...well, they're not zero," William concluded.

"No, William, they're not." I ran my hands through my hair, fighting the urge to call the whole thing off. But Garth's terrified face at the funeral flashed through my mind, followed by the image of foreclosure notices and the Family scattered to the four winds. "I need to put my wig on," I said, heading for the bathroom with leaden steps. "We have to get this done before Rita catches the real criminals."

Chapter Thirty-One

Walking into First National Bank as Diego Locksley felt like stepping through a portal into enemy territory. I had my burner in my coat pocket recording. Every security camera in the bank felt like it was tracking me, every employee looked like a potential threat, and I found myself identifying exit routes and defensive positions with the acute awareness of someone who knew he'd be returning to commit a felony.

If I'm this nervous just committing fraud, what the hell am I going to feel like when I'm actually robbing the place?

I pushed that thought to the back of my mind and focused on inhabiting Diego's character. Nervous energy could work in my favor. A collector handling valuable items had every reason to seem slightly anxious about security procedures.

"Good afternoon," I said to the receptionist, keeping my voice steady despite my hammering heartbeat. "I'd like to inquire about renting a safety deposit box."

The young woman directed me to a middle-aged man behind a desk whose nameplate read "Douglas Hartwell,

Manager." He looked up from his paperwork and gave me a genuine smile.

"Mister...?" Douglas asked, rising to shake my hand with old-fashioned courtesy.

"Locksley. Diego Locksley," I said, suddenly realizing how ridiculous I sounded.

"A pleasure to meet you, Mr. Locksley. Please, call me Douglas. What brings you in today?"

"The short of it? I need a safety deposit box. I'm a collector of vintage toys and prototypes," I said, settling into the character I'd rehearsed. "I deal primarily with private collectors and museums. Some of my pieces are worth considerable money, and I need secure storage while I arrange authentication and sales."

Interest sparked in Douglas's eyes. "Collectibles have become quite the market lately. I've read about some remarkable prices being achieved at auction. Nostalgia is very lucrative."

"I've heard it said that nostalgia may be the most powerful drug there is," I whispered, getting a real feel for Diego now. He's a bit of a gossip.

For the next few minutes, we discussed the collectibles market while Douglas had me fill out paperwork. I found myself relaxing slightly. His enthusiasm seemed authentic, and he treated me like a legitimate businessman rather than someone to be scrutinized.

But then came the moment of truth.

Douglas pulled out a scanner and ran my fake ID through it, comparing the information on his screen with what I'd written on the forms. My heart pounded so hard I was certain he could hear it across the desk. This was where everything could fall apart. If the ID didn't pass their verification systems, if something in their database flagged Diego Locksley as suspicious, if Francis's contact had made even the smallest error...

My entire future now rested in the hands of Francis fucking Donahey.

Douglas frowned slightly at his screen, and I felt my blood go glacial.

"Hmm," he murmured, clicking through something on his computer.

Fuck. We're blown.

"Is there a problem?" I asked, surprised by how steady my voice sounded.

"Not at all," Douglas said, looking up with that same warm smile. "Just wanted to make sure I had all the information entered correctly. Everything looks perfect, Mr. Locksley. Shall we get you set up with a box?"

Relief flooded through me so powerfully I nearly laughed out loud. The fake ID had passed. Francis's contact was as good as advertised. I should've known he'd be good at being bad.

Douglas led me through the secure area toward the safety deposit box room, explaining bank policies as we walked. "Now, Mr. Locksley, I need to go over what can and cannot be stored in safety deposit boxes. Obviously, valuable items like your collectibles are exactly what these boxes are designed for. However, we cannot store anything illegal, hazardous, or perishable..."

As he continued his explanation, I scanned the room with what I hoped was professional awareness. The space was lined floor to ceiling with metal boxes of various sizes, each secured with dual locks. No security cameras in the security deposit box vault. Exactly what we needed—no eyes to watch me work, no cameras that needed to be hacked nor hidden from.

And then I saw it. Box 103055. Charity's box. Two million dollars in untraceable cash, sitting less than three feet away.

"Excellent," I managed. "I actually have a preference for my box number, if possible. It's somewhat superstitious, but 130500 has been my lucky number since my first major sale."

Douglas raised an eyebrow, intrigued. "Now that's an interesting story, I'm sure."

Like I said, Diego Locksley is a bit of a gossip.

"Oh, it is. A Japanese prototype of Unicron—one of the villains from that Transformers cartoon movie from the '80s," I said, warming to the tale William had told me more than once. "The prototype was never put into production, but I managed to authenticate it and sell it to a private collector for $130,500. It was my first big score; I've used that number as my lucky charm ever since."

"Transformers, eh? My grandson would be impressed." Douglas checked his tablet. "Let me see if 130500 is available... You're in luck! That box is currently unoccupied."

Perfect. Box 130500 would put me right next to Charity's 103055, close enough to film everything Floyd would need, hopefully.

"The dual-key system ensures maximum security," Douglas was saying as we approached my assigned box. "The bank holds one key, you hold the other. Both keys are required to access your box—one person alone cannot open it."

I made sure I angled myself so my phone would record Douglas as he demonstrated the procedure, using his master key on the right side while instructing me to use my customer key on the left. The mechanism clicked smoothly, and Douglas pulled out the inner container.

"This removable box is where you'll store your items," he explained. "This area is completely private. Please feel free to use this table behind you to arrange your belongings in your box. When you're finished, simply return the container to its slot and lock it."

"Very thorough security," I said approvingly. "How often can I access my box?"

"During normal banking hours, as often as you like. Simply present your key and identification to any staff member." Douglas handed me my customer key, a small piece of metal that represented the gateway to our entire operation. "Is there anything else you need to know about the process?"

"I think I understand perfectly. Could I have a few minutes to organize some items I brought with me today?"

"Of course. Take all the time you need. I'll be at my desk if you have any questions."

The moment Douglas's footsteps faded down the hallway, I slipped in my earbud and speed-dialed the Family.

"I'm in," I whispered, scanning the room one final time to ensure I was alone.

"P-p-physical or e-e-electronic locks," Floyd's voice crackled through the connection.

"Physical keys," I said.

"P-p-perfect," Floyd's voice crackled through the connection, barely containing his excitement. "I need detailed photos of everything. The locking mechanisms from multiple angles, the interior of your open box, the surrounding boxes, measurements of the space between the banker's lock and the customer's lock. Then take video of it all just to be safe."

For the next ten minutes, I methodically documented everything Floyd requested. As I worked, I found myself staring at the interior of the safety deposit box. Just a metal-lined rectangular space. It looked exactly like what it was: a secure container designed to hold valuable items. But in my mind, I could see it filled with stacks of cash, the financial salvation that would keep my Family together and safe.

I was mere inches away from two million dollars. So close to security, to independence, to never having to worry about foreclosure or Charity's threats again. And so fucking far away.

But maybe that would change once we analyzed this footage.

Back home, the Family gathered around Floyd's laptop like we were in the Situation Room observing a military operation in real time. I had been thorough.

"This is ex-x-xcellent intel," Floyd said, studying the lock mechanisms. "Really, Nicholas. G-g-good job."

"How does it look?" I asked. "Can you work with what we've got?"

"Actually, y-y-yes. These mechanical locks can be picked using manual methods. It's just a m-m-matter of building the r-r-right tool for the job. With the f-f-footage you recorded, I h-h-have a clear image of the banker's k-k-key. I can approximate the number of tumblers of the banker's lock based on that im-im-image. Then I can approximate the number of tumblers of the customer's lock, b-b-based on Diego's customer k-k-key, which we have here."

"What kind of tool? Can you build it?" Vinnie asked.

"A specialized dr-dr-rone, designed specific-ally-ally to manipulate these lock mechanisms. From the measurements Nicholas gathered, I can b-b-build something tiny enough to fit into a bag, with articulated ap-ap-appendages capable of oper-ating on both locks. Theo-theoretically."

"How long would that take?" I asked.

"For the drone con-con-construction? Few weeks if I adapt Mo-Mozart," he replied.

Garth had been listening quietly, but now he spoke up. "What about getaway?"

"Vinnie's our driver," I said. "Rita's been teaching him, and he's getting better every day. And I sure as hell will have enough anxiety the day of that I don't want to worry about driving or traffic cameras or..."

Vinnie nodded eagerly. "I can do it, Nicholas. The Vinman can."

Finally, we'd found our true north.

"So, our plan is simple," I said, looking around at my Family. "When Floyd's drone is ready, Diego Locksley will walk into the bank, enter the safety deposit box room, Floyd will use Mozart to pick the locks from the getaway van, I pack up Charity's money and walk out. Vinnie drives us home clean."

William frowned. "That's remarkably...mundane."

"Exactly," I said with growing confidence. "No rappelling down buildings, no *Ocean's Eleven* bullshit or secret catch-phrases. I think we all assumed we were going to live some kind of movie moment, an exciting heist full of danger and adrenaline." I paused, looking at each of their faces in turn. "But if all goes according to plan, it's going to be boring as hell."

"Boring?" Vinnie asked.

"Yes, boring," I reiterated. "Life's not a movie. Boring means we don't go to prison. Boring means we save the house. Boring means we stay together."

"Boring is perfect," Garth said, convinced.

The doorbell rang, cutting through our moment of satisfaction.

My body tensed automatically. "Remember," I said quietly, making eye contact with each member of the Family, "first rule of Heist Club."

"You don't talk about Heist Club," they responded in unison, like some kind of criminal catechism.

I moved toward the front door while the Family calmly rearranged themselves in the living room. Through the peephole, I saw a teenager in a pizza delivery uniform, holding what appeared to be an extra-large pizza box.

Not Rita. Good.

I opened the door. "Can I help you?"

"Pizza delivery. Extra-large meat lovers!" the kid announced cheerfully.

Behind me, I heard the Family cheer with excitement.

"We didn't order any pizza," I said, confused.

The delivery kid's smile faltered slightly as he checked his phone. "Is there a Garth Cartwright at this residence?"

I called back into the house, "Garth, come here for a second."

Garth appeared in the doorway, curious. The delivery driver looked him up and down carefully.

"Are you Garth Cartwright?"

"Yes," Garth said, his smile growing at the prospect of unexpected pizza.

The kid opened the pizza box. It was completely empty except for a manila envelope lying where pepperoni and cheese should have been. He pulled out the envelope and handed it to Garth.

"You've been served."

Then he was gone, jogging back to his car and peeling out of our driveway before any of us could process what had just happened.

Garth stood frozen in the doorway, staring at the envelope in his hands like it was a live grenade. The excited murmurs from the Family died immediately. With shaking hands, Garth tore open the envelope and pulled out the legal documents inside. I watched his face as he read.

Without a word, he handed me the envelope, reached up to remove his hearing aids, and walked to his bedroom. The door closed with a soft click that somehow sounded louder than if he'd slammed it.

"What happened?" Vinnie asked, his voice small.

I scanned the legal paperwork, my stomach cramping with each sentence. "Conservatorship hearing," I said quietly. "Charity's petition has been accepted by the court. Garth has thirty days to respond, and then there'll be a hearing to determine if he's mentally competent to manage his own affairs."

The room fell silent except for the distant sound of traffic outside. Somewhere down the hall, I thought I heard Garth crying, but I couldn't be sure.

I looked at the Family. William's anxious tapping, Floyd's worried face, Vinnie's clenched fists. They were all looking at me, waiting for me to say something that would make this okay, that would give them hope.

I had nothing.

"We should get some sleep," I said finally. "Tomorrow, we figure out next steps."

As they dispersed to their rooms, I stood alone in the living room holding Charity's legal summons.

Boring wasn't going to cut it anymore. We needed perfect.

And perfect was a hell of a lot harder to guarantee than boring.

Chapter Thirty-Two

The Family needed a break from the world. Or maybe it was me. It's difficult to tell. Being buried alive underneath repeated avalanches of injustice and grief had that effect. I couldn't tell where my grief ended and the Family's began. And we needed more than what the Pint & Proper could provide.

The smell of burning rubber and gasoline hit me the moment we stepped out of the van at SpeedZone Go-Karts. The track sprawled before us like a miniature NASCAR circuit, complete with hairpin turns, straightaways that begged for maximum velocity, and tire barriers that had seen their share of collisions.

Vinnie stood frozen beside me, watching other drivers zip around the track. His hands were clenched at his sides, and I could see fear building with each go-kart that rocketed past us.

"I don't think I can do this," he said quietly, his voice barely audible over the whine of engines and squealing tires.

"Sure you can," I said, though I wasn't entirely convinced

myself. Teaching Vinnie to drive in an empty parking lot was one thing. This was real.

The track attendant, a college-aged kid with grease-stained coveralls came over. "First time here?" he asked, taking in our unusual ensemble.

"My brother is learning to drive. We thought this might help build his confidence," I said.

The kid's gaze settled on Vinnie, and I braced myself for the usual awkwardness. The uncomfortable stare, the talking-to-me-instead-of-him routine. Instead, the attendant smiled directly at Vinnie.

"Cool, man. I'm Jake. What's your name?"

"Vinnie," my brother replied, some of the tension leaving his voice at being addressed normally.

"Well, Vinnie, unlike a real car, if you mess up here, worst-case scenario is you spin out."

Jake walked us through the safety procedures. He explained the helmet requirements, track boundaries, what to do in case of mechanical problems. But I could see Vinnie getting overwhelmed, his eyes darting between the track and Jake, his anxiety rising by the second.

"Any questions?" Jake asked as he finished his spiel.

That's when Floyd wheeled closer, his small duffel bag positioned across his lap. "A-actually, Jake?" he called out. "C-can karts accommodate p-passengers?"

"Just need you to sign an additional liability waiver." Jake pulled out a clipboard. "Who's your driver going to be?"

"Nicholas," Floyd said, signing the forms. "I want to r-ride shotgun."

After putting on our helmets and selecting our karts, we were all geared up and ready to roll out like a group of Auto-bots. Vinnie sat in his single-seater kart, gripping the steering wheel with white knuckles as he watched other drivers zip past at speeds that probably seemed terrifying from his stationary position. Floyd had transferred into the passenger seat of my kart with minimal assistance, his duffel bag secured between his feet. Garth looked like Donkey Kong stuffed into Super Mario's kart, with William driving his own kart too.

"Remember, gas, brake, steering. Don't overthink it," I called to Vinnie.

"Right," Vinnie replied, his voice tight with anxiety. "Do like Rita taught me."

Floyd suddenly perked up in the seat beside me. "V-Vinnie, pretend this is *M-M-Mario Kart.*," he said unexpectedly.

"This is not *Mario Kart,*" Vinnie protested.

The flag dropped, and chaos erupted around us.

Immediately, it was clear that Vinnie was struggling. While other drivers accelerated confidently into the first turn, Vinnie crept forward at speeds that made elderly pedestrians look aggressive. Kart after kart zipped past him, some drivers shouting encouragement that probably sounded like criticism from inside his helmet.

"Move it!"

"Come on, drive!"

"You can go faster than that!"

I pulled alongside Vinnie's kart, trying to offer encouragement. "You're doing fine! Just give it a little more gas!"

But I could see his panic building. His head was swiveling frantically between the track ahead and the drivers passing him, his shoulders hunched.

"Nicholas," Floyd said urgently beside me, "he's about to q-qu-quit. I can see it."

I followed Floyd's gaze and realized he was right. Vinnie's kart was slowing even further, drifting toward the outer barrier like he was preparing to pull over and give up.

"P-p-pull up be-beside him," Floyd called out to me. "When I say punch it, p-p-punch it!"

I watched Floyd extract what appeared to be a portobello mushroom from his bag. An actual portobello mushroom, but painted bright red with large white spots.

What. The. Fuck?

"Vinnie!" Floyd bellowed, cutting through the engine noise. "This i-i-is *Mario Kart!*"

He hurled the mushroom through the air with surprising accuracy, landing it directly in Vinnie's lap.

"P-p-punch it!" Floyd shouted at me.

I mashed the gas pedal, our kart surging forward just as Vinnie looked down to see the mushroom sitting in his lap. For a moment, confusion flickered across his face. Then understanding dawned like a Nintendo sunrise.

"Dash mushroom!" Vinnie yelled, his voice transforming from panic to pure joy.

His kart shot forward as he finally committed to the gas pedal, and I watched my brother's entire demeanor change in real time. The fear melted away, replaced by the confidence of someone who knew exactly what he was doing.

"This is Mario Kart!" he shouted, as I watched Vinnie aggressively steer into the next curve, making my heart stop and my pride soar simultaneously.

Floyd was beaming beside me. "I knew it would work," he said with satisfaction. "S-s-sometimes you just need-need the right power-up."

What followed was absolute and utterly enjoyable mayhem.

Within two laps, Vinnie had transformed from the slowest driver on the track to one of the most aggressive. He was darting between other karts with video game precision, taking corners at speeds that seemed impossible for someone who'd been terrified five minutes earlier, and hitting more karts than he'd ever admit.

That's when Floyd reached into his bag again.

"Banan-na-nana time," he announced with wicked glee, producing an actual banana and peeling it half-way.

He tossed the banana peel directly in front of Vinnie's kart.

"Banana!" Vinnie screamed with delight, swerving dramatically to avoid the yellow hazard.

Garth, who'd been circulating behind us with William, suddenly found his path blocked by strategically placed fruit debris. His kart went into a controlled slide as he overcompensated, spinning gracefully into the tire barrier, laughter echoing.

"Banana peel!" William shouted as he swerved out of the way.

The other drivers on the track had started watching our Family's increasingly elaborate interpretation of *Mario Kart*. Floyd continued his assault, pulling out tennis balls that had been painted to resemble green and red turtle shells.

"Gr-green shell!" he announced, lobbing a green turtle shell tennis ball that bounced off the track surface and rolled harmlessly into the infield.

"Red shell incoming!" A red-painted turtle shell tennis ball followed, this one aimed at Garth's kart.

Our gentle giant caught the red shell one-handed without missing a beat, then hurled it back at Floyd. Soon tennis balls were flying in every direction as the Family engaged in full-scale *Mario Kart* warfare at twenty-five miles per hour.

The transformation was complete when other drivers started joining in. A teenager caught one of Floyd's tennis balls and threw it at his friend's kart. An old man, who'd probably never played a video game in his life, found himself dodging banana peels while laughing like a child.

"Rainbow Road!" Vinnie shouted as he took the final turn, somehow managing to make a go-kart track sound like the most magical place on earth.

The chaos continued for another five minutes until Jake appeared trackside, waving a checkered flag.

I drove up next to Vinnie. "Loser does dishes for a week!" I yelled to Vinnie over the roar of engines.

Vinnie gave me a mischievous smile, and I watched him gun it without hesitation to expertly outmaneuver me, cut off Garth and William, slide into the last curve, and beat us all to the finish. As Vinnie crossed the finish line first, the whole go-kart arena exploded in cheers.

"The Vinman can! Losers do dishes!" Vinnie yelled at me like we were kids again.

As we climbed out of our karts, I expected to see Jake annoyed or concerned about the tennis balls and fruit debris scattered across his track. Instead, he was grinning like he'd just witnessed the most entertaining shift of his career.

"Sorry about the mess," I said, though I wasn't really sorry at all.

"Are you kidding? That was epic." Then his expression shifted to apologetic professionalism. "Unfortunately, my manager saw the whole thing, and you're all banned for life."

"Banned for life?" Vinnie asked, though he was still grinning.

Floyd wheeled closer with his now-empty duffel bag. "Worth it," he said simply.

As we loaded back into the van, the lifetime ban became a badge of honor. We'd been treated like typical troublemakers getting kicked out for horseplay, not like people with disabilities who needed special handling. In its own weird way, that ban was the greatest compliment they could have given us.

"Best day ever," Vinnie announced from the passenger seat.

"I understand driving better. It's not scary when you know what game you're playing."

"Just remember," I said, "real roads don't have bumpers, and you can't ram other cars."

"But they have the same situations," Vinnie replied with newfound confidence. "Speed, braking, turning, knowing what's around me. I can do this, Nicholas. I just need practice."

I glanced in the rearview mirror at Floyd, who was still wearing that satisfied expression of someone whose plan had worked perfectly.

As we drove home through the darkening evening, I found myself marveling at what I'd just witnessed. For two hours, we'd been a Family at play. Not a caregiver managing his charges, not people with disabilities struggling to fit into a typical world, just five guys having the time of their lives with go-karts and improvised power-ups.

For just a moment, all the pressure and anxiety about our impossible situation had disappeared. No foreclosure notices, no legal threats, no bank heist. Just pure, uncomplicated joy.

Chapter Thirty-Three

"Nicholas!" William announced without looking up. "The VR environment is complete, so we can begin training protocols."

The next morning, I found William hunched over his laptop at the kitchen table. Empty energy drink cans formed a small pyramid beside him. His usual caffeine monument that attested to the fact that he'd been at this all night.

I poured myself coffee and sat down across from him. "I don't need to train any longer. I know how to walk into a bank."

William's fingers stopped mid-keystroke. He looked up at me like I'd just announced the earth was flat. "What do you mean, you don't need to train!? I've spent weeks coding this environment. The bank layout is perfect down to the millimeter. Every camera angle, every exit route, the exact dimensions of the safety deposit box room..."

"I know, and it's incredible work," I interrupted gently. "I don't think we need it anymore."

"Don't need it?" William's voice climbed an octave. "How can we possibly not need it?"

I took a sip of coffee, choosing my words carefully. "When we started this, we all had this idea in our heads about what a heist would look like. But the actual job is simpler than that. I walk into the bank as Diego Locksley. I go to the safety deposit box room. Floyd's drone picks the locks. I transfer Charity's cash to my bag. I walk out. That's it."

"That's it?" William repeated, his anxiety manifesting in the rapid tapping of his fingers against the table. "Nicholas, you're describing the ideal scenario. What about deviations? Unexpected variables? Environmental factors that could compromise the operation?"

"Like what?"

"Like anything!" William stood up, his agitation forcing him into motion. "What if there's an earthquake? A power outage? What if the bank manager decides to escort you personally? What if another customer enters the safety deposit box room? What if..."

"William..."

"You need to memorize the layout," he continued, his words coming faster. "Every step, every turn, every possible exit. If something goes wrong, and something always goes wrong, you need to know that bank as well as I do. Better than I do. You need to be able to navigate it blind, count your steps to the exits, identify alternate routes..."

Vinnie wandered into the kitchen, drawn by William's raised voice. "What's going on?"

"Nicholas doesn't think he needs to train. He doesn't believe things can go wrong," William said, appealing to Vinnie like a lawyer presenting evidence to a jury.

"But everything always goes wrong," Vinnie said immediately. "That's what happens in movies. Someone has a plan, and then something happens and they have to change the plan."

"Exactly!" William seized on this. "Murphy's Law is very clear: anything that can go wrong, will go wrong. It's a fundamental principle of..."

"That's a law?" Vinnie interrupted, his eyes going wide. "Why would they name it after our family? Nicholas, are we cursed?"

I smiled. "No, Vinnie. Murphy's Law is just an expression. It means that—"

"We're screwed if Nicholas doesn't train properly," William cut in. "Remember that old show I made you watch? *Farscape*? Crichton and D'Argo always had a plan, and what happened?"

"Everything went wrong," Vinnie said quietly, his concern deepening. "Every single time."

"Because they didn't prepare for contingencies," William pressed. "They assumed the simple plan would work, and then...well, it didn't."

"I don't like Murphy's Law," Vinnie said with finality.

"Alright, alright," I held up my hands in surrender. "You've made your point."

William's face brightened immediately. "Outstanding decision."

"While we're on the subject of preparation," I said, an idea forming, "could you code a VR driving simulation for Vinnie? Something that shows him the exact route from here to the bank and back? The most direct path, minimal traffic complications?"

William's eyes lit up. Puzzles were his catnip, and I just sprinkled some in front of him. "A driving simulator customized for Vinnie's specific needs. Brilliant! I could include traffic patterns, pedestrian behavior, stop lights, turn signals..." He was already pulling up his coding software. "I'd need to map the actual route, incorporate realistic physics, maybe add a tutorial system for...”

“Just make it as simple as possible,” I said. “More *Mario Kart*, less *Gran Turismo*.”

“*Mario Kart*,” Vinnie repeated. “I’m really good at *Mario Kart*.”

“You drove off Rainbow Road seventeen times last week,” William pointed out.

“Because you always get the red shells!” Vinnie protested.

“Be that as it may,” William said, turning back to his laptop, “if we don’t want Vinnie driving off the metaphorical Rainbow Road during our getaway, he needs to practice the actual route until it’s muscle memory. You know, the best way to get to Carnegie Hall.”

Vinnie shook his head. “I don’t know how to get there.”

“Practice, practice, practice,” William chimed.

I watched William’s fingers fly across the keyboard, already deep into planning Project Vinnie Kart. William was right. We needed to prepare for everything that could go wrong.

“William,” I said, pulling him back from submerging into his coding. “Thank you. For the VR environment, for pushing back when I was being shortsighted. This is exactly what we need.”

He looked up, momentarily surprised by the gratitude in my voice. “It’s simply logical preparation. Mr. Darcy would say that proper planning prevents poor performance.”

“Mr. Darcy probably never planned a bank heist,” I said.

“No,” William agreed. “But if he had, he would have done it properly. Oh, and you’re welcome, Nicholas.”

“Can I play *Mario Kart* while we wait for the VR stuff? I want to practice my driving skills,” Vinnie asked.

“Rainbow Road?” William asked with obvious trepidation.

“Rainbow Road,” Vinnie confirmed.

As they set up the game console, I found myself hoping that William's obsessive preparation would be enough. That memorizing every step, practicing every turn, planning for every contingency would somehow make things go smoother.

Fuck Murphy.

As Vinnie played *Mario Kart* and William dove back into coding *Vinnie Kart*, I found myself standing outside Garth's closed door. The go-kart adventure had lifted his spirits temporarily. I'd watched him laugh and compete and forget about the legal nightmare waiting for him. But the moment we'd gotten home, he'd retreated back into his room like a wounded animal seeking its den.

Two days now. Two days of closed doors and silence.

I opened the door slowly, making sure to step into Garth's line of sight so I wouldn't startle him.

Garth was sitting on his bed, tablet propped on his knees, watching what appeared to be powerlifting competition footage. Some massive Eastern European guy was attempting a clean and jerk that looked physically impossible. The volume was off, of course. I wondered if that's why he gravitated toward powerlifting videos; the sport needed no audio commentary to understand the struggle, the victory, the defeat written across the lifter's face.

The room smelled like a stale gym locker. Empty protein shake bottles lined his nightstand alongside a plate with sandwich crusts that had probably been there since yesterday morning. At least he was eating.

I moved closer and waited for him to notice me, giving him the courtesy of controlling when the conversation began. When he finally looked up, his eyes were red-rimmed but dry. Whatever crying he'd done, it was finished now.

"Hey, big guy. What are you up to?" I tentatively asked.

Garth set the tablet aside with deliberate care, like he

needed a moment to gather his thoughts before responding. His hands remained still in his lap for what felt like an eternity. Then they began to move.

<Been hiding,> he signed, his movements heavy and slow.

"I noticed. The Family's worried about you." I settled into the chair beside his bed. Garth needed a friend right now, not a caregiver. "Want to talk about what's going on?"

Garth was quiet for a long moment before he signed, *<Conservatorship hearing scares me. Charity wants to make me...less.>*

"Less how?" I asked gently.

<Controls everything. When I work. When I eat. When I exercise. Makes all decisions for me. I become nothing.> Garth's hands paused and clenched into fists before he added, *<No, less than nothing! If declared mentally incompetent, that's how world sees me.>*

The raw honesty of his fear cut straight through me. This wasn't just about losing independence. It was about losing his very identity as a human being capable of making choices.

"That's why we're risking everything to stop her," I said firmly. "Charity and everyone like her will always see people like you and Vinnie and William and Floyd as less than human. You're not, Garth. Look at me."

He looked at me directly as I signed.

<The Family doesn't see you that way. I don't see you that way. And we never will,> I replied, leaning forward. *<You know who else never saw you that way?>*

<Momma,> Garth signed, his expression softening.

"Agnes saw exactly who you are. A good man. Someone worth fighting for."

Garth nodded slowly, then patted the stack of envelopes scattered across his bedspread. *<That's why I've been in here.*

Reading Momma's letters I took from her room. Got caught up in them past couple days.>

I noticed the letters for the first time. Dozens of them, some yellowed with age, others more recent.

Garth's expression grew more serious. *<This is why Charity hates me.>* He gathered up the letters and handed the stack of envelopes to me. *<Read them, Nicholas. Learn for yourself.>*

I accepted the letters, feeling their weight in my hands. Whatever secrets these contained, Garth believed they held the key to understanding Charity's cruelty toward him.

<Love letters,> Garth signed. *<Between Momma and my real father.>*

Real father?!

If Garth and Charity had different fathers, it would explain so much about the family dynamics and Charity's resentment. My mind was already racing through the implications. Two fathers. Two different relationships with Agnes. And somewhere in these letters lay the truth about why Charity had grown up hating her half-brother.

As I left his room and closed the door behind me, I stared down at the bundle of letters in my hands. Agnes Cartwright's elegant handwriting stared back at me from the top envelope, the paper yellowed with age but the ink still clear.

I couldn't wait to read them.

But I also dreaded what I might find.

Chapter Thirty-Four

Rita said I needed to understand driving better, and movies about driving seemed like a good way to learn. Looking through William's movie collection, I picked *Driving Miss Daisy* first because it was about driving and I needed to practice for Heist Club. It did not help the way I wanted it to. Then I found a movie about race car drivers called *Rush* that looked good too.

Nicholas, Garth, and William went to Cost$hare Warehouse to buy groceries and supplies for the house. I was happy they left me and Floyd alone because that meant I got to pick what I watched on TV. No William making everything about Mr. Darcy. No Nicholas making us watch the news. No Garth and wrestling, even though I really liked wrestling. Just me and the remote.

While I watched, I thought about Garth. Nicholas told me he talked to him yesterday about the conservatorship hearing. That made me feel better. Garth needed help, and Nicholas and Garth had always understood each other. Both of them were quiet and strong and thought about things before they talked. Then I heard a buzzing from Floyd's room.

I was worried about Floyd.

Floyd's nightmares were getting worse. They happened more now, and when they happened, they were louder and scarier. I could hear him through the walls sometimes, making noises like he was fighting invisible monsters. Nicholas didn't know how often they were happening because Floyd's room was farther from Nicholas's room than mine was and Floyd was marking green checks, which means Floyd was lying. Something was wrong with Floyd, and I wanted to help him. I didn't know how.

That's when I heard Floyd yell really loud from his room. Not a nightmare yell. An angry yell.

I turned off the TV and went to see what was wrong. Floyd was at his desk with Mozart. Pieces were all over the place. Tiny screws and metal parts were scattered everywhere. Floyd's face was red and he looked really mad.

"What's wrong, Floyd?" I asked.

Floyd spun his wheelchair around to face me, his hands shaking with frustration. "Ev-ev-everything's wrong!" he stammered, gesturing wildly at the scattered drone parts. "I c-c-can't get this st-st-stupid thing to work!"

I looked at the mess on his desk. Mozart looked like someone had taken him apart with a sledgehammer. "Can I help?" I asked.

Floyd rubbed his face with both hands, leaving grease smudges on his cheeks. "N-n-no, Vinnie. This is...this is r-r-really complicated stuff."

"Talking always helps you," I said, sitting on his bed so we were at the same level. "Explain it to me."

Floyd stared at me for a moment, like he was deciding

whether to trust me. Then he sighed and pointed to a small metal device among the scattered parts.

"See that? That's a b-b-bump key gun. It's supposed to p-p-pick locks automatically." His stutter was getting worse as he talked faster. "I used the i-image of the banker's key to fffigure out how many t-t-tumblers a banker's master lock has. Then I m-m-matched it to Diego Locksley's safety deposit box key that Nicholas g-g-got. I used that to extrapolate how many t-t-teeth Charity's customer key would have."

I nodded even though I didn't understand what "extrapolate" meant.

"If I can get the motors in, the bump key gun sh-sh-should be able to pick both locks," Floyd continued, his frustration building. "But I can't get the m-m-mechanism to fit inside Mozart's body and still leave room for the c-c-camera and flight controls."

I could see how scared Floyd was. His hands were shaking and his voice was getting higher as he talked.

"Is this why you've been having nightmares?" I asked. "Because you're stressed about Mozart?"

Floyd went very quiet before he said, "Yes. No. M-m-maybe?" He looked at me really serious and asked quietly, "Vinnie, can you k-k-keep a secret?"

I perked up. I loved secrets. "Yes, Floyd. I'm good at keeping secrets. Rita has no idea she's training a criminal to drive. What's your secret?" I asked.

Floyd closed his eyes and took a deep breath before he admitted, "I stopped t-ta-taking my med-medi-medications."

I didn't know what to say. Nicholas taught me to always take my medications. They were important to keep me healthy. This made no sense.

"Why? That doesn't make sense," I said to Floyd.

Floyd wouldn't look at me. And then I understood. "That's why your nightmares are bad. Why would you do that?" I pressed.

Floyd was quiet a long time. When he began talking, he sounded scared and sad.

"I c-c-can't figure out how to make the b-b-bu-bump key gun wo-wo-work. If I can't solve this, Garth will be ffffforced to live with Charity and we'll all get scattered to the quantum w-w-winds or worse!" Floyd yelled. He was really upset. I was really confused.

"I'm confused, Floyd," I admitted.

Floyd closed his eyes and leaned back in his wheelchair, like Nicholas does when he wants to explain something big to me. After a second, he said, "The man I was before the lightning s-s-strike, he was an engineer. *He* could fix Mozart. But I k-k-eep getting lost in my br-brain fog. It's like r-r-right when I think I'm clos-s-se to figuring it out, it s-s-slips away in my head."

"I know that feeling," I said. "I don't like it either."

Floyd nodded agreement. "I th-th-think the meds were fogging my brain," Floyd said quickly. "Making it harder to r-r-remember who I used to be. The nightmares are c-c-coming back because the meds are leaving my system. But with them gone, I'm st-st-starting to remember more."

That made sense now. It wasn't just stress about Mozart. It was his old memories fighting to come back. "You think if you can remember more, you can fix Mozart," I said to him, now understanding what he really wanted.

Floyd was hurting himself to help us. Just like Nicholas always hurt himself to help us.

"Floyd, that's really brave," I said. "And really stupid."

Floyd laughed, but it sounded sad. "Yeah, I kn-kn-know.

But V-Vinnie, if I can't figure out M-Mo-ozart, the Family gets b-b-broken up forever."

"But can I help you? I want to help," I said.

Floyd's eyes got watery. "You're already h-h-helping, Vinnie. Just by listening. You were right. It h-h-helps to talk about it."

"Tell me more then," I said.

Floyd wiped his eyes and took a deep breath. "The night-mares are ch-ch-changing. I'm starting to remember things when I wake up. N-n-not the blind terror, but r-r-real memories."

"What kind of memories?"

"I remember working in a lab. Building things. Fixing things. It feels like...like I was r-r-really good at it." Floyd's voice got stronger as he talked about the good memories. "And I remember college. Studying late at night. Learning about how things work."

"That sounds nice," I said.

"But then there's always the other one," Floyd said, and his voice got quiet and scared again. "The b-b-baseball game. The count is t-t-th-hree and two, bases loaded. I can see it s-s-so clearly, but I don't un-under-derstand what it means."

I thought about this. "Do you think the baseball memory is when the lightning hit you?"

Floyd nodded slowly. "I th-th-think so. But Vinnie, I've been thinking about why I can't remember more."

"Because the lightning hurt your brain?"

"Yes, but m-m-maybe not the w-wa-ay I thought." Floyd leaned forward, like he was going to tell me a secret. "You kn-know how when you h-h-h-hurt yourself really bad, like when you c-c-cut your finger cooking, you can't rem-remember exactly what the pain felt like after it st-stops hurting?"

I thought about this. "Yeah, it's weird. I know it hurt, but I can't remember how much."

"Our brains do that to p-p-pr-rotect us. What if my b-b-bra-rain is doing the same t-t-thing with my memories? What if I c-c-ca-an't remember because remembering will hurt too m-m-much?"

That made sense to me. "So, if you can handle the pain of remembering, your brain will let you remember?"

"That's my the-the-theory," Floyd said, getting excited. "If I c-can live through the p-pain of rem-remembering what I l-lost, maybe I'll get my full f-f-fa-faculties back. Then I'll be able to ffffix Mozart and s-save our Family."

I felt scared for Floyd. "What if it's too much pain? What if it hurts so bad you can't handle it?"

Floyd was quiet for a long time. When he answered, his voice was very serious. "I d-d-don't know, Vinnie. But for the s-s-sa-ake of our Family, I'm going to ffff-ind out."

"Floyd..."

"Pp-pr-promise me you won't tell Nicholas," Floyd said quickly. "He'll make me t-t-take my medications. He'll try to protect me from the p-p-pain. But I need to hurt to get b-b-bet-better."

I didn't like this. But I understood it. It was Floyd's turn to carry everyone else.

"I promise," I said. "But Floyd? Be careful. We love you."

"I will," Floyd said. "Thanks, Vinnie."

When I left his room, I felt scared and proud at the same time. Scared because Floyd was taking a big risk. Proud because he was being brave for all of us.

As I walked back to the living room, I thought about what Floyd was doing. He was hurting himself because he loved us. That's when I understood something I never really understood before.

Love isn't just the good feelings. Love is also when you hurt so other people don't have to hurt. Love is when you give up things you want so other people can have what they need.

You carry the pain so your Family doesn't have to.

That felt big and sad and beautiful all at the same time.

Chapter Thirty-Five

BANG.

The gunshot punched through the air like a fist through drywall, the sharp crack echoing off the concrete walls of the indoor range. I flinched despite wearing hearing protection, watching Rita's target paper shudder as the bullet tore through its center mass.

Rita lowered her Glock 19 with the practiced ease of someone who'd fired thousands of rounds, her stance relaxed but controlled. She popped the magazine, checked the chamber, her muscle memory making her movements smooth and efficient. She turned to me with that half-smile that said she knew exactly how much I enjoyed watching her work.

"Your turn," she said, gesturing to the lane beside hers.

I looked down at my own target. Or more accurately, at the blown-up poster of Charity Cartwright's face that Rita had printed and attached to the target. Charity's fake smile stared back at me, all teeth and cold calculation, blown up to nearly life-size and stapled over the standard silhouette.

"This is incredibly therapeutic," I admitted, raising Rita's spare nine-millimeter and trying to remember everything she'd taught me about grip and sight alignment.

BANG.

My shot went wide, punching a hole somewhere in Charity's left shoulder. Not fatal, but satisfying enough.

"Breathe," Rita coached from beside me. "You're anticipating the recoil. Squeeze, don't pull."

I lined up another shot, focusing on Charity's smug face, thinking about Garth's terror at the funeral, about the legal summons, about everything Agnes's letters had revealed to me last night.

BANG.

Closer this time. Caught her ear. A piece at a time then.

"Better," Rita said. She was reloading her own weapon, sliding a fresh magazine home with a decisive click. "So, tell me about these letters. You said you stayed up all night reading them?"

I lowered my weapon, keeping it pointed downrange like she'd taught me. "They're love letters. Between Agnes and a man named Gideon. Garth's biological father."

Rita raised her Glock and fired three rapid shots—BANG BANG BANG—all center mass on her target. When she spoke, her voice was conversational, as if we were discussing weekend plans instead of organized crime and murder. "Gideon. Not Thomas Cartwright?"

"No. Gideon Gallagher was Thomas's number two. His capo." I raised my weapon again, lined up another shot at Charity's paper face. "They called him The Gun. He was Thomas's enforcer, the man he trusted to handle his dirtiest work. Kind of like King Arthur, Guinevere, and Lancelot, except this story doesn't end with noble sacrifice and Camelot falling. This one ends with murder and revenge."

BANG.

I caught Charity's other shoulder. I was getting closer.

"Start from the beginning," Rita said. "Give me the whole telenovela."

"Agnes was married to Thomas Cartwright first. Charity's father. By all accounts, it was an arranged marriage. Old money consolidating with older money, that kind of thing." I paused to reload, my fingers clumsy compared to Rita's. "What I didn't know...what Garth didn't know, was that Thomas was deep in organized crime. The Cartwrights didn't make their fortune through legitimate business; they were mob. Thomas bought up banks specifically to launder money for himself and other criminal families."

Rita's expression didn't change, but I saw her eyes narrow slightly. "The Cartwright Foundation started as a money laundering operation?"

"Essentially." I raised my weapon again, but didn't fire yet. "Agnes was the classic mob wife back then. A regular Carmela Soprano. She knew what Thomas did, benefited from it, but stayed willfully ignorant of the details. That is, until she met Gideon."

BANG BANG.

Rita fired twice more, both shots devastatingly precise. "Let me guess. Gideon was different. Noble. Everything Thomas wasn't."

"According to the letters, yes. As noble as a criminal can be. He was Thomas's most trusted man, his Lancelot. And Agnes fell in love with him." I finally took my shot, catching Charity somewhere near her collarbone. "They had an affair. Agnes got pregnant with Garth. And for a while, they thought they might actually get away with it."

"But Thomas found out," Rita finished.

"He found out." I lowered my weapon, the weight of the story making it hard to keep my arms steady. "He had Gideon murdered. Just...disappeared him. The letters stop abruptly right after Agnes tells Gideon about Garth's first words, his first steps. The next letter in the stack isn't from Agnes to Gideon. It's from a private investigator confirming Gideon's death."

Rita was quiet for a moment, methodically loading another magazine. When she spoke, the warmth had drained from her voice. Professional. Detached. "So, Agnes had her husband killed."

"Not immediately. She was patient." I set my gun down on the shelf in front of me, no longer interested in shooting Charity's face. "According to what I pieced together from the later letters—letters she wrote but never sent to Gideon, like she was still talking to him beyond the grave—Agnes became Thomas's partner in the business for the first time. Learned everything. Made herself indispensable. And then, years later, Thomas...disappeared. No body. No evidence. Just gone."

"Agnes took over the operation," Rita said, not a question.

"She took his everything. But here's where it gets interesting. Agnes didn't just inherit a criminal empire and keep running it. She legitimized everything. Took the dirty money operation and transformed it into something that catered to the obscenely wealthy. Hedge funds, market manipulation, the kind of financial crime that's technically legal if you have enough lawyers and political connections." I finally met Rita's eyes. "She became everything Thomas was, but smarter. Cleaner. More dangerous because she operated in the light instead of the shadows."

BANG.

Rita's shot took out one of Charity's paper eyes. "And Charity knows all of this?"

"She knows Garth isn't Thomas's biological son. She knows her father loved her and hated Garth, probably suspected the truth even if Thomas never confronted Agnes about it. And when Thomas disappeared, Charity blamed Garth for 'making Daddy leave'." I made air quotes with my fingers, the gesture feeling inadequate for childhood trauma and inherited hatred.

"Jesus Christ." Rita lined up another shot. "So, Charity's spent her whole life hating her half-brother for her mother's choices. For being the living proof that her mother betrayed her father."

"And for being disabled," I added quietly. "Don't forget that part. Charity sees Garth as defective. Less than human."

BANG BANG BANG.

Three shots, rapid fire, obliterating Charity's other eye and most of her nose. Rita's jaw was tight, her movements controlled but aggressive.

"You know what the worst part is?" I continued, needing to finish the story even though every word felt like swallowing glass. "The last few letters before Gideon disappeared, they're Agnes telling him about Garth. About how strong he is, how gentle. How much Gideon would love his son if he could meet him. She was so full of hope, Rita. She thought maybe they could all run away together, start over somewhere Thomas couldn't find them."

Rita lowered her weapon, turning to face me fully. "But Gideon was killed before that could happen."

"Yeah. And Agnes became... I don't even know what to call her. A monster? A survivor? A godmother?" I shook my head. "She killed her husband to avenge her lover. She transformed a criminal empire into a 'legitimate' business that probably does just as much damage through legal means. She accumulated more wealth than God. And she used all of it to protect Garth from the half-sister who hated him."

I raised the gun, lined up Charity's forehead in my sights, and squeezed the trigger.

BANG.

Wide left. I still couldn't shoot for shit.

Rita's gaze drifted from her target to my face as she processed the conversation. "Nicholas, can I ask you something?"

"Shoot." I winced at my own word choice. "I mean, yes. Ask."

"Agnes... You and Garth always talked about her like she was a saint. The benevolent benefactor who saved your group home, who believed in your mission, who understood that people with disabilities deserved dignity and independence." Rita's voice was careful, probing. "But this woman you're describing... She had her husband murdered. She ran a criminal empire, even if she eventually legitimized it. Does that change how you see her?"

I was quiet for a long moment, really thinking about the question. Did it change how I saw Agnes? Should it?

"You know what's funny?" I finally said, raising my weapon for another shot. "I keep thinking about this movie Vinnie and I love. *The Dark Knight*. You remember the ending?"

"The ferry scene," Rita said immediately. "Two boats, each with a detonator to blow up the other boat. One full of civilians, one full of prisoners. The Joker makes the people choose who dies."

"Exactly." BANG. Another miss, this one not even close to Charity's face. "And in Christopher Nolan's version, neither boat pushes the button. The civilians don't kill the prisoners. The prisoners don't kill the civilians. Nolan's saying that when pushed to the brink, humanity chooses to be good. That we're inherently decent, even when we're terrified."

Rita made a sound that might have been a laugh or a scoff, I couldn't tell which. "You're about to tell me you agree?"

"I think Nolan's full of shit," I said, surprising myself with the vehemence in my voice. "Or maybe not full of shit, but...idealistic in a way that feels naive now. Agnes wasn't inherently good or evil. She was a person who did terrible things for reasons she convinced herself were justified. She loved Gideon, so murdering Thomas became acceptable. She loved Garth, so building a financial empire through morally questionable means became necessary."

"That's not how you usually think," Rita observed, ejecting her magazine and loading a fresh one.

"No, it's not. I want to believe people are basically good. That given the choice, they'll do the right thing. But..." I gestured at Charity's bullet-riddled face on my target. "Agnes did monstrous things. And she did them all for love. Is she a monster or a saint? Can she be both?"

Rita raised her Glock, lined up her shot, and spoke without looking at me. "The ones who seem like saints are usually just better at hiding their sins. Agnes did what she thought she had to do to protect what was hers. That doesn't make her good or evil. It just makes her human."

BANG.

Right between the eyes. Perfect shot. Charity's forehead exploded with the impact, the paper target shredding where the bullet passed through.

"There," Rita said with satisfaction, lowering her Glock.

Chapter Thirty-Six

"Vinman, you are a culinary magician," Rita said, taking another bite of coq au vin. "Seriously, you could charge forty dollars a plate for this at a restaurant."

Vinnie beamed from across the table, his pride evident in the way he sat up straighter. "Mom's recipe. You have to brown the chicken first, get those brown bits stuck to the bottom of the pot, then deglaze with wine. That's where all the flavor comes from. Though Nicholas's is vegetarian, so no chicken to brown, no flavor."

I laughed as I took a bite of my vegetarian au vin, "Still good though. Thanks for making a separate version for me."

"Fond," William said. "That's the caramelized bits that stick to the pan, they're called fond."

"Fond. Weird word," Garth said aloud.

I smiled, feeling the pleasant warmth of a good meal with people I loved. The shooting range had been cathartic, and now this. Rita fitting seamlessly into our Family dinner, everyone relaxed and happy. Vinnie's cooking working its usual magic.

"How's the driving practice going, Vinnie?" Rita said, "I

haven't had time to take you out again this week, but I hope you're still practicing."

"It's going really good!" Vinnie said enthusiastically. "I've been practicing every day. William's been helping too."

"Oh, yes," William said excitedly as he had Rita's full attention which he loved. "I've built a driving program. We're calling it *Vinnie Kart*. It simulates every aspect of driving and will help Vinnie practice the route to—" He stopped abruptly, his mouth snapping shut.

Here we go.

Rita waited, her expression open and curious. "What route?"

William stared at his plate, clearly struggling with how to finish that sentence. The silence stretched uncomfortably as everyone at the table watched him squirm.

"You can't leave me hanging like that, William. A route where?" Rita asked playfully.

William looked directly at her, tone grave: "Lawyer."

I had just taken a sip of water when the word hit my brain and I inhaled sharply, sending water down the wrong pipe. I coughed violently, my eyes watering as I tried to get air back into my lungs.

What the fuck, William?

Rita patted my back with concern. "You okay, Nicky?"

"Fine," I managed between coughs. "Wrong pipe."

But Rita's attention was already back on William, a mixture of amusement and confusion playing across her face. "Did you just say 'lawyer'?"

William looked utterly panicked now, clearly realizing he'd made some kind of mistake but not knowing how to fix it.

Floyd jumped in quickly. "It's a j-joke William started doing after a *CSI* mar-mar-marathon. You know, like when you're in tr-trouble in those shows, the only word you should say to a c-c-op like yourself is 'lawyer.' It's f-funny."

Rita laughed, clearly charmed by what she thought was our usual Family weirdness. "Very *Law & Order* of you, William."

I felt my pulse start to race. This was bad. And about to get worse.

Rita turned to Garth, who'd been quietly eating his chicken. "How about you, Garth? How's work been treating you?"

Garth looked up, chewing thoughtfully before swallowing. "Good. Busy."

"Yeah? What's been keeping you busy?" Rita asked conversationally.

"Lots of lifting. Lots of deliveries." Garth's expression shifted the moment the word left his mouth, realization dawning that he'd said something he shouldn't have.

"Deliveries?" Rita's voice carried genuine curiosity, asking the very question that was now rattling around in my brain. "I thought you collected shopping carts at Cost$hare?"

Garth's eyes darted to Vinnie, who gave the slightest headshake. Garth nodded once and turned back to Rita.

"Lawyer," Garth said firmly.

I choked on nothing, my throat seizing up as panic flooded through me. I coughed again, harder this time, trying to cover my reaction. What the fuck had Vinnie and Garth been up to? Deliveries? Clearly, I needed to do some interrogations of my own after this disastrous dinner.

Floyd laughed nervously and motioned for everyone else to laugh too. The whole Family started to fake giggle and then the fake giggles became real and infectious. "G-good one, Garth," Floyd said to cover.

Rita turned her attention to Floyd, "What about you,

Floyd? What drone have you been working on lately? Wait, I know the answer. 'Lawyer.'"

"No, it would be 'law-law-lawyer.'"

The whole table laughed at Floyd's self-deprecating joke. Before the laughter stopped, I took the opportunity to change the subject, so Rita wouldn't start thinking about how weird everyone was being.

"Since everyone here has lawyered up apparently, maybe we should ask you some questions, Rita. How's the task force going? Any progress on the Happy Face Killers?"

Rita's laughter finally died as her expression shifted to frustration.

"Nothing concrete yet," she said. "These guys are ghosts. They hit four banks in three months, kill someone at each robbery, then disappear without a trace."

The table went quiet. I felt my shoulders sag with relief that we'd successfully changed the subject.

"That's...horrible," Vinnie said quietly.

"It's calculated," Rita corrected. "These aren't crimes of passion or desperation. This is strategic terrorism. They kill one person at every robbery, completely random, specifically to make everyone else comply. And it works. Every witness we've interviewed says the same thing. Once someone dies, everyone else does exactly what they're told."

"How do they get away so cleanly?" I asked. "No forensic evidence at all?"

"They cut the power in a one-block radius before they hit the bank," Rita explained. "Kills the security cameras, throws everything into chaos, makes it impossible to track their movements. By the time power's restored and we arrive on scene, they're long gone."

"Jesus," I muttered.

"And the masks," Rita continued. "They always wear these

cheap happy face masks, the kind you can buy at any party store for two dollars. Makes them memorable but completely anonymous at the same time. Every witness remembers the masks. No one can describe the people wearing them."

"That's actually quite clever," William observed. "Create a distinctive visual signature that ultimately reveals nothing about one's true identity."

"It's psychotic," Rita said flatly. "And effective. The commissioner is chomping at the bit to bring these bastards down, but we've got nothing. No leads, no suspects, no idea when or where they'll strike next."

"Anyway," Rita said after a moment, visibly shaking off the dark mood, "enough work talk. This was supposed to be a nice dinner." She smiled at Vinnie. "The chicken really was amazing."

"Thanks, Rita," Vinnie said.

As we finished eating and the Family began clearing dishes, Rita leaned close to me, her breath warm against my ear. "Let's make it an early night," she whispered, her hand finding mine under the table.

I felt my pulse quicken. "Yeah?"

"Yeah." Her voice was low, playful. "It's been a long week."

I glanced at the Family, who were busy loading the dishwasher. "They're supposed to have movie night."

"They can do that without you," Rita said, her hand sliding up my thigh. "Come on, Nicky," she said seductively.

"Movie night!" William announced from the living room. "What shall we watch?"

"You guys pick," I called back, standing and pulling Rita up with me. "I'm taking the night off."

"Taking the night off?" Floyd repeated, grinning. "Is th-that what we're calling it now?"

"Shut up, Floyd," I said, but I was smiling.

As Rita and I headed toward my bedroom, I could hear the Family's debate starting.

"*Pride and Prejudice*," William said.

"You watched that yesterday!" Vinnie protested.

Rita laughed as we closed my bedroom door. "Your Family is insane." And then she was kissing me.

But in the back of my mind, even as Rita's hands found the button of my jeans, I couldn't quite shake the image of her processing the Family's strange behavior.

She'd let it go tonight, buying Floyd's lawyer joke cover.

But Rita never really let anything go.

She just waited for the right moment to circle back.

And I had no idea that she'd been in my bedroom earlier, while I was in the living room.

No idea that she'd already found exactly what she was looking for...

Chapter Thirty-Seven

"Ready, Nicholas?" William asked. I could hear it in his voice—that blend of excitement and anxiety that meant he was about to be insufferable.

The VR headset felt heavier than it should have as I positioned it over my eyes, the foam padding pressing against my temples with uncomfortable intimacy.

"As I'll ever be," I muttered, adjusting the straps.

The world dissolved into pixels, then reformed as the interior of First National Bank. The detail was staggering. William had meticulously recreated everything from our reconnaissance footage. The marble floors with their subtle veining, the brass fixtures that caught imaginary light, even the slight scuff marks on the teller counter.

"You're standing at the entrance," William narrated. "Take twenty-three steps forward to reach the customer service area."

I began walking, or rather, walking in place while the VR environment scrolled around me. The sensation was disorienting at first, my brain struggling to reconcile the visual information with my stationary body.

"Twenty-one, twenty-two, twenty-three," William counted with obsessive accuracy. "Now turn sixty degrees right and proceed fourteen steps to the safety deposit box entrance."

I followed his instructions, the virtual bank responding to my movements with unsettling realism. The Family had gathered around to watch, though all they could see was me standing in the middle of our living room, waving my arms and shuffling my feet like an idiot.

"This feels ridiculous," I said.

"You look ridiculous," Vinnie confirmed. "Keep going."

The VR bank corridor stretched before me, and I entered the safety deposit box room. It was lined with those familiar metal boxes. Everything was exactly as I remembered it, down to the positioning of box 103055—Charity's box—right next to my rental, 130500.

"Excellent," William said. "Now, let's introduce some variables."

Before I could ask what that meant, the lights in the VR bank suddenly flickered and died, plunging everything into darkness.

"Power outage," William announced. "Emergency lighting only. What do you do?"

"Are you fucking kidding me right now?"

"Language," William chided. "And no, Murphy's Law is very clear: anything that can go wrong, will go wrong. You need to know this bank in the dark."

Dim emergency lighting kicked in, casting everything in sickly green. The shadows were all wrong, the familiar layout suddenly alien and threatening.

"You've already walked this route," William continued. "How many steps from the entrance to your box?"

I tried to recall. "Thirty-seven steps total?" I shuffled forward in the darkness, counting under my breath, my hands reaching out instinctively even though I knew nothing was really there.

"Good," William said. "You're at your box. Now access it and remain calm."

For the next hour, William threw increasingly absurd scenarios at me. Fire drills. Chatty customers in the main lobby. Each time, I had to improvise a response that kept Diego Locksley looking like a legitimate businessman rather than a criminal.

By the time William finally said, "Simulation complete. Overall score: seventy-eight percent," I was sweating despite not having physically exerted myself.

I pulled off the headset, blinking in the sudden brightness of our living room. The Family applauded with varying degrees of enthusiasm.

"Seventy-eight percent?" I asked. "That's passing, right?"

"Barely," William said with his classic bluntness.

"I need a break," I said, handing him the headset.

"Perfect timing," William said. "Vinnie needs to practice *Vinnie Kart* anyway."

As William helped Vinnie into the VR headset, I sat down next to Floyd and we watched Vinnie's first solo run through the virtual streets. He made the first two turns perfectly, then blew right past Jasmine Street. William called out the miss. Vinnie reset and tried again. Same result—he sailed past the intersection like it wasn't there. Three more attempts. Three more misses. William's corrections grew more insistent with each run.

Vinnie's frustrated voice cut through the moment. "I can't find Jasmine Street! William, where is it?"

William's frustrated sigh was audible. "I've shown you three times, Vinnie. You take a left going south onto Jasmine Street, then—"

"I don't know which way is south!" Vinnie protested, the VR headset still covering his eyes.

I moved closer and could see what Vinnie was seeing reflected on William's laptop screen. The *Vinnie Kart* interface had a clean, minimalist design. A small compass in the corner showing N-S-E-W. A street sign reading "Jasmine Street" with an arrow pointing left. A text overlay that read "Turn LEFT (South) onto Jasmine Street."

All information that made perfect sense to William's logical, organized mind.

All information that was completely meaningless to Vinnie.

"It intersects with High Street," William explained with strained patience, pointing at the map on his screen. "We've driven past it dozens of times."

Vinnie pulled the headset up to his forehead, squinting at the laptop. "But I've never seen a street sign that says Jasmine Street," he insisted, his confusion genuine.

I watched Vinnie stare at the interface—at the compass rose he couldn't interpret, at the street signs that held no meaning for him, at the directional arrows that might as well have been hieroglyphics. His eyes darted across the screen, searching for something familiar, something he could anchor himself to. But William had built the simulator the way he himself saw the world: logical, sequential, based on abstract concepts like cardinal directions and municipal planning.

"William," I said carefully. "Jasmine and High. Where exactly do they intersect?"

"At the 7-Eleven," William said immediately. "The one with the—"

"The broken window!" Vinnie suddenly exclaimed, pulling off the VR headset completely. "The Seven-Eleven with the broken window that they never fix! I know exactly where that is! It's right past the Popeye's where we get fried chicken!"

William and I looked at each other, understanding dawning simultaneously.

"Oh," William said softly. "*Oh.*"

"Landmarks," I said. "He navigates by landmarks, not street names."

Vinnie nodded enthusiastically. "I don't know street names. I know places. Like, there's the gas station with the really tall sign. And the house with the weird purple mailbox. And that pizza place that always smells like garlic even from outside."

William was already pulling up the *Vinnie Kart* code on his laptop, his fingers flying across the keyboard. "I can fix this. I can add visual landmarks, highlight the places Vinnie actually remembers..."

"We should walk through it together," I suggested. "The whole route. Have Vinnie identify every landmark he uses to orient himself."

For the next hour, the three of us sat around William's laptop, virtually driving the route from our house to First National Bank and back. Vinnie called out every landmark, every detail that stuck in his memory. The peculiar things that would never appear on any map but that made perfect sense to him.

"There's the church with the really pointy roof."

"The Mexican restaurant with the giant sombrero sign."

"That corner where there's always a guy selling flowers."

William coded frantically, adding each landmark to *Vinnie Kart*, highlighting them with glowing markers that Vinnie could easily spot. By the time we finished, the driving simulator looked less like a navigation tool and more like a treasure map, each landmark shining like a beacon guiding Vinnie home.

"Try it now," William said, handing the VR headset back to Vinnie.

Vinnie put it on, and this time, something magical

happened. His movements became fluid, confident. He navigated the route without hesitation, calling out landmarks as he passed them.

"Broken window 7-Eleven, turning left... Purple mailbox house, staying straight... Pointy church, turning right..."

He completed the entire route—to the bank and back—without a single wrong turn.

When he pulled off the headset, he was grinning. "I did it! I can drive there!"

"The Vinman can," I confirmed, feeling hope stirring slightly in the back of my mind despite Floyd's earlier confession of failure.

Garth had been watching quietly from his recliner, but now he sat forward. "I have idea," he said carefully. "For getaway."

We all turned to look at him.

"William said Winter Avenue," Garth continued, "the one-way streets. Block Winter Avenue while Nicholas is inside, police have to go around. Longer route. More time for us. For Murphy's Law."

William pulled up a street map, studying it. "He's right. If Winter Avenue is blocked, emergency vehicles would have to detour approximately 1.2 miles to reach the bank from the nearest precinct. That's an additional three to five minutes of response time."

"How do we block a street?" Vinnie asked.

Garth smiled, a rare expression these days. "I work at Cost$hare. Orange cones. Hard hat. Safety vest. I look like construction worker. Nobody questions construction."

"That's..." William paused to process the permutation. "That'll work nicely."

"I have my moments," Garth said with simple pride.

"But you'd n-n-need to position yourself before Nicholas enters the b-b-bank."

"There's one more thing," I said, remembering a detail I'd been working on. "We need to disguise the van. I already stole a license plate from the mall parking garage last week. But we need something that makes the van look different going to the bank than coming back."

"Like what?" Vinnie asked.

"Magnetic decals," I said. "Something innocuous that can be peeled off after the heist. I was thinking maybe a plumbing company or—"

"Meals on Wheels," Vinnie interrupted suddenly.

We all looked at him.

"It will work," Vinnie said, his excitement building. "A Meals on Wheels van. Who's going to look twice at a van delivering food to old people?"

"Meals on Wheels it is," I said, making a mental note to order the magnetic decals. "We put them on before we leave, take them off after we pick up. Change the plates back."

"Murphy's Meals on Wheels," Vinnie added with a grin. "Because our last name is Murphy."

"Let's maybe not put our actual name on the fake business," I said.

"Right. Good point."

Floyd had been quiet through this exchange but then he asked, "W-William, can you s-s-show me a twenty-five-m-m-meter radius from the s-s-safety deposit box room?"

William overlayed a marker clearly delineating twenty-five meters from the safety deposit box room on the map we were all studying.

"Why?" I asked Floyd.

Floyd looked at me to explain, "All the extra w-w-weight

from the b-bump key mechanism, plus miniaturizing every-thing to fit... M-M-Mozart's range is twenty-five meters. And that's if there's no in-interference." Floyd studied the map a moment. "I c-c-can't be in the get-getaway van. I'll have to be on the sidewalk outside the bank."

"Alright," I said, looking around at the Family. "So, let's review. I go into the bank as Diego Locksley. Floyd operates Mozart remotely and picks Charity's locks. I transfer the money to my bag and exit. Vinnie drives the van with the Meals on Wheels decals and stolen plates, picks me up and we meet two blocks away in the alley with no cameras. We remove the decals, change the plates back, drive home."

"Don't forget my traffic diversion," Garth added. "I block Winter Avenue while you're inside. Police have to go long way, if they come."

"Right. Garth provides our escape buffer." I ran my hand through my hair, trying to see the holes in the plan, the places where Murphy's Law would inevitably fuck us. "What are we missing?"

"Contingencies," William said immediately. "What if Floyd loses connection to Mozart? What if the locks don't open? What if—"

"William," I interrupted gently. "We've planned for the contingencies. If shit hits the fan, we go home and try again another day."

"But—"

"We can't plan for everything," I said, surprising myself with the words. "At some point, we have to trust ourselves and execute. We've trained. We've prepared. We're as ready as we're going to be."

The room fell quiet.

"When?" Vinnie finally asked. "When do we do it?"

"Soon," I said. "But not yet. We need to run through everything a few more times. Make sure we're all comfortable with
our roles. And Floyd needs time to finish Mozart."

Chapter Thirty-Eight

Thursday afternoon sunlight filtered through our kitchen windows as I prepared Floyd's weekly setup. With everything going on the last couple of months, we'd been caught flat-footed a few times when Grace arrived for her weekly visits. Not this week. This week we were prepared and all Heist Club paraphernalia had been hidden away.

Grace would arrive any minute. Floyd watched from the kitchen table as I wiped it down one last time to make sure he and Grace had a clean surface to play *Magic: The Gathering*.

The doorbell rang with its familiar two-note chime.

Grace stood on our porch, her fingers fidgeted with the cross on her necklace, most likely praying to God for a last-minute miracle. The late afternoon light caught the grey streaks in her brown hair, and I found myself noticing how much older she looked than when these visits first started. Five years of hope deferred had a way of aging people.

"Grace," I said, stepping aside. "Come on in."

"Thanks, Nicholas. How's Floyd been this week?"

"Good. Still no nightmares," I lied. We couldn't afford Grace looking at Floyd and the Family too closely right now, and if she knew about Floyd's worsening nightmares, she'd insist on getting involved.

I led her to the kitchen, where Floyd was waiting. He looked up as we entered, his eyes widened in surprise, but then his face changed to an expression of polite curiosity.

Strange.

"Floyd," I said gently, "Grace is here for your weekly *Magic* game."

Floyd studied her face and predictably asked, "Have we...p-p-played before?"

"Yes," Grace said, settling into her chair with the ease of long practice. "Every week. You're quite good at it."

I took my usual observation post as Grace began unpacking her decks. She explained the basic rules as she always did. Floyd absorbed the information like he was hearing it for the first time, which, from his perspective, he was. But there was something different today. A sharpness to his attention that I couldn't quite place. He kept smiling at Grace and asked pointed questions about the gameplay and rules, which prolonged her explanations. She talked, and he listened.

They played through their first game, and their pain fractal began anew.

"You always did have a gift for seeing three moves ahead," she said softly.

Floyd tilted his head. "Did I?"

"You..." Grace caught herself, that familiar pain flickering across her face before she pushed it away. "You're very good at strategy games."

Floyd gathered up the *Magic* cards and set up another game. "Grace, d-d-do you have a p-pa-partner? Ch-children?" Floyd asked.

Grace stopped shuffling her deck. She was quiet for a moment trying to decide how best to answer without triggering Floyd's memory reset. This was new; Floyd had never inquired about Grace's life before. Usually, he just kept the conversation to the game and its rules. Finally, Grace said, "No, I always wanted to have children and start a family, but I've been waiting for the man I love to come back to me."

"Th-th-that's too bad. You deserve to be h-h-happy and l-live a fffull life," Floyd said as he touched the back of Grace's hand. Floyd was about to move his hand away, when Grace took his hand in hers and held it tight.

"That's a lovely thing to say, Floyd. Thank you, but I'm happy to wait; he's worth waiting for." I saw Grace squeeze Floyd's hand, and he squeezed back. Then Grace returned to shuffling, and they started another game. As they continued playing, Floyd kept watching Grace and smiling. These were new and different behaviors for Floyd and Grace, and I hoped that maybe, for once, they'd leave on a happy note this time.

Grace looked at her watch and realized they'd played for almost two hours. "Wow," she said, "we haven't played this long in years."

"Time never ma-ma-matters when you're having f-f-f-un." Floyd smiled at her. "Cut m-m-e." Grace cut Floyd's deck as she set up for the fifth game. It was a raucous game with several game resets and board wipes. Floyd and Grace laughed and screamed at each other as the game twisted and turned. It was so much fun watching them have a good time. Then, I saw Floyd make an error in strategy that allowed Grace to pummel him for thirty points in one turn. They both laughed as she did a happy little victory dance.

Floyd said, "You know I l-l-let you win."

Grace countered, "Sure, you did." They both continued to giggle as they gathered up their cards. As Grace shuffled her deck, I saw her expression change. That look of dogged determination I'd learned to recognize. The look that said she was going to push, going to try one more time to break through the wall between Floyd's present and past. I couldn't blame her this time. Floyd was so open and warm, perhaps this was the day she'd break through.

"Do you remember the Chaos Orb game?" Grace asked, her voice carefully casual.

Floyd's hands paused over his cards. "Ch-Chaos Orb?"

Here we go. She's flying too close to the sun again.

"I had this white weenie deck," Grace continued, leaning forward slightly. "All these little soldier creatures that would swarm the battlefield. And you were about to lose, but then you had this one card. Chaos Orb. You could throw it and whatever cards it landed on would be destroyed."

Floyd went very still.

His hands stopped moving mid-shuffle, cards frozen between his fingers. His eyes lost focus, that same expression I'd learned to recognize over the years. Grace's face was caught between hope and dread. We'd seen this pattern before, the moment where Floyd briefly touched something, then lost it again.

"Floyd?" I said carefully, taking a half-step forward.

But Floyd's eyes were refocusing. Not with the usual confusion that followed his resets, but with something else entirely. Something that made my breath catch.

Recognition.

Floyd stared at Grace with an intensity that was almost uncomfortable to witness. His mouth opened slightly, as if he was trying to form words... Then he found them.

"Grace," he said. "Your name is...Grace McCallister."

No stutter. The words came out smooth, clear, certain.

Grace's hands flew to her mouth. "Floyd? Do you... Do you remember me?"

I felt hope surge despite every instinct I'd developed to suppress it. This was different. This was finally happening.

Grace reached across the table, tears already streaming down her face. "Oh my God. Floyd, I've been waiting so long for you. I love you so much." Floyd's expression softened for a moment then—

"GET OUT!"

The words exploded from Floyd with such violence that both Grace and I flinched backward. His face had transformed from recognition to something feral, something I'd never seen on him before.

"Floyd, what—" Grace started, but Floyd was already moving.

"Get out! Get out of my house!" Floyd's voice cracked with rage, his hands working the wheelchair controls to advance on her. "Leave me alone! I never want to see you again! Do you hear me? I never want to see you!"

Grace stood and stumbled backward, her chair clattering to the floor. "Floyd, please, I'm—"

I was frozen, my mind unable to process what I was witnessing. This wasn't a reset. This wasn't confusion. This was deliberate, targeted, unbridled fury.

Grace was backing toward the door now, her face a mask of terror and heartbreak. "I don't understand," she sobbed. "Floyd, I love you, I've been—"

"I don't care! I hate you! I've always hated you! You should have let me die! I'm dead! Nothing! GET OUT!" Floyd roared, still chasing her with his wheelchair. "Leave! Go! Never come back! I hate you! I don't want to see you ever again!"

Grace hit the front door with her back, fumbling for the

handle. Floyd's wheelchair slammed to a stop, inches from her, and for a terrible moment I thought he might actually try to strike her.

"Floyd!" I finally found my voice, moving forward. "Stop this right now!"

But Grace was already wrenching the door open, fleeing onto the porch. Running from the wreckage Floyd had just made of her heart. I heard her footsteps on the driveway.

"Nicholas," Vinnie's voice came from behind me, small and scared. "What's happening?"

I didn't answer. I was already moving toward the door, chasing after Grace. Whatever the fuck had just happened to Floyd, I needed to—

Grace was at her car, keys shaking in her hand as she tried to unlock it. Her entire body was trembling.

"Grace, wait," I called, jogging down the driveway. "Please, just— I need to understand what happened in there."

"Don't." The word came out sharp. She finally got the key in the lock.

"He's been having episodes, his memory's been fragmenting, this wasn't—"

"Nicholas." She turned to face me, and I saw something I'd never seen in her before. Not heartbreak. Not even anger. Resignation. "Do you know what the worst part of loving someone with a brain injury is?"

I didn't answer.

"It's not that they don't remember you. It's not even that they might never remember." Her voice was steady now, almost clinical. "It's that you can't tell the difference between the injury talking and the person talking. When Floyd said he hates me, when he said he's always hated me—was that the lightning? Or was that him?"

"Grace, that wasn't—"

"You don't know." She cut me off. "And neither do I. I can't spend the rest of my life wondering if the man I loved is trapped in there hating me, or if he's just gone and what's left is..." She gestured helplessly toward the house. "That."

"He doesn't hate you."

"Then what was that?" Grace's composure cracked slightly. "Because in there? In that moment? He knew exactly who I was, Nicholas. He spoke my full name. No stutter. No confusion. He *knew* me. And he chose that."

I opened my mouth but had nothing to say. Because she was right. Floyd had recognized her. Had spoken clearly. Had made a choice.

"I'm so stupid. I thought, well, I don't know what I thought. That love conquers all? I've been waiting for him to come back," Grace said quietly. She shook her head. "I can't do this anymore."

"Grace—"

"I'm done." She got in the car. "I'm sorry, Nicholas. I know you care about him. But I'm done waiting for someone who either can't come back or doesn't want to. The man I know is simply gone."

She closed the door and the car pulled away, too fast, tires squealing slightly on the pavement. I stood in the driveway and watched her go. Just before she turned the corner, brake lights flared red. She was stopping, maybe changing her mind, maybe—

Then the lights went out and she was gone.

It was the last time I ever saw Grace McCallister.

When I walked back inside, I found Floyd's wheelchair overturned in the middle of the living room floor. He must have thrashed so violently after I'd left that he'd toppled the entire thing. He lay sprawled on the carpet, his paralyzed legs twisted at awkward angles, his upper body curled into itself.

He was weeping.

Not the quiet tears I'd seen before during his episodes. This was raw, guttural sobbing. The sound of something fundamental breaking inside a person.

"It's gone," Floyd gasped between sobs. "It's never coming back. It's gone."

The Family stood frozen, none of them knowing what to do. William's stimming had accelerated to the point where he looked like he was about to bounce off the walls. Vinnie was on the verge of tears himself. Even Garth was paralyzed by Floyd's breakdown.

I moved without thinking, kneeling beside Floyd on the carpet.

"Floyd," I said quietly. I carefully unbuckled him from his wheelchair, pulled him away from it as I set the wheelchair upright. Then I gathered Floyd into my arms. His body was rigid with grief, every muscle locked. "I've got you. You're okay."

"It's gone," Floyd repeated, the words coming out in gasps. "Never coming back. It's gone."

I held him, one hand supporting his back, the other cradling his head against my shoulder. He felt smaller somehow, diminished by the emotional storm that was tearing through him.

Around us, the Family remained motionless. I could feel their eyes on us, their collective helplessness filling the room like a physical presence.

This wasn't a medication issue. This wasn't a reset or a confusion spiral.

Something had fundamentally changed in Floyd, and I had no idea what it was or how to fix it.

I held him, his tears soaking into my shirt, his body shaking with each breath. One by one, the Family came down to the floor around us. No one spoke. No one needed to.

We stayed until the shaking stopped.

Chapter Thirty-Nine

I walked into the restaurant kitchen carrying my recipe binder. Today I was going to ask Sous Chef Dave for help with something really important.

I was glad to have to work today. Everything at the house was tense. Floyd remembered his old life and made his wife hate him.

It was a lot.

Sous Chef Dave was at the prep station chopping vegetables. His knife moved so fast I could barely see it. When he saw me, he stopped and smiled.

"Vinman! Right on time," Dave said. "What's up?"

I set my binder down on the counter and took a deep breath. "I need help, Dave. I want to take Celia out on a really special date. Like at the best restaurant in town. I came into some money, and I want to treat her."

Dave wiped his hands on his apron. "The best restaurant in town? That's probably Chez Laurent. French place. Really expensive. You'd need a reservation way ahead though."

My heart sank. Way ahead meant it was too late.

"Wait," Dave said, and I could see him getting an idea. "Chef's going on vacation this week. Leaving tomorrow. While he's gone, I'm in charge."

"Okay," I said, not understanding what this had to do with Celia.

"Why don't you bring Celia here?" Dave said, getting excited. "Tell her to meet you here at the restaurant. I'll put one of your mom's recipes on the menu as a special. You can surprise her. And Vinnie?" He smiled really big. "You'll cook it."

I felt my whole body get warm. "Really? You'd let me cook? For her? Here in the restaurant?"

"Hell yes, and not just for her, for all our customers," Dave said. "Your mom's recipes are restaurant quality. This is your chance. What do you think?"

I thought about it. Cooking for Celia in a real restaurant. Making one of Mom's recipes. Having real people pay money for my food. This was on my bucket list.

"Yes," I said. "Let's do it."

"Which recipe?" Dave asked.

I opened my binder and flipped through the pages. Mom's handwriting was on every page. I stopped on one that always made me think of her.

"Braised short ribs," I said. "Mom's version with the red wine."

Dave leaned over to look. "Beautiful. You can prep everything ahead, braise it low and slow. The meat falls off the bone. Perfect for a special night."

"When should I tell Celia?" I asked.

"Friday night. Seven o'clock. I'll have the best table ready." Dave put his hand on my shoulder. "This is going to be great, Vinman."

. . .

Friday came fast. I showed up to work early so I could prep everything. Dave already set up my station with all the ingredients.

"Remember," Dave said. "Low and slow. Don't rush."

I followed Mom's recipe exactly. Sear the short ribs until they're brown. Remove them and cook the onions and carrots. Deglaze with the wine and stock. Put the ribs back in. Cover and put in the oven for three hours.

The kitchen smelled amazing. Other cooks kept walking past asking what I was making.

"Braised short ribs," I told them. "My mom's recipe."

At 6:30, Dave came over to check. He lifted the lid on my pot, and the smell made his eyes close. He took a spoon and tasted it.

"Vinman, this is perfect," he said. "Your mom would be so proud."

That made my throat feel tight. I had to look away.

At seven o'clock, I watched from the kitchen as Celia walked in. She was wearing a blue dress that made her look really pretty. Her hair was down and curly.

The server seated her at the best table. It was in the corner with candles. I watched Celia look around. She looked confused about why I wasn't there.

The server said something to her. Probably that I would be late. Celia nodded.

"Ready?" Dave asked me.

I plated the short ribs exactly like Mom used to. The meat arranged just right. The sauce spooned over. The vegetables around the edge. A sprig of thyme on top.

"Go get her, chef," Dave said.

I carried the plate through the doors. My hands shook a little, but I didn't spill. Celia looked up when she saw me and her mouth opened.

"Vinnie? What are you doing?" she asked.

I set the plate down. "I made this for you. It's my mom's braised short ribs. I cooked it myself."

Celia's eyes got really big. Then watery. "You cooked this? For me?"

"For you and for everyone else who orders it tonight," I said. "It's the special tonight. Sous Chef Dave put it on the menu. People are going to pay money for my food."

Celia stood up and hugged me tight. "Vinnie, this is so good! I'm proud of you!"

When she let go, we sat down. The server came over, and Dave had told her what to bring. All the best things. The risotto. The chocolate gâteau for dessert.

"Everything tonight is free," the server said. "From Chef Dave."

We ate and talked and Celia kept saying how good the short ribs were. She took pictures with her phone. She was so happy, it made me happy too.

Between dinner and dessert, I decided to talk about the important thing.

"Celia," I said. "I want to talk about something important."

She put down her fork. "Okay."

"Nicholas and Rita explained sex to me," I said. "About how it works. I understand better now."

Celia's face turned red. "Oh."

"I want to have sex with you," I said. "Because I love you. But I want to make sure you want it too."

Celia took my hand. "Vinnie, I love you too. Sex with you would be amazing, but I can't have sex until I'm married. It's important to my religion. Do you understand?"

I thought about what Nicholas and Rita said about respecting what your partner wants. "Yes. I understand. We aren't ready to get married though."

"No we aren't. Sex can wait until we are ready. Thank you for understanding," Celia said.

"Can I ask you something else?" I said.

"Yes."

"You believe that God is good and takes care of you?"

"Yes," Celia said. "God takes care of us."

"What if someone you loved was trying to hurt you? What if one of your brothers tried to put you in state care? Would you do bad things to stop them?" I asked.

Celia looked confused and scared. "Why are you asking that?"

"Just pretend," I said.

Celia thought for a long time. "I've never been in state care. But I heard stories from others. Bad stories."

"The stories are true," I said. "State care is bad. They hurt me there."

Celia squeezed my hand. "I'm sorry, Vinnie."

"So, if someone was trying to send you there, would you do something bad to stop them?"

Celia was quiet. "No. I would pray. I would ask God to show me what's right." She looked worried. "Vinnie, are you going to state care? Is someone trying to send you away?"

I didn't want to lie. "Maybe. Me and William and Floyd. We might get sent away if we can't fix our problem."

"What problem?" Celia asked.

I remembered the first rule. "I can't tell you. But I wanted to know what you would do. Your opinion is important to me."

Celia squeezed my hand. "Two wrongs don't make a right, Vinnie. Even if someone is hurting you, doing something bad back doesn't make it okay."

I nodded. We talked about this before with Goldilocks. Celia believed doing bad things was always bad.

"Okay," I said and squeezed her hand back.

The server brought the chocolate gâteau, and we ate it together. It was really good. Warm with ice cream. But I was thinking about what Celia said.

When we finished, I said, "I'm sorry we can't have sex tonight. But I finished one of my bucket list things. I cooked in a real restaurant and real people paid money for my food."

Celia smiled. "That's wonderful, Vinnie."

"Since we're waiting for sex, maybe we could make out instead?" I asked.

Celia smiled bigger. "I would like that."

We left, and Celia kissed me in the parking lot. It was a long kiss that made me feel warm and tingly. When she stopped, she said, "Thank you for tonight, Vinnie. It was perfect."

"You're welcome," I said.

I watched her drive away in her ride share. Then I stood there thinking about everything. About God and prayer and doing the right thing. About how Celia believed if she prayed, God would show her the answer.

Maybe that would work for me too?

That night before bed, I knelt down like when I was little and Mom was alive. Mom always made me pray before bed. After she died, I stopped because I was mad at God for taking her.

But tonight, I wanted to try.

"God," I said out loud. "It's me, Vinnie. I know we haven't talked in a long time. I was mad at You for taking my mom. But Celia says You're good and You take care of people."

I closed my eyes and put my hands together.

"I'm confused. I don't know if what we're planning is right or wrong. Charity is trying to hurt Garth. We're going to lose our house and our Family. We have to do this heist to save everyone."

My voice got quieter.

"But Celia says two wrongs don't make a right. She says even if someone is hurting you, doing something bad back doesn't make it okay. I don't know what to do, God. Please show me the answer. Please give me a sign. It would help me a lot."

I waited.

Nothing happened.

And then I waited even more.

More nothing happened.

"Please, God," I said. "I need help. Show me what's right."

I kept my eyes closed and waited for something. A feeling. A voice. A sign. Anything.

But there was nothing. Just quiet.

I opened my eyes and looked around. No signs. No angels. No special feeling.

Nothing.

I felt disappointed. It felt like when Floyd gave me that lottery scratcher for my birthday. I scratched it hoping to win, but I got nothing. A rip-off.

I climbed into bed and stared at the ceiling.

I thought about Celia and how believing in God made her feel safe. How she trusted that if she prayed, the answer would come. I respected that. It was important to her.

But it wasn't working for me.

God didn't answer. He didn't give me a sign. He didn't tell me if doing the heist was right or wrong.

Maybe God was too busy. Maybe He only answered prayers for people like Celia who went to church and did everything right.

Or maybe God wasn't real and Celia just believed because it made her feel better.

I didn't know.

What I did know was that if I wanted something done, I had to do it myself. Nicholas always said that.

We couldn't wait for God to save us.

We had to save ourselves.

I thought about the first rule of Heist Club. You don't talk about Heist Club.

From now on, when I was with Celia, I would follow that rule. I loved her. I respected her beliefs. But I couldn't tell her what we were planning because she would never understand.

Celia lived in a world where God answered prayers and two wrongs didn't make a right.

I lived in a world where my Family was about to get torn apart unless we did something bad to stop it.

Those two worlds couldn't be together.

So, I would keep them separate. With Celia, I would be the Vinnie she knew. The one who cooked her dinner and respected her wishes about waiting for marriage.

With my Family, I would be the Vinnie who helped plan a heist. Their Doug Judy.

And I would never let those two worlds be together.

I rolled over and closed my eyes. Tomorrow I would tell Sous Chef Dave how the date went. Tomorrow I would practice driving with *Vinnie Kart*. Tomorrow I would help the Family get ready.

Tomorrow I would keep being two different Vinnies.

But tonight, I was just tired and sad that God didn't answer.

Then I thought about Mom's short ribs and how happy Celia looked when I brought them to our table.

I fell asleep happy.

Chapter Forty

Yesterday's court-appointed psychologist evaluation had left Garth rattled. I could see it in the way he'd barely touched dinner, in the silence that followed him like a shadow. Two hours of invasive questions designed to build Charity's incompetency case, and now here we were at the Special Olympics, trying to pretend everything was normal.

The parking lot was pandemonium. Families unloaded wheelchairs, athletes in matching team uniforms stretched, volunteers directed traffic with aggressive cheerfulness that only came from too much coffee and not enough sleep.

Rita squeezed my hand as we walked toward the entrance. "I'm excited to see Garth compete. We usually volunteer and have to work."

"He's trained so hard for this," I said. Though whether his head would be in the game after yesterday was another question entirely.

Floyd had stayed home, still wrecked from the Grace situation and throwing himself into Mozart's final construction with single-minded focus. The van felt emptier without him.

Inside, the venue was massive. The Special Olympics took over a college campus with multiple competition areas and families clustering in bleachers. Volunteers in neon vests directed foot traffic like they were landing planes.

William had gone completely silent the moment we entered, his shoulders rigid with tension. When he spoke, his voice had transformed entirely.

"One must navigate such gatherings with considerable discernment," he announced in his full Mr. Darcy register. "The crush of persons assembled here is quite overwhelming to one's sensibilities."

I glanced at him. This was survival mode. The crowd had triggered him so hard he'd disappeared completely into the character.

"Don't worry, William. It'll get better when we find Garth's area and stick to it," I said.

We spotted Garth near the weightlifting platform, his orange Special Olympics shirt stretched tight across his massive shoulders. When he saw us, his face brightened.

"You made it," he said.

"Wouldn't miss it, you know that, big man," I told him. "Where and when are you competing?"

"Third heat, men's heavyweight division. Clean and jerk." Garth gestured to the main platform. "Probably forty-five minutes. Lighter weight classes first."

"We'll be cheering loud enough for Floyd too," Vinnie said.

Rita gave Garth a hug. "Go warm up. We'll find good seats."

As Garth headed toward his coach, I noticed William looking increasingly uncomfortable with the crowd, his fingers starting their anxious tapping against his leg.

William cleared his throat with aristocratic formality. "I

find myself in need of refreshment. Perhaps a beverage to fortify oneself for the proceedings ahead?"

"We'll come with you," Rita said, catching my eye.

The four of us made our way to the concession stand, William maintaining his rigid Mr. Darcy posture as he navigated through the crowd. When we reached the line, he positioned himself with careful dignity, hands clasped behind his back.

"What can I get you?" I asked him.

"A modest refreshment shall suffice. Perhaps water, or if available, tea prepared in a civilized manner, though I harbor doubts regarding the latter in such an establishment."

Vinnie had been scanning the area when he suddenly grabbed my arm, then Rita's. "Look," he whispered, nodding excitedly toward the volunteer station.

A young woman in a volunteer vest was watching William. Maybe mid-twenties, short dark hair, glasses. But it wasn't casual people-watching. Nope, her expression held recognition, understanding, and quite obvious interest.

"William," Rita said quietly, leaning close. "That volunteer. She's checking you out."

William's disbelief echoed in his words. "I beg your pardon?"

"The woman with the glasses," Vinnie added, trying to be subtle and failing completely. "She keeps looking at you."

William glanced at the woman with the glasses, then straightened his posture even more. "It is far more probable that she observes the general assemblage rather than directing her attention toward my person specifically."

"She's definitely looking at you," Rita said.

"Such a notion is most improbable," William replied, his Mr. Darcy voice becoming even more formal under stress. "I possess neither the distinguished bearing nor the social graces that would warrant such—"

"Tell her yourself. She's coming over," Vinnie interrupted.

William's eyes widened slightly as the woman began walking toward our group with obvious purpose.

"Oh, dear," William managed.

Rita and Vinnie both placed hands on William's back and gently but firmly pushed him forward, away from the concession line. He stumbled slightly, then caught himself with as much dignity as he could muster.

The woman in question reached him with a warm smile. "Hi. I'm sorry to interrupt, but I couldn't help noticing..." She paused, choosing her words carefully. "You seem like you might appreciate a quieter spot away from the crowd noise?"

William bowed slightly, actually bowed, his formality reaching new heights. "Your observation demonstrates considerable perspicacity, Miss... I regret I have not yet had the honor of making your acquaintance."

"Sophie," she said, and I caught the flicker of recognition in her eyes. She'd clocked his coping mechanism immediately. "And you are?"

"William," he managed, then added with painful formality, "It is a pleasure to meet you, Miss Sophie, though I confess the circumstances are somewhat irregular given the informality of the setting."

The three of us had taken a subtle step back, giving them space while remaining close enough to watch. Rita squeezed my hand, a small smile playing at her lips. We weren't missing this.

"Would you like to step over there?" Sophie gestured to a less crowded area near the wall. "It's a bit quieter. Easier to have a conversation."

William glanced back at us with barely concealed panic. Rita made a small shooing motion with her hand.

"That would be...most agreeable," William said carefully. "If you are certain it would not impose upon your duties as a volunteer?"

"I'm on break," Sophie assured him.

They moved to the quieter spot, William walking with such careful, formal bearing that he looked like he was attending a state dinner. We followed at a discreet distance, pretending to examine the concession menu while actually watching them intently.

"This is better than movie night," Vinnie whispered.

"Shh," Rita said, though she was grinning.

We couldn't hear everything they were saying, but we could catch fragments. Sophie was doing most of the talking at first, her body language open, encouraging, and she was bouncing from foot to foot, clearly her own stimming routine. William's posture was perfect—hands clasped behind his back, nodding occasionally.

Then Sophie said something in between bounces that made William's formal bearing crack slightly. His hands came forward, gesturing as he responded. The Mr. Darcy accent was still there, but his movements were becoming more his as he started to bounce on his toes a bit.

"She's good," Rita observed quietly. "Look at how he's mirroring her body language. She's made him feel comfortable."

After a few more minutes of conversation, Sophie's expression became more serious. She said something that made William go very still.

"I wish I could hear what she's saying," Vinnie muttered.

Whatever it was, William was listening with complete attention. Then Sophie pulled out her phone. William fumbled for his own phone with less grace than usual, the Mr. Darcy mask slipping as he tried to navigate the exchanging of numbers.

They talked for a few more minutes before Sophie checked her watch and gestured back toward the volunteer station. She said something that made William nod seriously, then she waved at our group, acknowledging that she knew we'd been watching, before bounding away back to her post.

William stood there for a moment, staring at his phone, before turning and walking back to us.

"Well?" Rita asked immediately.

William's formal bearing had softened, though the aristocratic speech patterns remained. "Miss Sophie expressed... She expressed hope that in future encounters, I might feel sufficiently comfortable to introduce her to the authentic William, rather than the mask I employ."

"What did she mean by that?" I asked, though I had a good idea.

William's voice was quieter now. "Miss Sophie explained that she too possesses autism. That she once engaged in similar masking behaviors, attempting to present as neurotypical through considerable effort and emotional expenditure."

He paused, his hands tightening slightly at his sides.

"She described it as exhausting," William continued. "Said she was perpetually drained from the performance of normalcy. But she has ceased such efforts. Now she simply...exists. As herself." He looked at us with something vulnerable in his expression. "She suggested that perhaps the considerable energy I invest in maintaining my façade might be better directed...elsewhere." William's gaze drifted back to Sophie working at the volunteer tent.

Rita reached over and squeezed his shoulder. "What do you think?"

"I think..." William's Mr. Darcy voice wavered. "I think she may possess insight I have not previously considered. Though the prospect of existing without this persona is rather terrifying."

"Did you get her number?" Vinnie asked.

The formality cracked entirely as William actually smiled, a real, awkward William smile. "I did. She suggested we might begin a formal courtship."

"Perhaps you've finally found your Eliza Bennett," Rita said.

William smiled. "Perhaps." And then he gave Rita a look of sorrow and said softly, "I'm sorry, Rita. But it would've never have worked between us. I see that now. I hope I didn't hurt you."

I squeezed Rita's hand so hard to stop her from laughing while simultaneously not making eye contact with her or we'd both lose it. She later confessed she drew blood from biting her tongue so hard. To her credit, she shook her head, and told William she understood. We both walked away as fast as we could for fear of laughing at what was clearly an enchanted moment for William.

And I was grateful I could stop watching William watch Rita.

We made our way back to the bleachers as they were setting up for Garth's heat. William was quieter now, thought-ful. The Mr. Darcy bearing remained, but I noticed something subtle had shifted. Like he was wearing it rather than being consumed by it.

"Sophie is really cool, William, and pretty," Vinnie said as we took our seats.

"Indeed," William replied, then caught himself. "She is...quite remarkable."

By the time we found seats, the weightlifting competition

was about to start. Down on the competition floor, athletes were taking their positions. When they called Garth's name for his first lift, the Family erupted in cheers.

"Let's go, Garth!" Vinnie shouted.

Garth approached the bar loaded with weights that looked impossibly heavy. He positioned his hands, took a breath, and lifted.

The clean and jerk was flawless. Perfect form. The crowd applauded enthusiastically.

His second lift was even better. More weight, equally perfect form. After two rounds, Garth was in first place.

"He's going to do it," Vinnie said, gripping my arm. "Nicholas, he's really going to win gold!"

Garth loaded the bar for his third attempt. A personal record weight that would guarantee gold if he could lift it. I watched him position himself, saw the determination in his face, the way his entire body coiled with readiness.

He lifted.

For a moment, it looked perfect. The bar rose smoothly, Garth's form textbook. But halfway through the jerk, something went wrong. Maybe his grip slipped slightly. Maybe the weight was just too much. Maybe yesterday's evaluation was still echoing in his mind, Charity's lawyers asking him to count backwards from one hundred, to explain what he'd do in an emergency, to prove he was competent.

Whatever the cause, Garth couldn't lock out his elbows.

He dropped the weight.

The buzzer sounded.

Failed lift.

The crowd applauded his effort anyway, but I could see the devastation on Garth's face. When the final scores were posted, he'd placed second.

Silver. Again.

Damn.

When Garth joined us after the medal ceremony, the silver hanging around his neck, his face was carefully neutral. But I could see the disappointment in every line of his body.

"You were amazing out there," Rita said, hugging him.

"Close. No cigar," Garth said.

"You lifted more than anyone else in the second round," I pointed out. "That last weight was insane. You almost had it."

"Almost isn't gold," Garth said in defeat.

"Next year," Vinnie said firmly. "Next year you'll get it."

William stepped forward, and I expected Mr. Darcy's flowery consolation. Instead, William just put his hand on Garth's massive shoulder and said, simply, "You're still the strongest person I know."

No affected accent. No aristocratic bearing. Just William, speaking his truth.

Garth looked surprised, then pulled William into a crushing hug.

On the drive home, Rita and I rode in comfortable silence, the sunset painting the sky in oranges and reds as the Family carried on their antics in the back.

"I've been thinking about apartment hunting," Rita said suddenly. "Looking at some places this weekend. Want to come with?"

"I'd love that," I said.

"Yeah?" Rita smiled. "We could grab lunch after, make a day of it."

"Sounds perfect."

We drove in silence for a few more minutes before Rita spoke again.

"I love you," she said quietly.

The words stopped my breath.

"I know I don't say it enough," she continued, eyes on the road. "But watching you with the Family today, seeing how much you care about them, how hard you work to give them a happy life full of experiences. You're a good man, Nicholas Murphy. I'm grateful I found you."

My throat closed up completely.

"I love you too," I heard myself say.

We pulled into the driveway. The Family piled out of the van behind us, Vinnie still chattering about Garth's lifts, William quiet but somehow more present than usual.

That night, after everyone had gone to bed, I found myself standing outside Floyd's room. The door was slightly ajar, and I could see him hunched over his workbench, Mozart's components spread across the surface.

I knocked softly. Floyd looked up, and the clarity in his eyes was almost unsettling after years of watching him struggle through fog.

"Can't sleep?" he asked. No stutter.

"Something like that." I leaned against the doorframe. "How's Mozart coming?"

"Before my accident, I built robotic surgical systems," Floyd said. "Specifically, teleoperated manipulators for minimally invasive procedures. You need multiple robotic arms working in perfect synchronization. One holds the camera, others hold surgical instruments, all responding to a surgeon's hand movements in real time with zero lag."

His hands moved over Mozart's frame as he spoke.

"The core challenge is identical to what I'm facing with Mozart. Multiple motors that must execute coordinated movements with sub-millisecond precision."

Floyd pulled up a schematic on his tablet.

"I used to solve this with distributed timing controllers. Each motor has its own processor, but they all sync to a master clock signal. I'd been trying to control Mozart's motors sequentially. But I can build a dual-processor system now. It's not complex engineering. I was just too confused before to see the elegant solution."

Floyd set down the servo motor he'd been examining. He was quiet for a long moment, his hands resting on Mozart's frame. When he spoke, his voice was raw. "I finally know what happened the day I was hit by lightning. It was a company picnic. During a departmental softball game, I was at bat. I remember standing at that plate, bases loaded, talking shit with my colleague who was the catcher. I remember the smell of rain coming. I heard a crack of thunder, and then—" Floyd's voice broke completely. "What I remembered next was waking up in a hospital bed unable to move my legs, unable to remember Grace's face, unable to understand that my entire life had ended while I was unconscious. Do you know why I couldn't remember?"

"The lightning damaged—"

"No." Floyd shook his head. "I mean, yes, physically it damaged my brain. But I've been thinking about what I told Vinnie. About pain. How when you hurt yourself badly, you can't remember what the pain felt like after it stops."

I moved into the room and sat in the chair beside his workbench.

"Our brains protect us," Floyd continued. "They won't let us hold on to agony that could destroy us. For five years, my mind kept me in the dark because remembering would have been too much pain delivered too fast. The lightning didn't just damage my body and brain. It obliterated my entire existence in a single instant. My career, my marriage, my future, my identity. Everything I was, just...gone. My nightmares weren't horrible dreams. They were dreams about my past."

His voice cracked.

"I couldn't process that. I couldn't face what I'd lost. My mind wouldn't let me. So, I wandered in the fog, building little drones, playing games..."

"And now?" I asked quietly.

Floyd's gaze drifted to his workstation, where two *Magic* decks sat in their worn boxes—Grace's and his own, side by side. He reached out and picked up his deck, turning it over in his hands. "This is me facing it. When I saw Grace this week, everything came flooding back. I knew exactly who she was and exactly how our games had gone in the past. She was so beautiful, but so sad. I knew what I had to do, but I wanted one last moment with her. Knowing her, loving her. One last memory of...us."

Floyd slid the deck from its box, the cards whispering against cardboard. He looked down at them—at all those years, all those games. Floyd's eyes brightened with tears. "So, I strung out the *Magic* session as long as I could, soaked in every moment with her before I had to let her go. I let her win that last game because I wanted to see that little victory dance she always does."

"Oh, Floyd, I'm so sorry," I said.

Floyd began to shuffle, the familiar riffle and bridge a kind of meditation. "It's fine. It was nice. I got to remember the person I was with her. The engineer who designed robotic surgical systems and went on outdoor adventures. The husband planning a family. The avid *Magic* player. I allowed myself to pretend to be that old person for those two hours with Grace while we played *Magic*. And then she asked about the Chaos Orb, and I knew...I had to let her go."

He stopped, his breath shaky. Floyd slid the deck back into its box and set it down beside Grace's. The deed was done, but the wound was still fresh. Open and hurting. Only time could heal this. Maybe. I wasn't placing any bets.

We sat in silence for a moment.

"Grace deserved better than what I did to her, driving her away like that," Floyd said finally. "But Nicholas, she would have waited forever. She *was* waiting forever. You heard her, she wouldn't start a family until the man she loved came back to her. That man can never come back. I love her too much to let her live like that."

His voice shattered completely on those last words. Floyd's shoulders began to shake, then the sobs came. Deep, wrenching sobs that seemed to tear something fundamental from his chest. He bent forward over his workbench, his hands covering his face as years of suppressed grief finally broke through.

I moved closer, putting my hand on his shoulder. There was nothing to say. Nothing that would make this hurt less. So, I stayed with him while Floyd wept for everything he'd lost and everything he'd sacrificed.

After a few minutes, the sobs gradually subsided. Floyd straightened slowly, wiping his eyes with the back of his hand.

"Sorry," he managed.

"Don't be."

Floyd turned back to Mozart, his hands still trembling slightly. "Thank you, Nicholas. For the five years you took care of me. Gave me dignity when I had nothing. Made me part of something that mattered. You didn't see a broken engineer or a disabled burden..."

"You're Family," I said quietly. "But weaning yourself off your meds? That was dangerous."

"I know. It was my reckless Hail Mary!" Floyd nodded. "Desperate times and all. I won't do it again. I promise."

"How long until Mozart's ready?"

"Few days. Maybe a week for testing." Floyd's hands moved over Mozart's components with new certainty.

I left him there, surrounded by circuits and the ghost of who he used to be, building something new from the broken pieces that remained.

Chapter Forty-One

"This is it, Nicky," Rita called down to me, slightly breathless. "Unit 3B."

The apartment was a third-floor walk-up in a converted Victorian, the kind of place that looked charming in photographs and exhausting in reality. Rita was already halfway up the second flight of stairs, her enthusiasm carrying her forward despite the climb.

I followed at a slower pace, my mind churning through the conversation we'd had in the car. How she'd picked this specific apartment because it had enough space for me and Vinnie when the foreclosure came through.

When, not *if*.

Rita had already accepted it as inevitable. She'd planned for our homelessness with the same pragmatism she applied to everything else. Found us a landing spot. Calculated square footage. Made sure we'd have somewhere to go when everything fell apart.

The landlord, a woman in her sixties who'd introduced herself as Mrs. Chen, unlocked the door with a flourish. "Two-bedroom, one bath. Original hardwood floors, updated kitchen. Rent includes gas and water."

"Nicholas, look at this light," she said, gesturing to the bay window that overlooked the street. "And the ceilings. God, these ceilings."

I followed her gaze upward. Twelve feet, maybe more. The kind of architectural detail that had disappeared from modern construction, replaced by eight-foot drops and cost efficiency.

"It's beautiful," I said, and meant it.

Mrs. Chen excused herself to take a phone call, leaving Rita and me alone in the empty apartment. Rita immediately grabbed my hand and pulled me toward the bedrooms.

"Okay, so this one could be for you and me," she said, stepping into the larger of the two rooms. "And Vinnie gets the smaller one. There's a closet in the hallway we could use for linens and overflow."

She was walking the perimeter, measuring with her eyes, already seeing past the freshly painted walls and new carpet to whatever vision she'd constructed in her mind.

"We could put the bed here, facing the window. Dresser on that wall. Maybe hang some art—nothing too expensive, but something that feels like us, you know?" She turned to face me, her excitement palpable. "What do you think?"

"I think it's perfect," I said.

Rita moved closer, looping her arms around my neck. "The task force money is actually making this possible. I know the overtime is brutal, but the extra pay means I can afford a place big enough for all three of us." Plus, you'll land a nursing gig somewhere, and it will all work out." She paused, her expression becoming more serious. "What happens to the others? William, Floyd?"

The question landed like a direct hit to my solar plexus.

"I don't want to talk about it," I said quietly. "It's too painful."

Rita's arms tightened around me. "I'm sorry. I shouldn't have—"

"No, it's okay. I just…" I pulled back slightly, needing the distance to breathe. "I'll fall apart if I think about where they'll end up."

Maybe prison.

Rita studied my face for a moment, then nodded. "Okay. We don't have to talk about it."

She turned back to surveying the room and changed the subject. "You know what's fucked up?" Rita said suddenly, still looking out the window. "My friend who recommended me for the task force is now getting railroaded by Internal Affairs. It's like every good meal in life comes with a free side of shit, no substitutions allowed."

I felt my attention sharpen. "What happened?"

"They ran a routine background check—the kind they do periodically, making sure nothing's changed that could compromise an officer." Rita's voice carried an edge of anger I only heard when she talked about injustices. "Turns out this AI system they're using flagged a distant cousin. Like, third or fourth cousin he's never even met. Guy has a criminal record. Drug trafficking, I think."

"And they're going after your friend for that?"

"Michael's a twenty-year veteran. Spotless record. Commendations. The works." Rita turned to face me, her expression troubled. "But now IA is treating him like he's compromised because of some family member he didn't even know existed until the algorithm spat out his name. They're saying he should have disclosed it, but how the fuck do you disclose a family connection you're not aware of?"

I felt something cold crawl up my spine. "Can they actually punish him for that?"

"They're trying. Making him prove he had no knowledge, no contact, no potential conflict of interest." Rita's hands clenched into fists. "It's not even about whether he did anything wrong. It's about covering their asses in case it ever becomes a problem. Guilty by association with someone he's never even spoken to. AI is turning into the precogs from *Minority Report*. Slightly useful but mostly wrong."

The implications crashed over me like a wave. If we got caught? If they traced the heist back to me? If Rita's connection to our family became public knowledge?

She'd lose everything.

Her career. Her pension. Her reputation. Twenty years from now, she could be in Michael's position, except instead of a distant cousin, it'd be her husband. The man she loved. The man she'd been living with, helping, supporting.

No IA board would believe she hadn't known. No investigation would clear her. Even if she was completely innocent the association alone would destroy her.

"That's horrifying," I managed. "How's Michael holding up?"

"Not well. He's got a family, mortgage, kids in college. If they force him out, he loses everything." Rita shook her head. "The worst part is how unfair it is. You can't control who your family is. You can't be responsible for someone else's choices."

Rita was right. You couldn't control who your family was.

But you could be destroyed for their choices.

Floyd had shown me what real sacrifice looked like. Choosing Grace's future over his own happiness. Destroying her hope so completely that she'd have no choice but to move on. It had been cruel and necessary and an act of profound love.

If I walked away now. If I created enough distance that no investigation could reasonably connect us. If I made the break clean and decisive enough that Rita would have plausible deniability.

She'd be hurt.

But she'd survive.

And when this was all over—when we'd saved the house and stopped Charity and kept the Family together—maybe I could walk this back. Maybe I could explain. Maybe she'd understand that I'd done it to protect her.

Or maybe she'd hate me forever.

But I knew Rita couldn't be part of what came next.

Rita moved back to the window, gazing out at the street below. "I can see us here, you know? Coming home after work, cooking dinner together. Vinnie experimenting with your mom's recipes in the kitchen. Maybe getting a cat eventually."

She turned to face me, and the love in her eyes was so pure and uncomplicated that I felt my resolve waver.

"We could build something really good here, Nicholas. A real home. A real life." She smiled. "I know the timing's terrible with everything going on. But after the foreclosure, after the dust settles and you and Vinnie are settled in...we could start planning something permanent."

This was it. The moment.

Do it. Do it now. Like a Band-Aid.

I took a breath. Steadied myself. Then I dropped to one knee in the empty master bedroom of an apartment neither of us had signed a lease for yet.

"Nicholas?" Rita's voice carried confusion. "What are you—"

"Marry me," I said.

The words hung in the air between us like a grenade with the pin pulled.

Rita's eyes went wide. Her mouth opened, then closed. Her hands, which had been relaxed at her sides, suddenly came up in a defensive posture, not quite warding me off, but not welcoming either.

"What?" she managed.

"I know I don't have a ring," I continued, committing fully to the bit now. "But standing here, looking at this place, imagining our future together, I don't want to wait anymore. I love you. I want to marry you. I want to build that life you're talking about. I want—"

"Nicholas, stop." Rita's voice was sharp, almost panicked. "Just stop. Stand up."

I stayed down. "Rita—"

"Stand up!" The command in her tone made me obey automatically.

She was breathing faster now, her composure cracking in a way I'd never seen before. Rita Reyes, who could walk into active crime scenes without flinching, who held her ground against armed suspects, who faced down the worst humanity had to offer with steely calm...

She was freaking out.

"I can't. We can't—" She ran her hands through her hair, pacing now.

I watched her spiral, feeling equal parts relief that my gambit was working and crushing guilt at the manipulation.

"Rita, I love you. I thought—"

"I love you too." She stopped pacing, turning to face me with tears starting to gather in her eyes. "God, Nicholas, I love you so much. But this, right now? I can't—"

Her voice broke on the last word.

I moved toward her, knowing I needed to seem hurt but understanding. Like a man who'd genuinely miscalculated the moment but would graciously accept rejection.

"I need time," she said finally. "Maybe we should..." Rita swallowed hard. "Maybe we need some space. Just for a little while. To think about our futures separately, so we can come back together with clear heads."

I felt something twist in my chest. This was exactly what I wanted. Exactly what I'd manipulated her into suggesting.

It felt like dying.

"If that's what you need," I said, making my voice gentle. Understanding. "Take all the time you need."

She was giving me exactly the out I'd been hoping for.

I should have felt triumphant.

Instead, I felt like Floyd. Like I'd just voluntarily ripped out my own heart.

"Okay," I said quietly. "Some space. Time to think. I understand."

Timing is everything.

Mrs. Chen chose that moment to return, knocking lightly on the doorframe. "So? What do you think? Should we talk about signing a lease?"

Rita and I looked at each other. The moment stretched uncomfortably.

"I need a few more days to think about it," Rita said finally. "Can I get back to you by the end of the week?"

"Of course, dear. Take your time." Mrs. Chen smiled warmly, completely oblivious to the emotional carnage that had just unfolded in her empty apartment.

The drive back was quiet. Rita kept her eyes on the road, one hand on the wheel, the other resting on the gear shift. I could see her working through everything in her head—the proposal, the timing, the logistics of merging our chaotic lives.

When we pulled up to my house, Rita put the car in park but didn't turn off the engine. She finally turned to look at me.

"I do love you. That hasn't changed. I just can't do this right now."

"Okay."

I got out of the car and watched her drive away, her tail-lights disappearing around the corner.

I went to my room and closed the door.

Only then did I let myself feel it. The full weight of what I'd just done.

It was the best I could do.

Chapter Forty-Two

I sat in the passenger seat of our van, watching Vinnie complete his pre-drive checklist with the meticulousness of a pilot preparing for takeoff. Three weeks of near-daily practice had transformed this abandoned mall parking lot into something almost sacred.

"The seat is too close," Vinnie said as he wiggled to get comfortable.

"I'll show you how to adjust it later. Ready?" I asked.

Vinnie nodded, his expression serious. "Ready."

He turned the key. The engine rumbled to life. Then, without the hesitation that had plagued his early attempts, he shifted into drive and eased onto the gas.

The van moved forward smoothly. No jerking. No overcorrection. Just steady, controlled acceleration.

"First landmark?" I prompted.

"The 7-Eleven with the broken window," Vinnie said immediately, his eyes scanning the empty lot as if the convenience store might materialize between the faded parking spaces. "Turn left after 7-Eleven."

We'd transformed the parking lot into a makeshift version of our route to First National Bank. Garth had spray-painted crude landmarks at strategic intervals—a bright orange X marking the broken window 7-Eleven, a purple square representing the weird mailbox house, a hand-painted church spire that looked more like a melting ice cream cone.

Vinnie navigated between them with increasing fluidity, calling out each landmark as he passed. His turns were smooth, his speed consistent. The van responded to his commands like an extension of his will rather than a foreign object he was trying to control.

"Beautiful," I said. "Now let's try the figure eight."

Garth had painted two large circles at opposite ends of the lot, connected by crossing paths that formed the infinity symbol. The exercise was designed to build Vinnie's spatial awareness, his ability to judge turning radius and maintain speed through curves.

Vinnie approached the first circle, slowing slightly as he entered the curve. The van leaned into the turn, tires gripping asphalt as he maintained steady pressure on the gas. Around the first loop, smooth and controlled. Through the crossover, his hands adjusting the wheel with small, precise movements. Into the second loop, completing the pattern.

Then again. And again. Each repetition more confident than the last.

After a few more successful loops, Vinnie spoke without taking his eyes off the painted lines. "I'm sorry about Rita."

I really didn't want to talk about that. Vinnie either didn't care or knew I needed to.

"You broke up with her to protect her from what we're doing," he continued. "I'm not stupid, Nicholas. I see what you did there."

I didn't respond immediately, watching the landmarks slide past the windshield.

"After the heist," Vinnie said with quiet certainty, "you can fix it. You can explain everything. Rita will understand."

"I hope it's that simple."

"It is," Vinnie insisted. "Rita loves you. Love means you understand when people do things to protect you. You can fix it after."

I felt my throat tighten, not trusting myself to speak.

"That's it," I said finally, changing the subject. "You've got it. One more time, then we'll call it."

Vinnie nodded, his focus absolute as he began another figure eight. He was approaching the final curve when something happened.

Movement in his peripheral vision—a piece of trash blown by wind—made him instinctively hit the gas harder than intended. Or maybe his foot slipped? Maybe it was just the culmination of three weeks of muscle memory meeting a moment of overcorrection?

Whatever the cause, the result was spectacular.

The van's rear end slid sideways as momentum carried us forward. Vinnie's hands spun the wheel into the skid—exactly the right response, though I doubted he knew—and suddenly we were drifting through the turn like something out of *The Fast and the Furious*. The van rotated smoothly, tires screaming against asphalt, the world spinning past the windshield in a controlled blur of unfocused motion before Vinnie straightened out and we shot forward, perfectly aligned with the exit path.

My heart was trying to punch through my ribcage.

Vinnie's hands were locked on the steering wheel white-knuckled. His face had gone the color of chalk. He eased off the gas and brought the van to a stop, then carefully shifted into park with hands that trembled slightly.

For a moment, we just sat there in the sudden silence, the engine idling, both of us breathing like we'd just finished a sprint.

"What the fuck was that?!" I managed, my voice climbing several octaves higher as panic lodged in my throat.

"That was an accident," Vinnie said finally, his voice small.

I stared at him. "An accident?"

"I didn't mean to hit the gas." He turned to face me, and I could see the fear in his eyes. "I have to change my underwear, Nicholas."

The absurdity of it hit me all at once. The terror melting into relief, the relief colliding with the ridiculous image of Vinnie accidentally Tokyo drifting because he'd overcorrected on a turn. I started laughing.

Vinnie stared at me for a second, then started laughing too. Soon we were both losing it, tears streaming down our faces, the tension of three weeks of training and the fear of the upcoming heist all pouring out in hysterical giggles.

"I thought you were showing off!" I gasped between laughs.

"I thought I was dying!" Vinnie shot back.

We sat there in the van, two grown men laughing like idiots in an abandoned parking lot.

"You know what?" I said when I could finally breathe again. "You're ready. You can drive."

Vinnie wiped his eyes. "Really?"

"Really. If you can accidentally pull off a Tokyo drift like that and not crash, you can handle whatever the actual route throws at you."

"The Vinman can," Vinnie said with a grin, though I noticed he didn't start the van again right away.

We sat there for another minute, letting our heart rates return to normal, before we switched seats so we could head home.

Vinnie was ready.

That's one.

Floyd's room had been transformed into something between a laboratory and a cockpit. Monitors lined his desk, displaying camera feeds from Mozart's perspective. His hands moved across a modified gaming controller, each minute adjustment translating to Mozart's movements with near-perfect fidelity.

I leaned against the doorframe, watching him work. Mozart hovered in the center of the room, its four propellers humming softly as it held position.

"Maneuverability test," Floyd announced. The words crisp and clear. No trace of the stutter that had plagued him for years.

Mozart shot forward, pulled up at the last possible second before hitting the ceiling, then descended in a perfect spiral before coming to rest hovering exactly one meter above Floyd's desk.

"Impressive," I said.

"Watch this." Floyd's concentration intensified. Mozart drifted forward toward the practice lock setup he'd constructed —a wooden board mounted with six different types of locks, ranging from simple padlocks to more complex deadbolts.

Two small appendages extended from Mozart's undercarriage, impossibly delicate manipulators that Floyd had designed specifically for this purpose. They positioned themselves at the first lock—a standard tumbler mechanism similar to a household deadbolt.

The appendages inserted themselves into the keyhole. Five seconds. Ten. Fifteen.

Click.

The lock opened.

"That's the easy one." Floyd's eyes were distant, completely absorbed in the task. Mozart moved to the next lock, then the next. Each mechanism yielded to his remote manipulation with increasing speed.

"You built a fucking Decepticon," I said with genuine admiration.

I watched Mozart execute a perfect landing on Floyd's desk, its propellers spinning down. Floyd set down his controller and turned to face me.

"Mozart's ready," Floyd said with pride and certainty.

That's two.

Cost$hare Warehouse's parking lot had shopping carts scattered across the asphalt like metallic tumbleweeds, the aftermath of too many customers loading too many vehicles with too many bulk purchases and the incessant flow of humanity engaged in the eternal pursuit of deals and discounts.

Capitalism at its finest.

I sat in the van at the far end of the lot, watching through binoculars as Garth executed his plan. He'd been "borrowing" equipment for some time now—an orange safety vest here, a hard hat there. They mysteriously disappeared from Cost$hare's storage area and reappeared in our garage.

Today's acquisition was more ambitious.

Garth had positioned himself near the loading dock where maintenance equipment was stored. As he pushed a massive train of shopping carts past the area, his movements seemed casual, unhurried. Just another employee doing his job. But I watched his hand snake out and grab an orange traffic cone, tucking it smoothly into the cart at the front of his train where it became just another piece of cargo.

He continued across the lot, collecting more carts, building his train. Another pass by the loading dock. Another cone disappeared. Then another.

By the time Garth's shift ended thirty minutes later, he'd accumulated six traffic cones, all hidden among the legitimate equipment in his work area, ready to be "forgotten" and accidentally taken home at day's end.

When he finally emerged from the employee entrance, his Cost$hare vest exchanged for a regular jacket, he directed me to park in the back, where he loaded his borrowed loot into the van undetected.

When he climbed into the passenger seat, I could smell the day's work on him.

"Successful harvest?" I asked.

Garth nodded. "Last shopping trip. Have everything now."

That's three.

William's contribution to our training montage was characteristically thorough. While the rest of us focused on physical skills—driving, drone operation, equipment acquisition—William had taken on the role of strategic coordinator, running thousands of simulations through the VR environment to identify potential failure points.

I found him in the living room, VR headset on, his hands moving through empty air as he navigated the virtual bank. He'd been at this for three hours straight, and I knew from experience that trying to interrupt him mid-simulation would only result in irritation.

Instead, I waited. Watched him work through whatever scenario he'd constructed.

Finally, he pulled off the headset, blinking in the sudden return to reality.

"Nicholas," he said, not sounding surprised by my presence. "I've completed the final simulation series."

"And?"

"Our preparation is more than adequate for our needs." William carefully set down the headset. "Barring truly catastrophic variables, we should succeed."

"You've really thought of everything," I said when he finished.

"I've tried. Whether it will be enough..." William shrugged. "That remains to be seen. But we've prepared as thoroughly as possible."

That's four.

That evening, the Family gathered in the living room for what had become our final planning session. Floyd had Mozart resting on the coffee table. Garth had arranged his liberated construction equipment in the corner like a costume waiting for its actor. William's laptop displayed the VR bank environment, ready to run through any scenario we needed to review. And Vinnie sat on the couch, keys in hand, ready to drive us anywhere we needed to go.

"Status check," I said, falling into what had become my role as de facto mission commander. "Floyd, what's Mozart's operational readiness?"

"Ninety-five percent," Floyd replied without hesitation. "Flight systems are perfect. Mozart's range of operation is twenty-five-meters. Lock manipulation is functional."

"Garth, equipment acquisition?"

"Complete. Practiced setup three times. Ready to deploy cones, divert traffic."

"William, contingency planning?"

"Comprehensive and documented. We are a go."

"Vinnie, driving proficiency?"

Vinnie grinned. "The Vinman can," he said a little too confidently, but I allowed it.

"And Diego Locksley is ready for his closeup, Mr. DeMille," I said.

Despite everything, despite the weight of what we were about to do, I felt myself smile.

"Alright," I said, looking around at each of them. "We've done everything we can to prepare. The plan is solid. Our skills are sharp. Now, we need to set a date."

"Tomorrow's out," Vinnie said immediately. "I have work."

"Me too," Garth added.

"Day after tomorrow then," I suggested. "All in favor?"

Five hands rose as one.

We were united and determined.

And even though I knew my life wasn't a movie, in that brief instant, it sure as hell felt like one.

I was finally ready.

That's five.

"Then it's settled," I said. "Day after tomorrow. Operation Heist Club is a go."

Chapter Forty-Three

Going to work when I knew the heist was tomorrow was hard. I tried to concentrate on stocking the food shipment, but my mind was filled with landmarks of the route I had to drive, and I realized I had put the potatoes in the freezer instead of the pantry. I was walking back to the freezer to fix my mistake when Sous Chef Dave stopped me.

"Chef's back from vacation, Vinnie. He wants to see you," Sous Chef Dave said.

"Now?" I asked. "I accidentally put the potatoes in the freezer."

"Yes, now. I'll get the potatoes." Dave said as he patted my shoulder and pushed me towards Chef's office.

I was sure I was in trouble. Sous Chef Dave had put Mom's braised short ribs on the menu as a special while Chef was gone.

I walked to Chef's office in the back of the restaurant. The door was open but I knocked anyway because Nicholas taught me to always knock even when doors are open.

"Come in, Vinnie," Chef said without looking up from his papers.

I walked in and stood there. My hands were sweating. I wiped them on my apron.

"I know what happened while I was away," Chef said.

"I'm sorry, Chef. I didn't mean to—"

Chef held up his hand to stop me. "Sit down."

I sat in the chair across from his desk. It was a nice chair. Nicer than the chairs in the kitchen where we ate family meal.

Chef finally looked at me. Not the way he usually looked at me.

"Your dish," Chef said. "The braised short ribs. It sold more than any dish has in the past three months."

I was so nervous I didn't know what to say. My brain was trying to understand if this was good or bad.

"That's...good?" I asked.

"It's very good, Vinnie." Chef leaned back in his chair. "Dave tells me it's your mother's recipe. That you prepared it yourself."

"Yes, Chef. Mom taught me how to cook before she died."

Chef nodded slowly. "I'm giving you a raise. Effective immediately. And I'm adding prep work to your duties. You'll help with vegetable prep, stock preparation, basic sauces. Dave will supervise, but you'll be working in the kitchen proper, not just unloading trucks."

"Thank you, Chef, I'll work hard. I promise. This is my dream," I said.

Chef was quiet a moment as he looked at me, "I was wrong about you. I said some things that were...inappropriate. Maybe hurtful. You're more capable than I gave you credit for, Vinnie."

I felt my face get hot. Chef was saying sorry without saying sorry.

Typicals.

My heart was beating fast. "Really?"

"Really. And with your permission, I want to put your mother's braised short ribs on the menu as a rotating special. We'll call it Vinnie's Short Ribs. Your name on the menu. What do you say?"

"No," I told him. "Josephine's Short Ribs. That was my mom's name."

"Josephine's Short Ribs it is," Chef said with a small smile.

My throat felt tight, like when I wanted to cry but I was too happy to cry. I nodded.

"Now back to work. Dave's waiting for you."

I stood up. "Thank you, Chef."

"You earned it, Vinnie. Keep it up."

I walked out of Chef's office and my legs felt weird. Like they were floating. Sous Chef Dave was waiting by the prep station with a big smile.

"He told you?" Dave asked.

"I got a raise. And I get to do prep. And my dish is going on the menu with my mom's name on it."

"You're a real chef now."

A real chef. Like a typical.

I worked the rest of my shift helping Dave prep vegetables for dinner service. He showed me the right way to brunoise carrots and how to make stock from chicken bones. My hands knew what to do because Mom had taught me, but doing it in a real restaurant kitchen made it feel different. Special.

When my shift ended, I felt like I was walking on clouds. The sun was still out and everything looked brighter. The grass was greener. The sky was bluer. I was a real chef now. Chef even said so.

. . .

I was walking home when I saw Francis and Scott at their table in the park. As usual, they were not playing chess at the chess table.

I should have kept walking. Nicholas would have told me to keep walking. But I was so happy about what happened at work that I wanted to tell someone. And Francis was right there.

"Vinman!" Francis called when he saw me. "Look who it is. Come over here, buddy."

I walked over to their table. Francis was smiling his big Francis smile that made him look friendly even though I knew he wasn't always friendly.

"What's got you so happy?" Francis asked. "You're glowing, man."

"I got a promotion at work," I said. I couldn't help smiling. "Chef gave me a raise. And my dish is going on the menu with Mom's name on it. I'm doing prep now. Real kitchen work!"

"No shit?" Francis stood up and put his hand on my shoulder. "Vinnie, that's huge! That's fucking incredible, man. You're a real chef."

"That's what Sous Chef Dave said."

"We gotta celebrate," Francis said. He looked really happy for me. "This is a big deal, Vinman. You can't just go home after news like this. Take a load off. Play some checkers with me. Scott, get the board. I'm about to whip Chef Boyardee's ass in checkers!"

Scott got up and went to Francis's car to get the checkers.

I should have said no. I should have remembered that Francis always had a plan for me. But I was so proud of myself that I wanted to sit and enjoy it for a while longer. A day like this doesn't happen every day for me.

"Okay," I said. "Just for a little bit."

"Excellent." Francis pulled out a chair for me. "You know

what? This calls for some refreshments." Francis reached under the table and got two energy drink cans from his backpack. They were the fancy kind with lots of colors and lightning bolts on them. He handed me one.

I looked at the can. "I don't know, Francis. Nicholas says I shouldn't—"

"It's not candy, Vinman," Francis said. He opened his can and took a big drink. "See? Just an energy drink. You can buy these at any gas station. Your brother's paranoid because he's a control freak."

That was true. Nicholas was a control freak. And it wasn't candy. I could see Francis drinking his energy drink. And I was thirsty.

"Okay," I said.

I opened my can and took a drink. It tasted like artificial fruit and chemicals. Not good but not terrible. Like most energy drinks.

Scott came back with the checkerboard and set it up. We started playing. Francis was talking a lot about how proud he was of me, asking questions about the restaurant, telling me stories about his own jobs when he was younger.

The checkers game went fast. I won. We started another one.

That's when I started to feel different.

At first, I felt warm. Like I had drunk hot chocolate on a cold day, and the warmth was spreading through my whole body. Starting in my stomach and moving out to my arms and legs and head. Which was weird, because the energy drink was cold.

"You feeling good, Vinman?" Francis asked. He was watching me with a weird smile.

"Yeah," I said. "I feel really good."

I did. I felt better than good. I felt amazing. Like I could do anything. Like I was the smartest, strongest, best version of me that ever existed.

I was a superhero.

"That's what I like to hear," Francis said. "Tell me more about the restaurant. What'd Chef say exactly?"

I started talking. The words came out fast. Very fast, but I didn't mind. I told Francis everything about my conversation with Chef, about working prep with Dave, about how my hands knew what to do because Mom taught me. But I was talking faster than I usually talked. The words were running into each other, but I couldn't slow down.

"And then Dave showed me how to brunoise the carrots, which is when you cut them into really small cubes and it has to be precise and even, and I did it, and Dave said I did it perfect, and—"

"Pump the brakes," Francis laughed. "Slow down, buddy."

But I couldn't slow down. I felt so good. So alive. Like everything in my life had been leading to this moment. I finally understood my purpose. I was a chef. A real chef. And I could do anything. Anything I wanted.

I won the second checkers game even faster than the first. Jumpjumpjump, KING ME! My brain could see all the moves before they happened. Everything was so clear.

"You're on fire tonight," Scott said.

"I feel like I'm on fire," I said. And it was true. I felt hot. Really hot. Like the sun was inside me.

I stood up. "I need to cool down."

"You okay?" Francis asked, but he was still smiling that weird smile.

"Yeah, I just need to move. I need to run or something."

The playground was right there. Kids were playing on the

swings and slides. I walked over and started running around. The wind felt good on my face. It cooled me down.

I ran faster. Everything was so bright and clear and perfect. I hated running, but now it felt amazing to run. It felt like I could run forever. I jumped on the merry-go-round and pushed it as fast as it would go. Kids were laughing. I was laughing. This was the best day ever!

I ran to the jungle gym and climbed up really fast. Faster than I'd ever climbed before. I felt like Spider-Man. No, not Spider-Man. I felt like I could fly.

"Vinnie!" one of the kids yelled. "You're being crazy!"

"I know!" I yelled back. "I'm a superhero! I can do anything!"

I jumped down from the jungle gym and started running again. I had so much energy. So much power. I needed to tell Nicholas about my promotion. I needed to tell the whole Family. This was the best news ever and they needed to know right now. Right now!

I started running home. My legs were moving so fast. Faster than they'd ever moved before. The park was behind me and then the streets were flying past and I was running and running and running.

Behind me, far away, I heard Francis call out: "Hey, Casey Jones, watch your speed!"

That's weird. Casey Jones wears a hockey mask and is friends with the Teenage Mutant Ninja Turtles. I didn't understand what Francis meant. I didn't care. I was invincible.

I couldn't slow down. I didn't want to. I felt perfect. I felt like I could run all the way around the world and back home again.

I ran up our driveway and burst through the front door.

I was in the kitchen reviewing William's final equipment checklist when our front door exploded open with enough force to rattle the windows.

"Nicholas!" Vinnie's voice carried a manic edge I'd never heard before. "You won't believe what happened! Chef gave me a promotion and put my dish on the menu and I'm a real chef now and I did one of my bucket list things and Ifeelsogood! Iranallthewayhomeand—"

The words came out in a torrential rush, each syllable crashing into the next without pause for breath. I looked up to see Vinnie practically vibrating in the doorway, his eyes unnaturally bright, pupils dilated to the point where I could barely see any color around them.

Oh fuck.

"Vinnie?" I stood slowly, my nurse practitioner training immediately cataloging symptoms. Rapid speech. Dilated pupils. Excessive energy. Inability to stand still. "Are you high?"

"I AM SUPERHERO!" Vinnie was bouncing on his toes, his hands gesturing wildly. "Icandoanything! Nicholas, you should have seen me at the park, I was running so fast and climbing and everythingwassobrightand—"

"Slow down." I moved toward him carefully, the way you'd approach a spooked animal. "Take a breath. Tell me what happened."

"I told you! Chef promoted me! My dish is on the menu! With Mom's name on it!" Vinnie's voice climbed higher and faster with each word. "Then I saw Francis and we played checkers and I won twice and I ran all the way home and I didn't get tired! I could run forever!"

The mention of Francis made my hackles rise.

"Francis." I kept my voice level despite the rage flooding my system. "You saw Francis today?"

"At the park! He was happy about my promotion! We celebrated and—" Vinnie stopped mid-sentence, his attention frac-
turing as William emerged from his room to investigate the
commotion. "William! I got promoted! I'm a real chef now!
Chef said so!"

William took one look at Vinnie and his expression shifted
to alarm. "Nicholas, what's wrong with him?"

"Vinnie," I said, moving closer. "Did Francis give you
anything? Anything to eat or drink?"

"He gave me an energy drink." Vinnie was pacing now,
unable to stand still. "It wasn't candy. I checked. You said no
candy from strangers or Francis but this was an energy drink
and Francis was drinking one too so it's okay—"

"Oh fuck." The pieces clicked together with horrifying
clarity. Francis hadn't given him an energy drink. He'd given
him something laced with stimulants. Amphetamines, maybe
MDMA, cocaine possibly?

And Vinnie, in his excitement about his promotion, had
walked right into the trap.

"I need you to sit down," I said, reaching for his arm.

Vinnie pulled away, still moving. "I don't want to sit down!
I want to tell everyone about my promotion! Where's Floyd?
And Garth? They need to know! This is the best day of my
life!"

Garth wandered in with Floyd trailing behind him, both
aghast at Vinnie as I attempted to calm him down and get to the
bottom of this.

"Vinnie, listen to me." I tried to catch his eye, but his gaze
kept darting around the room. "I think Francis put something
in that drink. Something that's making you feel this way."

"What? No!" Vinnie shook his head emphatically. "I feel
great! Better than ever!"

Vinnie's words accelerated, tumbling over each other like

dominoes falling in cascade. His hands were everywhere at once. Gesturing, flailing, touching his face, his chest, the wall, the doorframe.

"... and Chef said I earned it and Dave showed me how to brunoise which is this really specific cut and my hands just knew what to do and I won checkers twice and I ran so fast and—"

"Vinnie, you need to calm down," I said, but he wasn't listening. Couldn't listen. His brain was firing too fast to process input.

"... everything is so bright and clear and I can see everything and I understand everything—"

His hand went to his chest.

His left hand. Palm flat against his sternum.

Then his face changed.

The manic joy drained away, replaced by confusion. Then fear.

"Nicholas?" His voice came out small. Wrong. "Nicholas, my arm feels weird."

"Vinnie—"

His left arm. He was rubbing his left arm.

Oh fuck no.

"My chest—" Vinnie's eyes went wide. "Nicholas, my chest hurts..."

His knees buckled.

I lunged forward but wasn't fast enough. Vinnie hit the floor hard, his body convulsing once before going terrifyingly still.

"Vinnie!"

The scream tore out of me as I dropped beside him. My hands went to his neck, feeling for a pulse.

Nothing.

No no no no no—

Fuck.

"William!" I roared. "Medical bag! Now!"

William stood frozen, his hands flapping at his sides, mouth opening and closing without sound.

"William, move!"

He bolted toward my room.

"Garth!" I grabbed Vinnie under the shoulders. "Help me get him flat! Floyd, call—"

Floyd already had his phone out, fingers moving toward 911.

"NO!" I knocked the phone from his hand. It skittered across the floor.

Floyd stared at me like I'd lost my mind. "Nicholas, he needs—"

"He can't go to the hospital high on drugs!" The words came out in a snarl. "Charity will use this! She'll take Garth! She'll take the house! We'll lose everything! Fuckfuckfuck!" I was teetering on the brink of a Chernobyl meltdown.

"He's dying!" Floyd shouted back.

"I know!"

Garth had Vinnie stretched out flat. I positioned myself over my brother's chest, laced my fingers together, found the center of his sternum.

Vinnie's face was already going gray.

One. Two. Three. Four.

Don't die, Vinnie...

I lost count. Fuck.

One. Two—

Wait, what number was I on?

"Mmmmmmmmmm—" William dropped my medical bag next to me as his high-pitched keening filled the room making thinking impossible.

"Shut up!" I screamed without looking up. "I can't count!"

The keening stopped. I heard him breathing hard, on the edge of his own meltdown.

One. Two. Three. Four—

Was that four or five?

"Nicholas!" William's voice cracked. "You can time compressions to songs!"

"I don't need a fucking music lesson!"

He picked up Floyd's phone off the ground and I heard him frantically scrolling. "'Staying Alive' works but that's ancient, nobody knows— Wait, here! Dua Lipa, 'Break My Heart.' The chorus has perfect timing for CPR!"

I wasn't listening. Couldn't listen.

My brother's heart had stopped.

Vinnie was dead.

Please God please God no—

Music suddenly blared from Floyd's phone. Pop music. Dance music. Completely inappropriate for watching someone die.

Dua Lipa began to sing her smash hit "Break my Heart."

William started singing.

His voice was off-key, uncertain, but he was singing the words, and Floyd joined in, and even Garth read the words as they flashed on the phone's screen and Floyd tapped Garth's leg in rhythm to the beat, and suddenly all three of them were singing with Dua Lipa while my brother lay dead on our living room floor.

The Family sang the first line as their voices struggled to merge.

They pushed into the second line, finding their rhythm.

My arms were burning. Sweat dripped into my eyes.

The third line hit louder, the Family leaning into it.

Then the chorus. Their voices cracked at the high notes.

Eight. Nine. Ten.

Please. Please. I'll do anything. Let him live. Please.

Fourteen. Fifteen. Sixteen.

And do you know what happened?

A miracle.

My compressions synced to their singing without me realizing it. The rhythm locked in. My hands moved in time with the music, and even though I wanted to scream at them to shut the fuck up, to stop singing this fucking pop song while Vinnie died—

It was working.

The compressions were even. Timed. Perfect.

The absurdity of the moment was absolute. The Family sang with Dua Lipa to help me keep rhythm on CPR compressions because a high school bully gave cocaine to my twin with Down syndrome who was dying on the floor of our living room.

I checked for a pulse.

Still nothing.

"Fuck!" I rocked back on my heels. "It's not working!"

William had set my medical bag beside me. I yanked it open, hands moving on autopilot through supplies until I found what I needed.

Adrenaline. Syringe.

The Family kept singing, but their voices had gone shaky. They were crying now. All of them. Still singing through the tears because they didn't know what else to do.

I drew the adrenaline into the syringe with shaking hands, 0.6 milligrams. Straight to the heart.

"Nicholas." William's voice cut through the singing and they stopped. "If you're going to inject directly into his heart, you need a black magic marker."

I looked up at him. "What?"

"A marker. To mark the spot. Like in *Pulp Fiction*—"

"I don't need a black magic marker!" I ripped Vinnie's shirt open, buttons scattering.

"But in the movie—"

"This isn't a movie, William!"

"A black magic maker might help—"

"I know where his fucking heart is!"

William flinched back.

I found the spot. Just left of the sternum, between the ribs. I had to go through the intercostal space, had to hit the left ventricle, had to break through—

My hands were shaking.

I closed my eyes and inhaled.

As my breath slowly filled my lungs to capacity...

Sound muted. Time stopped.

I opened my eyes. Vinnie's face was gray. Lifeless. My twin. My responsibility. My brother.

The one person I'd promised Mom I'd always protect.

I raised the syringe.

Mom, if you're there...

I drove the needle down with everything I had, feeling it all. The resistance of skin. Muscle. The terrible crack as it punched through cartilage. The pop as it penetrated the pericardium.

Then I PUSHED.

Adrenaline flooded directly into Vinnie's heart.

For three seconds, nothing happened.

Dead silence.

Then—

Vinnie's body exploded off the floor with a roar that sounded like he was being born and dying at the same time. His back arched, every muscle contracting at once, and his eyes flew open wide and wild and—alive!

He gasped, hands scrabbling at his chest. "WHAT—Where—"

"Don't move." My voice came out steadier than I felt. I grabbed his wrist, found his pulse.

Strong. Fast, but strong.

I checked his pupils. Reactive. I pressed my stethoscope to his chest.

Heart rate elevated but steady. Lungs sounds clear.

He was okay.

He was going to be okay.

"Vinnie?" I kept my voice calm. Professional. "Can you hear me?"

He blinked up at me, confusion and pain warring on his face. "What happened? Why does my chest—"

"Don't talk. You need rest. And fluids." I stood, my legs unsteady. "Floyd."

Floyd looked shell-shocked, his face pale. "What do you need?"

"Get him water and monitor him. If anything changes—respiratory distress, chest pain, anything—you call 911. Understand?"

"I—yeah. Okay." Floyd moved to Vinnie's side mechanically.

I stood there, motionless, as I allowed a Zen calmness to unexpectantly wash over me.

"Nicholas?" William's voice was small. "What are you doing?"

I grabbed the keys to the van. Walked toward the front door.

"Nicholas?" Floyd's voice had gone sharp with alarm. "Where are you going?"

I turned back to look at Vinnie on the floor with Garth kneeling protectively at his side. Vinnie was completely out of it, but on the mend. And in my head, a crystal clear, existential epiphany struck.

I finally understood Agnes Cartwright.

And I was suddenly certain of what I had to do next.

I was going to kill Francis Donahey.

I walked out the front door, my heartbeat steady and slow.

Time to make the donuts.

Chapter Forty-Four

Vinnie had been dead for two minutes.

I didn't remember driving to the park. Didn't remember getting in the van, starting the engine, navigating the streets. One moment I was walking out our front door, the next I was pulling into a parking spot with no memory of the journey between.

Autopilot. Muscle memory. The same route Vinnie must have ran earlier today.

I turned off the engine and sat there, hands still on the wheel.

Through the windshield, I could see them.

Francis and Scott at their usual table. The one they pretended to play chess at. Laughing. Heads thrown back. Scott slapping the table. Francis holding a phone up, watching something, his face lit by the screen's glow.

They had no idea.

No idea that a few minutes ago, I'd driven a needle through my brother's sternum and flooded his heart with adrenaline because one of them had thought it would be funny to drug him. No idea that Vinnie had collapsed on our living room floor and I'd performed CPR to save his life. No idea that my twin—my responsibility, my entire fucking world—had been dead for almost two minutes because Francis Donahey wanted entertainment.

They were laughing.

I sat there and watched them laugh, and something crystallized in my mind with the kind of clarity you only get when you've stopped giving a shit about consequences.

This wasn't an isolated incident. This was the world.

This was what typicals did to people like Vinnie. Not all of them, I know, but enough. Enough that every trip to the grocery store required strategic planning. Enough that every family gathering meant fielding the same invasive questions about Vinnie's "situation." Enough that I'd learned to recognize the look in people's eyes when they first met him. That fractional pause, that recalibration, that decision tree processing: *Special needs. Disabled. Different. Lesser. Invisible.*

Some people hid it better than others. Some buried it under performative kindness or inspiration-porn sentimentality. Others, like Francis, didn't bother hiding it at all.

But the bias was there. Woven so completely into the tapestry of society that most people didn't even register it as bias. It was just...the way things were. The natural order. The hierarchy of human value.

People with disabilities weren't quite real to them. Weren't productive members of society. Weren't quite *people* in the way that counted.

So, mocking them didn't really count as cruelty. Drugging them was just a prank. Filming their suffering was content. Because deep down, on some level most typicals would never consciously acknowledge, they didn't believe people like Vinnie had the same capacity for pain, for fear, for humiliation.

Or love.

They didn't think people like Vinnie were fully human.

And that's what allowed them to do shit like this without losing sleep. That's what allowed Francis to dose my brother with cocaine and then film him having a drug-induced psychosis at a playground. That's what allowed Scott to watch and laugh and hold the fucking camera steady.

The cruelty was unconscious. Reflexive. Cultural.

I'd spent my entire adult life trying to change this. Educating. Being a advocate of the disability community. The patient explainer. The reasonable one. The bridge-builder between worlds.

And what had it gotten me?

A dead mother who'd worked herself into an early grave trying to prove her son was worthy of existence. A system that saw people like Vinnie as problems to be managed rather than humans to be respected. And Francis fucking Donahey, still laughing at the chess table.

Almost every major advancement in human history had come from someone different. Someone who saw the world sideways. Someone whose brain didn't work the typical way. Curie. Einstein. Mozart. Tesla. Turing. Van Gogh.

Different minds changed the world.

But society didn't celebrate "different." Society tolerated it, at best, and at worst, it punished it. Mocked it.

Drugged it and filmed it for laughs.

Vinnie had learned to smile through the mockery. To pretend he didn't notice when people talked about him like he wasn't there. To accept "special" as a euphemism for "less than."

Where did that leave the caregivers, the family members, the people who loved someone the world had decided didn't matter?

Where did that leave me?

I opened the van door and stepped out into the summer evening.

Society taught us that violence only made things worse. That we couldn't take the law into our own hands. That there were proper channels, correct procedures, appropriate ways to address grievances.

And that was all well and good.

But what happened when society itself was the problem? What happened when the proper channels didn't give a shit? When the correct procedures were designed to protect people like Francis and control people like Vinnie?

The system wouldn't protect Vinnie. Society wouldn't protect him. The law wouldn't protect him.

I would.

Even if it killed me.

I rounded the back of the van and opened the rear doors. Garth's sports equipment was neatly organized—football, basketball, tennis racket, and three aluminum bats of various lengths.

I pulled out the middle one. Thirty-two inches. Two pounds.

I hefted it, feeling the balance. Garth had excellent taste in sports equipment.

The walk across the park felt longer than it should have. Each step measured. Calm. My heart beat steady and slow, like I was heading to work, not murder.

Because that's what this was. I had no illusions about that.

Francis and Scott still hadn't seen me. Too focused on Scott's phone, held between them. Utterly absorbed watching their video of Vinnie as if it were a comedy special.

As I got closer, I could hear it.

Vinnie's voice, manic and wrong, coming from the phone's speaker: "... need to run or something—"

Scott's voice: "Holy shit, look at him go!"

Vinnie's voice: "I'm a superhero! I can do anything!"

Francis, laughing so hard he could barely breathe: "Oh my god, send me that. This is fucking gold."

I was ten feet away when Scott's peripheral vision finally caught me. He looked up, saw me, saw the bat. He didn't have time to warn Francis.

I swung.

The bat connected with Scott's face with a sound like a watermelon splitting. His nose exploded in a spray of blood and cartilage. The phone flew from his hand. He went down hard, hitting the ground before his brain fully registered what had happened.

Francis bolted up from his bench, stumbling backward, keeping the table between us. His eyes found mine, then traveled to the bat, then back to my face.

For a moment, neither of us moved.

Then Francis smiled. Not his usual charming, shit-eating grin. Something else. Something eager.

"Took you long enough," he said. "I was starting to think you didn't care. Your response time on protecting the Vinman is down. You usually come a running the moment he squirts out a tear."

I didn't respond.

"How is the Vinman doing?" Francis asked, circling slowly, keeping the table between us. "Been keeping his nose clean?"

Still, I said nothing. I adjusted my grip on the bat.

And that unnerved him. I could see it in the way his smile faltered, in how his eyes kept darting to the bat, in how his casual stance became forced.

"Say something," Francis said, and now there was an edge

beneath the bravado. "Come on, man. This isn't fun if you don't react."

The silence stretched.

"Say something!"

"I'm going to kill you, Francis," I said.

Then I came around the table.

Francis dodged the first swing. Barely. The bat whistled past his head close enough to ruffle his hair. He backpedaled, hands up, and I followed. Measured. Patient.

The second swing, he ducked. Third swing, he managed to catch the bat mid-arc, both hands wrapping around it, stopping its momentum.

We stood there, locked together, both gripping the bat. His face was six inches from mine.

"You still don't get it," Francis grunted, trying to wrench the bat away. "All these years, you think you're so much better than me—"

I drove my knee into his stomach. His grip loosened, but he held on, and we stumbled together, wrestling for control, neither willing to let go.

"You're not! We're the same. That's right, the same!" Francis yelled as we struggled for control. "The high-and-mighty Nicholas Murphy is just like good ol' Frank Donahey!"

I was nothing like this piece of shit. I wrenched sideways with my body weight and the bat slipped from both our hands and clattered across the pavement.

Fine.

We'd do this like we did in high school.

Francis threw the first punch—wild, aiming for my jaw. I slipped it, countered with a jab to his ribs. He grunted and grabbed my shirt to throw me. I hooked his leg; we both went down, grappling.

We rolled on the concrete, trading positions. I got on top,

managed two good hits to his face before he bucked me off. We scrambled up, and suddenly we were sixteen again, trading punches behind the gym, except this time there'd be no principal to break it up.

This time, one of us was going to die.

I'd trained for this. Years of hitting the bag in the backyard. Years of angry nights working through my frustration on something that couldn't feel pain. I was faster, more skilled, and absolutely fucking enraged.

But Francis didn't fight fair.

He never did.

"If I'd known all it took was to coke up your better half to make you see we're the same, I'da done it a long time ago, little Nicky," Francis said between punches, backing up, circling.

He was trying to bait me. Make me sloppy.

"But because you have a retard sidekick, you think you're holier-than-thou, always looking down at everyone, the pillar of society. Take the tard outta the equation and merry ol' St. Nic is exactly the same as good ol' Frank Donahey," Francis taunted.

It worked.

I charged, not meaning to telegraph the punch. Francis sidestepped, and I realized too late that he'd maneuvered me— that my back was now to where Scott had fallen.

I started to turn, but something caught me at the base of my skull—a crack of aluminum on bone that turned my vision white.

My legs went out. I hit the pavement face first, tasting blood and concrete.

Above me, Scott stood swaying, holding my own bat, his face a mask of blood from his shattered nose.

I tried to get up. Made it to my knees before Scott hit me again. Something cracked—rib, maybe.

Then Francis was on me, kicking. Collarbone. Stomach. Kidneys. Each impact punctuated with grunts of effort and epithets I barely processed.

Scott swung the bat again. Caught me in the ribs on the left side. Definitely broken now.

I curled into a fetal position, arms over my head, knees tucked, protecting my vital organs the way I'd learned in the self-defense class I'd taken a lifetime ago. Make yourself small.

This was it, then.

I was going to die in a park at the hands of Francis fucking Donahey.

It didn't matter.

Because all I could think about was...

Who's going to take care of Vinnie?

Another impact. This one to the hea—

Chapter Forty-Five

I woke up on the couch and everything hurt.

My chest felt like someone put a hot iron on it. My arms were sore. My head was fuzzy.

The Family was in the kitchen. I could hear them talking loud but the words didn't make sense yet. Like when you turn on the TV in the middle of a show.

"—just walked out without saying anything—" That was William's voice, high and scared.

"He took the van keys," Floyd said. "That's all I saw."

"But where would he go? It's late! The heist is tomorrow!"

My brain was starting to work better. I remembered things in pieces.

Francis gave me a drink.

I ran home.

My chest hurt.

Then nothing...

Then I woke up on the floor with Nicholas looking down at me.

Nicholas leaving...

I tried to sit up but my chest screamed at me to stop. I made a sound without meaning to.

The Family rushed into the living room like I was on fire.

"Vinnie!" William said. "Don't move! You died! You were dead for almost two minutes!"

That explained why I hurt so much.

"Where's Nicholas?" I asked. My voice sounded wrong. Scratchy.

Floyd and William looked at each other deciding who should tell me the news.

"We don't know," Floyd said. "He just...left."

Nicholas always told us where he was going. Always.

"Was he mad or yelling when he left?" I asked.

William and Floyd looked at each other again.

"That's what was strange," William said slowly. "He wasn't yelling at all. He was...calm. Very calm. He grabbed the van keys and just walked out like he had errands to run."

My stomach dropped, like when you're on a rollercoaster that goes down too fast.

I understood what that meant.

"He went to fight Francis," I said. "At the park."

"What?" William's voice went high. "Why would—"

"Because of what Francis did to me!" The words came fast. "We have to stop him!"

I grabbed the arm of the couch and pulled myself up. Everything hurt. My chest burned. My legs felt like they were made of gelatin.

But Nicholas was in danger.

Nicholas and Francis fought all the time. And Nicholas didn't always win.

"Garth," I said, looking at him. "I can't run. I'm too hurt. But you can."

Garth's eyes got wide and he leaned toward me.

"Run to the park as fast as you can. Stop Nicholas. We'll be right behind you."

Garth nodded once, hard, and ran out the door. I heard his feet pounding down the driveway.

"William, help me walk," I said. "Floyd, let's go."

We went outside. Every step hurt, but I kept moving. Floyd's electric wheelchair hummed beside us. William held my arm.

Nicholas needed us.

When we got to the park, I saw the crowd first. A big circle of people. Some holding up their phones to film.

I pushed through without looking at anyone. The Family came right behind me.

Then I saw.

Garth was kneeling on the ground, holding Nicholas.

Nicholas's face was covered in blood. His eyes were closed. He wasn't moving.

Nicholas was dead.

Then I saw his chest move. Just a little.

Breathing.

"Vinnie!" Garth's voice was too loud. "No Francis! Just Nicholas!"

Someone in the crowd said, "I called 911. Ambulance should be here any minute."

No.

No 911. No police. No ambulance.

They would ask questions. They would investigate. Charity would find out.

If the authorities got involved, we were done. The heist was done. Everything was done.

I knelt down next to Garth and Nicholas. Nicholas's face

was a mess. Blood from his nose and mouth. Cuts everywhere. One eye swollen shut.

I reached into his pocket and found the van keys.

"No ambulance," I said to Garth. "We're taking him to the hospital. I'll drive."

Garth's eyes got wide. "You drive?"

"Yes," I said, even though my hands were shaking. "Pick him up. Let's go."

We walked through the crowd. People moved out of our way.

Garth carried Nicholas to the van and gently laid him on the backseat. William climbed in with him. I think Floyd felt guilty because his chair took so long to load. After a long time waiting, I got in the driver's seat. My hands were shaking.

I had never driven anywhere except the heist route.

"Vinnie," Floyd said, "I'm pulling up hospital directions on GPS."

"Vinnie can't—" William started from the back.

"I can do this!" I said. "But I need help. All of you have to help me."

Floyd pulled up the GPS. The phone lady started talking.

And we did it together.

Floyd called out landmarks I would know—the gas station with the blue sign, the grocery store, the church with the tall steeple. William watched out the back and told me when cars were behind me. Garth pointed from the passenger seat when I needed to turn. The phone lady said the directions, and I turned them into places I could understand.

It was scary. My chest hurt. My hands were sweating on the steering wheel. But the Family helped me see. Helped me know where to go. Helped me drive my dying brother to the hospital.

It wasn't far.

Just a few minutes.

That took forever.

The emergency room doors opened automatically.

Garth carried Nicholas in his arms. I walked behind him, my chest still burning. Floyd's wheelchair hummed beside me. William followed, his fingers tapping.

A nurse at the desk looked up and her face changed when she saw us.

I watched her eyes move from person to person.

Big deaf Garth, carrying an unconscious beaten man.

Me, with Down syndrome, walking like I might fall over.

Floyd, in his wheelchair, body branded by lightning.

William, standing too straight, fingers tapping, not making eye contact.

It was the same look people gave us everywhere.

The look that said: *You don't belong.*

The look that said: *Someone normal must be in charge of you.*

"My brother needs help!" I said loud. "He had a bicycle accident!"

The nurse pressed a button. More nurses came running with a stretcher. Garth put Nicholas on it.

"What happened?" one of them asked.

"Bicycle accident," I said again. "He wasn't wearing a helmet."

If I said he was attacked, they would call the police. We couldn't have police.

They wheeled Nicholas away fast. Through doors we couldn't go through.

.   .   .

We sat in the waiting room a really long time. The lights were too bright. The chairs were uncomfortable. And we were miserable.

William paced. Floyd stared at the doors. Garth sat very still. I felt my chest hurt and thought about Nicholas somewhere behind those doors.

This was the first time we'd been in a hospital without Nicholas. Without a typical.

William stopped and started bouncing on his toes, his fingers tapping even faster.

I didn't know what to do.

Then a doctor finally came through the doors. She was old, with gray hair. She looked at our family, and I watched her decide who to talk to.

Her eyes landed on William because William looked the most typical.

"Are you the family of Nicholas Murphy?" the doctor asked William.

William opened his mouth, but I stood up first.

"I'm Nicholas's twin brother," I said. My voice came out strong. I had to be now.

The doctor's eyebrows went up. She looked at me for a long moment.

Then she nodded.

"Your brother has several broken ribs, extensive contusions, and significant cranial trauma," the doctor said. "The accident caused his brain to swell. We're placing him in a medically induced coma to allow the swelling to subside."

"Is he going to die?" I asked.

The doctor's face was serious. "It's touch and go. The next twenty-four to forty-eight hours are critical."

Touch and go. That meant maybe yes, maybe no.

"I want to see him," I said.

"He's unconscious. He won't know you're there."

"Then it doesn't matter if I see him."

I walked toward the doors. The Family came right behind me.

We followed the doctor down white hallways to a room. Then she left to give us privacy to see Nicholas.

My brother was in a bed with rails. Machines beeping. Tubes in his arms. A tube down his throat connected to a machine that breathed for him. His face was swollen and purple.

"We need to call Rita," William said. His voice was shaking. "She needs to know."

"No," I said.

"What?" William turned to me. "Vinnie, she's his girlfriend—"

"Ex-girlfriend," Floyd said. "He broke up with her."

"To protect her!" William said too loud. "But this is different! This is—we have to tell her!"

"If Rita gets involved, the heist is done," I said. "Nicholas wanted her protected. We're not calling her."

William's face went red. "The heist is done! Don't you understand? We needed Nicholas! A typical! To get into the bank! To be Diego Locksley! Without him, we're finished. We're dead! We're all dead!"

His words echoed in the sterile room.

I looked at Nicholas in the bed. At the machines keeping him alive.

All my life, people told me what I couldn't do.

Can't go to regular school. Can't have a real job. Can't live alone. Can't be trusted. Can't be normal.

Can't can't can't can't can't.

And I believed them. Because everyone said it. Teachers.

Doctors. Social workers. Strangers. Even Chef before he saw I could really cook.

So, I became what they expected. I let Nicholas make all the decisions. I stayed safe and protected.

But right now, I wasn't the one who needed protecting.

I was the one who *did* the protecting.

The long Tetris piece fell down in my head. The straight piece that makes everything fit.

I looked at my Family. Floyd and William and Garth and Nicholas.

"I've been dead before," I told them. "The heist is still happening," I continued. My voice was calm. The kind of calm Nicholas used when he was absolutely sure.

"Vinnie—" William started.

"We trained hard for this," I said. "Nicholas got us this far, we'll carry him across the finish line."

"But our plan requires a typical," Floyd said.

"We have one," I said.

I turned to look directly at William.

William's eyes went wide. He shook his head fast. "No. No no no. Vinnie, I can't—"

"You can," I said. "You're the only one who can."

"I'm not typical!" William said. His voice got high and squeaky. "I'm autistic! I stim! I hide behind Mr. Darcy! How am I supposed to be Nicholas?!"

"You don't have to be Nicholas," I said. "You'll be Diego Locksley. Diego Locksley is already not real. You just have to be not real for an hour."

William was breathing fast, like when there aren't enough eggs.

"You wrote the VR program," I said gently. "You know every step better than any of us. You ran millions and millions of simulations."

"That's different!" William said. "That's code! That's not real people!"

"Like Mr. Darcy?" I pressed.

"That's different—"

"How?"

"Mr. Darcy is safe," he finally said. "Mr. Darcy is a shield. I know exactly what he'd say because he's from a book. He's fixed. Predictable. I don't know who the fuck Diego Locksley is."

"You watched Nicholas be Diego Locksley in the VR for hours. You know what he does. Be that," I said.

"What if I panic? What if I have a meltdown in the bank?"

I looked at Garth. "Garth goes to live with Charity. She gets conservatorship. She controls him forever."

William flinched.

I looked at Floyd. "Floyd loses his home. Gets sent to a nursing facility."

Floyd's jaw clenched.

I looked at William. "You get sent to a group home. Maybe one with bad Wi-Fi. Definitely one where you can't watch *Pride and Prejudice* whenever you want."

William's eyes locked on mine.

"I get sent to state care. And Nicholas," I said, gesturing to the bed. "Nicholas wakes up and finds out he sacrificed everything for nothing."

"Or we do the heist," William squeaked out.

The room was quiet except for machines beeping.

Everyone looked at William.

William looked at Nicholas in the bed. At the tubes and machines. At his swollen face.

Then William looked at Garth. At Floyd. At me.

He was quiet for a long time.

Then he took a deep breath and nodded once.

"Okay," William said. His voice was shaky but sure. "I'll do it. But tomorrow's out of the question. I'm going to need some time. We reschedule Heist Club until I'm ready."

"Why do you need time?" I asked.

"First, we have to fix the prosthetics to make me look like Diego Locksley," William said, like we should have known that already. Then his face scrunched up like he bit into a lemon as he sighed, "Then...I need to learn how to pass as a typical."

Chapter Forty-Six

Floyd had all the supplies spread out on the kitchen table—
silicone pieces, adhesive, makeup, brushes, sponges. He'd
watched Nicholas practice this so many times he said he could
do it in his sleep. Plus, he had socials to watch for backup.

"Sit still," Floyd told William for the third time.

William was not sitting still. His fingers were tapping on
his leg. His foot was bouncing. His whole body wanted to run
away from Floyd touching his face.

"I can't," William said. His voice was high and tight. "I
don't like people touching me."

"I am aware," Floyd said. He was being very patient. "But if
we can't get the prosthetics right, this is all for nothing."

William took a deep breath and tried again to sit still. Floyd
pressed a piece of silicone to William's nose bridge. William
flinched.

"Think of something else," Garth suggested. He was
watching from across the table.

"Like how fucked we are?" William asked without moving
his mouth much.

"Language," Garth reminded William.

"How about thinking of your favorite scene from *Pride and Prejudice*?" I offered.

William's eyes lit up a little. "The one where Mr. Darcy confesses his love in the rain, or the BBC version where—"

"Either," I said. "Just sit still."

Floyd worked for a few minutes in silence. William's fingers kept tapping, but he stayed mostly still.

"This is impossible," William said after a while. "Even if you make me look like Diego Locksley, I can't act like a typical. I can't. I'll panic. I'll say the wrong thing. Typicals will know. It's impossible."

I sat down across from him. "Our Family overcomes impossible every day we wake up."

"That's different."

"How?"

"We overcome impossible things that involve our disabilities," William said. "This is asking me to pretend I don't have one. For an extended period. Around strangers. In a high-stress situation. I can't—I literally cannot interact with typicals for that long. It's why I can't hold a real coding job. Why I work from home. Why I—"

"You already know how," I interrupted.

William blinked at me. "What?"

"You coded a tool to do it. Your VR bank."

I watched his face change. The same way mine changed in the hospital when the long Tetris piece fell into place. Or in a movie, when everything suddenly made sense and the camera moved forward and backward at the same time to tell you it's important.

"I can practice," William whispered. "In VR. Social interaction scenarios. Different typicals. Different conversations. I can run simulations until—"

He tried to jump up but Floyd grabbed his shoulder.

"Stay. Still," Floyd said firmly.

William froze. But he was smiling now. A real smile, not his Mr. Darcy smile.

Floyd worked for two more hours. I watched him apply each piece of silicone like he was building one of his drones as he matched William's face to Diego Locksley's picture the best he could.

William got twitchy again after a while. His eyes kept moving. His fingers kept tapping.

"You know what helps?" Floyd said while he blended the edges of a cheek piece. "I saw this interview once with Danny DeVito. When he played the Penguin in the old Batman movie, he had to sit in makeup for hours every single day."

"*Batman Returns*. A golden oldie. How did he endure it?" William asked.

"He kept his eyes closed the whole time," Floyd said. "Until the makeup was done. Then he'd open his eyes and see the monster that was the Penguin staring back. He said he loved experiencing the transformation every day. Because his mask made it so easy to be the Penguin."

William listened to this story like there was a test later.

Then he closed his eyes.

"Tell me when you're done," William said quietly.

Floyd smiled and kept working.

When Floyd finally put down his brushes, he said, "Okay, William. Open your eyes."

William opened his eyes. He looked in the mirror Floyd held up.

The person looking back wasn't William. It wasn't Nicholas either. It was someone new. Someone in between.

"It's not exact, but you definitely look like Diego Locksley's first or second derivative," Floyd said as he watched William stare into Diego Locksley's eyes in the mirror.

"Floyd, you are a sorcerer," William whispered.

William touched his face gently. "This is...very convincing."

"Thanks." Floyd looked proud. "Now, let's see if you can act the part."

William stood in the middle of the living room with his VR headset on.

To us, he looked silly. Standing there with a big headset on, moving his hands in the air, talking to people we couldn't see.

But to William, he was in the bank.

"Good morning," William said in his Mr. Darcy voice. Very proper. Very stiff. "I require access to my safety deposit box, if you would be so kind."

"No!" I said. "That's Mr. Darcy! Diego Locksley doesn't talk like that!"

William lifted the headset. "But I don't know how Diego Locksley talks!"

"Like Nicholas," Floyd said. "Casual. Normal. A little bit friendly."

"I don't know how to be casual!" William said.

"Pretend the bank people are us," Garth suggested.

William made a face. "That seems psychologically unhealthy."

"Just try," I said.

William put the headset back on. He took a deep breath.

"Hey, morning," William tried. His voice was less Darcy but still weird. Too cheerful. Like he was trying too hard. "I need to get into my safety deposit box. Number 130500. Thanks a bunch!"

"Better," Floyd said. "But you sound like you're in a Mentos commercial."

"What's that?"

"Nobody's that happy. You look psychotic," Floyd explained. "Nicholas is polite, not excited."

William adjusted. "Good morning. I need access to my safety deposit box. Number 130500."

"Better!" I said. "But make your voice sound more bored."

"Bored?"

"Like when Garth tells you about his workout," I added.

"Hey!" Garth said.

William tried again. And again. And again.

Each time we gave him notes like we were his director.

"Don't stand so straight. Slouch a little."

"Nicholas doesn't say 'indeed.' Stop saying 'indeed.'"

"When the bank person talks, you have to look at them. Not at their forehead. At their eyes."

"You're tapping your fingers again. Diego Locksley doesn't do that."

After an hour, William got frustrated. He pulled off the headset and threw it on the couch.

"This is impossible! Every time I think I'm doing it right, one of you tells me I'm wrong!"

"You're getting better," I said.

"I'm a disaster!"

"William," Floyd said calmly. "In the last hour, you went from Regency gentleman to slightly awkward but acceptable typical person. That's progress."

William looked at him. "Really?"

"Really. You just need more practice to get to Carnegie Hall," I said.

William picked up the headset again. "Okay."

We practiced for the rest of the day. William would go into

the VR bank and interact with the virtual people. We would watch him and give him feedback. Sometimes Garth would demonstrate how a typical person stands. Sometimes Floyd would show him how to make small talk. Sometimes I would remind him to breathe normally and not hold his breath when he talked.

By dinner time, William could walk into the virtual bank, talk to the virtual teller, and get into the virtual safety deposit box room without acting like Mr. Darcy or having an attack.

This went on for a week.

Every morning, Floyd would apply the prosthetics while William kept his eyes closed and thought about Danny DeVito becoming the Penguin. Every afternoon, William would put on his VR headset and practice being Diego Locksley in the bank. And then every night, William made us watch *Breaking Bad*.

All of *Breaking Bad*.

I hated *Breaking Bad* at first. It was so slow. Nothing happened for like three episodes.

But William said we had to watch it. He said it was important.

By episode four, I understood.

Walter White's family was threatened. He had cancer. He had no money. The system failed him. So, he became a criminal to protect his family.

Just like us.

"See?" William said during one episode. "Walter White is breaking bad. That means doing wrong things for the right reasons."

I thought about that a lot. Walter White wasn't bad. He made bad choices for good reasons.

Just like us.

While we watched *Breaking Bad* at night, Nicholas stayed

in the hospital in his coma. The doctors said he was stable. Not getting worse. But not getting better either.

And William made great progress. By the end of the week, he could be Diego Locksley for almost an hour without slipping into Mr. Darcy or having a meltdown.

Floyd said the prosthetics looked perfect. He could apply them in thirty minutes now without William fidgeting.

We were as ready as we were going to be.

Tomorrow was the heist.

I drove the route by myself that night.

The whole route. From our house to the bank to the alley and back home. I drove it twice to make sure I remembered every landmark. Every turn. Every street.

I could do this.

Then I set my GPS for the hospital and drove there. It was a different route. Streets I didn't know. But the phone lady helped me, and I found the landmarks, and I got there without getting lost.

I parked in the visitor lot and went inside.

The nurse at the desk recognized me. She smiled and nodded me through.

Nicholas's room was dark except for the machines. They beeped softly. The breathing tube made a whooshing sound.

I sat in the chair next to his bed.

"Hey, Nicholas," I said quietly. "It's me."

He didn't answer. He couldn't answer. The tube down his throat breathed for him.

"The heist is tomorrow," I told him. "I wish you could be there. I wish you could be Diego Locksley and be in charge. But you can't."

The machines beeped. The tube whooshed.

"This past week I had to take care of the Family like you," I said. "I had to make decisions and check on everyone and make sure we were ready. Floyd helped, but it's a lot. It's only been a week, and I'm so tired. You did this forever."

I looked at his swollen face. At the tubes and wires keeping him alive.

"Thank you," I said. My throat felt tight. "For everything. For rescuing me from state care. For always protecting me even when I didn't want to be protected. For being my brother."

I took his hand. It was warm but limp.

"I understand now," I said. "What you sacrificed. How much you gave up for me. For all of us."

The machines kept beeping. Nicholas kept breathing. But it was the machine, not him.

"I'm terrified," I admitted. "But one way or another, Heist Club ends tomorrow."

I squeezed his hand and stood up. Kissed his forehead like he used to do to me when I was scared.

"I love you, Nicholas."

I walked to the door. Put my hand on the handle.

Then I stopped.

I turned back around.

Nicholas lay there in the bed. Unconscious. Maybe dying.

"If you're with Mom," I said quietly, "I need you both to do something for me."

My voice came out soft but certain.

At my side, my hands clenched into fists.

"Look away," I said. "I'm about to break bad."

Chapter Forty-Seven

Oh, I think we're back where I started telling my story too late at the beginning. Where was I? Oh yeah, in the middle of Heist Club—

Outside First National Bank...

"Game time, everyone. Stick to the plan," I told my Family through the earpiece. "We do this right, it'll all be over in five minutes—"

TAP TAP TAP.

I turned to see a police officer tapping at my window.

Oh shit.

We looked at each other through the glass. Both of us shocked.

I was shocked because I was robbing a bank.

The police officer was shocked because...well, I had Down syndrome and was driving a getaway van.

I didn't know what to do...

The officer motioned for me to roll down the window.

I couldn't move. Couldn't breathe. Couldn't think.

My hand moved to the window button like it belonged to someone else. The glass slid down with an electric whine.

I watched the police officer take a long, confused look at my Down syndrome face.

"I'm sorry, can you drive?" he blurted out.

My brain froze like I drank a milkshake in one slurp.

I wanted to say something, anything...

Nothing came out.

In my earpiece, William's voice suddenly spoke. Calm. Clear. And in a voice I hated more than anything.

"I'm an excellent driver," he said.

No.

"I'm an excellent driver," William repeated.

Then Floyd's voice joined in. "I'm an excellent driver."

"*Say it*, Vinnie," I heard William tell me over the comms.

My brain was too panicked to—

"I'm an excellent driver!" William said firmly over comms.

And then it happened.

I blurted, "I'm an excellent driver."

The words came out loud. Flat. Not my normal voice. It was that stupid *Rain Man* voice, the one I promised I'd never do.

The police officer blinked at me. "What?"

In my ear, William and Floyd started talking faster, saying quotes over and over until I said them to the police officer.

"Definitely, definitely," William said.

"One minute to Judge Wapner, *oh boy*," Floyd said.

My mouth opened and the words came out before I could stop them.

"Definitely, definitely, one minute to Judge Wapner, *oh boy*," I repeated to the police officer.

"Sir—" the police officer started.

"Course I don't have my underwear. I'm definitely not wearing my underwear," I heard myself say. "K-Mart. I get my underwear at K-Mart. Definitely have to watch Wapner at four o'clock. I'm an excellent driver. Definitely, definitely."

I finally ran out of breath.

The police officer's expression changed from confused to something else. His eyes narrowed. I watched him understand.

He knew I was quoting *Rain Man*.

He thought I was mocking him.

I can't believe Rain Man is going to send me to prison.

Then the officer's face got hard. He clenched his jaw and said, "Jesus, Rain Man, I'm sorry. You don't have to bite my head off!" His face was red when he stepped back from the van, shaking his head like he couldn't believe someone with Down syndrome just made fun of him.

The police officer got very annoyed and asked, "Can I see some ID, sir?"

I pulled out my wallet and handed him my fake ID. The police officer was surprised as he studied it. I could see him reading the fake name I picked.

"Mr. Mario Bourdain?" the police officer asked me.

"Yes, how can I help you, officer?" I said as he handed me back my fake ID.

"I was trying to tell you you're in a fifteen-minute parking zone. You have a nice day, sir," he said and definitely didn't mean it. Embarrassed, the police officer grabbed his bicycle and pedaled away at lightning speed, like he couldn't get away from me fast enough.

I watched the police officer disappear as he turned down Winter Avenue where Garth was setting up his traffic cones.

I started breathing again. I hated *Rain Man*, but today that stupid movie kept me out of prison.

"I see what you did there," I said quietly into the comms. "I hate you all. Thanks."

"You're welcome," William said.

"Definitely welcome, *oh boy!*" Floyd added in his Rain Man voice.

"William, you're up," I said into the comms.

William's voice came through my earpiece. Shaky but determined. "Acknowledged. I'm going radio silent until I reach the safety deposit box room. But I can still hear you all. If I slip into Mr. Darcy instead of Diego Locksley, feel free to...Cyrano de Bergerac me."

"Are you speaking like Mr. Darcy again?" I asked because I didn't understand.

"It means we'll help him if he freezes," Floyd explained quickly. "Like we helped you."

"Copy that," I said.

I looked across the street to check on Garth. He was easy to spot in his bright orange construction vest. He was placing the last traffic cone on Winter Avenue. Cars were already starting to go around. Garth said through comms, "I'm set." He couldn't hear our comms, but he could read the captions of our conversation using his phone's accessibility feature.

William's voice came through my earpiece. Quiet. Like he was talking to himself more than us.

"Here goes everything."

I could hear William walking in the bank. And then I heard, "Good morning," William's voice said through my earpiece loud and clear. He sounded...confident. "I am Diego Locksley. I require access to my safety deposit box, if you would be so kind."

"If you would be so kind" was definitely Mr. Darcy.

"William," I whispered into the comms. "You sound like Mr. Darcy at a tea party."

William couldn't answer back. But I hoped he heard me.

The bank manager stood up. It was the same voice of the man Nicholas met when Diego first rented the box. "Mr. Locksley! Good to see you again," the bank manager said to William. "How can I help you today?"

I heard William pat his duffel bag. The bag with Mozart hidden inside. "I need to access my box. I'm working on a new prototype I need to secure. Top secret. Very hush-hush. It's for a major Hollywood franchise. I cannot disclose which one at this juncture, but I assure you, it's quite significant."

"*Diego*," I said into the comms. "Take it down a notch."

I heard William try to correct himself. "The intellectual property contained within this bag represents years of innovation and—"

"Just breathe," Floyd's voice cut in. "Less is more."

William stopped talking mid-sentence. Took a breath. Started again, calmer this time.

"Forgive me. I get excited about my work," William said. More natural now. "Just need to access my box."

"Better. Much better," I encouraged William.

I could hear the bank manager start typing. "No problem at all, Mr. Locksley. Let me just pull up your account." After a bunch of typing he continued, "You know, Mr. Locksley, you look different."

William froze.

Then the bank manager added, "'Have you lost some weight since last we met?"

Then Floyd's voice came through. Calm. Clear. Feeding William the line.

"Thank you. Been working out. It's good to get noticed," Floyd said in our ears.

William sounded like a puppet. "Thank you. Been working out. It's good to get noticed."

The bank manager said, "Well, it shows. Keep it up."

"I shall endeavor to do so," William said.

I made a face. Mr. Darcy was slipping through.

But the bank manager didn't notice. I heard him get up and say, "Alright, Mr. Locksley. Let's get you to your box."

I could hear the bank manager lead William toward the back of the bank where the safety deposit boxes were.

"Here we are," the bank manager said. "Box 130500."

I heard the sound of keys. Two locks clicking. One after the other.

"There you go," the Bank Manager said. "Take all the time you need. Just close the box when you're done and give me a holler."

"Thank you kindly," William said.

Footsteps. The door closing.

Silence.

Then William's voice, barely a whisper. "I'm in."

I let out a breath I didn't know I was holding.

Floyd's voice came through the comms. "William, turn on your phone camera. We need eyes."

I heard rustling. William moving. Then William's laptop screen sitting in the passenger seat lit up with a split-screen that showed video from William's phone on one screen and Mozart's camera on the other screen, just like Floyd planned.

We could see what William was seeing now.

The safety deposit box room was small. Maybe as big as my bedroom. Gray walls. Lights that buzzed. Rows and rows of metal boxes on every wall. Each one with a number.

William's camera moved to two boxes right next to each other.

Box 130500. Diego Locksley's box. Our box.

Box 103055. Charity Cartwright's box.

Two million dollars was sitting right there. Just on the other side of that metal door.

"Floyd," I said into the comms. "Get Mozart ready."

"Already on it," Floyd said.

I watched Floyd through my windshield. He was outside the bank, sitting in his wheelchair with Mozart's controller in his hands. His fingers were moving across the buttons like he was playing a video game. Except this wasn't a game. This was our lives.

William reached into his duffel bag and pulled out Mozart. The little drone looked like a toy, which is what we wanted people to think if they saw it. But Mozart was much more than a toy. Mozart was our key to everything.

William set Mozart on the table.

"Set," William said into the comms.

Floyd's voice came through my earpiece. "Activating Mozart now."

On my laptop screen, I saw Mozart's propellers start spinning. The little drone lifted off the table and hovered in the air. It moved toward Box 103055. Charity's box.

Mozart was so steady. Like it was held by invisible hands.

Two small arms came out from Mozart's body. They looked like thin robot fingers. Floyd had spent weeks making those arms perfect.

The arms moved toward the two locks on Charity's box. One lock was hers. One lock was the bank's.

Mozart inserted two fake keys into the locks. Keys that Floyd made special. Then Mozart's arms started moving. Trying to pick both locks.

I held my breath.

"Should be done in a jiffy," Floyd said over the comms, but his voice sounded nervous.

Time passed. Mozart kept working on the locks. The arms kept moving.

But nothing was happening.

"Floyd?" William asked quietly. "How long is a jiffy?"

Floyd didn't answer right away. Then he said something that made William worry even more.

"Please refrain from talking. I only have three shots at this."

"What?!" William's voice got high and squeaky.

"I'm kidding. Be quiet and let me work," Floyd said.

I watched my laptop screen. Mozart's arms kept working. Picking the locks.

Time felt weird. Like it was going too fast and too slow at the same time.

I watched the screen. I watched Floyd outside. I couldn't breathe.

Mozart's arms were moving. Working the locks. Trying to get them to turn.

Please work. Please please please work.

Nothing was happening.

We were going to fail.

Then—

CLICK.

Both locks turned.

It was the best sound I ever heard.

"Yes!" Floyd yelled so loud in my ear it hurt.

Mozart's propellers wound down. The little drone landed on the table like a bird coming home to rest.

William was breathing hard. I could hear him through the comms.

"William?" I said. "You okay?"

"I'm okay," William said, but his voice was shaky. "I'm opening the box now."

I watched the screen as William reached for Box 103055. He pulled it out of the wall. Set it on the table. Opened the lid.

And there it was.

Money.

So much money.

Stacks and stacks of hundred-dollar bills crammed inside the box. Some stacks had rubber bands. Some didn't. It looked like someone had just thrown money in there without caring how it fit.

Two million dollars.

William just stared at it. I could see his hands shaking on the screen.

"Holy shit," William whispered.

"William?" I said. "What's wrong?"

"It's...there's so much of it," William said. His voice sounded weird. Like he couldn't believe what he was seeing. "It's overflowing. Like Scrooge McDuck's vault of gold coins. I could swim in this."

"William," I said. "Start packing. We need to get the hell out and dodge."

"Get the hell out of Dodge," William corrected me automatically. "But, yes."

I watched the screen as William opened his duffel bag. He reached for the first stack of money.

Then the lights went out.

The screen on my laptop went black.

"Vinnie?" William's voice came through my earpiece. Scared. "Vinnie, the power just went out."

A chill ran down my back and bumps on my neck and arms suddenly rose.

"William?" I said. "What's happening?"

But before William could answer, I saw something through my windshield that made me get very very cold.

Two people were marching toward the bank.
They were wearing happy face masks and carrying guns.

Chapter Forty-Eight

"WILLIAM!" I yelled into the comms. "The Happy Face Killers are here! They're storming the bank!"

"What?!" William's voice went high.

"Two perps, heavily armed, William, they're going inside now!" I watched them walk through the bank's glass doors. "They're robbing the bank!"

Through William's phone camera on my laptop, I could see what was happening inside. William crawled to the security deposit box room door and pointed his camera into the bank. The emergency lights had turned on. Everything was dim and lights flickered on and off.

"What do I do?" William gasped more than asked.

Before I could answer—the bank doors burst open.

Two men in happy face masks walked in. One was tall. One was shorter. The leader had a shotgun and the other had hand guns.

The leader fired his shotgun into the ceiling.

BOOM!

People screamed.

William screamed, but stayed on the floor of the security deposit box room. "What do I do?! I can't pack the money and get out. What do I do? WhatdoIdowhatdoIdo?" he said very fast.

"Stay calm and stay hidden," I said to reassure him. It didn't work.

"Good afternoon, ladies and gentlemen!" the leader announced. His voice was loud and theatrical, like he was having fun. "I'm sure you've heard of us." He pointed to his mask. "We're your friendly neighborhood Happy Face Killers come to make a withdrawal!"

He cocked his shotgun one handed.

"Everyone in the middle of the room! NOW!"

The shorter one started grabbing people. Shoving them toward the center of the bank. Bank employees. Customers. Everyone.

I watched through the camera as the Happy Face Killers led the bank manager, customers, and bank tellers at gunpoint toward the middle of the room. William was shaking. I knew because the camera was shaking and William was holding the camera.

The leader walked around the group of people. His shotgun moved from person to person.

"As long as you remain quiet," he said, "no one gets hurt."

He paused.

"Well, that's not entirely true. One lucky person gets to meet God today, but you have my word, I'll make sure it doesn't hurt."

My heart stopped.

"Which one?" the leader continued. He pointed his shotgun at different people as he talked. An old woman. A young man. A mother holding her baby.

Then he laughed.

That laugh.

I knew that laugh.

I'd heard it a thousand times. At school. At the park.

Francis.

Francis fucking Donahey.

"That's Francis," I said into the comms. "The leader is Francis Donahey."

"What? How do you know?" Floyd's voice asked in my ear.

"I know his laugh," I said. "I heard it all my life. That's Francis. The shorter one must be Scott."

On my laptop screen, I watched Scott move from teller to teller. Opening cash drawers. Stuffing money into a bag.

Francis kept moving his shotgun. Playing with people.

I couldn't breathe. I couldn't think.

Someone was going to die, and we were watching it happen.

"Vinnie," Floyd said in my ear. Urgent. "What do we do?"

I looked at my laptop screen. At the hostages in the bank. At Francis with his shotgun. At Scott robbing the tellers.

I looked across the street at Garth in his orange vest. At Floyd in his wheelchair with Mozart's controller.

My Family.

We came here to save ourselves. To steal money so we could keep our house. So we wouldn't get separated. So we could stay together.

But if we did nothing right now, someone was going to die.

I thought about Nicholas in the hospital.

My heart hurt.

It hurt so bad I thought I might cry.

Because I knew what we had to do.

"I love you all very much," I said to the Family over comms. "I'm going to miss you. But I can't...I can't live another day of my life if we let Francis kill someone."

And then I made the most dangerous decision of my life.

"Abort the heist," I said. "Do whatever you can to save those people. Floyd, you have the comms. I'm calling Rita. Repeat: abort, abort, abort!"

My hands were shaking as I pulled out my burner phone and dialed.

The phone rang. Once. Twice. Three times.

Come on, Rita!

Then Rita's voicemail picked up.

"You've reached Rita. Leave a message." BEEP.

I made my voice really low like Batman.

"Um, hello, this is a tip from a concerned citizen who is very concerned," I said. "The Happy Face Killers are robbing First National Bank on Winter Avenue. Right now! They have guns! Please hurry! Thank you, goodbye!"

I hung up and looked at my laptop screen in the passenger seat.

On the screen, I could see Francis walking toward someone through William's camera.

An old man. Gray hair.

"You," Francis said, pointing his shotgun at the old man. "You look like you've lived a good long life."

The old man couldn't speak. He just stood there shaking.

"Bet no one'll miss you, old timer," Francis said.

He raised the shotgun to the old man's head.

"William, initiate Contingency Plan Alpha Omega 84," Floyd's voice said over comms.

William set the phone down on the ground still pointing at the bank. Then I saw William's hand slowly open the door and Mozart fly into the bank.

The little drone hovered in the middle of the bank. Its propellers made a buzzing sound that filled the whole room.

Everyone stopped. Francis. Scott. The hostages. Everyone looked up at Mozart.

"What the fuck is that?" Francis said.

Floyd's voice came through my earpiece. Two words.

"Chaos Orb."

Then Mozart exploded.

Not like a bomb. Like a flower opening. The drone split into four pieces. Four separate mini-drones. Each one with a single propeller. They flew in different directions. Fast. Chaotic. Buzzing around the bank like angry bees.

"Police drones!" Scott yelled. "They found us!"

Francis started shooting. BOOM! One of the mini-drones exploded in a shower of sparks.

Scott pulled something from his jacket. A smoke grenade. He pulled the pin and threw it.

PSSSSSHHHHH.

Gray smoke filled the bank. It spread fast. Within seconds, I couldn't see anything on the laptop screen except smoke and shadows.

"Now's your chance, William. Get out of there!" I yelled over comms.

William grabbed the phone and crawled out into the main bank area. Through all the smoke, I couldn't see clearly what was happening in the bank, but I heard—

"Cover me!" Francis yelled at Scott. "We gotta get outta here!"

I heard more gunshots. People screaming. The mini-drones buzzing.

I looked across the street at Garth and said, "Garth, it's time to go." I saw him read his phone screen, then he dropped the traffic cone he was holding and sprinted toward Floyd.

On the laptop screen, the smoke was still too thick to see

clearly. But I heard William's voice. Very quiet. Very Mr. Darcy.

"I say, I find myself quite immobile—"

We didn't have time for Mr. Darcy. Then I remembered what he told me about Sophie.

"William," I said into the comms. Gentle. Like Nicholas would. "Mr. Darcy never planned a heist. Never robbed a bank. But William has. You trained for this. You memorized everything. You planned for every problem. Mr. Darcy can't help you. He can't help the people in the bank. You can."

Silence.

Then William's voice came back. Different now. Stronger. "You're right. I...I know what to do. I trained for this."

Through the laptop, I heard movement. William breathing. Counting under his breath. "Twelve steps. Ten. Eight."

I saw the camera lean down toward a woman who was taking cover behind a pillar and I heard William say, "Hold on to my shirt. I know the way out." Like he was a hero in an action movie.

On the laptop, people were crawling, ducking, and panicking. William grabbed every one he could as he counted his steps out of the bank. I could hear him coughing from the smoke. More gunshots.

Then, William erupted out of the front door of the bank, smoke billowing behind him, with a train of frightened hostages holding on to him about ten people deep.

Once outside, everyone ran in different directions, coughing, looking for cover to get away from the smoke and bullets.

I looked down the street to check on Floyd and Garth.

Garth had reached Floyd's wheelchair. Floyd was frantically working the controller. The last three mini-drones were still flying around inside the bank.

"We have to go!" Garth said to Floyd. He started to wheel Floyd toward the van.

"Wait!" Floyd said. "The wheelchair lift takes too long! Leave me!" Floyd yelled. "Get yourself to the van! I'll slow you down!"

Garth shook his head. Then he did something amazing. He bent down, slid his arms under the wheelchair—Floyd and all—and lifted. Two hundred pounds of person and metal rose into the air. Then Garth ran, carrying Floyd in his wheelchair like a wounded soldier to a helicopter.

"You could've warned me!" Floyd yelled as Garth ran with him.

I opened the van's back doors. Garth reached me in seconds. He set Floyd and the wheelchair down inside the van.

"Thanks," Floyd said, breathing hard.

Garth just nodded.

I looked at the bank. More people were running out. The smoke was pouring out the doors now. I could hear sirens in the distance.

Rita was coming.

"Where's William?!" I yelled.

Floyd pointed. "There!"

I saw William running the wrong way. Away from us. Toward the other side of the street.

"William!" I yelled. "Wrong way!"

William kept running.

I didn't think. I gunned the engine.

The van shot forward. Tires squealing. I drove straight toward William.

"Vinnie!" Floyd yelled. "What are you doing?!"

I remembered my accidental Tokyo drift from practice. I could do this.

I hoped.

I slammed on the brakes and yanked the wheel hard to the left like I did by accident in the parking lot with Nicholas. But this time I did it on purpose.

The van's back end swung around in a perfect arc. The tires screamed. The world spun. And when it stopped spinning, the van's back doors were facing William.

"Get in!" I yelled.

William leaped into the van. Garth caught him and pulled him inside.

"Go, go, go!" Floyd yelled.

I was about to hit the gas when Garth yelled something that made me stop.

"Look!" he bellowed.

He was pointing at a car parked behind us.

A fancy car. One we knew. One with a license plate that said CANDYMN.

Francis's car.

"Fuck that guy!" Garth yelled.

Garth jumped out of the van before any of us could stop him!

He ran to Francis's car.

Then he did something we would all remember for the rest of our lives.

Garth bent down. Got his hands under the car's side part. Took a deep breath.

And lifted.

The car started to tilt. Slowly at first. Then faster.

Garth was roaring. Like the Hulk. Like every weight he ever lifted at the gym was practice for this one moment.

The car went up. Up. Up.

Then it crashed onto its side with a sound like thunder.

Francis's getaway car was going nowhere now.

Garth ran back to the van and jumped inside.

"Punch it!" he yelled at me.

I stomped on the pedal.

The van peeled out. Behind us, I could hear the sirens getting louder and louder.

"Floyd!" William yelled. "Can you see anything?!"

I pulled the van into the alley where we needed to change out the license plates and take off the disguise decals. Before we got to work, we all huddled around the laptop screen. Floyd was typing. His fingers moving fast. "I'm trying to connect to the last mini-drone! One made it outside!"

The laptop screen changed. Now it showed a view from the ground. Sideways and upside down. The mini-drone had fallen and was lying on the pavement.

But we could still see.

We watched Francis and Scott run out of the bank. Smoke billowing behind them. Happy face masks still on. Guns in their hands.

They ran toward the CANDYMN car.

Then they stopped.

Their car was on its side. Completely wrecked.

"What the fuck?!" Francis screamed. His voice came through the laptop speakers. "How did... Who could have..."

Then we heard it.

Sirens.

"We're in deep shit now, Francis," Scott said as he looked ahead.

Police cars screeched around the corner. Three of them. Lights flashing. Sirens wailing.

Rita's car was in front.

The police cars stopped. Doors opened. Officers got out. All of them had guns drawn.

But Rita walked ahead of all of them. Calm. Steady. Her gun pointed at Francis and Scott.

"Drop your weapons!" Rita yelled. "Get on the ground, Now!"

Francis raised his shotgun.

"Don't!" Rita yelled.

Scott fired.

Rita didn't flinch. She fired back.

BANG!

Scott grabbed his shoulder and fell. Blood spreading on his shirt.

Francis tried to aim at Rita but she was already moving. Through the smoke. Through the danger. Like she was made of iron.

BANG!

Francis's leg exploded. He went down hard. The shotgun clattered away from him.

"Need a bus at First National Bank!" Rita yelled into her radio. "Two suspects wounded! Send backup!"

Then the mini-drone's screen went black.

Battery dead.

We all looked at one another in shock.

"Did Rita kill Francis and Scott?" William asked us all, unable to mask the delight in his voice.

Garth shrugged.

Floyd lifted up his hands with his fingers crossed.

"That...is why they call her Mother," I said proudly.

We changed out license plates, removed our disguise decals, and headed home.

Back inside the van, nobody spoke for a very long time.

I drove us home in a weird silence.

When I parked in our driveway, we still sat in the van. Still quiet.

Floyd started giggling first. William joined in. Garth's laugh boomed through the van. And suddenly, I was laughing too.

We were all laughing and crying and hugging each other in the back of the van in our driveway.

Rita got them.

She got Francis and Scott.

The Happy Face Killers were done.

The guys who beat up Nicholas were shot and going to prison. Sorry, not sorry.

And we were alive.

All of us.

The Family was alive.

And suddenly, we couldn't stop talking about it. Everyone was talking over each other in the van.

"I can't believe Mozart worked!" William said. His prosthetics were starting to peel at the edges, but he didn't care. "The Chaos Orb actually worked!"

"Did you see Garth flip that car?!" Floyd said for the third time.

"Vinnie Tokyo drifted to save me," William added, hitting my shoulder from the back seat. "Tokyo drifted!"

"And this time I don't have to change my underwear!" I yelled.

Garth spoke loud with pride, "The Incredible Hulk ain't got shit on me!"

"William, you helped nine civilians escape. You're a hero!" Floyd said to William.

"Yes, and *William* saved them," William said in his real voice.

"That was better than any gold medal," I said and slapped Garth on his shoulder. He flexed like Lou Ferrigno.

"This was the best day of my life," William said.

"And the worst," Floyd added with a grin.

We all laughed.

"Nicholas would be so proud," I said. "When he wakes up, we can tell him everything we did today."

"If he wakes up," William said quietly.

Then we got quiet again.

Nobody wanted to think about that. About Nicholas not waking up.

"He'll wake up," I said. Because he had to. Nicholas always came back. Always.

Then Floyd said something we didn't want to hear.

"We won the battle, but lost the war."

Everyone looked at him.

Floyd's face got sad. "The heist failed. We didn't get the money. We lost."

Our celebration died when Floyd said that.

He was right.

We saved people. We stopped Francis and Scott. We did good things.

But it cost us everything.

William made a sound like he was in pain. "I was right there. *Right there.* Staring at it. Two million dollars," William said, his voice sounded hollow. "The answer to all our problems. Just sitting there in Charity's box. So much money it was overflowing. But there wasn't time to pack it," William continued. "The power went out. Francis and Scott arrived. There just...there wasn't time."

My heart hurt for him. For all of us.

"You did your best," I said. "We all did. And because of that, one person gets to go home tonight. That old man Francis was going to kill. He's alive because of us."

"Vinnie's right," Floyd said. "We did the right thing."

William was quiet for a long time.

Then he said something weird.

"I hate losing."

We all looked at him.

"William?" I said.

William's face changed. He got a smile. A real smile. Not his Mr. Darcy smile. A William smile.

"I said, I hate losing. Which is why I chose not to."

"What?" Floyd said.

"There wasn't time to pack the money," William explained. "But there was time for something else. A switcheroo."

My brain didn't understand yet.

"What do you mean?" I asked.

William's smile got bigger. "There was no way I was leaving that money behind. Not after everything we did to get it. Not after what it means to us. Not after knowing who we were stealing from."

"William," Floyd said. "What did you do?"

"I put Charity's cash-filled inner safety deposit box inside Diego Locksley's empty box," William said slowly. Like he was explaining something simple. "And I put Diego's empty inner box inside Charity's."

Nobody said anything.

We all just stared at William.

"So, if Charity ever opens Box 103055..." William continued.

"It's empty," Floyd finished. His voice was barely a whisper.

"And when we go back to open Box 130500 after the heat dies down..." William said.

"It has two million dollars inside," I said.

William nodded. "The Family is saved."

For a second, nobody moved.

Then Garth grabbed William's face with both hands and kissed him.

Then Floyd yelled so loud I thought the van windows would break.

Then I was crying and laughing at the same time.

We did it.

We actually did it.

Chapter Forty-Nine

Heist Club was done. We were home. Safe.

And eating pizza we ordered because I didn't feel like cooking.

We sat around the kitchen table, the pizza boxes spread out between us.

I sat at the table with my phone in my hand. I kept checking it every few minutes to see if the hospital called about Nicholas. They hadn't called yet. Nicholas was still in his coma, and I was worried about him.

But everyone else was happy. Really happy.

"We still have work to do," William said. He stopped counting crusts and looked at everyone. "In approximately two weeks, I'll return to First National Bank. I'll access Diego Locksley's safety deposit box and retrieve the two million dollars."

"Then we begin Phase Two," I said. "First, we pay off the house."

"Then," William cut in, "we need to set aside funds to incorporate ourselves as a legal entity, so our corporation can challenge Charity's conservatorship petition."

Garth jumped in, "We'll need lawyers, good ones, to fight Charity."

"And finally, we'll need to cover Nicholas's medical bills," Floyd said.

"How much?" Garth asked.

Floyd looked at the ceiling a moment and said, "Approximately four hundred thousand dollars, give or take, which leaves us with 1.6 million dollars for long-term stability and future needs."

William whistled. "That's a lot of money."

I checked my phone again. Still nothing from the hospital.

"The hard part is over," William continued. He sounded confident. "Everything from here is administrative. Boring paperwork and financial transactions. No more breaking laws. No more danger."

I looked at my Family again. They were smiling and joking and being happy. We did something impossible, and now we could stay together.

But Nicholas wasn't here to see it.

I checked my phone again.

"Vinnie, the hospital will call when there's news," William said. He used his gentle voice, not his Mr. Darcy voice. "Checking your phone every thirty seconds won't change anything."

"I know," I said. But I kept holding my phone anyway.

That's when William looked out the kitchen window and froze, like there was a T-rex looking back at him.

"Oh boy," he said.

"What?" Floyd asked.

"Rita's here!" William pointed at the window. "Her police cruiser just parked in our driveway."

I dropped my pizza slice on my plate.

"Shit," Floyd said.

We all looked at each other. The happy feeling disappeared fast.

"What do we do?" Garth asked. His voice was tight with worry.

"Stay calm," William said. He was using his Mr. Darcy voice now, which meant he was nervous. "We knew this might happen. Rita was Nicholas's girlfriend. She might just be checking on us."

"Or she knows," Floyd said.

"She can't know," William said. "We left no evidence. We were careful."

There was a knock on the door.

We all looked at each other again.

"Someone should answer it," Floyd whispered.

"Vinnie, she likes you the most," William said. "Act normal."

I stood up from the table and walked to the door. My heart was beating fast. I opened it.

Rita stood on our porch in her police uniform. She looked tired. Really tired. Her eyes had dark circles under them, and her hair was pulled back tight in a ponytail.

"Hey, Vinnie," she said. Her voice was flat.

"Hi, Rita," I said. I tried to sound normal. "What are you doing here?"

"Can I come in?"

I stepped aside, and she walked past me toward the kitchen. The whole Family was sitting at the table looking at her like she was a bomb that might explode.

"Hi, everyone," Rita said as she entered the kitchen.

"Hello, Officer Reyes," William said formally.

"Hey, Rita," Floyd said.

Garth nodded but didn't say anything.

Rita looked around the kitchen slowly. She was doing that

cop thing where they look at everything to find clues. I saw her eyes move across the table, taking in our phones, the pizza boxes, each of our faces.

"Long day?" Floyd asked.

"You have no idea," Rita said. She rubbed her face with both hands. "I just spent the last six hours booking and processing two suspects. So much paperwork. Then debriefing with my captain. Then more paperwork."

"Sounds exhausting," William said.

"It was." Rita moved to stand behind William's chair. "But it was worth it."

"Why?" I asked.

Rita looked at me. Her eyes were sharp now, not tired anymore. "Because I caught the Happy Face Killers."

The room got very quiet.

"The bank robbers?" William said. "The ones who have been terrorizing the state?"

"The same," Rita said. She started walking slowly around the table, her hand trailing along the back of each chair as she passed. "Turns out they're not as smart as everyone thought. They got sloppy today when they tried to rob First National Bank."

"Congrats on catching them," Floyd said. His voice sounded fake.

"Yeah, thanks," Rita said. She was standing behind Floyd now. "But here's the interesting part. Want to know who they are?"

Nobody said anything.

Rita continued her slow circle around the table. "Francis Donahey and Scott McCreedy." She stopped behind Garth. "Ring any bells?"

I felt cold.

She knew that we knew Francis and Scott.

"Turns out Francis and Scott are hardened criminals," Rita continued, moving again. "They've been robbing banks for months. Wearing happy face masks. Murdering people." She was behind my chair now. I could feel her presence. "But today, someone called in an anonymous tip, on my personal cell phone, no less. Told me exactly where they were and what they were doing. Just in time for me to stop them from killing hostages."

She came around to face the table, leaning against the counter.

"That's great," I said. My voice sounded small.

"It is great," Rita said. "I'm going to get a commendation. Probably make detective. My captain called me a hero." She paused. "All because of an anonymous tip."

The room was so quiet I could hear William breathing.

Rita pushed off the counter and started circling the table again. "So, here's my question." She looked at each of us as she passed. "Do any of you know anything about what happened at First National Bank today?"

Nobody said anything. We all just looked at each other, then back at Rita.

The silence stretched out too long.

Rita stopped behind William again. She reached down and picked up the pizza slice from his plate. William's eyes went wide, but he didn't say anything.

"Vinnie," Rita said, holding William's pizza slice. "Can I see your phone?"

I pulled out my phone and slid it across the table to her. She picked it up with her free hand, scrolled through some stuff with her thumb, then slid it back.

"Now give me your burner phone," she said. She took a bite of William's pizza.

"I don't have a burner," I said.

Rita chewed slowly, looking at me with her cop face. Then she dropped the pizza slice onto William's plate, pulled out her personal cell phone, pressed some buttons, and held it up.

My voice came out of her phone speaker: "Um, hello, this is a tip from a concerned citizen who is very concerned. The Happy Face Killers are robbing First National Bank on Winter Avenue. Right now! They have guns! Please hurry! Thank you, goodbye!"

The message ended.

Nobody moved.

I looked at William. William looked at Floyd. Floyd looked at Garth. We all looked at Rita.

She knew.

I felt scared and sick and like I might throw up.

Then Floyd started laughing. Not a little laugh. A big, loud, can't-breathe kind of laugh. He laughed so hard he had to hold his stomach. He almost fell out of his wheelchair!

"A concerned citizen who's concerned?" Floyd gasped between laughs. "Vinnie, what's with the Batman voice? Who're you fooling like that?" And then he kept laughing.

My face felt hot. I was so embarrassed.

"I was trying to disguise my voice," I said to defend my poor choice.

"You failed miserably," William said, but he too was smiling.

"There was a lot going on at the time," I said. But I knew it was kind of funny.

Rita wasn't laughing. She held out her hand.

"Burner. Now."

I reached into my pocket and pulled out my burner phone. I handed it to her.

Rita took the burner, opened the back, pulled out the battery, removed the SIM card and bent the SIM card until it snapped. Then she dropped the phone on the kitchen floor and stomped on it with her boot. It made a crunching sound and broke into pieces.

"Always destroy burners after use," Rita said. "Basic criminal tradecraft."

She said it like she was teaching us something we overlooked.

Then Rita reached into her jacket pocket and pulled out a plastic bag. Inside the bag were broken pieces of metal and wires and circuit boards. She tossed the bag onto the center of the kitchen table where we could all see it.

Floyd leaned forward and looked at the transparent bag. His face went white.

"Mozart," he whispered.

"I collected all the pieces after the Happy Face Killers were arrested," Rita said. Her voice was gentle now, not cop-voice anymore. "There may be some eye witness testimony about a drone, but without security cameras working or physical evidence, there's no way to link them to you now."

Floyd stared at the bag of broken Mozart parts. Then he looked at Rita.

"Are you going to tell?" I asked, my voice small and scared. "Are you going to arrest us?"

The room was so quiet I could hear my own heartbeat.

Rita stared at all of us a very long time in silence. Then she shook her head and then she scoffed. Her scoff turned into a laugh.

"Tell who?" she said. "Who the fuck is going to believe the Merry Band of Misfits pulled off a bank heist? You did something most professionals can't. When Francis and Scott robbed the bank, they cut the power. There is no security footage in a square block radius. I have no evidence linking you to any crimes. And no witnesses saw anyone but Francis and Scott. Not a single person besides me knows. Or will ever know."

"We didn't rob the bank," I said. The words came out before I could stop them. "We robbed Charity."

Rita stopped smiling.

"What?"

"We robbed Charity's safety deposit box," I explained. "It had two million dollars in there. Garth's money. We took it back. That's not wrong, Rita. That's right. I know it."

Rita stared at me. Then at Garth. Then back at me.

Rita pulled out the one empty chair, Nicholas's chair, and sat down at the table with us. She put both hands on her face and made a sound that was half laugh and half disbelief.

"Wow," she said. "Just...wow."

She looked at all of us like she was seeing us for the first time.

"Who do you think you are?" she asked like she was really confused.

I knew the answer immediately.

I looked Rita in the eyes.

"You know. You know exactly who I am," I said to her in a low voice. "Say my name," I commanded.

"What?" she asked.

"Say. My. Name."

Rita tilted her head to the side. Her mouth twitched like she was trying not to smile. She understood what I was doing. And after years and years, she finally confessed, "You're Doug Judy."

"You're goddamn right," I told her. "And you're Peralta."

There was a moment where I thought Rita was going to be mad. That she wouldn't get it. But she laughed at my joke.

Then she looked around the table and stopped laughing as she realized whose chair she was sitting in. Nicholas's chair.

"Wait," she said. "Where's Nicky?"

The happiness drained out of the room.

Rita's smile disappeared. She looked at each of our faces and saw something bad.

"Where is Nicholas?" she asked again. Her voice was different now. Scared.

I felt my eyes get wet.

"Rita," I said softly, "we have a lot to tell you."

Chapter Fifty

Three weeks passed since Heist Club.

A lot happened in those three weeks.

Rita became a Misfit. An honorary Misfit, even though she was the one who called us that in the first place. She was devastated about what Francis and Scott did to Nicholas. But she took satisfaction in knowing she shot both of those fuckers. Her words, not mine. They'd live, but they'd never be free again. She spent every moment she could at the hospital sitting next to Nicholas's bed.

I couldn't tell if Rita was mad at Nicholas or not. She was too worried about him to show if she was angry.

One day I asked Rita why she helped us, with her being a cop and all. Rita told me she still believed in the law. But there were some unwritten laws that were more important than the written ones.

I understood what she meant.

While Nicholas slept in his coma, the Family did everything we said we had to do. William became Diego Locksley one last time. He walked right into First National Bank all by himself. He went to the safety deposit box room. He opened box 130500. And he took Charity's two million dollars.

Then we used that money to fix everything Charity broke.

We paid off the house. Our home now. The bank couldn't take it away from us anymore.

We incorporated ourselves as a legal entity so we could hire lawyers to fight Charity's conservatorship petition. Good lawyers. The kind that cost a lot of money but win cases.

We could pay Nicholas's medical bills so Rita wouldn't have to worry about them, or us.

We did everything Nicholas would have done if he was awake.

But every single day, I got more and more worried. Because Nicholas wouldn't wake up. There was progress, though. He finally started breathing on his own. No machines breathing for him anymore. The doctors said he might wake up soon. Or he might not. Brain injuries were complicated. We just had to wait and see.

So, we waited.

And waited.

And waited.

Until finally, three weeks after the heist, the phone rang. It was the landline, so I prepared myself for bad news.

It wasn't.

Nicholas was awake.

I almost fainted when the nurse told me. My legs felt weak and my heart beat so fast I thought it might explode. I called Rita immediately. Then I gathered the Family. We all went to the hospital together.

But I wanted to see Nicholas first. Alone. Just me and my twin brother.

The nurse let me go in by myself.

· · ·

Nicholas was sitting up in his hospital bed. He looked terrible. His face was pale and thin. He had tubes in his arms and monitors beeping next to him. But his eyes were open. He was awake. He was alive.

"Vinnie," he said. His voice was rough and scratchy.

"Nicholas," I said. I felt tears in my eyes, but I didn't care.

I walked over and hugged him carefully. He hugged me back. Not as strong as normal, but he hugged me.

"What the fuck happened?" Nicholas asked when I pulled away. "I'm so sorry I wasn't there for Heist Club. I let you all down. They say I've been asleep for a month. Did Charity take Garth? What happened?"

I sat down in the chair next to his bed.

"No, we did Heist Club without you," I said. "We did it by ourselves."

Nicholas stared at me. "Tell me everything."

So, I told him everything.

I told him about William switching the boxes during the power outage. About how we thought we failed. About the Happy Face Killers being Francis and Scott. About the chaos and the escape and William's brilliant plan working perfectly even though Murphy's Law made everything go wrong. Everything.

Nicholas just stared at me the whole time. His mouth was open a little bit. He looked like someone told him he won the lottery.

"The heist worked?" he said quietly.

"Kind of," I said. "Murphy's Law is definitely real, that's for sure. But we beat Murphy. Everything is taken care of. We paid off the house. Saved Garth. Everything."

Nicholas's eyes went wide. He tried to sit up more but groaned and fell back on his pillow.

"Vinnie, you can't just spend that kind of money!" he said.

His voice was panicked. "You have to launder it first! The IRS will—"

I raised my hand. Just one hand. Palm out. Like a boss. Like the godfather.

Nicholas stopped talking.

"I took care of that too," I said.

Nicholas blinked. "You...what?"

I smiled. And then I told him.

One week ago...

Floyd and I sat at a roulette table in the Golden Nugget Casino.

The plan was simple. Floyd would bet on red. I would bet on black. We would bet the same amount every time. No matter what number came up, one of us would win and one of us would lose.

William explained it was the oldest trick in the book.

I put my chips on black. Floyd put his chips on red.

The dealer spun the wheel. The ball bounced around and landed on red seven.

Floyd won. I lost.

We did it again. And again. And again.

After about twenty minutes, the dealer called over to a big man who looked very serious. She talked to him quietly, but I heard her say "pit boss" and "suspicious activity." She pointed at me and Floyd. The pit boss looked at us.

I made my face go blank. I let my mouth hang open a little bit. I looked at the roulette wheel like I didn't understand how it worked. I was Slow Joe.

Floyd sat in his motorized wheelchair. He had some drool on his chin from concentrating so hard on the game. All on purpose.

The pit boss stared at us for a long time.

Then he laughed. Not a mean laugh. A tired laugh.

"They're not criminals," the pit boss said to the dealer. "They're retarded. Their money spends too."

He walked away.

The dealer kept dealing.

The pit boss was wrong.

We weren't retarded.

Just invisible.

"It took us seven casinos and about a week, but we laundered the money," I said finally.

Nicholas looked at me a long time without saying anything.

It was a lot for him.

"So, can you tell me what you've learned about fighting?" I asked him like Mom.

Nicholas was quiet for a moment. Then he said, "Can you tell me what you learned about taking things from Francis?"

I thought about that. About the cocaine. About trusting Francis when I shouldn't. About dying...

"Dua Lipa saves lives," I answered.

Nicholas burst out laughing. And he kept laughing. But then something changed. I saw a tear fall down his cheek.

Nicholas was crying.

I didn't understand. "Nicholas? Are you okay? Should I get a nurse?"

Nicholas shook his head. He wiped his eyes with his hand. "I'm fine," he said. His voice was shaky. "I'm crying because I'm happy. My bucket list is done," Nicholas said as he grabbed my hand. His grip was weak, but he held on tight.

We sat like that for a minute.

Just two brothers.

Then Nicholas asked me, "Who taught you how to launder money like that?"

"Rita."

Nicholas's face went ashen. All the happiness disappeared. He looked scared.

"Rita," he said. "Oh god. Vinnie—"

I raised my hand again. Nicholas stopped talking.

"She knows," I said.

"What?"

"Rita knows everything," I said. "About the heist. About Diego Locksley. About the fake proposal. Everything."

Nicholas looked like he might throw up.

"She shot Francis and Scott too, but I'll let her explain," I said.

I stood up and walked to the door. I looked back at Nicholas one more time. He looked terrified.

Then I opened the door and left.

***

The door opened and Rita walked in.

For a moment, we just looked at each other. Four weeks of silence between us.

"Hi," I said. My voice came out rougher than I intended.

"Hi," she said back.

She pulled the chair closer to my bed and sat down. Not too close. Professional distance. That hurt more than I expected.

"How are you feeling?" she asked.

"Like I got my ass kicked by my high school bully and then spent four weeks in a coma," I said.

Rita's mouth twitched. Almost a smile. Not quite.

"Vinnie told me what happened," I said quickly.

"About you lying to my face for months?" Rita interrupted. Her voice was calm. Too calm. "About you creating a fake identity to steal from Charity? About you proposing to me as a manipulation tactic?"

I flinched. "Rita—"

"Let me finish." She held out her hands. "I've had three weeks to think about this, Nicholas. Three weeks sitting next to your hospital bed, wondering if you'd wake up. Three weeks to process what you did. What the Family did. What I did."

"What you did?" I asked.

"I covered your tracks," Rita said flatly. "The Family was careful, but not perfect. Their loose ends, I tied them up. Destroyed evidence. Manipulated reports. Made sure no one would ever connect the Merry Band of Misfits to what happened at First National Bank."

I felt tears burning behind my eyes. "Rita, I'm so sorry. I was trying to protect you. I knew that if you knew what we were planning—"

"I would have arrested you," Rita finished. "Or tried to stop you. Or both." She leaned back in her chair. "The proposal. That was clever. Cruel, but clever. You knew I'd say no. You knew it would throw me off, make me think you were just having some kind of crisis we could circle back to later and fix."

"It worked," I said quietly.

"It did," Rita agreed. "Francis and Scott are going to prison for the rest of their lives," she added with satisfaction. "Multiple counts of armed robbery, parole violation, murder. They'll never see daylight again. And I got to be the one who put them there."

There was something fierce in her voice. Something protective and vengeful all at once. She'd shot the men who'd hurt me. She'd made sure they'd never hurt anyone again.

"Thanks," I said.

"Don't thank me yet," Rita said. "Not before we talk about what happens next."

I titled my head slightly and asked, "What do you mean?"

"I made detective," Rita said. "My captain put me up for promotion. The task force, the arrest, the commendation—it all paid off. I'm getting everything I wanted."

I should have felt happy for her. But all I felt was hollow. "That's great, Rita. Really."

"But there's one more thing you should know," Rita said. Her voice changed. Became sharper. More dangerous. "After your fake proposal, you really pissed me off."

I swallowed. "I'm sorry—"

"Don't be. I went down the Cartwright rabbit hole to take my mind off you," Rita continued. "Agnes's body was still at the funeral home, as Charity had challenged her will. Agnes's will specifically stipulated that she was to be buried. Charity petitioned to have Agnes cremated. After that red flag, I convinced a judge to place a hold on the cremation so I could have an autopsy performed."

The room tilted. "You what?"

"Agnes was prescribed digoxin for her heart condition," Rita said. "Common medication for elderly patients with atrial fibrillation. But the levels in her system when she died? Fatal. Either she accidentally took an entire bottle of pills at once, or someone with access to her medications gave them to her."

I couldn't breathe. "Charity."

"Agnes wasn't the type to accidentally overdose," Rita continued. "She was methodical. Organized. Careful. No, someone killed her. Someone who stood to inherit everything. Someone who needed her out of the way. Charity needed her mother's body cremated so there'd be no evidence of her crime. That's why she petitioned the court to ignore her mother's last wishes. She was going to burn all the evidence of her matricide. Luckily for us, I got to Agnes first."

"Holy shit," I whispered.

"When I questioned Agnes's recently fired staff, her butler was more than happy to inform me of a huge fight between Agnes and Charity. Charity had learned how her father 'left.' A few days after that fight, Agnes ends up dead. Clearly, Charity decided to get rid of her father's murderer once and for all. It's a tale as old as time."

"Tell me you arrested that bitch?" I asked.

Rita's smile grew wider. "Two days ago. Charity Cartwright was arrested for the murder of her mother, Agnes Cartwright. Her assets are frozen. Her conservatorship petition is dismissed. And thanks to certain documents I found..."

She paused, and I saw something mischievous in her eyes.

"Documents?" I asked.

"Remember that dinner? When the Misfits went all 'lawyer' on me?" Rita pulled a folded envelope from her jacket pocket. "I took these. The letters between Agnes and Garth's father, which somehow ended up in your bedroom."

My mind raced. The letters. The ones Garth had found. The ones that showed the Cartwright family's dirty dealings. The paper trail even money couldn't hide.

"Those letters gave us leads on other crimes," Rita said. "Tax evasion. Fraud. Bribery. Charity's apple fell from her father's tree, not Agnes's. The Cartwright Foundation is under investigation. Her father's legacy is being torn apart. Every-thing she cared about is gone. And here's the cherry on top," Rita said, her eyes gleaming. "When Charity eventually goes to withdraw her insurance policy, the two million dollars she hid from everyone, she's going to find an empty safety deposit box. Because your Merry Band of Misfits took care of that too."

I started laughing. I couldn't help it. It hurt my ribs and made my monitors beep faster, but I couldn't stop.

"We won," I said between laughs. "We actually won."

"If you ever lie to me like that again," Rita interrupted, "I will arrest you myself. Understand?"

"Understood," I said.

We sat in silence for a moment. The monitors beeped. The hospital hummed around us. And slowly, carefully, Rita reached out and took my hand.

"I love you," she said. "Even when you're an idiot."

"I love you too," I said. My voice cracked.

She squeezed my hand.

"Which brings me to my next point," Rita said.

She reached into her other pocket and pulled out a small ring. It was simple. A thin gold band with a small diamond. Worn with age but beautiful.

"This was my mother's," Rita said softly. "For twenty years, she wore it every day. She was wearing it when she died."

I stared at the ring. Then at Rita.

"Nicholas Murphy," Rita said. "Will you marry me?"

My brain short-circuited. "Rita, I...I don't know what to say."

"I need you to say 'yes,' Nicholas," Rita replied patiently.

"Yes. Of course, I'll marry you! I knew you were a hopeless romantic under that tough cop exterior," I chided.

"Married couples can't testify against each other, dummy," Rita said, her voice flat and practical.

For a moment, I couldn't speak. Couldn't move as I processed what she'd just said. Then Rita laughed, and I started to laugh with her. Rita leaned forward and kissed me. Deep and long and perfect. She tasted like coffee and mint and home.

When she pulled back, she handed me her mother's

wedding band. I slid it onto her left ring finger and held her hand.

We stayed like that for a long time.

Just holding each other.

Being together.

The Merry Band of Misfits had pulled off the impossible.

We'd won.

And somehow, against all odds, I got the girl too.

Epilogue

Timing is everything.

I know that better than most typicals.

Mom used to say that when she taught me to cook. She's not here anymore to say it, but I remember. And now I understand it in a way I didn't before.

Timing was everything for Heist Club. Too early and we would have failed. Too late and we would have lost everything. But we got the timing exactly right.

Kind of like eggs benedict.

Nicholas always told me that the world has good people and bad people. Heroes and villains.

I used to believe that. It made things simple.

But we broke laws to save our home. We lied to protect each other. We did bad things for good reasons.

That doesn't fit into heroes and villains.

We're Family. And Family is more important than worrying about good or bad.

Sometimes you have to break the rules to protect the people

you love. Sometimes being good means doing bad things. Sometimes the wrong decision is the right choice.

That's a lot.

I know.

But it's true.

Nicholas also told me that life isn't a movie. That real life doesn't work like movies do.

I think he's wrong about that too.

Because we got our happy ending. Just like in the movies.

The house is paid off. The Family is together. The bad guys are in jail. The good guys won.

Well, kind of. We're not exactly good guys. But we're not bad guys either.

We're us.

The Merry Band of Misfits.

Oh, I forgot, one more thing. Now that you know our story, you're an honorary Misfit. That means, *you* know the first rule of Heist Club... No, seriously, don't tell anyone. I don't want to go to prison.

Prison food is terrible.

www.ingramcontent.com/pod-product-compliance
Lightning Source LLC
Chambersburg PA
CBHW051128130726
47988CB00005B/1747